PRAISE FOR

RIVER MARKED

"This book is about famil
needs to be done for the g
you'll laugh out loud, snic
bing, not sniffing tears). S
give it your full attention, b
it down. This is an urban everyday world is believably twisted into the world of fae, werewolves, vampires, and myths made real."

—*SFRevu*

"An outstanding urban fantasy novel with some well-loved and well-traveled characters . . . I recommend this book highly, as well as all of the previous novels."

—Examiner.com (Reno)

"Thoroughly engaging . . . Patricia Briggs hit the ball out of the park . . . *River Marked* is full of the good stuff you are looking for."

—*Boomtron*

"The plotting of *River Marked* is the most impressive part of it, because it isn't the big bad that gets all of the spotlight, nor should it. It is finally, after six books, and bits and kernels, finally shedding some light on shifter history. That is where Ms. Briggs will grab fans of this series and keep them up past their bedtimes . . . *River Marked* is a turning point in the Mercy Thompson series."

—*Preternatural Reviews*

"The plot had depth and substance, and really kept the story moving right along. The pacing was perfect. Prose and dialogue were craftily woven together. Character development was stellar, even for some of the minor characters. World-building continues to be top-notch in this series."

—*Book Series Reviews*

"Mercy fans will enjoy both discovering more about her past and seeing her on the road to a (relatively) happily wedded future."

—*Kirkus Reviews*

"A wonderful urban fantasy that has characters who touch the souls of readers."

—*Genre Go Round Reviews*

continued . . .

PRAISE FOR

SILVER BORNE

"If the term 'ass-kicking chick' has ever found a more apt heroine, I—well, I can't think of who. These are fantastic adventures, and Mercy reigns . . . a good read. It's complex, surprising, filled with action [and] great characters, and it's touching . . . Patricia Briggs writes with a deft hand, seamlessly blending exposition into Mercy's internal dialogue and conversations." —*SFRevu*

"Exciting . . . Briggs creates both well-rounded characters and a complex mythology, resulting in a rich read that's far more than a series of action adventures strung together. Fans of the series will be thrilled." —*Publishers Weekly*

"There's a lot going on in *Silver Borne*, but its pacing is practically perfect as it shifts between introspection and sudden action . . . a must for anyone following the series, [and] one that should also be popular among fans of paranormal romance."

—*Booklist*

"Mesmerizing . . . Always an astonishing storyteller, Briggs keeps adding layers of rich complexity to her characters and their world. Fasten your seat belts—it seems Mercy is in for a very bumpy ride! Here's another for your keeper shelf."

—*Romantic Times* (top pick, 4½ stars)

PRAISE FOR

BONE CROSSED

"Briggs makes a well-deserved move into hardcover with the rousing fourth adventure for kick-ass werecoyote auto mechanic Mercedes Thompson . . . The preternatural culture of vampire seethes and wolf pack politics is deeply intriguing. Briggs provides plenty of detail about Mercy's complex world."

—*Publishers Weekly*

"Mercy is not just another cookie-cutter tough-chick urban fantasy heroine; she's got a lot of style and substance and an intriguing backstory. Series fans will appreciate the resolution of some ongoing plotlines, and the romantic tension is strong."

—*Library Journal*

PRAISE FOR
IRON KISSED

"The third book in an increasingly excellent series, *Iron Kissed* has all the elements I've come to expect in a Patricia Briggs novel: sharp, perceptive characterization, nonstop action, and a levelheaded attention to detail and location. I love these books."

—Charlaine Harris, #1 *New York Times* bestselling author

"Another top-notch paranormal mystery . . . Thompson is a sharp, strong heroine, and her lycanthropic love triangle is honest and steamy. Briggs never shies from difficult material, and she moves effortlessly from werewolf pack psychology to human legal proceedings, making this a tense, nimble, crowd-pleasing page-turner."

—*Publishers Weekly*

PRAISE FOR
BLOOD BOUND

"Once again, Briggs has written a full-bore action adventure with heart . . . Be prepared to read [it] in one sitting, because once you get going, there is no good place to stop until tomorrow."

—*SFRevu*

"Plenty of action and intriguing characters keep this fun. In the increasingly crowded field of kick-ass supernatural heroines, Mercy stands out as one of the best."

—*Locus*

PRAISE FOR
MOON CALLED

"An excellent read with plenty of twists and turns. [Briggs's] strong and complex characters kept me entertained from its deceptively innocent beginning to its can't-put-it-down end. Thoroughly satisfying, it left me wanting more."

—Kim Harrison, #1 *New York Times* bestselling author

"Patricia Briggs always enchants her readers. With *Moon Called*, she weaves her magic on every page to take us into a new and dazzling world of werewolves, shapeshifters, witches, and vampires. Expect to be spellbound."

—Lynn Viehl, *New York Times* bestselling author

Titles by Patricia Briggs

The Mercy Thompson Series

MOON CALLED
BLOOD BOUND
IRON KISSED
BONE CROSSED
SILVER BORNE
RIVER MARKED
FROST BURNED
NIGHT BROKEN
FIRE TOUCHED
SILENCE FALLEN
STORM CURSED

The Alpha and Omega Series

ON THE PROWL
(with Eileen Wilks, Karen Chance, and Sunny)
CRY WOLF
HUNTING GROUND
FAIR GAME
DEAD HEAT
BURN BRIGHT

MASQUES
WOLFSBANE
STEAL THE DRAGON
WHEN DEMONS WALK

THE HOB'S BARGAIN

DRAGON BONES
DRAGON BLOOD

RAVEN'S SHADOW
RAVEN'S STRIKE

Graphic Novels

ALPHA AND OMEGA: CRY WOLF: VOLUME ONE
ALPHA AND OMEGA: CRY WOLF: VOLUME TWO

Anthologies

SHIFTER'S WOLF
(*Masques* and *Wolfsbane* in one volume)
SHIFTING SHADOWS

River Marked

Patricia Briggs

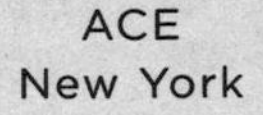

ACE
Published by Berkley
An imprint of Penguin Random House LLC
penguinrandomhouse.com

ISBN: 9780441020003

Ace hardcover edition / March 2011
Ace mass-market edition / February 2012

Printed in the United States of America
13 15 17 19 18 16 14 12

Map by Michael Enzweiler
Cover art by Daniel Dos Santos
Cover design by Judith Lagerman

For Derek, Michelle, Jodi, Kari, Elaine, and Megan—
it's about time you got one.
And for Laura and Genevieve—welcome to the family.

ACKNOWLEDGMENTS

If this book is enjoyable, it is due in no small part to the people who have helped me get things right. In no particular order, this book owes a lot to the following people: Michael Briggs—okay, he gets thanked first because he's my husband; Ginny Mohl, M.D., Ph.D., and my sister, who cheerfully answers questions about all things bloody and painful; Anne Sowards, who doesn't get cranky with late . . . late books and is a huge help in making each and every book the best that it can be; Jody Heath, intrepid guide and volunteer at Columbia Hills State Park; and last, but not least, the very nice women who helped me with Samuel's workplace in *Silver Borne*: Crystal Kalmbach and Danielle Hernandez.

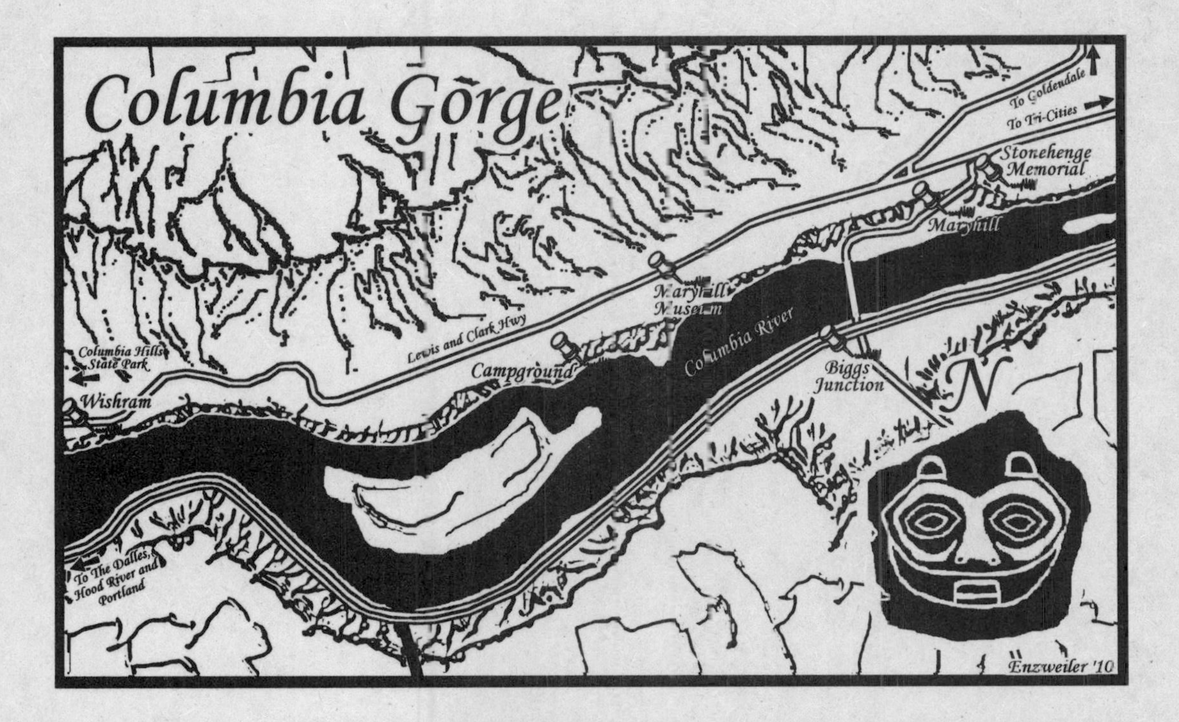
Columbia Gorge
To Goldendale
To Tri-Cities
Stonehenge Memorial
Maryhill
Maryhill Museum
Columbia River
Lewis and Clark Hwy
Campground
Biggs Junction
N
Columbia Hills State Park
Wishram
To The Dalles, Hood River and Portland
Enzweiler '10

FROM *THE DALLES CHRONICLE*

Two Local Men Still Missing
Thomas Kerrington (62) and his son Christopher Kerrington (40) are still missing, though the boat that they were fishing in has been recovered. The boat was found abandoned two miles downstream of John Day Dam yesterday. The men set out on a morning fishing expedition Monday but never returned. Sherman Co. marine deputy Max Whitehead says, "This has been an unusually bad year for boating fatalities on the Columbia. We're stepping up patrols and urging boaters to take their safety very seriously." Searchers are scouring the river, but after four days, hopes are low for a safe recovery of the two men.

FROM *HOOD RIVER NEWS*

This week's fish counts are drastically down at both John Day and The Dalles dams. Allen Robb of the Oregon Department of Fish and Wildlife says, "We are concerned that there was some sort of toxic dump in the river somewhere between the dams. There is a significant reduction in the numbers of fish, and our operators are telling us that this is especially true of our larger fish such as the adult coho salmon." Although extensive testing is under way, no sign of poison has been found in the river nor has there been an unusually high number of dead fish. "The fish are spooked," says local fishing guide Jon Turner Bowman.

1

UNDER THE GLARE OF STREETLIGHTS, I COULD see that the grass of Stefan's front lawn was dried to yellow by the high summer heat. It had been mowed, but only with an eye to trimming the length of the grass, not to making it aesthetically pleasing. Judging by the debris of dead grass in the yard, the lawn had been left to grow long enough that the city might have demanded it be mowed. The grass that remained was so dry that whoever had cut it wouldn't have to do it again unless someone started watering.

I pulled the Rabbit up to the curb and parked. The last time I'd seen Stefan's house, it had fit right into his ritzy neighborhood. The yard's neglect hadn't spread to the house's exterior yet, but I worried about the people inside.

Stefan was resilient, smart, and . . . just Stefan—able to talk Pokémon in ASL with deaf boys, defeat nasty villains while locked up in a cage, then drive off in his VW bus to fight bad guys another day. He was like Superman, but with fangs and oddly impaired morals.

I got out of my car and walked up the sidewalk toward the front porch. In the driveway, Scooby-Doo looked out at me eagerly through a layer of dust on the windows of Stefan's usually meticulously tended bus. I had gotten the big stuffed dog for Stefan to go with the Mystery Machine paint job.

I hadn't heard from Stefan for months, not since Christmas, in fact. I'd been caught up in a lot of things, and getting kidnapped for a day (which was a month for everyone else because fairy queens can apparently do that), was only part of it. But for the last month, I'd called him once a week and gotten only his answering machine. Last night, I'd called him four times to invite him to Bad Movie Night. We were a person short of the usual as Adam—my mate, fiancé, and the Alpha of the Columbia Basin Pack—was out of town on business.

Adam owned a security firm that, until recently, had dealt primarily with government contractors. Since the werewolves—and Adam—had come out to the general public, though, his business had started to boom on other fronts. Werewolves were seen as very good security people, apparently. He was actively looking for someone else who could do most of the traveling but so far hadn't found the right person.

With Adam away, I could give more attention to the other people in my life. I'd decided Stefan had had time enough to lick his wounds, but from the looks of things, I was a few months late.

I knocked on the door and, when that got no response, gave it the old "Shave and a Haircut" knock. I'd resorted to pounding when the dead bolt finally clicked over, and the door opened.

It took me a while to recognize Rachel. The last time I'd seen her, she'd looked like the poster girl for the disenchanted goth or runaway teenager. Now she looked like a crack addict. She'd lost maybe thirty pounds she didn't have to lose. Her hair hung in limp, greasy, and uncombed strings down her shoulders. Mascara smudges dripped over her cheeks in faded smears that would have done credit to an extra in *Night of the Living Dead*. Her neck was bruised, and she held herself like her bones ached. I tried not to show that I noticed she was missing the last two fingers on her right hand. Her hand was healed, but the scars were still red and angry.

Marsilia, the Mistress of the Tri-Cities' vampires, had used Stefan, her faithful knight, to oust traitors from her seethe, and part of that involved taking his menagerie—the humans he kept to feed from—and making him think they were dead by breaking his blood bonds to them. She seemed to think that torturing them had been necessary as well, but I don't trust vampires—other than Stefan—to speak the truth. Marsilia hadn't thought Stefan would object to her use of him and his menagerie once he knew that she'd done it to protect herself. He was, after all, her loyal Soldier. She'd miscalculated how badly Stefan would deal with her betrayal. From the looks of it, he wasn't recovering well.

"You'd better get out of here, Mercy," Rachel told me dully. "'Tisn't safe."

I caught the door before she could shut it. "Is Stefan home?"

She drew in a ragged breath. "He won't help. He doesn't."

At least it didn't sound like Stefan was the danger she had been warning me about. She'd turned her head when I stopped her from shutting the door, and I saw that someone had been chewing on her neck. Human teeth, I thought, not fangs, but the scabs climbed the side of the tendon between her collarbone and her jaw in brutal relief.

I shouldered the door open and stepped inside so I could reach out and touch the scabs, and Rachel flinched back, retreating from the door and from me.

"Who did this?" I asked. Impossible to believe Stefan

would let anyone else hurt her again. "One of Marsilia's vampires?"

She shook her head. "Ford."

For a moment I drew a blank. Then I remembered the big man who'd driven me out of Stefan's house the last time I was there. Half-changed to vampire and mostly crazy with it—and that had been before Marsilia had gotten her claws into him. A very nasty, scary guy—and I expected he'd been scary before he'd ever seen a vampire.

"Where's Stefan?"

I have very little tolerance for drama that ends in people getting hurt. It was Stefan's job to take care of his people, never mind that for most vampires their menageries existed as convenient snacks, and all the people in them died slow, nasty deaths over a period that might last as long as six months.

Stefan hadn't been like that. I knew that Naomi, the woman who ran his household, had been with him for thirty years or more. Stefan was careful. He'd been trying to prove that it was possible to live without killing. From the looks of Rachel, he wasn't trying very hard anymore.

"You can't come in," she said. "You need to leave. We're not to disturb him, and Ford . . ."

The floor of the entryway was filthy, and my nose detected sweaty bodies, mold, and the sour scent of old fear. The whole house smelled like a garbage heap to my coyote-sensitive nose. It would probably have smelled like a garbage heap to a normal human, too.

"I'm going to disturb him, all right," I told her grimly. Someone obviously needed to. "Where is he?"

When it became obvious that she couldn't or wouldn't answer, I walked farther into the house and bellowed his name, tilting my head so my voice would carry up the stairs. *"Stefan! You get your butt down here. I have a bone or two to pick with you. Stefan! You've had enough time to writhe in self-pity. Either kill Marsilia—and I'll help with that one—or get over it."*

Rachel had resorted to patting my shoulder and tugging at my clothes to try to get me back outside the house. "He can't go outside," she said with frantic urgency. "Stefan makes him stay in. Mercy, you have to get outside."

I'm tough and strong, and she was shaking with weariness and, likely, iron deficiency. I had no trouble staying right where I was.

"Stefan," I bellowed again.

A lot of things happened in a very short period of time, so that I had to think of them later to put them together in the proper order.

Rachel sucked in a breath of air and froze, her hand on my arm abruptly holding on to me rather than pushing me away. But she lost her grip when someone grabbed me from behind and threw me onto the upright piano that sat against the wall between the entryway and the living room. It made such a huge noise that I mixed up the sound of my impact with the pain of my back hitting the top of the piano. Reaction to countless karate drills kept me from stiffening, and I rolled down the face of the piano. Not a fun thing. My face hit the flagstone floor. Something crashed into a limp pile beside me, and suddenly I was face-to-face with Ford, the big scary guy who inexplicably seemed to have thrown himself down beside me, blood dripping out of the corner of his mouth.

He looked different than he had last time, leaner and filthier. His clothing was stained with sweat, old blood, and sex. But his eyes, staring momentarily at me, were wide and startled like a child's.

Then a faded purple T-shirt spilling over ragged dirty jeans, and long, tangled dark hair blocked my view of Ford.

My protector was too thin, too unkempt, but my nose told me that he was Stefan almost before my brain knew to ask the question. Unwashed vampire is better than unwashed human, but it is not pleasant, either.

"No," Stefan said, his voice soft, but Ford cried out, and Rachel let out a squeak of sound.

"I'm all right, Stefan," I told him, rolling stiffly to hands and knees. But he ignored me.

"We don't harm our guests," Stefan said, and Ford whimpered.

I stood up, ignoring the protest of sore shoulders and hip. I'd have bruises tomorrow, but nothing worse thanks to sensei's sometimes-brutal how-to-fall sessions. The piano looked like it would survive our encounter as well.

"It wasn't Ford's fault," I said loudly. "He's just trying to do your job." I don't know if it was true or not; I suspected Ford was just crazy. But I was willing to try anything to get Stefan's attention.

Still crouched between Ford and me, Stefan turned his head to look at me. His eyes were cold and hungry, and he gazed at me as though I were a complete stranger.

Better monsters than he had tried to cow me, so I didn't even flinch.

"You're supposed to be taking care of these people," I snapped at him. Okay, so he did scare me, which is why I was snippy. Get-scared-and-get-mad wasn't always smart. I, raised in a pack of werewolves, certainly knew better. But looking at Stefan and what had happened to his home made me want to cry—and I'd rather get scared *and* mad than do that. If Stefan thought I pitied him, he'd never let me help. Criticism was easy to take.

"Look at her—" I gestured toward Rachel, and Stefan's gaze followed my hand in response to the command in my voice, command I was just learning to borrow from Adam. There were a few perks to being the Alpha werewolf's mate.

Stefan jerked his gaze back to me as soon as he realized what I'd done, baring his fangs in a way that reminded me more of one of the werewolves than a vampire. But the snarl died from his face, and he looked at Rachel again.

The tension eased from his shoulders, and he looked down at Ford. I couldn't see the big man's face, but his body language clearly said "surrender" to my pack-trained sight.

"Merda," said Stefan, releasing his hold on Ford.

"Stefan?"

The menace was gone from his face, but so was all trace of any emotion. He appeared almost dazed.

"Go get showered. Comb your hair and change your clothes," I told him briskly, striking while he was still weak. "And don't dawdle and leave me at the mercy of your people for very long. I'm taking you out tonight to watch some bad movies with Warren, Kyle, and me. Adam is out of town, so there's a slot open."

Warren was my best friend, a werewolf, and third in the Columbia Basin Pack. Kyle was a lawyer, human, and Warren's lover. Bad Movie Night was our therapy night, but sometimes we invited people we thought needed it.

Stefan gave me an incredulous stare.

"You obviously need someone to hit you with a cattle prod to get you moving," I informed him with a sweeping gesture that took in the disreputable state of his house and his people. "But you got me instead, your friendly neighborhood coyote. You might as well give in because I'll just annoy you until you do. Of course, I know a cowboy who probably has a cattle prod somewhere if it comes to that."

One side of his mouth turned up. "Warren is a werewolf. He doesn't need a prod to get cows moving." His voice sounded rough and unused. He glanced down at Ford.

"He's not going to hurt anyone soon," I told the vampire. "But I can drive most people to violence given enough time, so you should get moving."

Abruptly, there was a popping noise, and Stefan was gone. I knew he could teleport, though he seldom did it in front of me. Both of his people jerked reflexively, so I guessed they hadn't seen him do it much, either. I dusted off my hands and turned to Rachel.

"Where is Naomi?" I asked. I couldn't see her letting things get into this state.

"She died," Rachel told me. "Marsilia broke her, and we couldn't put her back together. I think that was the final straw for Stefan." She glanced up the stairway. "How did you do that?"

"He doesn't want me to get the cattle prod," I told her.

Her arms were wrapped around herself, her mutilated hand clearly visible. She was bruised, bitten, battered—and she said, "We've been so worried about him. He won't talk to any of us, not since Naomi died."

Poor Stefan had tried to curl up and die because Marsilia had sold him out—and he'd done his best to take the remnants of his menagerie with him. And Rachel was worried about him.

About him.

"How many of you are left?" I asked. Naomi had been a tough lady. If she was gone, she wouldn't have been the only one.

"Four."

No wonder they looked bad. Four people couldn't feed a vampire all by themselves.

"He's been going out hunting?" I asked.

"No," she said. "I don't think he's been out of the house since we buried Naomi."

"You should have called me," I said.

"Yes," said Ford from the ground, his voice deep enough to echo. His eyes were closed. "We should have."

Now that he wasn't attacking me, I could see that he was thin, too. That couldn't be good in a man transitioning from human to vampire. Hungry vampire fledglings have a tendency to go out and find their own food.

Stefan should have fixed this before it got so bad.

If I'd had a cattle prod, I might have been tempted to use it, at least until the stairs creaked and I looked up to see Stefan coming down. I have a dusty degree in history for which I'd sat through a number of films of the Third Reich, and there were men who'd died in the concentration camps who were less emaciated than Stefan in the bright green Scooby-Doo T-shirt he'd filled out just fine when I'd seen him wear it a few months ago. Now it hung from his bones. Cleaned up, he looked worse than he had at first.

Rachel said that Marsilia had broken Naomi. Looking at Stefan, I thought that she'd come very close to breaking him, too. Someday, someday I would be in the same room with Marsilia with a wooden stake in my hand, and, by Heaven, I would use it. If, of course, Marsilia were unconscious, and all of her vampires were unconscious, too. Otherwise, I'd just be dead because Marsilia was a lot more dangerous than I was. Still, the thought of sinking a sharp piece of wood into her chest through her heart gave me great joy.

To Stefan, I said, "You need a donor before we go out? So no one pulls us over and makes me take you to the hospital or the morgue?"

He paused and looked down at Rachel and Ford. He frowned, then looked puzzled and a little lost. "No. They are too weak. There aren't enough of them left."

"I wasn't talking about them, Shaggy," I told him gently. "I've donated before, and I'm willing to do it again."

Ruby eyes gazed hungrily at me before he blinked twice, and they were replaced with eyes like root beer in a glass with the sun shining behind it.

"Stefan?"

He blinked. It was an interesting effect: ruby, root beer, ruby, root beer. "Adam won't like it." Ruby, ruby, ruby.

"Adam would donate himself if he were here," I told him truthfully, and rolled up my sleeve.

He was feeding on the inside of my elbow when my cell phone rang. Rachel helped me dig my phone out of my pocket and opened it. I don't think Stefan even noticed.

"Mercy, where the hell are you?"

Darryl, Adam's second in command, had decided it was his job to keep me in line when Adam was gone.

"Hey, Darryl," I said, trying not to sound like I was feeding a vampire.

My eyes fell on Ford, who had never risen from the floor but was staring at me with eyes that looked like polished yellow gems—citrine, maybe, or amber. I didn't remember what color his eyes had been a few minutes ago, but I think I would have remembered the funky eyes if they'd been there then. He was getting very close to becoming vampire, I thought. Before I could get too scared, Darryl's voice interrupted my thoughts.

"You left for Kyle's house an hour ago, and Warren tells me you aren't there yet."

"That's right," I said, sounding astonished. "Look at that. I'm not at Warren's yet."

"Smart-ass," he growled.

Darryl and I had this love-hate thing going. I start to think he hates me, and he does something nice, like save my life or give me a cool pep talk. I decide he likes me, and he rips me a new one. Probably I just confuse the heck out of him, and that's okay, because the feeling is mutual.

Darryl, of all of Adam's wolves, hates vampires the most. If I told him what I was doing, he'd be over here with reinforcements, and there would be bodies on the floor. Werewolves make everything more complicated than necessary.

"I've lived without babysitters for thirty-odd years," I told him in a bored voice. "I'm sure I can manage to get to Kyle's house without one." I was getting a little dizzy. Lacking another method, I tapped Stefan on the head with the hand I held the cell phone in.

"What was that?" asked Darryl, and Stefan gripped my arm harder.

I sucked in my breath because Stefan was hurting me—and realized that Darryl had heard that, too.

"That was my lover," I told Darryl. "Excuse me while I finish getting him off." And I hung up the phone.

"Stefan," I said. But it was unnecessary. He let me go, backed up a few steps, and knelt on one knee.

"Sorry," he growled. His hands rested on the ground in front of him, fisted tight.

"No trouble," I told him, glancing at my arm. The small wounds were sealed, healing quickly from his saliva. I'd learned more about vampires over the past year or so than I'd known the rest of my life. Ignorance had been bliss.

I knew, for instance, that because of my bonds with Adam, there would be no repercussions from letting Stefan feed from me again. A human without that protection who was food for the same vampire more than once could become a pet—as all the people in the menagerie were: dependent upon the vampire and ready to follow any orders he might give them.

My cell rang, and, with both of my hands available to me, I took the time to check the number: Darryl. Okay, there might be repercussions to letting Stefan feed from me, but they would have more to do with Darryl tattling on me to Adam than they did with Stefan. I hit a button on the side of my phone, so it quit ringing.

"I've gotten you into trouble," said Stefan.

"With Darryl?" I asked. "I can get myself into trouble with Darryl on my own just fine—and hand his butt to him if he steps too far out of line."

Stefan came to his feet, tilted his head, and gave me a little smile—suddenly looking much more like himself. "You? Miss Coyote versus the big bad wolf? I don't think so."

He was probably right.

"Darryl isn't my keeper," I told him stoutly.

He snorted. "No. But if something happens to you while Adam is away, it is Darryl who will bear the blame."

"Adam isn't that stupid," I said.

He waited.

"Jeez Louise," I told him, and called Darryl back.

"I'm fine," I said to him. "I thought Stefan might need a night out and stopped by to pick him up. I'll call you from Kyle's driveway, then you can call Adam and tell him I made it safely. You can also tell him that as long as I don't have crazy fairy queens, swamp monsters, or rapists with delusions of grandeur after me, I can take care of myself."

Darryl sucked in his breath. I supposed it was the rapist remark, but I was done flinching about it. The man was dead, and I'd killed him. The nightmares had mostly stopped, and when they emerged, I had Adam to fight them with me. Adam is a very good man to have beside you in a fight, even if all you are fighting is a bad memory.

"You forgot demon-possessed vampires," said Stefan into the silence. Vampires, like werewolves, can hear private phone conversations—so can I, actually. I've become quite fond of text messaging since I moved into Pack HQ.

"So she did," said Darryl. His voice had softened to molasses and gravel. "We try to give you the air you need to breathe, Mercy. But it is hard. You are so fragile and—"

"Rash?" I offered. "Stupid?" I have a newly minted brown belt in karate, and I fix cars for a living. Only in comparison to a werewolf am I fragile.

"Not at all," he disagreed, though I've heard him call me both rash and stupid as well as a number of other unflattering things. "Your ability to survive anything that gets thrown at you sometimes leaves the rest of us swallowing ulcer medication for days afterward. I don't like the taste of Maalox."

"I'm safe. I'm fine." Except for a few bruises from my

encounter with the piano—and, as I took a step, a little dizziness from blood loss. Darryl wouldn't catch my little fib, though. While he can smell a lie as well as most any werewolf, he wasn't the Marrock, who could pick up my lies before they left my mouth, even over the phone. Besides, I was mostly safe—I eyed Ford a little warily, but he still hadn't moved from where Stefan had thrown him.

"Thank you," Darryl said. "Call me when you are at Kyle's."

I hung up. "I think I liked it better when the pack would have been happy to see me dead," I told Stefan. "Are you ready to go?"

Stefan reached a hand down and pulled Ford to his feet—and then shoved him up against a wall. "You leave Mercy alone," he said.

"Yes, Master," said Ford, who hadn't struggled at all when Stefan pushed him around.

All hint of violence dropped from Stefan's body, and he leaned his forehead into the bigger man's shoulder. "I'm sorry. I will fix this."

Ford reached up and patted Stefan on the shoulder. "Yes," he said. "Yes, of course you will."

I admit I was surprised that Ford could say more than "Ogg smash."

Stefan backed away from him and looked at Rachel.

"Is there food in the kitchen?"

"Yes," she told him. Then she swallowed, and said, "I could make hamburgers and feed the others."

"That would be good, thank you."

She nodded, gave me a small smile, and headed for the depths of the house—presumably to the kitchen, with Ford trailing behind her like a big puppy, a really big puppy with sharp teeth.

We walked out the door, and Stefan looked around at the remnants of his lawn. He paused beside the van, shook his head, and followed me to my car. He didn't say anything until we were on the highway along the Columbia.

"Old vampires are subject to fugues," he told me. "We don't handle change as well as we did when we were humans."

"I grew up in a werewolf pack," I reminded him. "Old wolves don't deal with change very well, either." Then, just in case he thought I was sympathizing with him, I added, "Of course, usually they don't bring down a bunch of people who depend upon them."

"Don't they?" he murmured. "Funny. I thought that Samuel almost brought down a lot of people with him."

I downshifted and passed a grandmother who was going fifty in a sixty-mile-an-hour zone. When the roar of the Rabbit's little diesel engine relieved enough of my ire, I shifted back up a gear, and said, "Point to you. You are right. I'm sorry I didn't come sooner."

"Ah," said Stefan, looking down at his hands. "You would have come if I had called."

"If you had been in any shape to call for help," I told him, "you probably wouldn't have needed it."

"So," he said, changing the subject, "what are we watching tonight?"

"I don't know. It's Warren's turn to pick, and he can be kind of unpredictable. We watched the 1922 version of *Nosferatu* the last time he chose, and before that it was *Lost in Space*."

"I liked *Lost in Space*," Stefan said.

"The movie or the TV series?"

"The movie? Right. I had forgotten about the movie," he said soberly. "It was better that way."

"Sometimes ignorance really is bliss."

He looked at me, then frowned. "Orange juice will help with the headache."

So I was waiting in the line at a drive-thru, having ordered two orange juices and a burger at Stefan's insistence, when my phone rang again. I assumed it was Darryl fussing again, so I answered it without looking at the display. Someday I'm going to quit doing that.

"Mercy," said my mother, "I'm so glad I got in touch with you. You've been hard to reach lately. I needed to tell you that I've been having trouble with the doves. I can find people who have pigeons, but the man who had the doves just disappeared. I found out today that he apparently also had fighting dogs and is doing a few years behind bars."

My headache got abruptly worse. "Pigeons?" I'd told her no doves. Doves and werewolves are just a . . . Anyway, I'd told her no doves.

"For your wedding," said my mother impatiently. "You know, the one you are having this August? That's only six weeks away. I thought I had the doves under control"—I was sure I had told her no doves—"but then, well, I wouldn't want to give money to someone involved in dogfights anyway. Though maybe it wouldn't bother Adam?"

"It would bother Adam," I said. "It bothers me. No doves. No pigeons, Mother. No fighting dogs."

"Oh good," she said brightly. "I thought you'd agree. It comes from an Indian legend, after all."

"What does?" I asked warily.

"Butterflies," she said airily. "It will be beautiful. Think of it. We could release helium balloons, too. Maybe a couple of hundred would do. Butterflies and gold balloons released into the sky to celebrate your new life together. Well," she said, her voice brisk and determined, "I'd better get on it."

She hung up, and I stared at my phone. Stefan was convulsed in the passenger seat.

"Butterflies," he managed through bouts of helpless laughter. "I wonder where she found butterflies."

"Go ahead and laugh," I told him. "It's not you who is going to have to explain to a pack of werewolves why my mother is going to set loose butterflies—" I set him off in whoops again. It was too much to hope that it was one or two. No, my mother never did anything by halves. I pictured a thousand butterflies and, dear Lord help me, two hundred gold helium balloons.

I leaned forward and banged my head on the steering wheel. "I'm eloping. I told Adam we should, but he didn't want to hurt my mother's feelings. Doves, pigeons, butterflies—we are going to end up with a plane with a banner and fireworks . . ."

"A marching band," said Stefan. "And bagpipes with handsome Scottish pipers wearing nothing but their kilts. Belly dancers—there are a number of local belly-dancing troupes. Tattooed bikers. I bet I could help her find a dancing bear . . ."

I paid for my food while he was still coming up with new and wonderful additions to my wedding-day angst.

"Thanks," I told him, taking a big swig of orange juice, and drove back out into traffic. I hate orange juice. "You are such a big help. My new life's ambition is to see to it that you and my mother are never alone in a room together until after Adam and I are married."

LAUGHTER AND BLOOD HAD REVIVED STEFAN SO much that beyond an observation by Kyle that "Someone needs to remember that the runway model look doesn't even look good on runway models," Kyle and Warren didn't seem to notice anything wrong with Stefan. They also, tactfully, didn't comment on the orange juice I normally wouldn't have touched with a ten-foot pole.

We grabbed three huge bowls of microwave popcorn and headed up to the theater room. Kyle is a very successful lawyer; his house is big enough to have a theater room. Adam's house has a theater room, too—but then, it is unofficial home to the whole pack. At any given time we have a couple of extra people sleeping over. Kyle's house just has Kyle and Warren. Warren would be happy living in a tent out on the range. Kyle prefers Persian carpets, marble countertops, and leather chairs. It says something—I'm not sure what—that they are living in Kyle's idea of home rather than Warren's.

Warren's pick for our feature film turned out to be *Shadow of the Vampire*, a fictional movie about the making of *Nosferatu*. Someone had done a lot of research into the legends about the old film and played with them.

At one point, watching Stefan's intent face, I said, in a stage whisper, "You know, you *are* a vampire. You aren't supposed to be scared of them."

"Anyone," said Stefan with conviction, "who ever met Max Schreck would be scared of vampires for the rest of their lives. And they've got him dead to rights."

Warren, who was sitting on the floor in his favorite position—leaning back against Kyle's legs—hit the pause button, sat forward, and twisted around so he could see Stefan, sitting on the other side of the couch. I, as the lone girl, got the big new recliner.

"The movie has it right? Max Schreck really was a vampire?" Warren asked. Max Schreck was the name of the man who played the vampire in *Nosferatu*.

Stefan nodded. "Schreck wasn't his real name, but he used it for a century or two, so it will do. Scary old monster. Really scary, really old. He decided he wanted to be on film, and none of the other vampires felt like challenging him over it."

"Wait a minute," said Kyle. "I thought that one of the complaints about *Nosferatu* was that all the scenes with Schreck were obviously filmed in daylight. Don't you vampires all go to sleep in the daytime?"

Kyle, as Warren's lover, knew a lot more about the things that go bump in the night than most humans, to whom vampires were movie monsters, not men who wore Scooby-Doo shirts and lived in upscale houses in real towns. It wouldn't be long, though, I thought, before vampires were outed. Werewolves had outed themselves a year and a half ago—though they were careful what they told the public. The fae had been out since the 1980s. People were gradually learning that the world was a scarier place than the scientific reasoning of the last few centuries had led them to believe.

"We die during the day," said Stefan. "But Max was very old. He was capable of all sorts of things, and it would not surprise me to know that he could walk in the day. I only met him once—a long time before *Nosferatu*. He attended one of the *festas* of the Master of Milan, the Lord of Night, without invitation. It was odd to see so many powerful people cower before one unwashed, poorly dressed, amazingly ugly man. I saw him kill a two-hundred-year-old vampire with a look—just disintegrated her to dust with one glance because she laughed at him. The Lord of the Night, who was her Master, was very old and powerful, even then—and he did not voice an objection though she was the youngest of his get and dear to him."

"Is Schreck still alive?" Warren asked.

"I don't know," said Stefan, and added, half under his breath, "I don't want to know."

"Was he always that ugly, or did he get worse with age?" asked Kyle. Kyle was beautiful, and he knew it. I was never certain if he was really vain, or if it was one of a dozen things that he used to camouflage the sharp mind behind the pretty face. I suspected it was both.

Stefan smiled. "That's the question that haunts the older vampires. One doesn't ask questions about age, but we can tell, more or less. Wulfe is probably the oldest vampire—other than Max—I've ever met. Wulfe is not ugly or monstrous." He paused, then continued thoughtfully, "At least not on the outside."

"Maybe he was fae or part fae," I ventured. "Some of them are very . . . unusual-looking."

"I have never heard that about him," said Stefan. "But who would know?"

Warren hit the play button and, somehow, knowing that Max Schreck, who had played the original Count Orlok, had been a nightmare for vampires, made the movie a lot scarier—and it had had plenty of that going for it anyway. Only Warren seemed impervious to the effect.

When the movie was over, he glanced at Stefan. "Vampire," he said without insult, "why don't you come down to the kitchen with me while these two look through Kyle's amazing library of video wonder for something that will keep Mercy from speeding all the way home."

"Hey!" I said indignantly.

He grinned at me as he rose from the floor to stretch, his lanky body reaching for the ceiling under Kyle's admiring eyes. Warren wasn't as pretty as Kyle, but he wasn't Max Schreck, either, and he knew he was playing for an audience. Maybe Kyle wasn't the only one who was vain.

"Hey, yourself, Mercy," Warren said. "How about we do a second movie? Stefan's used to staying up late, and you have no Adam to go home to. You two find something else, and Stefan and I will refill the popcorn bowls."

Kyle waited until Warren and Stefan were downstairs before saying, "Stefan looks hungry. You think Warren is going to feed him before bringing him back?"

"I think," I said, "that might be a good idea. He already had a bite of me today and was starting to look at you like you might be dinner. I don't think Warren would let Stefan feed from you if he asked, and you consented. Werewolves are possessive that way. Probably better if Warren does it. Being a werewolf with a pack, Warren won't end up Stefan's good friend Renfield."

Kyle grimaced.

"Don't start the conversation if you don't want an honest answer," I told him, hopping out of the chair and perusing one of the bookcases stuffed with Blu-rays, DVDs, and VHS tapes.

When Warren and Stefan came upstairs, it was obvious to me that Stefan had fed again. He was moving with something close to his usual grace.

"Don't you have *Bride of Frankenstein*?" he asked, when Kyle held up *The Lost Skeleton of Cadavra* as our pick for the second movie. "Or *Father of the Bride*? *Four Weddings and a Funeral*?" He glanced at me. "Maybe *The Butterfly Effect*?" Yep, he was feeling better.

I threw a pillow at him. "Just shut up. Shut. Up."

Stefan caught the pillow, tossed it back to me, and laughed.

"What's up?" asked Kyle.

I buried my head in the pillow. "My mother has given up on doves for the wedding and—though I didn't know they were in contention—apparently pigeons. She wants to release butterflies and balloons instead."

Warren looked properly appalled, but Kyle laughed.

"It's a new trend, Mercy," he said. "Right up your alley because it's supposed to be based on an Indian legend. The story is that if you catch a butterfly and whisper your wish to it, then let it go, the butterfly will take your request to the Great Spirit. Since you released the butterfly, when you could have killed or captured it, the Great Spirit will be inclined to view your request favorably."

"I am doomed," I told the pillow. "Doomed to butterflies and balloons."

"At least it isn't pigeons," observed Warren practically.

2

"SO WHAT DID YOU DO TO DARRYL?" ADAM ASKED as he shut the driver's-side door of my Rabbit.

Usually I drove the Rabbit, but Alpha wolves don't deal well with commercial airline travel. Having to trust some stranger to fly the plane had left Adam with a need for control, so when his daughter Jesse and I picked him up from the airport, he got to drive.

"I didn't do anything to Darryl," I protested.

Adam gave me a long look before he backed out of the parking spot and drove toward the exit of the airport parking lot.

"I stopped by Stefan's on the way to movie night," I said. "Adam, Stefan is in real trouble. He's lost a lot of his menagerie, and he hasn't replaced them. They're dying; he was dying."

Adam reached out for my arm and turned it so he could see the inside of my elbow. I looked at the flawless skin with interest, too.

"Mercy," Adam said, as Jesse snickered in the backseat. "Quit screwing around."

"It's on the other arm," I told him. "Just a couple of marks. In a day or so, they'll be gone. You know it won't hurt me. Our mate bond and the pack keeps him from connecting to me the way he would a human."

"No wonder Darryl was upset," Adam told me as he pulled up to the ticket booth behind another car. "He doesn't like vampires."

"Stefan needs to gather more people into his menagerie," I said. "He knows it, I know it—but I can't *tell* him so."

"Why not?" asked Jesse.

"Because a vampire's menagerie is made up of victims," Adam answered. "Most of them die very slowly. Stefan's better than the average vampire, but they are still victims. If Mercy encourages him to go out hunting, she's telling him that she approves of what he's doing."

"Which I don't," I said staunchly. The driver of the car in front of us was arguing with the ticket lady. I picked at the seam of my jeans.

"Except that it's Stefan," Adam said. "Who's not such a bad guy for a vampire."

"Yeah," I agreed soberly. "But he's still a vampire."

The lady in the ticket booth apparently won the argument because the driver handed her his credit card. I noticed that the ticket lady had a bouquet of helium balloons beside her; in the center was a Mylar balloon that said, "Happy Birthday, Grandma!"

"I have a request," I told Adam, as he handed the parking ticket to the lady in the booth.

"What's that?" He looked exhausted. This was his second trip this month to the other Washington on the opposite side of the country, and it was wearing on him. I hesitated. Maybe I should wait until he'd gotten a good night's sleep.

In the backseat of the Rabbit, Jesse giggled. She was a

good kid, and we liked each other. Today, her hair was the same dark brown as her father's. Yesterday, it had been green. Green is not a good hair color on anyone. After three weeks of hair that looked like rotting spinach, I think she finally agreed with me. When I got up this morning to go to work, she was in the process of dyeing it. The brown was somewhat more unexpected than the green had been.

"Hush, you," I told her with mock sternness. "No cracks from the peanut gallery."

"What do you need?" Adam asked me.

I already felt better with him home—the restless anxiety that was my constant companion when he was away had left and taken with it my panicky trapped feeling, too.

The lady in the parking booth nodded and waved us on because we'd timed Adam's flight right and had only been there fifteen minutes—still in the free-parking time allotment.

The balloons beside her made my stomach clench, especially the gold ones.

"I want to get married," I told him, as Adam put the Rabbit in gear and we put the balloons behind us.

He tilted his head and eyed me briefly before turning his attention back to the road. Likely his nose was giving him a taste of what I was feeling. Most strong feelings are vulnerable to detection when you live with werewolves. My nose was good, too, but all it told me was that he'd had a woman sitting next to him on the flight home, because her scent clung to his sleeve. Often our mating bond allowed us to know what the other was feeling or, more rarely, thinking, but it wasn't working that way right now.

"I was under the impression that we *are* getting married," he said cautiously.

"*Now*, Dad." Jesse stuck her head between the bucket seats of my Rabbit. "She wants to get married *now*. Her mom called on Friday and has given up on the doves—"

"I thought you'd already told her no doves?" Adam asked me.

"—*and* the pigeons," his daughter continued on blithely.

"Pigeons?" said Adam thoughtfully. "Pigeons are pretty. And they taste pretty good, too."

I hit him in the shoulder. Not hard, just enough to acknowledge his teasing.

"—but finally decided that butterflies would be better," continued Jesse.

"Butterflies and balloons," I told Adam. "She wants to release butterflies and balloons. Two hundred balloons. Gold ones."

"I expect she's trying to get monarch butterflies if she wants gold balloons," Jesse said helpfully.

"Monarch butterflies," said Adam. "Can you imagine the poor things trying to figure out their migration route from the Tri-Cities?"

"She has to be stopped before she destroys the ecosystem," I told him, only half-joking. "And I can only think of one way to do it. My sister eloped under the pressure of planning her wedding with my mother. I guess I can, too."

He laughed—and looked a lot less tired.

"I love your mother," he said with honest satisfaction that lowered his voice to a purr. "I suppose preserving the Tri-Cities' ecosystem is a valid reason for jumping the gun. Let's get married, then. I have my passport with me. Do you have your birth certificate, so we can get the license, or do we need to go home first?"

IT WAS A LITTLE MORE COMPLICATED THAN THAT, so it took us two days to get married. Eloping just isn't as quick as it used to be unless you live in Vegas, I guess. Of course, we still might have made it in one except that I insisted on Pastor Arnez doing the honors. He'd had a funeral and two weddings to work us around.

Adam had lost a lot of things fighting in Vietnam. His humanity and belief in God were just a few of them, he told me. He wasn't thrilled about a church wedding, but he couldn't really object without admitting that it was anger, not disbelief, he felt about God. I was just as glad to avoid that argument for a while.

We meant the ceremony to be a small thing, Adam, Jesse, and me, with a pair of witnesses. Peter, the pack's lone submissive, stopped in at the house at just the right time and so was pressed into service as a witness. Zee, my mentor, who would step in and run my business while we were gone on our impromptu honeymoon, was thus brought into our plans almost immediately and claimed the privilege of second witness. Despite rumor, the fae have no trouble going into a church of whatever denomination or religion. It is the steel that the early Christian Church brought along with it that was deadly to the fae, not Christianity itself—though sometimes the fae forget that part, too.

Somehow, though, word got out among the pack, and most of them managed to be at the church on Tuesday morning by the time Jesse and I drove in. Adam was coming separately with Peter in a nod to tradition. He had had to stop for gas, so Jesse and I arrived first, and when we parked, there were a lot of familiar cars in the lot.

"Word travels fast," I said, getting out of the car.

Jesse nodded solemnly. "Remember when Auriele was trying to throw a surprise party for Darryl? We might have managed to keep the pack out of this if we could have gotten it done yesterday. Do you really mind?"

"No," I said. "I don't mind. But if we have a lot of people here, Mom's going to feel bad." My stomach began to tighten with stress. One of the reasons to have a planned wedding was to avoid hurting people's feelings. Maybe this hadn't been such a good idea after all.

When we walked into the church, though, it became obvious that more than just the pack had found out. Uncle

Mike greeted us at the door—I supposed Zee had told him. Looking over his shoulder, I saw that the old barkeeper had brought a few other fae, including, somewhat to my dismay, Yo-yo Girl, whom I'd last seen eating the ashes of a fairy queen. Yo-yo Girl wasn't really her name, which I had never learned; it was just what she'd been doing the first time I'd met her. She was dangerous, powerful, and looked like a ten-year-old girl with flowers in her hair, wearing a summer dress. She smiled at me. I think she knew how much she scared me and thought it was funny.

I hadn't intended on walking formally up the aisle. But as people started to arrive, Samuel—werewolf, previous roommate, and long-time-ago boyfriend—pulled me aside and gave me a bouquet of white and gold flowers.

He pulled my hair away from my left ear and bent down to whisper, "My, but you are going to have your hands full with Jesse, aren't you? A little over three days, and she has the whole thing organized."

"Three?" I said. "We just decided to elope yesterday."

He smiled at me and kissed my forehead. "I heard about it on Saturday." *Before* Adam returned from the East Coast.

I glanced at Jesse—who smiled brightly at me, and mouthed, "Surprise." Then I took a real look around. While we waited for Adam, the church foyer had been acquiring a festive air as people brought out boxes with flowers and wide white ribbons—and if I wasn't mistaken, a few of the fae were using magic to add their own touch.

I wore my wedding dress, purchased the month before. I'd thought it would be odd, with such a quick ceremony, but since I already had the dress—a great frothy thing from the waist down and formfitting white silk on top with narrow sleeves—Jesse had decided I should wear it. And Jesse had chosen to wear her bridesmaid gown because "What else would I wear?" I hadn't been suspicious at all, probably because I loved the dress and would have accepted any excuse to wear it.

Someone opened the chapel doors so people could go sit down, but there were a lot of people already seated. Not just wolves and fae—I could see some of Adam's business contacts and some of my regular customers at the garage. Gabriel, my right hand at the garage, and Tony, my contact with the Kennewick Police Department, were sitting next to each other. I took a step closer to the chapel, trying to see everyone Jesse had made come to my elopement. There were a lot of them.

Samuel held me back as the foyer emptied until it was just us, Jesse, and Darryl—and the organ began to play Wagner.

Jesse, on Darryl's arm, led the procession toward the mouth of the sacrament hall. She paused there, to let my sisters, Nan and Ruthie, who'd evidently been hiding just inside the chapel doors where I couldn't see them, lead the way, escorted by Warren and Ben, another of Adam's wolves.

At the front of the chapel, Adam waited for me next to the minister.

I blinked back tears, sniffed—and Samuel dropped my arm.

I looked over to see what he was doing, but another man had taken his place.

"Zee wanted to have the honor of giving you away," said Bran, Samuel's father, the Marrock who ruled all the wolves anywhere I was likely to ever go, and the Alpha of the Montana-based wolf pack who had raised me. "But I had prior claim."

"They argued for a good while," Samuel whispered. "I thought there would be blood on the floor."

I glanced in the church and realized that a lot of the Montana pack I'd grown up with were here. Charles, Samuel's brother, sitting next to his mate, smiled at me. Charles seldom if ever smiled.

About that time, humiliatingly, I started to cry.

Bran leaned closer as we walked slowly, and said in a bare whisper that didn't carry beyond us, "Before you start feeling overwhelmed by how nice we all are to do this for you, you really should know a few things. It all started with a bet . . ."

When we lined up in the front of the church, as smoothly as if we'd practiced it, Bran was right: I wasn't overwhelmed anymore. Nor was I crying. Nan, Ruthie, and Jesse stood on my side of the church, along with Bran, who still had my hand. Darryl, Warren, and Ben lined up on the other side, next to Adam.

My mother, the traitor seated in the front row of pews, sent my stepfather up to pin a silk monarch butterfly on my bouquet. He kissed my cheek, exchanged a nod with Bran, then sat back down at my mother's side. My mother gave me a delighted smile and looked nothing at all like the nefarious plotter she was.

"Balloons," I mouthed at her, raising an eyebrow to show what I thought of her subterfuge.

She discreetly pointed up—and there, clinging to the ceiling, were dozens of gold balloons with silk butterflies tied to the strings.

At my side, Bran laughed—no doubt at my dumbfounded expression.

"Like the fae," he murmured, "your mother doesn't lie. Just leads you where she wants you to go willy-nilly, all for your own good. If it helps, you are not alone; she came to me with a coyote pup to raise, and look what happened to me. At least you don't owe her a hundred dollars."

"Serves you right for betting against my mother," I told him, as the music drew to a close, and he led me across to Adam.

Bran stopped just short, pulled me back against him, and frowned at Adam—and let the weight of his authority be felt throughout the chapel. Bran could disguise what he was, and he usually did so, appearing as a wiry-muscled young man of no particular importance. Every once in a while, though, he let the reality of what he was out. Bran was an old, old wolf and powerful. He ruled the wolves in our part of the world, and no one in this room, not even the humans, would wonder that he could make Alpha wolves obey him. The organ music faltered under the weight of it and stuttered to a halt.

"Pup," he said into the sudden silence, "today, I'm giving you one of my treasures. You see that you take proper care of her."

Adam, not visibly cowed, nodded once. "I'll do that."

Then the threat of what Bran was disappeared, and he became once more an unremarkable young-looking man in a nicely cut gray tux. "She'll turn your life upside down."

Adam smiled and, out of the corner of my eye, I saw my mother fan her face—Adam cleans up very nicely and, in a tux, is breathtaking even without the smile.

"She's been doing that this past ten years, sir," he said. "I don't imagine it will change anytime soon."

Bran let me step forward, and Adam took my hand.

"Have you lost any money lately?" I whispered.

"Do I look stupid?" he whispered back, raising my hand to his lips. "I have to sleep sometime. I didn't know about this until your mom called me at my hotel after she gave you the butterfly call. She apparently has been talking to Jesse for a couple of weeks. You and I were the last to know."

I stared at him, then looked at the mirthful gaze of Pastor Arnez. Have to wait for a funeral, indeed.

"I didn't bet anything, either," the pastor whispered to me.

"Most people," said Adam thoughtfully—and loud enough that even the audience members without preternatural gifts could hear him—"have surprise birthday parties. You get a surprise wedding."

And, almost as if they were coached—which at least a dozen people later assured me was not the case—they all shouted, *"Surprise!"*

In the brief silence that followed, one of the helium balloons popped and its remains, including a silk butterfly, fell down to the floor behind the minister. If it was an omen, I had absolutely no idea what it meant.

THERE WAS AN IMPRESSIVE ARRAY OF FOOD AND drink in the church basement, and I took the opportunity to corner my little sister Nan.

"How come you got to elope, and I get a surprise wedding?" I asked her.

She grinned at me. "You have cake on your chin." She reached over and wiped it off—looked around for a napkin, then stuck her finger in her mouth to clean it off.

"Ick," I told her.

She shrugged. "Hey, at least I didn't lick my fingers first. Besides, it's good frosting, a pity to waste it. And, in answer to your question, *I* eloped before Mom and my new mother-in-law killed each other. A surprise wedding like this would have left bodies on the ground. You got a surprise wedding because Mom, Bran, and . . . a few others were feeling guilty."

"Guilty," I said. "You have to have a conscience to feel guilt. I don't think Mom is capable of it."

Nan giggled. "You might be right. The bet thing wasn't our fault anyway; it's yours."

I raised my eyebrows in disbelief. "My fault?"

"It started when we all noticed that you would get this—this deer-in-the-headlights look on your face as we discussed the wedding, and we started to play you a little because it was pretty much impossible to resist."

There *had* been a few commiserating phone calls from my sister. I narrowed my eyes at her, and she flushed guiltily.

"The bet just sort of happened," she continued. "One

day, Dad said, 'Ten to one she bolts with Adam before you get to the wedding date.'"

"*Dad* was in on it?" I seldom called my stepfather "Dad." Not that I didn't adore him—but I'd been sixteen when I first met him, though he and Mom had been married for almost twelve years at that point. I started calling Curt by his first name and never got in the habit of calling him anything else.

"Of *course* not." My youngest sister, Ruthie, trotted up with a cookie in one hand. Nan, tall and soft-featured, took after her father; Ruthie was a miniature of Mom. Which meant she was tiny, gorgeous, and pushy. "Dad was appalled at what he'd started. Nan, Mom, and I all were the first to bet, but Bran got in on it pretty early on."

She casually snagged a glass of punch off the table, and I snagged it out of her hands and put it back.

"Not twenty-one yet," I told her.

"Next month," she whined.

I smirked at her. "You bet on my wedding. You don't get any favors." I straightened up. I had a sudden, delightful idea. "Wolves," I said, and reinforced my call with a touch on the pack bonds I was only just getting the hang of. I didn't have to speak loud, either. All over the church the wolves, all wearing their human faces, perked up and turned toward me. "My sister Ruthie isn't twenty-one yet. No alcohol for her." Then, in case she didn't get it, I told her, "You go anywhere near that punch or any other alcohol today, my wolves are going to interfere."

Ruthie stamped her foot and looked at Nan. "You just wait. You bet, too. She'll get back at you, and I'm going to be the one smirking." She stalked off with an offended air while Nan and I watched.

Nan shook her head. "Some poor man is going to end up with her."

I laughed. "He'll never know what he's gotten himself

into. Curt still thinks our mother is a sweet thing who needs his protection, and he's perfectly happy about it." I remembered belatedly that I was supposed to be mad at her. I frowned. "Enough about Mom and Ruthie. You were going to tell me how you went from bet to surprise wedding."

"Well," she said, "like I said, it is your fault. When she saw how stressed you were getting about it, Mom offered to do the whole thing for you." She laughed at the look on my face. "I know. Terrifying thought, isn't it? But you obviously weren't going to enjoy planning it yourself, either."

She slanted a thoughtful look at Bran, who was talking animatedly with my stepfather. My stepfather was a dentist. Bran ruled werewolves. I didn't want to know what they had in common to get that excited about.

"So, anyway, we started egging you on," Nan said, "just for fun—and the betting got just a little more serious. As soon as the money at stake got over twenty bucks, Mom's competitive instincts overruled her motherly ones. The date Mom picked for your elopement was tomorrow. So she planned the butterfly-and-pigeon thing, but I guess about then she started feeling bad about robbing you of a real wedding. She decided to plan the wedding without you anyway. Which proves she must have a conscience, if a little underdeveloped. She enlisted Jesse as her woman on the ground and got this wedding together with her usual efficiency." Nan took a big swallow of alcoholic punch, and her eyes watered.

"I am so glad Todd and I eloped," she said sincerely. "There was no way to salvage the wreckage. But I think that you deserved this, and I'm very happy for you." She leaned forward and kissed my cheek. Then she whispered, "He is really, really a hottie. How did you manage that?"

"Brat," I told her, and gave her a hug. "Todd's not exactly chopped liver."

She smiled smugly and took another sip. "No, he's not."

"He could be," said Ben from behind me, his British

accent giving him a civilized air that he didn't deserve. "Do you want him to be chopped liver, darling?"

I turned, making sure I was between Ben and Nan. "My sisters are off-limits," I reminded him.

A flash of hurt came and went on his face. With Ben, it was even odds whether the emotion was genuine or not—but my instincts told me it had been. So I continued in a mock-chiding tone, "Ruthie is too young for you, and Nan is married to a very nice man. So be good."

Nan had caught the flash of hurt, too, I thought. She was softer than our mother, more like her father in temperament as well as looks. She couldn't stand to have anyone hurting and not do anything about it.

She sighed dramatically. "All the pretty men, and I'm tied to just one."

Ben smiled at her. "Anytime you want to change that . . ."

I poked him in the side—he could have slipped out of the way, but he didn't bother.

"Okay," he said, backing away with exaggerated fear. "I'll be good, I promise. Just don't hurt me again."

He was loud enough that all the people around us looked at us.

Adam pushed his way through the pack and ruffled Ben's hair as he went by him. "Behave, Ben."

The Ben I'd first met would have snarled and pulled away from the affectionate scold. This one grinned at me, and said, "Not if I can help it, I won't," to Adam.

I liked Ben. But if I catch him alone in a room with Ruthie or Jesse, I will shoot him without hesitation. He's better than he was when he first came to Adam's pack, but he's not safe. Some part of him still hates women, still looks upon us as prey. As long as that is true, he needs watching.

"I have someone I'd like you to meet," Adam told me, with a nod to Nan.

He took my hand and led me past the giant wedding cake. It was a beautiful thing of blue and white flowers and silver bells—and despite having been cut and served to everyone here, it was still huge. Someone else had ordered it for another wedding and hadn't paid for it, which was the only way—Jesse had told me—that she'd managed the cake. Whoever had originally ordered it must have been planning a much bigger wedding than this one. I glanced at the crowded basement and tried to imagine a bigger wedding.

"Quick, now," Adam told me, and tugged me out the side door and up the back stairs. "We're escaping."

We made it out to the parking lot without seeing anyone else. Adam's truck, inexplicably attached to a huge goose-necked travel trailer that looked bigger than the mobile home I'd lived in until this winter, when the fairy queen burned it to the ground, awaited us, poised for a quick getaway.

"What's the hurry?" I asked, as Adam boosted me in through the driver's side, got in behind me, and started the truck before he had the door closed.

"Some of the fae have an odd idea of bride send-offs," he explained, as I wiggled over to the passenger seat and he guided the truck out of the parking lot, "including, according to Zee, kidnapping. We decided not to chance Bran's feelings should such a thing happen, and Zee promised to run interference for us until we were off."

"I forgot about that." And I was appalled because I knew better. "Bran and Samuel are probably more of a danger than any of the fae," I told him. "Someday, I'll tell you about some of the more spectacular wedding antics Samuel's told me about." Some of them made kidnapping look mild.

I belted in, helped him to put on his own seat belt, and glanced behind us again. "In case you didn't notice, there's something very big stuck to the back of your truck."

He smiled at me, his eyes as clear and happy as I'd ever seen them. "And that's my surprise. I told you I'd plan the honeymoon."

I blinked at the trailer. "Bring your own motel room

along?" It loomed over us, taller than the truck—which was plenty tall on its own—taller and wider, too, with sections along the sides that were obviously intended to pop out. "I'm pretty sure it's bigger than my old trailer."

Adam glanced over his shoulder and huffed a laugh. "I think it might be. This is the first I've seen of it. Peter and Honey took the truck and hitched it up."

"Is it yours?"

"No. I borrowed it."

"I hope we're not going anywhere with little windy roads," I said. "Or small parking lots."

"I thought we'd spend the night in this really neat truck stop I know of in Boardman, Oregon," Adam said, guiding it onto Highway 395 southbound. "The smell of diesel and the hum of big engines to accompany our first night together as man and wife." He laughed at my expression. "Just trust me."

We did stop in Boardman to change out of our wedding clothes. Inside, the trailer was even more amazing than outside.

Adam unhooked the billion bitty buttons that ran from my hips to my neck. A billion bitty buttons from my elbows to my wrists still awaited. They required two hands to unbutton, so all I could do was look around the trailer with awe. "It's like a giant bag of holding. Huge on the outside, but even bigger on the inside."

"Your dress?" he said, sounding intrigued.

I snorted. "Very funny. The trailer. You know about bags of holding, right? The nifty magic items that can hold more things than would ever really fit in bags of their size?"

"Really?"

I sighed. "The *make-believe* magic item from Dungeons and Dragons." I craned my neck around, and said, "Don't tell me you haven't played D and D. Is there some rule that werewolves can't indulge?"

He leaned his forehead against my shoulder and laughed.

"I may have been born in the Dark Ages"—actually he'd been born in the fifties, though he looked like he was only in his midthirties; being a werewolf halts and reverses the aging process—"but I have played D and D. I can tell you for certain that Darryl has never indulged, though. Paintball is his game."

I took a minute to picture Darryl playing paintball. "Scary," I muttered.

"You have no idea."

Adam rubbed his cheek against mine and went back to his task. "I could just pull this apart, instead of unbuttoning it," he said ten minutes later. It was a serious offer, spoken in a hopeful-but-doomed voice.

"You do, and you get to sew all the buttons back on," I told him. "Jesse is planning on reusing this."

"Soon?" he asked.

"Not that I know of."

"Somehow," he grumped, "that's not as reassuring as it ought to be."

"Gabriel's going to college in Seattle in the fall," I reminded him. "I think you're safe this year." My right-hand man had a thing for Adam's daughter, and right now he was living in the tiny manufactured home that the insurance had replaced my old trailer with. A situation that made them happy and Adam antsy. He liked Gabriel, but Adam was an Alpha werewolf—which put him off-the-scale protective of his daughter.

Eventually, Adam managed the buttons. While I hung the dress up and put it in the closet (yes, there was a closet), Adam stripped off his tux and pulled on jeans and a T-shirt. He didn't often dress down that far. Except for when he was working out, usually slacks and a button-up shirt was as grubby as he got. My clean shirt and jeans were dressed up for me. I was a mechanic by trade, and it was a rare thing when my fingernails were clean. Somehow, we fit together anyway.

He bought us milk shakes and burgers (one for me, four for him) from the nearby restaurant, filled the diesel tanks in his truck, and we were back on the road.

"Are we going to Portland?" I asked. "Or Multnomah Falls?"

He smiled at me. "Go to sleep."

I waited three seconds. "Are we there yet?"

His smile widened, and the last of the usual tension melted from his face. For a smile like that I'd . . . do anything.

"What?" he said.

I leaned over and rested my cheek against his arm. "I love you," I told him.

"Yes," he agreed smugly. "You do."

THE COLUMBIA GORGE IS A CANYON THAT RUNS nearly eighty miles through the Cascade Mountains, with the Columbia River cutting through the bottom. It is part of the border between Washington and Oregon. Most of the travel is on the main, divided highway on the Oregon side, but there is a highway on the Washington side that runs most of the length of the gorge. Though the western part of the gorge is a temperate rain forest, the eastern section is dry steppe country with cheatgrass, sagebrush, and breathtaking basalt cliffs that sometimes form columnar joints.

Adam turned off the highway at Biggs and took the bridge back over the Columbia to the Washington side. That bridge is one of my all-time favorites. The river is wide, a mile or nearly so, and the bridge arches gracefully up and over the water to the town of Maryhill.

It was founded by financier Sam Hill (as in "where in Sam Hill?") in the early twentieth century. He'd envisioned a Quaker paradisaical farm community and named the town after his wife, Mary Hill. She might have thought it was cooler, I suspect, if it weren't out in the middle of the desert with about two inches of soil. There isn't much left of the town—a few small orchards, a couple of nearby vineyards, and a state-run campground—none of which made Maryhill special.

But Sam Hill hadn't stopped with the town. He built the very first WWI memorial, a full-sized replica of Stonehenge visible from the highway on the Oregon side of the river.

We turned west once we were over the bridge, though, away from Stonehenge and Maryhill. After ten or fifteen minutes of driving down a narrow highway that cut its way along the desert-steppe country of the Columbia Gorge, we came to a campground. Though it was groomed to within an inch of its life, there was no one inside. Adam pulled in the driveway, took a card off the map holder on his sunshade, and swiped it through the control box next to the gate. A green light flashed, and the gate slid open.

"We have it to ourselves for the next ten days," he said. "I did some of the security here, and they told me we could stay even though it doesn't officially open until next spring. I'm sure the shower in the trailer works, but the ones in the restrooms over there are a lot bigger."

I looked around the campground, where tall oaks and maples gave shade to the graveled RV spaces. The big trees weren't natural for this part of the state, any more than the green, green grass—someone had spent a lot of time tending them.

Adam pulled into a spot halfway between the gray stone restroom and the river. I found myself frowning at one of the trees. It must have been sixty feet tall, its roots buried deep in the earth where it wouldn't disturb the groomed campground.

"Ten days," I said.

He knew how my mind worked. "Zee has the shop," he said. "Darryl and his mate are watching Jesse, who told me before we left that she didn't need a babysitter."

"To which you answered that they were bodyguards, not babysitters," I said. "But she argued that bodyguards usually didn't get to tell the people they are guarding what time they have to be home."

"And you weren't even there for the argument," marveled Adam. "Darryl broke in, and said, 'Family does.' And that was the end of that. So what else are you worried about?"

"Stefan," I said. "I asked Warren to look in on him, but . . ."

"I had a talk with Stefan," said Adam. "Unlike you, my conscience didn't prevent me from telling him he needed to fill out his menagerie. One of his problems is that he doesn't want to hunt in his backyard, and he can't leave his menagerie alone. Ben offered to watch his people, and Warren should leave for Portland tomorrow with Stefan. Anything else?"

"Ten days," I said, giving him a broad smile. "Ten days of vacation with you. No interruptions."

Adam leaned over and kissed me—and that was the last time I worried about anything for some time.

3

WE SWAM IN THE RIVER—OR RATHER I SWAM AND Adam waded in chest-high because werewolves can't swim. Their muscle mass is too dense to be buoyant, so they sink to the bottom like anchors.

The campground was built around a fair-sized backwater that was fast enough not to be stagnant but slow enough to be really good swimming. Strategic growths of Russian Olive and a selection of shrub-sized plant life I couldn't name, as well as a ten- or fifteen-foot drop just before the river, gave the swimming area a feeling of privacy. The temperature had risen to somewhere around a hundred degrees Fahrenheit, so the water felt really good.

We splashed and dunked each other like a pair of kids, and I laughed until I had to go out and sit on the shore to catch my breath.

"Coward," Adam said from the river, his hands just below the surface where he could gather ammunition to splash me.

"Not a coward," I vowed, panting as the sun tried to bake the water out of my hair, skin, and swimming suit all at once.

"Then what are you doing up there?" he asked.

I opened my eyes wide and batted them at him. "Watching the wildlife." I lowered my gaze to his midsection, where all sorts of lovely muscles were displaying themselves. Werewolves are seldom out of shape, but Adam was a little more ripped even than the average werewolf. "Some nice scenery around here," I purred.

He made a soft sound, and when I raised my gaze, his eyes were hot. "I have to agree," he said, stalking out of the water with purpose.

I squealed and came to my feet, laughing—and something out in the water beyond him caught my eye. He spun around to see what I'd noticed, but it was gone. A log maybe, I thought, floating a little below the surface. Hard to judge the size at this distance, but it had been too big for a fish.

Before the dams went in, some of the sturgeon got pretty darn big, upward of twelve feet if I believed Zee. Whatever I'd seen had been bigger than that. But it was gone now, and I'd distracted Adam from his hunt.

He was looking behind him. I took advantage of his momentary distraction and bolted toward the trailer.

Werewolves are quick. Not cheetah fast, maybe, but faster than timber wolves or dogs. I, too, am very fast. Faster than most werewolves I know—so maybe I wasn't running as hard as I could. Or maybe sex inspires the male of any species to greater lengths. Either way, Adam caught me before I was halfway to the trailer. Without slowing down, he tossed me over his shoulder and ran all the way back while I laughed like a ninny and tried really hard to breathe. He pressed me against the side of the trailer and made sure I didn't mind my capture at all.

Somewhere along the way, we made it into the trailer and up on the soft queen bed that was made with clean, new sheets—in fact, the whole trailer smelled brand-new. Trailers like this were expensive. Who did he know who would loan him a brand-new trailer?

That thought left me, too, and when we were finished, I was as hot and sweaty as I'd been before I first jumped into the river, the trailer smelled like us, and Adam was asleep.

Mating is a lot more permanent than marriage. Partly, I think, it's that usually if you find your mate, he's not going to be someone you need to divorce. Abuse is almost not possible when two people are connected by a mating bond, and it gives you insight into your mate that allows you to avoid the nastier fights that snowball into cold distance. And partly it is that magic is somewhat harder to deal with than legal paperwork, and the mating bond is pack magic.

Given that, I hadn't really expected for the actual wedding to matter so much to me.

"I like having you wear my ring," said Adam, his eyes yellow and gleaming out from under half-opened lids. Sometimes the mate bond gives more insight to one or the other of us. He seemed to be responding to the gist of what I'd been thinking, while I was being kept in the dark. "I like that people can just look at you and know that you are taken, that you are mine." He closed his eyes and laughed. "And yes, I know that sentiment is at the top of the Women's Liberation Movement's list of things not to say to a modern woman."

Something was bothering him, I thought. The last sentence or two had been just a little too tight.

"Uhm," I said, rolling over so I could lick a bead of sweat off his chest. He tasted like Adam. Who needed champagne? "You better not take off your ring without a really good reason," I told him, letting my inner coyote out where he could see her. Maybe he needed to know his possessiveness was returned, in spades. "And if your ex-wife or any moderately attractive woman from thirteen to seventy is in the area, you should be aware that there *is* no reason good enough for you to take off your ring."

He laughed, and I rolled again, until I was all the way on top of him.

I hadn't gotten it right yet, hadn't worked out what was bothering him. Our bond might be talking to him, but it wasn't letting me know anything that was going on behind his eyes—which had gone dark again. That's the problem with magic. You start counting on it, and it disappears out from under your feet and leaves you floundering worse than if you'd never had it in the first place. So all I could go on was what most other women had to use to interpret their mates' moods.

I had known Adam for more than ten years—I'd known his ex-wife, Christy, too. Maybe his problem was rooted in his first marriage. She'd been big on personal freedom—as long as it was her freedom. She'd been jealous of the pack; jealous, also, I thought, of Jesse, their daughter. She didn't love him, but she had wanted to be the center of his world and would tolerate nothing else.

Maybe he felt that he was trying to do that to me. Maybe we both needed to lighten up the atmosphere a bit, give ourselves time to deal with all the changes.

I nipped his ear lightly. "If it were socially acceptable to tattoo my name across your forehead, I'd do it."

"I only see my forehead when I look in a mirror," he said. "I see my hand a lot more often."

"It wouldn't be for you," I told him. "You know who you belong to. It's for all the other women. Only fair to warn them when the wrong word might get them hurt. This coyote has fangs."

His chest vibrated under me, the laugh not making it all the way out yet. He relaxed subtly.

"I thought that if you're feeling primitive about this, it is only fair to let you know that I'm feeling pretty primitive, too," I informed him lightly.

Then I rolled off him and over the edge of the bed to drop down on the floor. I kicked my swimming suit, now cold and clammy, aside. "However, you ought to know that *I* can't work at the shop with my rings on unless I want to be known as Nine-Fingered Mercy. And"—I touched the pawprint just beneath my navel—"having gotten all the tattoos I ever intend to, I won't tattoo your name on my forehead or anything like that."

He jumped out of bed and strode to his suitcase. He unzipped the outer pocket and pulled out a flat box, which he handed to me.

I opened it to find a thick gold chain with a battered military dog tag on it. Hauptman, it read, Adam Alexander. The last time I'd seen it, it had been one of a pair on the same steel chain lying on Adam's chest of drawers.

"That's to put your rings on when you're at work," he said, taking the chain from me and putting it over my head. As he fastened the chain, he kissed the back of my neck. He stayed there for a moment, his fingers tight on the necklace.

He'd given me one of his dog tags. I was never a soldier, but I'm a historian. I know why they started using a pair of dog tags. When a man died, and his buddies couldn't get the body out, they'd leave one tag with the body so anyone who found it could identify him. The other would be used to report his death.

That dog tag meant more to him than the ring did—and so it meant more to me, too. I noticed that the chain looked to be tough enough that I could wear it when running as a coyote, too.

"I need to go for a run," he told me, taking a full step back and slapping me lightly on my naked rump. His fingers lingered a little, testing the faint buckshot scars left from when I'd gotten a bit too close to a gun-happy rancher. "You want to come with?"

"Long run or short run?" I asked warily. Wolves love to run, but even most of them don't love to run the way Adam does.

He pulled on underwear and running shorts, socks and shoes as he considered my question. "Long run," he said, sounding a little surprised. "I'm a little wound up about something . . ." He let his voice trail off and gave me a small, almost shy, grin. "Wolf instincts are good, but sometimes it's hard to figure out what's touching them off. Running helps connect the frontal lobe with the hindbrain."

"That helps?" I asked with sudden eagerness. It really irked me when I knew something and had no idea where it came from.

He laughed. "Sometimes. Sometimes I just get tired enough not to care. You staying here?"

"I am feeling extremely mellow," I told him. He'd run things off better if I wasn't with him. "I'll stay here. But you better put a shirt on, or your gorgeous self will cause an accident if you go running by the road, and someone sees you." He smiled at that; I think he thought I was joking. "I'll take a shower and read until you get back. By then we might think about food, making some or hunting some down."

He hesitated.

"Adam," I said, "we are out in the middle of nowhere. No one who hates me knows where we are unless you borrowed this rig from Marsilia. Go run. I'll be here for you when you get back—that's a promise."

He gave me one of his assessing looks, then left, closing the trailer door gently behind him.

THE SHOWER IN THE TRAILER WASN'T HORRIBLE. I'd expected something only pygmies would be able to use, but it wasn't bad. I had no intention of using it, though, not with the camp showers available.

Camp showers should be primitive. I've used camp showers that only had cold water, that had no shower curtains, and some that I came out of feeling dirtier than I had when I went in. The camp showers here were an entirely different thing.

The whole building was air-conditioned down to a civilized and chilly contrast to the outdoor temperature. The floors were slate tile. The mirrors in the lavatories had hand-carved wooden frames. The countertop was a slab of dark green marble that contrasted beautifully with the bronze faucets. There were four shower rooms, in which the slate tile and bronze fixture theme was continued.

I'd never seen such a place in a campground—or even in a hotel. The water pouring out of the giant-sized, ceiling-mounted showerheads was hot and sluiced the sweat out of my hair and worry for Adam off my shoulders. I stayed in the stall a long time, and the water never changed temperature.

When I was wrinkled and relaxed, I dressed in cutoffs and a T-shirt that had a picture of a ratty little house on it. The caption said, "Thieves welcome. Please don't feed the werewolves." Jesse had had it made for me.

On the way back to the trailer, the sun baked the water out of my wet hair. I ducked in the trailer, pulled my book out of my suitcase, and went back outside to lie in the grass and read until Adam got back.

He'd been running for a long time.

I read for about fifteen minutes, then the sound of something scuffing the ground jerked me out of the story. I looked up, but there was nothing but birds and insects within my sight.

I looked back down at the page I'd stopped on, and I heard it again. It sounded as if someone was rubbing the bottom of soft-soled shoes on pavement about ten feet in front of me, but there was no one on the road. I took a deep breath, testing for scent—my hearing is good, but my nose is better.

I expected to scent a mole or ground squirrel, something that could be making noise out of sight. Instead, the air carried old-fashioned tanned leather, campfire smoke, a whiff of tobacco, and the unmistakable smell of an unfamiliar man. I set the book down and stood up.

As I turned in a full circle, seeing nothing, the hair on the back of my neck began to shiver in a familiar way.

I am a walker. That means, basically, that I can shift into a coyote whenever I want to. It gives me sharper ears and nose than the rest of the human population. It gives me an edge of speed—and I can sense ghosts that other people can't.

There was a ghost here. I couldn't see it, but I could feel it—and smell it.

The scuffing sound started up again and, with the sun high in the sky, I walked over to the asphalt road, where the sound seemed to originate.

A hawk cried out, though the sky was clear of any predatory birds. I wasn't the only one who heard it, because all the birdsong that had been keeping me company while I read ceased. Maybe it was a real hawk, but my instincts were convinced it wasn't, though most of the ghosts I've seen have all been human.

The scuffs were rhythmic now, almost like a very slow polka. Scuff-scuff, pause, scuff-scuff, pause. The scent grew stronger—and I could pick out one more. Coyote.

I must have stood there for three or four minutes as the sound of dancing grew more solid before I saw him. I saw his leathers first; the rest of him was shadowy and dreamlike. But the fringe and the quill patterns on his sleeves and the outsides of his leggings were clean and distinct.

The leathers weren't the kind you see at powwows. Those are well-tended, best-dress kinds of costumes, mostly. Beautiful, brilliantly colored, handcrafted clothing brought out for special occasions.

These leathers looked as though he'd worn them long enough that they fit him like a second skin. Thin patches were rubbed on the insides of his legs, as if he'd ridden on horseback a lot. The hide was darker under his arms and in the small of his back, where sweat from his dance would have gathered. He wore a porcupine quill–worked belt from which a coyote tail swung freely at his hip. The colors on the quillwork were faded, and the coyote tail was a little ragged.

I started to hear the music he danced to, no mystical drummers or flute players. He was the musician, accompanying himself with his own song, a nasal, wordless tune that resonated in my bones. About the same time, I could see his hands. They were a workingman's hands, rancher's hands, callused and scarred. A man's hands, but not an old man. One finger had been broken and reset crooked.

His hair hung in two thick braids that were finished with a red leather tie and stopped just below his shoulder blades. I recognized some of the dancing moves from the two or three powwows I'd attended in college, when I was still trying to hunt down my heritage. As he danced, he became more and more real to my eyes and to the rest of my senses. Until, at last, if it had not been that I'd seen him slowly materialize, I would have sworn he was a living person, though he kept his head turned from me so I just got glimpses of his features.

The rhythm of his dance changed from furious to achingly slow and back. At all times, his weight was evenly distributed on the balls of his feet—this was a warrior's dance, full of power and magic and the promise of violence. The warrior was who he was, though, and the dancer's nature didn't stop it from being a joyous celebration.

The ghost stopped dancing with his back to me, his whole body working to regain the oxygen he'd spent in his dance. I wondered how long ago he had performed his dance in the flesh and why he'd done it here.

"Hey," I said softly.

There are ghosts that just repeat important moments of their lives. I was pretty sure that this was one of those because self-aware ghosts who can act independently are rarer—and they tend to interact right off. This had all the hallmarks of a repeater; that dance, full of passion and emotion, had looked as though it had been done at a pivotal moment in someone's life.

But my voice made his shoulders stiffen. Then he turned slowly toward me until I stared into the face of a man I'd never met, whose face was as familiar as the one I looked at in my own mirror, even though I only had one black-and-white photograph of it from a newspaper report of his death.

My father.

I couldn't speak, couldn't breathe. It felt just like someone had belted me in the diaphragm, so my lungs couldn't work.

He stared at me, unsmiling. Slowly, almost ceremonially, he bowed his head to me. Then he slid into a coyote shape as easily, as quickly, as I can. The coyote appeared, oddly, more solid than the man had been. He looked at me with the same bold stare he'd had when he appeared human. Then, without warning, he bolted across the grounds and into the bushes a dozen yards away.

In the photograph, my father had been wearing the uniform of a rodeo cowboy—jeans, long-sleeved Western-cut shirt, and a cowboy hat. My mother, a teenager fighting free of strict parents, had met him in a rodeo where she was winning prize money barrel racing her best friend's horse when she was younger than Jesse. She hadn't had a chance to tell him she was pregnant before he'd been killed in a car accident. The name he'd given her was Joe Old Coyote.

I'd never seen my father's ghost before. He hadn't come to me when I slunk out of Montana, fleeing the only home I had ever known. He hadn't come when I graduated from high school or college. Hadn't come when I'd fought for my life against fae and demons and all sorts of nasty creatures. He hadn't come to my wedding.

I looked for footprints. I feel pretty confident of my knowledge of werewolves and marginally comfortable with what I knew of vampires. The fae are another matter—and I knew that there were other things I knew nothing about, some of them unique and some of them just well hidden.

I'd been certain what I'd seen was a ghost until I had a moment to wonder how my father, who'd died hundreds of miles away in eastern Montana, would have gotten here. He'd turned into a coyote, just like I could, and run off into the bushes. Most ghosts don't need to run away; they just dissipate. But there were no tracks—and I know how to track. Not even in the soft dirt right in front of the bushes he'd run into.

I had gooseflesh on my arms though it was still hot out.

"SO YOU DON'T THINK IT WAS A GHOST?" ADAM asked, then took a big bite of his hot dog.

The trailer had a stove and an oven, but there were both a fire pit and a grill next to our spot, and we'd decided to roast hot dogs for dinner in the pit. He'd run until dusk, stopped by and given me a sweaty kiss, then grabbed clean clothes and a towel before heading to the showers.

By the time he came back, I had a fire going in the pit and the food ready to cook.

There were camp chairs tied to the back of the trailer, but we sat on the ground next to each other anyway. If I didn't notice that we were cooking right next to the Behemoth Trailer and sitting on a manicured lawn, I could pretend we were really camping. This was like "the good parts version" of camping. I could get used to it.

"Umm," I answered, then swallowed so I could talk. "I didn't say that exactly—my father is dead, after all. If it was my father, it was a ghost. But maybe it was something else. There are stories about the Indian supernatural population, but a lot of the old knowledge was lost when the government tried to assimilate the tribes into the Amer-European culture. A good portion of what *is* known was made up on the spot—no one tells a tall tale like an Indian—and no one knows for certain anymore which are the really old stories and which were faked."

Charles, Bran's half-Indian son born sometime in the early eighteen hundreds, could have shed some light on the subject—but, to my intense frustration, he seldom talked about his Native American roots. Maybe I could have pushed him into it, but Charles was one of the very few people who really intimidated me. So even back when I was looking into that half of my family history, I'd never prodded him too hard, much as I'd have liked to.

"You think it might have been some local spirit imitating your father?" Adam asked.

He'd finished his hot dog and was in the middle of cooking another. He liked them burnt on the outside—I liked mine just shy of hot.

I watched my hot dog warm and tried to pretend I could believe that. "Maybe. Maybe there is something like a weird doppelganger who appears to other people or a backward foreganger—a death's-head who appears after a man dies instead of three days before."

Adam tilted his head at me, then shook it. "If you really thought it was some native critter, you'd be calling Charles."

Adam was right. If Charles thought I was really in trouble, he'd help however he could. He might be scary, but he was family. Sort of.

Adam gave me a shrewd look. "You just don't like the idea that your father visited you, and you don't know why."

And why Joe Old Coyote hadn't shown up sooner.

Damn it, I chided myself. I knew better than that. A ghost wasn't a person; it was just the leftovers. That ghost might be the ghost of my father, but he *wasn't* my father.

He'd died before I was born. But I hadn't suffered. I'd been raised by Bryan and Evelyn, my foster parents, and they had loved me. When they died, Bran and the rest of his pack had stepped in—and then my mother. I'd never been unloved, never mistreated. I was an adult—so why did the sight of a ghost who looked like my father make me feel so raw?

"Okay," I said. "Yep. You're right. If he could visit anytime, why didn't he? Why now when I don't need him?" I'd rather have believed it wasn't my father.

He put his arm around me. "Maybe it was some sort of vision quest without the fasting part."

I shook my head. "Nope, I already did my vision quest."

He pulled back, so he could see my face. "Really?"

"Uhm," I answered. "The summer Charles taught me to fix cars. One day he just took me out into the forest. We fasted for three days, then he told me not to shift into a coyote and sent me off into the mountains."

"What did you see?" Adam asked. "Or is that supposed to be a secret?"

I snorted. "Sacred, not secret, I think." Though the only person I'd ever told what I saw had been Charles. "But mine was pretty weird. I asked Charles if I did it wrong, and he just gave me that look—" I tried to freeze my face into an emotionless but somehow terrifying mask—and Adam grinned.

"What did he say when you showed him that expression?" he asked.

Only an idiot would make fun of Charles to his face. Adam knew me so well.

"He asked me if I'd eaten something that made me sick," I said. "Though he turned his head, so I couldn't see his expression. I think he might have smiled."

Adam laughed. "So back to your vision."

"Right," I said. "So my vision was a little . . . Charles told me that there was no right or wrong way to have a vision. It just was. Then he told me about some guy who had a vision and found out he could talk to spirits. Elk Spirit came to him and told him he had to serve Elk Spirit and to do that he had to dress only in yellow. Or maybe that was blue. So this guy, he did that for a few years until Bear Spirit came and told him he'd been talking to Elk Spirit and decided that it should be Bear Spirit he listens to. So Bear Spirit told him to paint his face red and walk backward. When Charles's grandfather, the medicine man, met this man, he had been walking backward for years and years. Charles's grandfather heard the man's story, and told him, 'Just because you listen to spirits does not mean you must obey them.'" I'd almost forgotten that Charles had shared that story with me. It was a sign, I suspect, of how upset I'd been that I hadn't had the kind of vision quest I had expected—one with eagles and deer who guide me to enlightenment.

"What happened?" Adam asked.

"Your hot dog is on fire," I told him.

He pulled the black thing out of the fire, tapped it on the ground, and it broke into pieces. He got another hot dog and stuck it on the campfire fork while I ate mine.

"Mercy, what happened to the guy who was walking around backward?"

"He washed his face and started walking forward. After about five steps, he tripped and broke his leg."

"You are making that up," said Adam, pulling his hot dog in for inspection. It wasn't black, so he stuck it back in the fire.

I lifted my hand. "Scout's honor, that's the story Charles told me. You ask him if you can't tell if I'm lying or not." That was sort of a put-down among werewolves. Only a very new werewolf wouldn't be able to sense truth from falsehood. "Charles said that the man never did go back to walking backward, though."

"You have to be a boy to say, 'Scout's honor,'" Adam told me.

"Nah-uh. Girl Scout leader, here." I pointed my thumb

at my breastbone. "Sort of. When my mom couldn't do it. Anyway, you wanted to hear about my vision."

"Yes."

I opened my mouth to tell him a funny version, but what came out was different from what I'd intended.

"One moment I was sitting alone in the middle of a forest; the next I was walking in a different place. Everything was gray, almost like a black-and-white film except there was no white or black, just odd shades of gray. There was no grass or trees, just endless mounds of sand. It felt . . . empty. Like those postapocalyptic horror films, you know? Empty but scary, too."

I could feel it now as I had then: the tightness in my chest that made it difficult to breathe, the way the hair on the back of my neck had stood up because I knew that there was evil lurking, watching.

Adam pulled his hot dog out of the fire, but instead of eating it, he forced the blunt end of the fork into the ground, so it stuck up like a bizarre garden ornament. Then he pulled me against him, and my tension eased so I could breathe normally again.

"Sorry," I said. "I didn't expect it to bother me so much."

"You don't have to tell me."

"No," I said. "But I want to." It felt right. Charles had told me I'd know when it was time to share what had happened to me. Some people were required to tell their experience to every person they met, but most of us only shared with a few people.

"So I was wandering through this desolate place. The only thing I could see besides sand were remnants of buildings. In the beginning, some of the buildings were modern—tall structures made of glass and steel. On those, the glass was cracked or broken and the steel rusted nearly through. As I continued on, the ruins started to be older buildings, houses. I clearly recall seeing what was left of an old Victorian, tipped awkwardly on its side as if it had been a giant dollhouse some child had kicked over. Then it was like something you'd see on a Western film set, but decades later. Blackened poles from adobe buildings half-buried in the sand, hitching posts and broken boardwalks, with dead weeds poking out.

"I'm the only living thing in the place.

"Eventually, there are only tent poles, and I am walking by them, crying, sobbing, with snot dripping from my nose—the whole wretched business though I don't know what I am grieving for."

"How old were you?" Adam asked.

"That was after Bryan died," I answered. "Just after, I think." Just talking about what I'd seen rattled me, my jaw vibrating as if I were cold, though Adam was warm and solid against me. He was real, but somehow that long ago vision was real, too. "So fourteen or thereabouts."

Telling Adam was almost like living through it again. The emotions had been real and powerful, maybe the most real thing about the whole vision.

"Finally, I came up to this car—an old Model T Ford buried up to its axles. It was so sad, I could feel its sorrow weighing down my heart, distracting me from whatever had caused me to cry in the first place. I put my hands on it, but there was no way to dig it out or fix it. I explained that to the car, as if it could understand what I was saying because I felt as though it could. I told it I was sorry I couldn't do more.

"Then, under my fingers it began to vibrate, shaking until I couldn't hold it anymore. I had to close my eyes against the sand it stirred up, and when I opened them, I was alone in a forest."

I remembered how frightened I had been in the forest. My pulse picked up, and goose bumps covered my forearms. The forest should have been a relief from the dead grayness I'd been in. The forest had been my second home—but the forest of my vision had hidden watchers, dangerous watchers who didn't approve of me.

"It was a dark forest. Although all the trees were conifers, they'd formed a thick canopy over the top of me—like in a rain forest. I could feel that I was watched, but no matter how hard I looked, I never saw them. My watchers followed me as I walked. Eventually, I started running, and I panicked like a rabbit. It seemed as though I ran for hours. Every time I slowed down, I could feel them closing in on me. So I didn't slow down." Remembered fear had me sweating, and the muscles on the back of my neck were tight. "I never saw anything while I ran. Never knew what was chasing me. I just knew I was the prey in this race. I knew absolutely that if they caught me, I was dead.

"I looked over my shoulder as I ran full tilt through the forest, and my foot caught a downed tree. I tumbled down a hill and landed at the foot of a La-Z-Boy."

"A what?" Adam asked.

"I told you it was weird. A La-Z-Boy, one of those big recliners. This one had a big tag on it that said 'La-Z-Boy.' It should have felt out of place in the forest, but instead it was I who didn't belong." The recliner had been orange and blue plaid. Ugly.

"At first all I saw was the chair, then I could tell it was occupied by a tall, handsome Indian man who looked not at all impressed by me."

Funny. I could remember the color of the chair as if I'd just been staring at it, but I couldn't really remember the Indian man's face or what he was wearing. I don't think I noticed anything except his eyes.

"I got to my feet. My jeans were torn, my shirt was ripped, and there was a long, painful scratch on my side. There were sticks in my hair. I felt as if I were someplace I didn't belong, somewhere no one wanted me. I raised my chin and met his gaze, eye to eye, though I knew in my heart it was a stupid thing to do." The panic had been gone, replaced by a hollow emptiness that felt like nothing could ever fill it.

Adam's hand tightened on my shoulder.

"As soon as I began the stare-down, a fox, a lynx, and a bear came out of the woods. A huge bird that looked like a giant eagle dropped out of the sky, and they all stared at me, but I kept my eyes on the man in the chair."

It had been unexplainably horrible, knowing that I did not belong in that forest with the Indian man and the animals. I was an outsider, alone.

"Steady," murmured Adam.

"The man finally said, 'Who are you who walks in my forest, half-breed?' I could tell he didn't mean that he wanted to know my name. He wanted to know what I was." I couldn't explain it right. "The essence of the person I was."

"What did you tell him?" Adam asked.

"I told him that I was coyote." I cleared my throat. "He stood up. And up. He was a lot taller than I was, as tall as the trees around us and somehow more real than they were. I know that's an odd visual picture, but it was just the way it was. Without dropping my gaze, he said, '*I* am Coyote.' He sounded pretty offended."

I sucked in a breath. "I probably should have given him my name. It wasn't the right answer—but it wouldn't have been the wrong one, either. So I said, 'Okay. You can be Coyote. But I am *a* coyote.' He considered my answer, then he bent down to whisper in my ear." I felt stupid about this last.

"What did he say?"

"He said, 'Okay. You can be a coyote, too. But you're a silly little thing, and I am a silly old thing.' And then I woke up."

"Do you know what it meant?" Adam asked.

I laughed and shook my head.

"That's a lie," he whispered, pulling me closer.

"It meant that I'm not Indian enough," I told him. "I don't belong anywhere."

He burned another hot dog while we sat together and watched the flames.

"I think you're wrong," he told me, finally. "It didn't sound like Coyote was rejecting you."

"He was talking about my coyote half," I said.

Adam smiled and rocked me a couple of times. "How confusing it must be to have a coyote half, a human half, an Indian half, and a white half."

I snickered and felt better. It was seldom a good idea to take myself too seriously. "All four halves are pretty happy about being married to you right now. Maybe I'm wrong. Maybe it meant that we should get matching La-Z-Boys." Though I would pick better colors. "If you don't pull that hot dog out pretty soon, you're going to go to bed hungry."

"Mmm," he rumbled into my ear. "I thought that being married meant that I never go to bed hungry."

WE CAME BACK OUT AFTER A WHILE, STOKED UP the fire, and cooked the rest of the package of hot dogs.

4

THE NEXT DAY, WE LEFT THE TRAILER IN THE empty campground—Adam had been responsible for setting up the security, after all—and drove back across the river, on past the oddly named town of The Dalles and the less oddly named town of Hood River to Multnomah Falls. Someone once told me there is about a ten-mile stretch where the annual rainfall increases by an inch a mile. Truth or not, not far west of Hood River the scrub is replaced by lots and lots of trees and other green stuff. A few miles farther on, the waterfalls begin.

Multnomah is the most impressive, but there are dozens of waterfalls on Larch Mountain, and we spent most of the day hiking the trails that webbed the mountainside from one falls to another. Since it was a nice day in the middle of summer, there were a lot of other people doing the same thing.

I didn't mind the company, and I didn't think Adam did,

either. It felt like we were a friendly party of strangers, drawn together by the extraordinary beauty of water dropping in white sheets from rocky cliffs. There was a sense of awe that connected us all, bringing us together. The ties were not as real as the pack bonds, but it felt like the beginnings of the same thing. It was magic, just a little of it, built of fair weather and joy.

That feeling of belonging to something greater than myself was the gift Adam gave to me.

My whole life I'd been an outsider: first a coyote raised in a pack of werewolves, then a supernatural outsider in my mother's mundane household, finally an outsider who had too many secrets to really have friends. I was good at appearing to fit in, so no one really took notice of me.

Until Adam. With Adam beside me, I felt like I belonged, like he was my connection to the rest of the world. And because of him, I could be just one of these happy hikers who were out to enjoy themselves. I shook off the faint shadow that recalling my vision had left upon me. Indian or not, coyote or human, I wasn't alone anymore.

Some of the trails were easy, even handicap accessible. Not too far from Multnomah, those all went away, and the fun started in earnest. The top of the mountain is a little more than four thousand feet above the trailhead, and not much of that climb is gentle.

I HEARD THE CRYING BEFORE I SAW THEM. THINKing someone was in trouble, I broke into a jog up the trail, and Adam ran behind me.

"Honey, I can't carry you." The woman's voice was on the edge of tears. "I just can't. You have to be a big boy and help me, Robert."

There followed a boy's voice, unintelligible to me and interspersed with sobs.

Around a bend in the trail we came upon two very upset people. A frazzled woman in her forties and a boy with a tear- and dirt-streaked face.

"Hey," I said. "Sounds pretty rough. What can we do to help?"

She started to refuse help—and then her eyes fell on Adam and lit up with avarice. I sympathized with her entirely—but was happier when I realized it was the strength of his back she was excited about and not his pretty face.

Her son was not nearly as excited as his mother. Robert, his mother informed us, was eight, but he had Down's syndrome and was as wary of strangers as most two-year-olds. He wasn't happy about the idea of Adam hauling him down the mountain to the parking lot.

While his mother tried to reason with him, Adam got down on one knee and looked the boy in the eye. He didn't say anything at all. But after almost a full minute, the boy nodded, and when Adam stood up, he climbed onto Adam's back without another protest. He still wasn't happy about it, but he knew who was in charge.

"Well," said Robert's mother, flabbergasted.

"Adam's good at giving orders," I told her truthfully. "Even without saying anything."

So Adam carried one very tired and cranky eight-year-old boy who had a sprained ankle down the trail while the boy's even-more-tired mother thanked him all the way.

"I didn't know it would be so steep," the boy's mother said to me, when Adam stretched his legs a little and got ahead of us. I thought it was to stop her incessant thanks, but maybe I was being uncharitable.

"Robert was so tired of being in the car. Eugene is still a long way, and I thought it might be nice if he ran off some energy; then he would sleep the rest of the way. I hope your young man doesn't hurt himself. Robert weighs almost eighty pounds."

"Don't worry," I assured her. "Adam was in the army. He can carry an eighty-pound pack down the mountain. That's also why he knows the difference between a twisted ankle, a sprained ankle, and a break."

I wasn't going to tell her that he was a werewolf who could probably carry us all down if he could figure out a good way to make a manageable bundle of us. Adam was out to the public, but neither Robert nor his mother looked like someone who could deal with werewolves at this point in their trip. The army part was true—they didn't need to know that his army life was back in the Vietnam era.

"Get his ankle X-rayed anyway," advised Adam, who'd had no trouble hearing us. "I'm not a doctor, and sprains can be tricky."

By the time we made it down to the parking lot, Robert had recovered except for an exaggerated limp. His mother had lost the desperate edge to her voice. She thanked us again, and Robert gave Adam a wet kiss on his cheek.

"My hero," I told Adam, as they drove away. "You done here? Or would you mind going back up again?"

To my intense pleasure, Adam and I hiked for another couple of hours, then ate in Hood River. I'd never spent so much time with him without interruption. Here, there was no other demand on either of us.

I loved it. Loved watching the alertness fade and the strain of taking care of the pack, of me, of his daughter, of his business just wash away from his face and his body.

Usually, Adam looked like a man well into his thirties—though werewolves don't age at all. By the time we returned to the campground, he'd lost ten years of care and looked not much older than his daughter. Laughter lit his face in a way that I'd never seen before.

I had done this. Me. Okay, me and God's waterfalls and mountainside forest. Even though it had seemed I couldn't get through a day without throwing him in the middle of my hot water. Even though he'd had to fight vampires, demons, and waterlogged fae because of me. Even though he'd had to fight his own pack, I was good for Adam.

I'd seen him ticked off, in pain, in sorrow. It was indescribably better to see him happy.

"What?" he asked, finishing the second of his nine-ounce steaks, medium rare. "Why are you looking at me that way?"

The trendy little restaurant that occupied the old Victorian intimidated me a little, not that I'd let anyone, including Adam, see it. I don't think I've ever seen anything, except possibly my mother, intimidate Adam. But it was more than that.

He fit here. He'd fit in running around out in the trails—and packing the little boy down the mountainside. For someone like me, who'd had to fight to make my own place because I didn't fit anywhere, he was . . . Well, the truth of the matter was that he fit me, too.

Though, from their sideways looks, a lot of the rather affluent diners eating there obviously didn't think so. Adam might be going casual in jeans and a T-shirt, but he still looked like he just stepped off a modeling job. I looked like I'd been hiking all day even though I'd pulled the leaves out of my hair in the restaurant bathroom.

I sighed theatrically, resting my chin on my cupped hands and bracing my elbows on the table. "You are too gorgeous, you know?" I said it just loud enough that the people who'd been watching us surreptitiously could hear me.

Unholy laughter lit his eyes—telling me he'd been noticing the looks we'd been getting. But his face was completely serious, as he purred, "So. Am I worth what you paid for me, baby?"

I loved it when he played along with me.

I sighed again, a sound that I drew up from my toes, a

contented, happy sound. I'd get him back for that "baby." Just see if I didn't.

"Oh, yes," I told our audience. "I'll tell Jesse that she was right. Go for the sexy beast, she told me. If you're going to shell out the money, don't settle."

He threw back his head and laughed until he had to wipe tears of hilarity off his face. "Jeez, Mercy," he said. "The things you say." Then he leaned across the table and kissed me.

A while later he pulled back, grinned at me, and sat back in his chair.

I had to catch my breath before I spoke. "Best five bucks I ever spent," I told him fervently.

HE WAS STILL LAUGHING WHEN HE BUCKLED HIS seat belt. "It's a good thing that we don't live in Hood River," he said. "I'd never be able to show my face in that restaurant again. Five bucks. Jeez." Adam was a gentleman raised in the fifties. He tried really hard not to swear in front of women.

"I thought it was pretty cool when that little old lady tried to give you a twenty," I said, and set him off again.

"The thing that spooked me"—he drove back out on the highway toward our campground—"was that woman at the table next to us, who looked like she bought the whole act, even after everyone else was laughing."

Ah, Creepy Lady. She'd watched us both with her eyes wide and her jaw open, and still her expression managed to be blank. I was betting she was either a total psychopath—or fae, which was sometimes the same thing. I could have gone closer for a good sniff—I've learned what fae smell like—but it was my honeymoon. I didn't want to know.

"I'm never going to be bored with you around," Adam told me. The funny thing was that he sounded happy about it.

"WANT TO GO FOR A RUN?" ADAM ASKED, HOPping out of bed a few hours later.

We'd lain down to rest after our travels. Not much resting had taken place, but I wasn't going to complain. Still, every bone in my body was Jell-O, and he wanted to go run?

"Ungh," I said. That was the best I could do.

He grinned at me. "You can drop the act."

I waved a weak hand at him.

"I bet I catch a rabbit before you do," he said.

Oh. He meant a *run*. We'd gotten back to the campground about dusk, so it was full dark. Full dark meant that in the unlikely event that someone saw Adam as werewolf, they'd think he was a dog—helped along by pack magic that let people see what they expected to see. The magic works in broad daylight, too, but darkness helps.

"Well, why didn't you say so?" I grumped at him as I vaulted off the bed. I was wearing half a T-shirt—the left half—and my socks. The other half of my shirt was on the far side of the trailer. I was going to take an hour and clean the trailer really well before we returned it to its owner or I'd risk being embarrassed.

Which reminded me. "Hey, Adam?" I dropped the half shirt on the floor and stood on one foot to take off a sock. "Who loaned us the trailer? The only people I know who could have afforded it are you, Kyle, or Samuel. Samuel would not be caught dead with something this . . . bulky. You told me it isn't yours. Did Kyle buy it in an attempt to compromise with Warren's desire to go camping?"

"Uncle Mike."

I froze, one foot in the air. "What?" He'd borrowed something from a fae?

Adam steadied me with a hand on my shoulder. "I'm not wet behind the ears," he told me, a little bite in his voice. "Uncle Mike called me and told me he'd heard I was planning on taking you camping and didn't he have the sweetest little trailer we could take with us."

"You borrowed from Uncle Mike?"

"Uncle Mike offered it . . . Now, how did he phrase that? For services already rendered. You need to either get the sock off, Mercy, or put that foot down before you fall over."

I pulled the sock off and stood on my own two feet. "Fae never give you anything for nothing," I said urgently. "Not even Zee, and he's my friend."

The fae do things like make you pledge your firstborn child or your life's blood for a piece of bubble gum, and make it sound like a good deal at the time.

"When the fae who owns this campground called to offer it up about an hour before Uncle Mike called, I was pretty suspicious," Adam told me.

His voice had regained its usual relaxed tone, but he was irritated. I could tell by the way he stripped off his shirt. I could leave it alone . . . but he didn't know the fae the way I'd come to know them.

"After Uncle Mike called," he continued blandly, "I knew they wanted us here for some reason. I could have refused—I had reservations in San Diego—but I thought you'd enjoy this more than a hotel, and I knew I would."

I frowned at him.

"I didn't promise him anything," Adam said with exaggerated patience. "You need to remember who you are now. They can't just f—" He stopped speaking for a moment, then swallowed his temper with an effort—and not as much effect as he probably wanted because the bland tone deserted him entirely.

"Mercy, they can't mess with you without messing with me and the whole pack—and Samuel—and Bran—and Zee—and Stefan probably, for that matter. I don't know what they want. Maybe they needed us to *not* go to San Diego—Uncle Mike mentioned San Diego specifically though I hadn't told anyone where I was taking you. Maybe they needed us to stick closer to home. We werewolves are a potential ally against political attacks now since we are the only other supernatural group who admits its existence to the general public. Maybe there is something here—" He waved his hands to indicate the general area upon which the trailer sat. "It could be something as easy as using us as a deterrent to another fae who plans on destroying what Edythe has built here."

Edythe must be the fae who owned the place. Of course it was a fae who had set up this campground, with its big trees and supergreen grass.

Adam was right. I'd forgotten that if the fae screwed with me, they were taking on the whole pack and then some. I was more than just a mechanic who fixed VWs and turned into a coyote because I had Adam, and I had friends. What a difference a year or two could make.

If he'd stopped there, I wouldn't have gotten mad. Maybe I'd even have conceded that he'd been right, and I shouldn't have worried. But he didn't leave it alone—because Adam might be gorgeous and smart, but he wasn't perfect.

"I suppose I could have driven myself crazy—" he bit out because our peculiar bond apparently wasn't doing its thing. He didn't know that I agreed with him. That he'd won. "Or more to the point," he said, "I could have let you drive both of us crazy for the past few days speculating what nefarious plot Uncle Mike has hatched up—Uncle Mike, who has proved himself to be, at least, a valuable ally if you don't consider him to be a friend. Or I could keep it to myself until your curiosity got the best of you and you asked so we could at least enjoy a couple days of our honeymoon before we started worrying about what the fu—" He was breathing harder now and had almost let that four-letter word all the way out.

I leaned forward, kissed the white line on his cheek that came out like war paint whenever he clenched his jaw, and said lightly, "All you ever had to do was tell me you had it under control, dear." I batted my eyes demurely. "I'm just the wife. I don't have to strain my poor weak brain worrying about the fae because you are here to protect me."

Yep, I was ticked, too. He was patronizing me.

I could still, however, admit when he was right: the fae certainly weren't the ones he had to worry about.

He narrowed his eyes at me. "That is not what I said. Don't put words in my mouth."

I reached around him, popped the door of the trailer open, and changed into a coyote before he finished his sentence—and I was off and running.

It would take a while before he could follow because werewolves take a lot longer to change. I supposed he could have chased after me in human form—but on two feet he'd never catch me, werewolf or not. Besides that, he was naked. The campground was rendered mostly private by topography and greenery, but it wasn't completely private. Pack magic wouldn't do anything to hide a naked man running across the campground.

I took advantage of him and left before he could continue the argument.

"DO YOU UNDERSTAND WHAT YOU ARE DOING, marrying an Alpha werewolf?" my mother had said a few months ago, as I drove us to yet another wedding-dress outlet in Portland. Who knew there were so many white dresses? Who knew there were so many horrible white dresses? The oddest thing was that it seemed like the worse the dress, the more expensive it was.

"Yes, Mom," I said, narrowly avoiding a brownish '77 LTD being driven by a grandmother who could barely see over the dash. "I've known Adam for a long time. I know just what I'm getting myself into."

As if I hadn't said anything, my mother said, "Any kind

of alpha takes some serious managing. Werewolves are controlling bastards—and Alpha werewolves are worse than that. If you don't watch it, you find that you are doing exactly what they tell you to."

There was an interesting snap in her voice, and I wondered how often Bran had gotten her to do what he wanted her to. Not as often as he wanted, I'd bet, but evidently more than she was happy about.

"I know how to take care of myself." I wasn't worried. Adam was dominant—that was certainly true. But I'd more than proved to myself that I could hold my own against him if I needed to.

"I know you do," Mom said with satisfaction. "But remember, confrontations aren't productive with an Alpha. You'll just lose—or worse, make him lose control."

"He won't hurt me, Mom."

"Of course not," she said. "But a man like Adam, if he loses control, he'll feel terrible. He'll worry that he *might* have hurt you. Making him feel horrible isn't what you want." She paused, considered what she said, then modified it. "Unless it is useful for him to feel horrible, of course. Mostly, though, I've found that isn't productive. Men who are miserable can be unpredictable."

I wondered if my stepfather knew how lucky he was that she felt it was in her best interests that he was happy instead of miserable. Probably he did; he was a smart man.

"I am the queen of hit-and-run," I told her. "All the satisfaction, none of the danger."

"Good," she said. "Just make sure he doesn't turn you into the good little wife. You'd manage it for a while—you were the good little daughter in my house from the time you moved in until you went to college."

There was a little edge to her voice, as if I'd hurt her—which hadn't been my intention at all. When I'd left Bran's pack to live with my mother and stepfather, I'd been sixteen, and they'd already had a family without me. No.

They'd had the perfect family without me. I hadn't wanted to disturb them any more than I could help.

"But if you try that in a marriage," she continued, "the marriage will self-destruct eventually, and there will be casualties everywhere you look."

"Adam doesn't want a good little wife," I told her.

"Of course not," she said. But she didn't know Adam that well, and I figured she was just humoring me, until she kept going. "But he was taught how to be a husband when it was assumed that his wife would be a combination cook/housekeeper/mother who would need him to provide for and protect her. He knows in his head and his heart that you are an equal, but his instincts were instilled a long time ago. You are going to have to help him with that and be patient with him."

My mother would not be nearly as terrifying if she weren't right so often.

SO INSTEAD OF STICKING AROUND TO FIGHT WITH Adam, I ran to let us both cool off, and to let the hurt of his patronizing remarks ease so I could think. I can't be patient when I'm mad—unless I'm waiting to get back at someone, and I wasn't that mad. Not yet.

I ran the first mile or so as fast as I could, then dropped down to a dog-trot.

I couldn't let him treat me like his first wife. I couldn't live surrounded by cotton wool.

But he knew that.

I trusted him. What he'd kept from me hadn't been life threatening. He was right. The fae would not offend the Alpha of the Columbia Basin Pack. One werewolf was a tough creature—but the real power of the werewolves lay in their packs. I could understand him wanting to make sure our honeymoon was worry-free.

Okay. Okay.

So at what point had our discussion turned into an argument that left us both angry? And left me with an ache in my chest that felt as if he'd punched me instead of snapped at me. He hadn't even worked up to a good rage, and I felt miserable.

A rabbit bolted right out in front of me. I hadn't really intended on hunting, but if the stupid things want to present themselves for dinner . . . With a fresh turn of speed, I gave chase.

I WAS EATING THE LAST OF THE RABBIT WHEN Adam showed up in his glorious furred form. Adam is a beautiful man, and his wolf is beautiful, too. He is colored like a Siamese cat, though in bluish grays that deepen to near black.

He dropped a second rabbit at my feet and lay down in front of me, nose on his paws and his ears flattened.

Nothing says you're sorry like a dead bunny.

I remembered his first wife. Christy had made him apologize a lot, apologize for things that were not his fault. I didn't want an apology. I wanted to know why we'd just had a fight, and I hadn't even enjoyed it.

I *liked* to fight with Adam.

He'd been mad first.

I considered that.

Adam got mad for three reasons. The most common, and my personal favorite, was frustration. Usually, when Adam was mad at me, frustration was the spark that set him off. Adam frustrated and angry with me usually started with fireworks and ended in good ways with a lot of adrenaline engendered and spent along the way.

The second was if anyone was trying to harm someone under his protection. We'd established that the fae were probably not planning our deaths or even near-fatal entrapments.

The third was pain—physical or otherwise.

Having established that he wasn't frustrated and neither I nor anyone else was in any danger—I must have hurt him somehow.

I narrowed my eyes at him. Usually, Adam was pretty straightforward. It was one of my favorite things about him. Figuring out why he'd been mad should have been a lot easier.

He'd tried to protect me, and I objected. We did that all the time, and he seldom got mad unless or until I got hurt.

He'd tried to make sure our wedding and honeymoon were fun. He'd thought that I'd fret about borrowing the van from Uncle Mike but that I'd also have a better time out here than I would have in a more typical honeymoon.

He'd gotten mad when he thought I was going to get mad at him for not telling me about the trailer. It was his belief that I would get mad about it that had hurt him. I wiggled my hips into a more comfortable position and tried to think like Adam—a very smart person poisoned by testosterone.

First—he knew I'd get mad if he kept anything big from me, but that wouldn't hurt his feelings.

And suddenly I understood what had happened.

I got up and stepped over my kill, then over his. I licked his muzzle—and then shifted back into human.

"You made some assumptions," I told him. "Take a note: it usually works better if you wait until I do something stupid before getting mad at me."

Adam stared at me. I couldn't tell what he was thinking.

"This building a marriage is an ongoing project," I told him. "And we'll both make a lot of mistakes along the way. I did worry about borrowing the trailer. But after a half minute's thought, I knew you'd never borrow anything from any fae without making sure you had a handle on the consequences." I blew out a huff of air. "You got mad because you thought I wouldn't trust you to know the difference. Not fair. Not fair at all.

"Me, I keep important stuff from you all the time." I grinned at him. "But I know you're a better person than I am. Still, I think that my frailty means you don't owe me an apology for doing something I would do, so we're even as far as keeping information from me is concerned."

Now it was he who narrowed his eyes at me.

"Right," I said as if he'd spoken. It was chilly in bare skin with the sun down, so I stretched out against him and let him keep me warm. "I know what I said before I took off—but I was provoked. No apologies from me or from you—but I'll take the rabbit on account. However, if you try that patronizing sh— stuff on me again, not even a fat juicy rabbit is going to stop the fight we'll have."

Since it was unfair for me to keep being the only one who could talk, I shifted back into the coyote. And since I have a policy of accepting gifts graciously, I ate his rabbit. Besides, fighting always made me hungry, and there was no chocolate handy.

He thought it was funny that I ate the second rabbit without accepting his apology—so we were okay again. I expected that we'd have a lot more fights, and mostly I looked forward to them. Life with Adam wasn't going to be boring, either.

WE WERE HEADED BACK TO THE CAMPSITE WHEN we found the boat. On the way out, I hadn't run right along the river. Instead, I'd followed one of the ridges that lined the gorge, avoiding the few houses and vineyards scattered here and there, and Adam had followed my trail. On the way back, though, we ran along the edge of the river. The moon was new, just a sliver in the sky, and the stars reflected in the black water.

The highway on the Oregon side was always busy, and this night was no exception. Our side, the Washington side, was a lot quieter: the river was wide, the noise of the cars a distant symphony accompanying the sounds of the night. One of those sounds was made by a boat bobbing against the shore.

I paused because this wasn't a place I'd have expected to find a boat. As soon as my attention was drawn to it, I could smell blood and terror—the aftermaths of battle. A glance at Adam told me he'd noticed it, too. The fur along his spine was raised though he was silent.

The boat was tucked under the edge of three or four trees and accompanying brush that grew along the bank. From what I could see, and I wiggled a lot closer than Adam could, it was one of the small fishing boats, a bass boat, the kind that maybe two or three people could use to fish in. Small enough to row though there was a small outboard motor on the back of this one. I couldn't see into the boat because of the underbrush, but I could smell a man's fear and hear him talking.

"Don't let it find me. Don't let it find me." Over and over again, very softly, barely even a whisper. I hadn't been able to pick up his exact words until I was within a stone's throw of the boat, and I have very good hearing. The boat hitting the rocks with the gentle rise and fall of the river's waves was louder than his voice.

I backed out of the brush and met Adam's eyes. Naked was going to be hard to explain, and I knew all about what those bushes were going to do with my skin. But Adam took too long to change, would be equally naked—and if whatever this man was afraid of came back, Adam the werewolf was our best defense.

Maybe other people wouldn't have automatically assumed that whatever this man was afraid of would need a werewolf to fight it. There were no werewolves around here, vampires tended to be more of an urban monster, and the fae reservation was an hour the other side of the Tri-Cities—two hundred miles or more away from us. But the sheer magnitude of the terror he still felt made me think I wasn't being paranoid.

I shifted to human. "Hey," I called. "You in the boat. Are you okay?"

The man's voice didn't alter. He hadn't registered my words at all.

"I think I'll have better luck reaching him from the river side," I told Adam. "That boat's still floating. If he's as badly hurt as all the blood I'm smelling makes me think he is, it'll be easier if we're not trying to drag him through the underbrush anyway."

The nearest bit of clear riverbank was about thirty feet downstream. The sun long gone, the water was icy. I stum bled on a big rock on the river bottom and made a splash when I fell. I made some noise, too—frigid water on nice warm skin when I'm not expecting it tends to make me squeak. The man in the boat screamed—from the hoarseness of his voice, it wasn't the first time he'd screamed tonight.

"It's all right," I said, regaining my feet. "You're safe."

He quit screaming, but I don't think it was because he'd understood me. Sometimes fear is too big for that—so much of your being is focused on survival that anything else falls to the side. I've been there a couple of times.

The rocks under my feet were sharp, but once I was waist-deep, my weight didn't press me down on them quite so hard. If I'd been headed downstream instead of upstream, I could have swum instead. Adam paced back and forth unhappily on the river's edge.

The trees hung over the river, and the shore curved back under them. Finding a path through the debris that had collected in the small backwater along with the boat forced me to wade in through a bunch of underwater plants I didn't see until I was in the middle of them.

My eyesight is pretty darn good at night, but the river was an impenetrable black veil, and anything below the surface was hidden. I hated not seeing. Who really knew what was in the Columbia?

Something brushed against my leg with a little more force than the rest of the weeds, and I let out an involuntary yip. Adam, invisible on the other side of the tree, whined.

"Sorry, sorry," I told him. "I'm fine. Just caught my leg on one of those clumps of plants. I can't see a damned thing under the water, and that and this guy reeking of fear has me all hopped up. Sorry."

The stupid plant was persistent. It clung to my calf as I approached the boat, resisting my halfhearted attempts to shake it loose. The tendency of some water plants to wrap around arms and legs of unsuspecting swimmers is one of the leading causes of drowning. However, I reminded myself, I had my feet on the river bottom, so this one was only an irritant. Nothing to panic about.

I forgot about the plant as soon as I grabbed the side of the boat and got down to business. My eyes just barely cleared the side of the boat, so I couldn't get a good look at the wounded man.

"It's okay," I told him. "We'll get you out of this."

I gave an experimental tug on the boat, but I was now up to my chest in the water, and the current threatened to push me off my feet. When I pulled on the boat, it was I who moved.

I shifted my grip, moving nearer to the bow. If I pulled the boat the way it was designed to move instead of sideways, it should require a lot less effort. As a last resort, I could climb in and use the motor—but the tree limbs were only a few inches above the gunnel, and I didn't really want to scrape myself up getting in the boat.

I heard something and jerked my head up.

Four small heads poked out of the river about a dozen yards from the boat. Otters.

Great, that was just great. Just what the night needed.

"Otters," I told Adam, my teeth beginning to chatter with the effect of the water. "If I start screaming, it's because the otters have come to get me."

He growled, a low, menacing sound, and the four heads disappeared. It wasn't as reassuring as it might have been. But there were no sharp teeth fastened on any of my parts that were underwater, not yet anyway. The only thing grabbing me was the damned weed, which was still wrapped pretty tightly around my ankle.

I had a friend who swam once with sea otters just off the California coast. She said it was an unbelievable experience. They apparently were regular comrades to the divers in the area, playful and cute. They played a little rough—divers who swam with them regularly often had to replace their quarter-inch neoprene diving suits because otter teeth and claws are sharp—but most of the divers counted it worth the price.

River otters are smaller and even cuter than their ocean-going cousins. They also have the sweet temperament of a badger with a hangover. It wouldn't have worried me much—I have sharp teeth when I want them, too. But right now I was in their environment and not mine.

I couldn't see them. Worse for me, I couldn't smell them or hear them, either. I could wait around for them to attack, or I could get the heck out of the river.

I got a good grip on the nose of the boat and managed to persuade it to move out a little. Five or six feet more, and I'd have it out where the river current would push it the way I wanted it to go.

The man in the boat began thrashing. It took me a second to realize he wasn't just panicking—he'd gone for the pull on the engine. As the sudden roar of the engine broke the night, I grabbed onto the boat as hard as I could and let my feet leave the river bottom.

The boat lurched forward, and the weed around my ankle tightened painfully, and for a second I felt as though— But no weed is that tough, and the boat jerked me out of its hold and drove about fifteen feet downstream before I pulled myself into the boat. By that time he'd collapsed again, and his hand fell off the tiller just as I grabbed it.

I balanced on the seat and turned the boat back to shore, where Adam paced.

The man grabbed my arm, and I almost tipped the boat over before I braced against his weight. If I'd had shoes on, my feet would have slipped off the wet wood, and I'd have landed on him.

"Got to get away," he said. His skin was as dark as mine—he was Indian, too, now that I finally had a good look at him—and still his lips managed to look pale.

"Got to get you to shore," I yelled at him over the noise of the engine. "Before you bleed to death."

There was a crunch as the bow of the boat hit the shoreline, then a mighty jerk as Adam grabbed a bowline I hadn't seen or else I'd have used it. He pulled us up and all of the way out of the water onto the bank.

I managed to kill the engine because I'd already started the motion, and when the boat stopped suddenly, I used the momentum to roll all the way out of the boat and onto the ground. My other option would have been to land on the man we were trying to rescue. The drop was not far. I hit the ground with my unprotected shoulder, which was going to bruise, but mostly managed not to hurt myself.

Adam came over to me.

"I'm fine," I said. "Check him."

He raised himself over the side of the boat to look in. I got up at the same time. Either blood loss or the shock of seeing a huge wolf with big sharp teeth had finally driven our man, who was bleeding from the remaining half of his right foot, unconscious.

Adam glanced from me to him—and then bolted. In that brief glance, he told me to stay put while he went for help. Wolves communicate much more clearly than humans do in an emergency.

Adam would run all out, but we were probably five miles or more from the campsite. It would take him ten minutes to get there, maybe ten more to change back to human if he pushed it. I had no idea where the nearest hospital was or how long it would take for them to get the man there. Adam would figure it out.

With the sun down, the air was chilly, the river cold, and both the wounded man and I were wet and freezing. But there was nothing I could do about that at the moment.

I pulled him back down in the boat and propped up the damaged foot on the wooden cross member that doubled as a seat. The wound was just oozing blood, which seemed odd to me. Maybe the cold was useful, even if it was dangerous.

I was debating the benefits of shifting into coyote and sharing what warmth my wet fur would gain us both against trying to figure out how to get his wet shirt off and use it to bandage his foot without a knife. Both moves were likely to be useless or worse . . . when I heard the hum of an engine out in the water.

Lights tracked over the shore and stopped on the white boat I was standing in. I waved my arms to call them in to shore. There were excited voices, but I couldn't tell what they were saying because the sound of their engine drowned out the meaning. A small but much sleeker and more modern boat complete with lights approached us at speed.

Help was here. Unless these were the guys who'd sliced off the man's foot. And me wearing nothing but Adam's dog tags. Ah, well, it couldn't be helped; my modesty wasn't worth a man's life.

The boat hadn't quite beached itself when three men hopped into the river. One of them grabbed the bowline, and as soon as he did, the fourth man, who'd been staying the boat, cut the engine and jumped in, too.

"Benny?" "Faith?" and "Who are you?" gradually resolved themselves into Hank and Fred Owens, Jim Alvin, and Calvin Seeker—introduced to me by Jim Alvin, easily the oldest of them though only Calvin qualified as young.

It was only after the Owens brothers pulled out a first-aid kit and started to work on the wounded man that I realized we were all—victim, me, and the four in the rescuing boat—Indian.

Jim Alvin was in his sixties and smelled of woodsmoke and old tobacco. Calvin was somewhere in his late teens or early twenties. Hank and Fred were around my age, I thought, and close enough in appearance that they might well have been twins, though Hank didn't talk at all. I don't know if I would have noticed their dog tags if I hadn't just received Adam's. But I would still have noticed that they had some sort of emergency training by the efficiency of their movements and their focus as soon as they saw Benny Jamison.

Benny was the hurt man.

Jim interrogated me—for all that his questions were soft-spoken and quiet—while the Owens brothers did their best to save Benny.

"No sign of anyone else?" he asked me, after I told him how Adam and I had found the boat—and how Adam had run back to camp to get help and left me to do what I could.

"No." I pulled the blanket they'd given me more securely around myself.

Benny woke up briefly when they started wrapping his foot with vet wrap. It sounded like it hurt.

Jim sighed. "Benny's sister, Faith, was with him out fishing. They were supposed to be home for dinner. Julie, Benny's wife, she called Fred tonight when Benny didn't answer his phone. We were docking, but the Jamisons are good folk. We put the boat back in the water and started looking. What tribe did you say you were?"

I hadn't, in spite of the fact that they had introduced themselves that way. All of them were from the Yakama (with three a's, though the town was spelled Yakima) Nation. The Owens brothers were Yakama. Jim Alvin was Wishram and Yakama, as was Calvin Seeker. I didn't think of myself that way. I was a walker and a mechanic, both of which served more often than not to make me separate from other people. I was Adam's mate, which connected me to him and to the pack.

I was also cold and tired. It took me too long to remember.

"Blackfoot," I said, then corrected myself. "Blackfeet."

"You don't know which?" asked Calvin, speaking for the first time—though he'd been watching me since they came ashore. I'd almost forgotten I was naked until I saw his face just before I'd been tossed a woolen blanket. I supposed polite disinterest was too much to ask from everyone. Three out of four wasn't bad.

"I never knew my father—my mother is white. He told my mother he was from Browning, Montana," I told them. The wool was doing a good job of warming the skin it covered.

Naked and wrapped in a blanket among strangers didn't use to bother me. Maybe if Calvin would have quit staring at the various pieces of me that the blanket didn't cover, it still wouldn't have bothered me. As it was, I did my best to keep Jim between Calvin and me.

"So you were raised white," said Calvin in disapproving tones.

I should have told them I was Hispanic and any Indians in my bloodlines were South American and unknown. Half of my customers thought I was Hispanic. Telling them I was Hispanic felt like it would have been less of a lie than telling them I was Indian. As if I were claiming ties that weren't there.

"Browning, Montana, makes him Blackfeet," Jim told me kindly. "Piegan. The Blood and the Siksika are Blackfoot."

I knew that. It just hadn't tripped off my tongue.

"What were you doing out here? It's an odd place to be running around at this time of night." Jim didn't say naked. He didn't have to. "Boy," he said abruptly to Calvin. "Don't you make your mother ashamed of her son."

The young man's mouth tightened, but he looked away from me. A few years ago his regard wouldn't have bothered me the way it did now. But things had happened since that made me uncomfortable standing nearly naked with four strangers—five if I counted Benny, which I didn't.

"I just got married," I told him, reminding my too-jittery self that Adam would be on his way back by now. If something happened, and I had no reason to think it would—especially as they had handed over a blanket to cover me without a word—Adam would be here before anything too bad happened. I wouldn't be caught in the trap of assuming all men were bad—but I wouldn't have been human if I weren't wary. "We were swimming."

"Good thing for Benny," said Jim. "We've been by here twice. It would have been morning before we could have seen that boat under the trees. And morning would have been too late for him."

Fred (I could tell because he wore a red flannel shirt, and Hank wore a gray one) left Benny to his brother and came over.

Evidently he'd been listening because he said, "I called 911, Jim, and they had already gotten a call from her husband. There is an ambulance on its way. I told the operator that we could get Benny up to the road. It'll be a rough trip. The road's only a half mile or so as the crow flies, but this is horrible country for a fast trek in the dark. But they'd have to make the trip twice that we need to make once."

"What about taking him on the boat?" asked Calvin.

Fred shook his head. "We might get him to the hospital faster that way—but the ambulance will have medical personnel on board. He'll get faster medical care, and time matters. If he stays in shock, we could lose him—but when he warms up, that foot is going to bleed like a fountain."

"Whatever you and Hank think best," said Jim, which seemed to make the decision for everyone.

5

THE ONLY BRUSH OR TREES IN THIS PART OF the gorge that weren't cultivated—very little of the ground on either side of the river *was* cultivated—were right on the river. For the most part our footing was cheatgrass-covered basalt, not horrible hiking if I'd had shoes.

It would have been better if I could have shifted into coyote, but I didn't know these men—and I don't make it a habit of telling everyone what I am. Too many bad things happened to people who admitted too openly what they were without a powerful group behind them—and sometimes even with a powerful group behind them. I'd survived a long time by keeping my head down and blending in; I wasn't going to change that just to make my bare feet feel better.

The Owens brothers and Calvin took turns carrying Benny. Jim led the way and carried a couple of flares to flag down the ambulance with. We all, except for whoever was carrying Benny, carried flashlights, which did a fair bit to destroy my night vision. I brought up the rear—though they had all suggested I stay down by the river.

I could have done that, but what if they ran into Adam? Under normal circumstances, they'd be perfectly safe. But Adam had had to make two fast changes tonight and experienced a number of stressors. He'd been forced to leave me naked and vulnerable. Benny had been so afraid—in addition to all the blood and pain.

Adam was not human and hadn't been for a long time. His control was very good—but this was not a good night for him to be meeting up with strangers carrying a bleeding, hurt man.

So I insisted on going with them.

We might have been a half mile from the road, but that half mile was all up the side of a very steep hill that was broken up with basalt cliffs that ranged from two feet to twenty or thirty feet high. The first kind we scrambled over; the second we worked our way around.

We'd made it about halfway by my hazy reckoning when Adam caught up to us. He was human and clothed, but his eyes were yellow bright from the adrenaline and the pain of his rushed changes.

He handed me a backpack, and said, "Clothes, shoes, and first aid." His voice was a low, growling sound, and his hand shook.

"Thank you," I said. "I'm safe with them." I found that I believed that now, and it was a relief. "Can you get Benny up to the road to wait for the ambulance?" It would be dangerous, all that blood. But the men were tiring, and tired people make missteps.

Adam didn't look directly at any of the strangers—so they wouldn't have the opportunity to meet his eyes. That was good and bad. It told me he was still in control—but he didn't trust himself to stay that way.

He took Benny off Hank's back without a word, cradling the wounded man like a baby—which kept Benny's foot up higher though it was a much more difficult way to carry an unconscious person than the fireman's carry the Owens brothers had been using.

Hank didn't fight Adam—just held very still, as though he sensed how much danger he was in. Adam lifted his head once, then took a quick look at all the men before sprinting off for the road at a dead run.

"Who the hell was that?" asked Calvin.

He had to have had a fair idea of who it was—after all, Adam had brought clothes for me. What he meant, I thought, was how did Adam run up the side of the canyon carrying Benny at a speed that would have done credit to an Olympic sprinter. "That was my husband," I said nonchalantly to the adrenaline-filled air as I opened the backpack and pulled out my jeans. "He's a werewolf—and Hank was smart enough not to make an issue of handing Benny off to him."

Adam's status was not a secret, though there were still a lot of werewolves who hid what they were. Adam was almost a celebrity in the Tri-Cities, though we were hoping the fascination with him would die down. It did no harm for Calvin and the others to know what he was—and maybe it would give them a little caution when we caught up to him.

Putting on my jeans was slow work because I was still a little damp, but the warmth felt wonderful. He'd packed a sweatshirt that smelled like Adam, came down to my knees, and was warmer than anything I'd brought. I dusted off my sore and bleeding feet and stuffed them into a pair of socks, then into my tennis shoes. Heaven.

I looked up to see all four men watching me.

"Don't meet his eyes if you can help it—he's had a rough day," I told them. Then, with the blanket in one hand, I took off after Adam, leaving the others to follow however they would. They'd been swift and sure in the face of their friend's trouble. They'd recover from the werewolf pretty fast.

Adam was waiting for us at the highway's shoulder when I found him. He'd set the injured man down a few yards away, where there was a big rock he'd used to keep Benny's leg elevated.

"Hey." I spread the blanket over Benny and tucked it in around him. "How are you doing, Adam?"

"Not good," he admitted without looking at me. "I need someone to kill." I think he was trying to be funny, but it came out seriously.

I could hear the others approaching. My feet were battered, shoes or no shoes, and my calf ached where the water plant had been pulled off so abruptly. I hadn't made the best time up to the highway and, without Benny slowing them down, evidently they had been able to speed up a lot. I stood up and walked to Adam.

"No one here needs killing," I told him with quiet urgency. "These men were out looking for Benny here. They are the good guys, so you can't kill them."

Adam still wasn't meeting my eyes, but he laughed, and it sounded genuinely amused. "Shouldn't."

"Shouldn't what?"

"Shouldn't kill them, Mercy. Not can't."

I put my forehead against his shoulder. "It's the same thing for you," I told him confidently.

He took a deep breath and turned around to meet the four men who were approaching us a little warily—because they weren't stupid.

"Hello," he said, his voice still growly and about a half octave lower than usual. "I'm Adam Hauptman. Alpha of the Columbia Basin Pack."

"Jim Alvin," said Jim, stepping forward. I'd told them not to meet his eyes, but he did better than that. Maybe it was luck, maybe he knew something of werewolves or just wild animals, but he turned one shoulder forward and tipped his head sideways and down submissively even as he reached out a hand. "Of the Yakama Nation. Thank you for the help. Benny's a good man." I noticed that Adam didn't get the elaboration of tribal bloodlines that I had.

"Do you know what happened to him?" asked Adam, after giving Jim's hand a brief shake. His eyes were wolf-bright, ominous yellow in the illumination of their flashlights.

"No idea at all," Jim said.

Fred Owens stepped up. His head was lowered, too, but he was looking up into Adam's face.

"I've seen all kinds of kills. A bear might bite off half a man's foot the way Benny's was. A bear or some other big carnivore."

It was a challenge, of a sort, and I held my breath.

The tension dropped from Adam's shoulders, and he suddenly grinned. "You think I bit off his foot? Hell, Marine, I just got married. I have more important things to do."

"Barracuda," said Hank into the sudden silence. "It looks like a barracuda . . . or maybe a tiger shark. They have these odd teeth that they saw back and forth."

"The Columbia," said Jim slowly, "is freshwater."

"Tiger sharks have been found up fresh waterways," Hank persisted.

"Not up past dams," said Fred. "How did you know I was a marine?"

Adam's eyes were now honey brown, not quite his usual bitter chocolate, but safer than before. "Easier than spotting a cop," said Adam. "Might as well have it tattooed across your forehead." He paused for effect, then said, "It helps that you're still wearing your dog tags."

"You're not a marine."

Adam shook his head. "Army ranger. I never could swim—and since I became a werewolf, I'm all but useless in the water."

"Could his foot have gotten caught by one of those old

jaw traps?" asked Calvin, speaking up for the first time. "It looked sort of like that to me."

"I haven't seen one of those things being used since I was a kid," Jim said. "And it was illegal then. But he's right. It could do that sort of damage."

"A bear trap wouldn't catch two people," Hank said. Adam might have won over Fred with his military fellowship, but the other Owens brother was still suspicious. "Where is Faith?"

"He was afraid of something." I frowned at the unconscious man. "Really afraid. But it wasn't Adam."

Fred nodded abruptly at his brother. "No ranger would be dumb enough to leave a witness alive."

Apparently, he felt that left Adam in the clear.

Hank looked less certain and rubbed a hand along his ribs as if they hurt. Maybe he had strained something carrying Benny up the hill, or maybe it was a reflex thing.

About that time, the ambulance, followed by a sheriff's car, pulled up. With practiced speed, the EMT people slipped Benny onto a gurney, and the ambulance roared off to the nearest hospital. The officer took down names and statements. He seemed to know the other men, and, from their body language, they all got along pretty well. When Fred told him Adam was a werewolf, the officer tensed up and ran his flashlight over us.

His gaze brushed by me, then stopped. "You're bleeding," he told me. He aimed his flashlight at my leg—and damned if he wasn't right.

I pulled up my pant leg. It had been so cold, and my feet had taken such a battering, I hadn't really been paying attention. It hurt, but I hadn't connected that to actual damage. And there was quite a lot, really. Something had ripped the skin off my calf and taken some meat with it. It looked like a really nasty rope burn.

"I got caught up in some weeds wading out to Benny's

boat," I said. "Benny hit the motor while I was holding on to the boat and pulled me loose."

"That doesn't look like something a weed would do," Fred told me, shining his flashlight on it. "Some of those underwater plants can be sharp and slice you up some, but that looks more like you pulled free of a hemp rope."

"All sorts of garbage in that river," said the deputy. "Lucky you didn't get caught up in deeper water. Ambulance is in use, but I could run you to the hospital."

"No," I said. "It's nasty, but I'm up-to-date on my shots. Mostly it just needs cleaning and bandaging, and we have the stuff to do that."

Adam had knelt to get a good look. I heard him take a deep breath, then move closer. After a minute, he shook his head and stood up. "Thought I smelled something odd, but there's no telling what a rope might gather sitting in the river."

The deputy swallowed, having been reminded what Adam was. "You four can take your boat back? Okay. Leave Benny's boat there, and we'll get people to check it out and see what that tells us. Mostly we'll just have to wait until Benny can tell us what happened to Faith and his foot. At this point, I expect it's some sort of accident."

"I saw a man attacked by a barracuda once," said Adam. He looked at Hank. "I agree it looked a lot like your Benny's foot." He glanced at Calvin. "Not a metal trap. Those old jaw traps are built to dig in and hold the animal, not go all the way through the bone. A bear trap might crush a foot off, and there was some crushing on Benny's foot—but mostly it was sliced. Something with sharp teeth went after him."

"No barracuda in the Columbia," said Fred. But he didn't sound like he was arguing. "No sharks, either, for that matter. It looks to me like something a piece of farm machinery might do. But I've never run into a baler or harvester in the river."

My leg, once I'd noticed it, began to itch. It looked as though it ought to hurt more than it did, but right now, it itched. Maybe I'd gotten into some nettles or something while I was running around bare-legged.

Adam glanced at me. "I need to get Mercy to camp."

The deputy said, "You guys go get your boat and go home. Mr. Hauptman, I can take you and your wife back to your camp so you can take care of her."

He was scared of Adam. When we got in the car, the scent of his fear filled the air. I don't think a human would have noticed, though, and a little bit of fear wouldn't set Adam off.

Adam had a lot of experience dealing with scared people. By the time we reached the campground, the deputy was deep in a discussion about what the impact of a second campground in the Maryhill area would be.

"What we really need here is a good restaurant or two." The deputy's voice carried his conviction. "The museum has a nice deli, and there are a couple of places in Biggs, but they are always overflowing with highway traffic. You have to drive all the way to Goldendale, The Dalles, or Hood River for really good food. Those are too hard to find for the tourist business pulled in by the museum or Stonehenge. I figure we lose a lot of business because we don't have enough places to eat."

He pulled up to the gates and let us out. "I'd appreciate it if you folks stayed around here for a few days in case we need to ask you anything else."

"We were planning to," said Adam. "But if you need us, you have my cell."

He drove off, and I told Adam, "You'd better not let Bran see how diplomatic and reassuring you can be when you want. He'll make you go around the country and make speeches about how werewolves are gentle and not scary at all, too."

Adam smiled and picked me up. "Shh," he said.

I didn't argue. The itching hadn't gone away, but the pain had increased just on the short ride to the camp. Besides, carrying me wasn't much of an effort for a werewolf.

"Hey," I said. "You've been playing the hero pack mule all day. First Robert, then Benny, and now me."

He set me down in front of the trailer and opened the door for me. When I sat on the leather sofa, he turned on the interior lights and rolled my pant leg up to my knee. In the bright light of the trailer, it looked a lot worse than it had. Yellow stuff and blood crusted the cut, which was about an inch wide and deeper than I'd thought. The first hint of bruising was beginning to appear above and below the cut, and the edges had puffed up.

Adam put his nose down to my leg and sniffed again. He took a fluffy towel out of a cupboard and put that over his leg. Then he propped my calf on his thigh and poured liquid fire over the cut. I know some people claim that hydrogen peroxide doesn't hurt. Goody for them. I hate the stuff.

I jumped when the hydrogen peroxide hit and shrank down into the couch as it continued to bubble ferociously. Adam used the damp towel to clean my leg, then he sniffed again.

"That was no rope," he growled. "There was something caustic or poisonous on whatever grabbed you—I can smell it."

"Is that why it itches?" I asked.

"Probably." He handed me a couple of pills from a bottle in the kit.

"What is this?"

"Antihistamine," he said. "In case the swelling is an allergic reaction."

"If I take these, I'll be asleep in three minutes." I took them anyway. The need to dig my fingers into that cut and scratch was almost unbearable as soon as the burn of the hydrogen peroxide had worn off.

"We need to call Uncle Mike," I said in a small voice. I didn't want to start an argument again.

He must have heard it in my voice because he patted my knee. "I'll call as soon as I'm through here, but I doubt that Uncle Mike sent us here for this."

"Just to be clear," I said. "I didn't misunderstand you, right? You and the Owenses are thinking that there is some kind of fish that ate Benny's foot."

"Too soon to make assumptions," said Adam. "Maybe they stopped onshore for lunch and met a bear."

"Are there even bear around here?"

"Probably not here," Adam acknowledged. "But up where we were hiking there are. No telling how far Benny got his boat from the initial attack."

"So what was it that grabbed my leg?" I asked.

"*That* is something that Uncle Mike might know," Adam said. "How much of those otters did you see?"

I blinked, my brain already starting to haze from the antihistamine. Otters.

I sat up a little straighter. "Those weren't river otters." Their heads were a little differently shaped. I hadn't paid much attention to that at the time.

Adam nodded. "I saw one when I got back to the boat. What do you bet that they're a European species? Werewolves aren't the only shapeshifters in Europe."

"I've heard of selkies and kelpies," I said. "But not shapeshifting otters."

"Nor have I," said Adam, frowning at my calf. "But selkies interacted with people a lot. Kelpies are rarer, I'm told, but terrifying. You can see why there would be stories about them. Otters just aren't scary."

So speaks the man who hadn't been naked in the river with them. They may be small, but they are agile and mean.

There was a knock on the door, and Adam and I both stared at it in shock. The gate by the highway was shut, and it wasn't so far from the trailer that we wouldn't have heard someone stopping there. He glanced at me, and I shook my head—I hadn't heard anyone coming, either. Adam reached into his luggage, quietly pulled out a handgun, and tucked it into the back of his jeans, tugging his shirt down over it.

The quiet knock came again.

"Who is it?" asked Adam.

"I am Gordon Seeker, Calvin's grandfather, Mr. Hauptman. Jim Alvin said that your wife got hurt helping Benny, who is a young friend of mine."

Adam opened the door warily. He stepped back, and I saw the man at the door for the first time. His voice hadn't sounded old, but I didn't think I'd ever seen anyone older outside a rest home.

Sharp brown eyes peered at me out of a face that looked as though it had been left out in the sun to dry too long. Skin like beef jerky and white hair caught back in a smooth French braid down his back. He wore horn-rimmed glasses and small gold studs in his ears. His back was bent, and his hands were curled up from arthritis, his fingers twisted and knuckles enlarged. But his movements were surprisingly easy as he climbed into the trailer without invitation.

He wore jeans and a plain red T-shirt under a Redskins jacket. I wasn't sure if he was a football fan, if he wore it as a statement, or if it was just something to keep out the cool night air.

Over his shoulder he carried one of those leather bags that should look like a purse but doesn't. On his feet were the most lurid pair of cowboy boots I've ever seen—and that is saying something because I come from cowboy country, and cowboys wear some really gaudy stuff. The boots were bright lipstick red, each with a United States flag beaded in red, white, and blue across the top.

He smelled of fresh air and tobacco. But his tobacco hadn't come out of a cigarette. A pipe maybe—something without all the additives that make cigarettes smell so bad. It reminded me of my father's ghost.

"He told me about you, Mr. Hauptman," said Calvin's grandfather. "Been a long time since I saw a werewolf. Not a lot of them in this part of the country. And this must be your wife, Mercedes—" Then he looked at me and drew in a breath.

"You," he said. "I wasn't expecting *you.* Jim said you were Blackfeet married to an Anglo werewolf. I should have asked myself how many Blackfeet women would associate with a werewolf, shouldn't I? I had wondered what happened to you." He narrowed his eyes. "You don't look like Old Coyote. Oh, I can see him some in your eyes and in your coloring, but you look more Anglo than I'd expected."

He had known my father.

Suddenly, antihistamine or no antihistamine, I wasn't at all sleepy. But there was a disconnect between my tongue and the questions that were galloping through my head. I looked at Adam. His eyes were half-lidded, and his expression was neutral. His body language said, "Isn't he interesting? Let's see what he does."

The old man looked down at my leg and hissed. "That looks bad. River Devil is back for sure." He sat beside me and opened the purse that wasn't a purse and pulled out a bundle wrapped in a silk scarf. He opened it up and began singing.

If you've never heard Native American music, it is hard to convey the feel of it. Sometimes there are words, but Gordon Seeker didn't use any. The music flowed up from his chest and resonated in his sinuses—as had the music made by the dancing ghost of my father. Still singing, Gordon Seeker took out a homemade honeycomb wax candle and lit it. It looked as though he lit it with magic, but I can usually sense when someone uses magic. I didn't see a match though I could smell sulfur.

I sniffed suspiciously and he grinned at me and I noticed he was missing one of his front teeth. Still singing, he held up his empty hand and closed his fingers. When he opened the hand, he held a burnt matchstick.

Then he pulled a segment of leaf out and held it to the candle. It was dry and lit fast. He let it go, and I tensed to grab it before it burned the trailer—but the flames consumed the leaf before it hit the carpet, leaving only a smattering of ash and a surprising amount of smoke.

I recognized the plant by its smell when I hadn't recognized the leaf. Tobacco. I guess he didn't smoke a pipe.

Gordon leaned forward and blew the smoke from the tobacco and the candle toward my leg. The blowing didn't seem to affect his song. He tilted his head, and I could only see one of his eyes.

And in his eye I saw a predatory bird that looked somewhat like an eagle. It was so darkly feathered that at first I thought it was a golden eagle, which, despite the name, often looks almost black; but it moved differently.

He closed his eyes, blew again, and when his eye opened, it was bright and predatory—but it was also just an eye in which no bird flew. I decided the antihistamine I'd just taken must have been affecting me more than usual.

He opened a jar and took some yellowish salve out and spread it on the mark the not-a-hemp-rope-not-a-weed had left on my leg. The relief was almost immediate.

He stopped singing, wiped his greasy fingers on his jeans. Then he put the candle out.

Adam looked at me.

"It feels a lot better."

"Magic?" Adam asked our visitor.

The old man grinned. "Maybe." He still had the little earthenware jar and tipped it toward me. "Or maybe it's the Bag Balm. I use it on all my cuts and burns." I'd thought that salve had smelled familiar. He'd added something to it, but the base was definitely Bag Balm. My foster mother had used Bag Balm as a cure-all, too. I kept a tin of it at work. "I understand your feet took quite a beating, too. Why don't you get them out where we can see them?"

"How do you know me?" I asked, peeling off my shoes and socks.

Adam had decided to judge this frail old man a possible threat. I could tell because he'd taken a step back out of reach. He was standing guard, ready to do whatever the circumstances required, trusting me to handle the rest. Likewise, I'd trust his judgment about the threat.

Our opponent might be an old man, but both Adam and I had lived around very old things that were dangerous. We wouldn't underestimate this man who smelled of tobacco, woodsmoke . . . and magic. It wasn't fae magic, so I hadn't noticed it right away. This was sweeter and subtler, though I didn't think it was any less potent.

Charles smelled a little like this sometimes.

The old man smiled at me and held the unguent pot. "And how would I not know Mercedes Thompson who is married to Adam Hauptman, Alpha of the Columbia Basin Pack?"

He did the not-lying thing very well. There are a lot of Other creatures who know when you are lying. Some of the fae, werewolves, some of the vampires—and me. The art of not lying without telling the truth is a valuable skill if you're going to have to deal with people who are Other.

He hadn't known who I was when he came into the trailer. But he'd taken one look at me, and his surprised recognition had been genuine.

"You know what I am," I said, suddenly certain of it. My heartbeat picked up with the excitement of it. He knew what I was and who my father had been.

"Use that salve on your feet," he said. "They look sore." He canted his head toward Adam without taking his eyes off me. "Do you have something for an old man to drink?"

"Soda or apple juice."

"Root beer?" The old man's voice was hopeful.

Adam got a cloth out of a drawer near the little sink and dampened it. Then he opened the miniature fridge and pulled out the silver can and handed it over Gordon's shoulder. He tossed me the damp cloth, then went back to his self-appointed observation post.

I wiped my feet. My calf was still sore, but it wasn't the bone-deep throbbing, and there was no itching. It felt like a rope burn and nothing worse. There had been some sort of magic on whatever had cut my calf, magic that the old man had nullified.

I'm immune to a lot of magic—but not all. Usually, the worse the magic is, the less likely I am to be immune.

The old man opened his pop can and drank it down. He drank the whole thing without taking a breath. When I was a kid, we used to say anyone who could drink a can or bottle dry had killed it. We'd tried it a lot, but the only one of us who could do it was one of the older boys. I'd forgotten his name. He died before I left Montana—a victim of the Change.

Gordon Seeker and I could bandy words back and forth all night—I grew up in a werewolf pack; I knew how to not-lie, too. However, sometimes straightforward was more useful.

"I'm a walker," I told the old man as I rubbed his magic Bag Balm on my feet. "How did you know what I was?"

He laughed, slapping his hands on his thighs. "Is that what they call it?" he said. "After those abominations down south, I suppose? You don't go around wearing the skins of those you kill, do you? How can you be a skinwalker, then? Abominations." He hissed through his teeth, and the sound whistled a little as the air escaped in the gap where the tooth was missing.

"Not a skinwalker but a shapechanger, you are. Coyote, right? Ai." He shook his head. "Coyote brings change and chaos." His head tilted sideways, and he looked as though he was listening to someone I couldn't hear. I glanced at Adam, but he was frowning at the old man.

Gordon Seeker laughed. "Better than death and destruction, surely—but those often follow change anyway. Very well." The eyes he turned to me were fever-bright.

He reached out and tapped my injured leg. "River marked. It meant for you to be its servant—good thing for you that coyotes don't make good servants. But it means more than that. It tells me that tomorrow you need to go to Maryhill Museum. Enjoy the art and the furniture built by the foreign queen—and then go see what they have in their basement. At noon, you meet my young grandson at Horsethief Lake, and he'll take you to see She Who Watches."

I knew what She Who Watches was, though I hadn't ever actually seen her in person. She was the most famous of the pictographs at Horsethief Lake.

"The tours are only open on Fridays," commented Adam. "At ten in the morning."

The old man grunted. "Indians go anytime they want to—it is our place." He tapped me. "She's Indian, no matter what she believes. My grandson is Indian. The two of them can take one Anglo wolf who belongs to an Indian coyote girl."

He stretched and tossed the empty pop can to Adam—who caught it. "Time for this old Indian to go." He looked at me again. "If you are going to use white man's words to describe yourself, 'avatar' is more accurate than 'walker.'"

He took his bag and indicated the little pot with his chin. "Better you keep that, little sister. A coyote will get herself hurt a lot if she runs with wolves."

And then he left.

Adam and I both waited, holding our breaths, but we heard neither footsteps nor car or boat.

After a moment, I shed my clothes and took coyote shape—I had about one more change in me tonight. But it was better that I changed than Adam. He opened the door of the trailer and walked out behind me as I put my nose to the ground and scent-trailed the old man. He'd headed for the river and not the road.

I followed him down to the little backwater where Adam and I had played in the river. About ten feet from the drop-off to the beach area, Gordon Seeker's scent and the imprint of his cowboy boots just disappeared.

"WHAT DO YOU THINK? WAS HE A GHOST?" ASKED Adam, as he scrubbed my feet again while I sat on the couch.

I'd told him they were fine. But he'd ignored me and insisted on cleaning them again after I'd gone out running around on them, even though I'd been on paws and not bare feet. It didn't hurt as much as it should have because the salve had healed the minor cuts better than any mundane Bag Balm could have. All I had left was a whole bunch of bruises.

"I think that there is more in heaven and earth, Horatio," I said. "I can usually tell if someone is a ghost. Or if I can't, I've never found out. How about you?"

"He smelled like woodsmoke and predator," said Adam. "He breathed, and I could hear his heart pump. If I had to guess, I'd say not a ghost. But I've never actually seen a ghost, so it's just a guess. A ghost was the first explanation that occurred to me for his disappearing act."

"You've never seen a ghost?" I saw them all the time, so I forgot how seldom other people could perceive them.

"No. So what do you think Gordon Seeker was?"

"You know," I told him, "there's an old Indian custom that Charles told me about once. If a visitor comes to your lodge and admires something out loud, you are supposed to give it to them. Charles says there are three reasons for the custom. The first"—I held up a finger—"is because generosity is a virtue to be encouraged. The second"—I put up another finger—"is to teach you not to be too attached to or too proud of things. Family, friends, community are important. Things are not. Can you guess the third one?"

He smiled. "Charles told me that one. Be careful who you invite into your lodge. I didn't think of it until after Seeker was already in the trailer. Maybe he was the Indian version of a witch. Medicine man."

"Charles says that medicine men and witches aren't very much alike."

My leg itched, and I pulled up my pant leg and contemplated scratching.

"River marked," said Adam, touching the mark lightly.

"He was as bad as the fae," I complained. "He didn't answer anything and just left us with more questions."

Adam kissed my knee, which should not have done anything to my pulse. I mean—the kneecap is as far from an erogenous zone as I know of. But it was Adam, so my heart rate picked up nicely.

He put my feet down. "The magic salve did its job. I don't think you'll need another application tonight. I have a funny feeling that you might need it more later. Speaking of the fae, though, when we start getting people missing and bloody, it's probably time to give Uncle Mike a call and see what he's set us into the middle of."

He pulled out his cell phone and dialed Uncle Mike's number. I heard the sound of loud music, and someone answered in Cornish.

"It's Hauptman," Adam said. "Get Uncle Mike for me." He started pacing the length of the trailer as he sometimes did when he was on the phone. I pulled my feet up—resting them on the towel to keep the couch clean. Without my feet on the floor, Adam had an extra half pace to use. My eyes drooped, and I had to fight to keep them open.

There were several clicks, and the music died down abruptly, as if Uncle Mike had gotten on a quieter extension.

"Adam," he said. "Congratulations. And why would you be calling me while you're on your honeymoon?"

"Otters," said Adam. "More precisely, otters that look like they'd be more at home in the Old Country and who smell of glamour."

He'd sensed it, too, then. That little bit of magic when I was trying to get the boat out from under the tree. It hadn't been Benny or the boat. The otters were the next best thing.

There was a little silence, then Uncle Mike gave a sigh of relief. "They are there, then. Edythe told us that none of her people had seen them for a while."

"Which is why you and Edythe sent us down here?"

Uncle Mike cleared his throat. "Not exactly. Edythe gets hunches sometimes. One of them was when a Roman ex-slave named Patrick came back to Ireland. We all wish we'd killed him right off just as she advised—except probably that would have only meant the Church would have sent someone else, and there would be a Saint Aiden or Saint Conner or some such instead of Saint Patrick. Harbingers are often like that old seven-headed dragon that grew two new heads whenever you cut one off."

"Hydra," Adam said.

"That's the one. Anyway, she doesn't have those moments very often, maybe no more than once a century. Last one was right before Mount St. Helens blew. After that Patrick thing, we all listen to her. A week ago she told me that she had a premonition that it might be a good idea if you and Mercy honeymooned at her campground and took a look at what the otterkin had been up to."

"What have they been up to?" Adam had stopped pacing and was looking wary. Edythe, whoever she was, had a premonition once a century or so—and had had one about us being here. That sounded a lot more serious than a man losing his foot to a bear or ghosts dancing beside the river, no matter how much they had affected me.

"Surviving, evidently." Uncle Mike's voice was suddenly grim. "Which is better than we had feared. Otterkin aren't like the selkies, who are their closest kin. There are other fae who wear otter shapes, but they aren't really related to otterkin. For one thing, otterkin don't interact with people well. We brought all that were left to the Walla Walla reservation and turned them loose in our waters."

"You don't have waters there," said Adam, pinching the bridge of his nose. "It was one of the things that the government made sure of—no running water that went into any of the reservations could come running out." He wasn't arguing. He was just telling Uncle Mike that they both knew there was something odd going on in the Walla Walla reservation.

Running water was supposed to enhance the powers of a number of fae. I was surprised anyone in the government—who wasn't fae—knew that little gem.

It had been a useless precaution, though. I've seen oceans in the reservation where they've somehow managed to open entry points into Underhill. That was one of the things I couldn't tell Adam—or anyone else. I'd promised, and the ones who'd suffer if I broke my promise included my mentor, Zee, so I kept my mouth shut.

"We have ponds," said Uncle Mike, not-lying even better than Gordon Seeker had. "But they weren't enough. So Edythe bought a scrub piece of desert and turned it into a campground."

"And turned the otters loose here."

"Otterkin. Edythe had a sanctuary built for them near the swimming hole. They should have been happy there, but they disappeared from it, and we haven't been able to find them for about six months. None of them were in good health when we put them there, and we assumed that they were gone until Edythe suddenly decided to send you."

"Tell me about the otterkin," said Adam.

"You should feel a kindred spirit with them," Uncle Mike told him. "They are shapeshifters who can take human form though their true shape is otter. As humans, they tend to resemble someone with severe autism. In the past, it got many burned at the stake."

"Do they kill people?" asked Adam.

There was a rather long pause.

"Not for food," said Uncle Mike.

"Neither do werewolves. Nonetheless, there are bodies wherever there are packs. Are there bodies where there are otterkin?"

"Not of the kind that would bring attention," said Uncle Mike. "They are territorial. Sometimes people drown near otterkin lairs."

"And you put them near the swimming hole."

"Which is protected by rune and magic," snapped Uncle Mike. "They couldn't even drown a baby in that swimming hole. They can swim and fish, but they can harm none therein."

"So they moved to where they could," Adam said. "We found them a few miles upriver. Are we supposed to stop them?"

"For that we wouldn't need you." Uncle Mike's voice was impatient. "There are seven of them. You could eat them for lunch and be hungry by dinner. They have very little magic of their own though they are clever with what they have, and they cooperate with each other. When there were hundreds of them, they were dangerous. There are otter-shaped fae who are powerful—but they are still back in the Old Country and doing fine."

"Otterkin are minor fae," I told Adam. Not too long ago, I'd read a book about the fae, written by a fae woman. It took me a while to remember them because they'd gotten the barest mention. "They used to be very common, but they aren't powerful. Probably no more trouble than real otters would be. River otters usually avoid people, which is good for the people."

"Ah, is that Mercy I hear? What does she say?"

That didn't mean that Uncle Mike couldn't hear me. Maybe he just didn't want Adam and me to know that he could hear what we said. Still, Adam politely repeated my words to Uncle Mike.

"Otterkin were supposed to be friendly and helpful," I added.

"Right," Uncle Mike agreed. "Being hunted to near extinction changes a lot of things. Still, they're not big enough to seriously threaten anyone."

Unless he was hurt and defenseless, as Benny had been.

"Ask Uncle Mike if they'd be able to do what something did to Benny's foot," I said. I couldn't see how they could, but it would be stupid not to ask.

After Adam relayed my question, Uncle Mike said, "No. They might be able to sever a toe or finger. They could kill someone, I suppose, just as a regular river otter could under the proper circumstances. But it would be because they opened up an artery." Then slyly, he said, "Sort of like a coyote might kill a werewolf." Which I had done—and didn't plan on doing again anytime soon. Sheer dumb luck is not something I felt like counting on.

"And Edythe thought that it was important that we check out seven otterkin?" Adam said.

Uncle Mike made a neutral noise. "Her premonitions aren't specific to the fae," he said. "Something bad is going to happen unless the two of you somehow manage to stop it. Or not. Her predictions aren't perfect." His voice got very serious. "You have to understand. This is not a favor you are performing for the fae. It may have nothing to do with the fae at all. We just saw to it that you are in the right place."

"Fine," said Adam coolly. "Have it your way for now. We'll discuss this again when Mercy and I return."

He hung up the phone.

"I was wrong," I said.

"About what?"

"Gordon Seeker wasn't as bad as the fae. At least he didn't engineer our presence at a disaster."

"You think seven otter-sized fae with very little magic comprise a disaster?"

"No," I told him. "But something bad is coming. It doesn't sound like Edythe has premonitions about stubbing your toe or even about some poor guy getting his foot taken off. And Uncle Mike knew it when he sent us here."

6

ONE OF THE REASONS I HATE TO TAKE ANTIHISTAmines is because of the dreams. They never make any sense, but they are consuming and difficult to throw off the next day.

That night I dreamed I was encased in stone. No matter how hard I struggled, no matter how hard I fought, I could not move. I grew hungry, and there was no surcease, no ease of the great appetite of my captivity.

I dreamed that I was freed at last, and I feasted on an otter that filled me more than an otter should, appeasing my hunger for a moment. So I didn't eat the other otters who swam around me.

They looked like the otters who had watched me pull Benny's boat out of the brush.

I woke up with the dry mouth and feeling of impending doom that were not unfamiliar after I'd taken antihistamines. I felt the same way after vampire, demon, or fae attacks, too. After, because, not being prescient, I never knew when the sword of Damocles was going to fall.

It didn't matter that I knew quite well that the dream meant nothing. It didn't take a Carl Jung to see where the otters had come from. And I suspected that the imprisoned feeling was the effect of the antihistamine itself, which left me sluggish. The hunger? That was even easier. I'd been hopping back and forth from human to coyote yesterday; it would make anyone hungry.

I almost matched Adam's appetite when we sat down for breakfast—cooked in utter civilization on the quarter-sized stove.

"Bad dreams," he said matter-of-factly. The mating bond had clearly given him insight at an inappropriate time again.

"Are we ever going to be able to control the mating bond when it does that?" I asked, shoveling in hash browns as fast as I could without having them dribble out the side of my mouth. "Did you get the whole thing?"

He smiled and nodded. "Otters and all. At least you ate one of them." He ate almost as fast as I did, but he was better at it. Unless I really paid attention, I never noticed him getting the food from his plate to his mouth. It was not so much a matter of speed but of exquisite manners and distraction.

"How's your leg and feet?" he asked as I washed up. He'd cooked, so I cleaned.

I wiggled my bare toes and did a few deep knee bends. "The calf aches a little, but the feet are fine."

"ARE WE DOING THIS BECAUSE GORDON SEEKER told us to?" I asked Adam, as he drove us the short distance to the Maryhill Museum of Art.

"I'd intended to take you this morning," he answered slowly. "But I have to admit that I'm curious."

I put my hand on his thigh, and said, "We could head home—or drive to Seattle, Portland, or even Yakima and find a nice hotel." I looked out from the highway and down onto the river. From where the highway was, the river looked small and relatively tamed. "I have the feeling that if we stay, things might get interesting."

He gave me a quick smile before looking back at the road. "Oh? What gave you that feeling? People getting their feet bitten off? The ghost of your father? A mysterious old Indian who disappears at the river without a sign of how he left? Maybe Yo-yo Girl's prophecy of the apocalypse?"

"Yo-yo Girl?" I yelped. "Edythe is Yo-yo Girl? *Yo-yo Girl* sent us here?"

He showed his teeth. "Feeling scared yet? Want to go somewhere safe?"

I couldn't help myself. I set my cheek against his arm and laughed. "It won't help, will it?" I said after a moment. "We'd just run into Godzilla or the Vampire from Hell. Trouble just follows you around."

He rubbed the top of my head. "Hey, Trouble. Let's go find out what your mysterious Indian wanted us to know."

IN SEATTLE OR PORTLAND, THE MARYHILL MUseum would have been a nice museum. Out in the middle of nowhere, it was spectacular. The grounds were green and well tended. I didn't see any of the peacocks as we walked from the parking lot to the entrance, but I could hear and smell them just fine. I'd seen it from the highway on the other side of the river while driving to and from Portland, but I'd never actually been in it before.

The first time someone tried to tell me about the museum, I thought they were crazy. In the middle of eastern Washington state, a hundred miles from Portland, a hundred and fifty miles from the Tri-Cities, the museum contained the furniture of the Victorian-era Queen of Romania and work by Auguste Rodin.

That was the first question answered by the slick brochure they handed us at the front door. Sam Hill, financier and builder of roads and towns—and this museum, which was meant to be his home—was a friend of Loïe Fuller. Loïe Fuller was a dancer of the early nineteen hundreds, famous in Europe for her innovative use of fabric and veils—and she was a friend of royalty and artists, notably Marie, Queen of Romania, (who designed furniture as a hobby) and the French sculptor Auguste Rodin.

Thus came the furniture of the Queen of Romania and a good-sized collection of Rodin's sculptures to the middle of nowhere.

Given its isolation, I expected that Adam and I would be the only ones in the museum, but I was wrong. In the first room, where the furniture and assorted memorabilia of the Victorian age held court, there were several groups of people. A pair of older women, a family of five that included a stroller, and a middle-aged couple. The room was big enough that it didn't seem crowded at all.

I found the heavily carved furniture beautiful, but stark and uncomfortable-looking—more suitable for a stage production than as something to have in your living room. Maybe a few cushions would have softened the square contours and made it more inviting.

The remainder of that floor was given over to a collection of paintings displayed in a series of interconnecting rooms.

Adam and I separated in the first room of paintings, taking different paths around the artwork. Most of it was very good, if not spectacular, until I came to an oil piece by a familiar painter. I must have made a noise because Adam slid up beside me and put his face against my neck.

"What?" Adam asked, keeping his voice low so as not to disturb the other visitors.

"Do you see that?" I said, nudging him toward the painting I was looking at.

It wasn't the most beautiful painting in the room, not by a long shot. There were also others more detailed, better executed even, but it spoke to me in a way the others did not. Here among English and Greek landscapes, portraits of maids and wildflowers, the cowboys looked a little out of place.

Adam leaned forward, which pressed him more tightly against me without being too flagrant, to read the display information. I snorted at him in mock dismay.

"I can see that you are not a true Westerner, or you'd have recognized him right off."

"No, ma'am," he drawled mildly, though I could see a dimple peeping out. I loved his dimple—and I loved it even more when he dropped into the accent of his youth. I especially loved the warm strength of him against me. I was so easy. "I'm a Southerner."

"Just like most of the cowboys he painted," I told him. "The West was populated by Southerners who didn't want to fight in the War Between the States—or who came here after they lost. That, my dear uncultured wolf, is a Charlie Russell—cowboy turned artist. Without him, Montana's history would just be a footnote in a Zane Grey novel. Charlie drew what he saw—and he saw a lot. Not a romantic, but a true realist. Every once in a while, some old Montana rancher still finds a few of his watercolors rolled up and forgotten in the bunkhouse. Like winning the lottery, only better."

Adam's shoulders shook. "I sense passion," he said, his voice soft with laughter, tickling my ear as he spoke into it. "But is it the art or the history that speaks to you?"

"Yes," I said, shivering. "I showed you mine. Which one is your favorite?"

He pulled away and directed me to a painting on the next wall. The woman sat in a cave, a dim waterfall to the left and behind her, a pool of water at her feet. The extraordinary thing about the work was the luminescence of the central figure achieved by some alchemy of the color and texture of her skin and of the fabric of her clothing combined with the shape of her pose. *Solitude* was its title.

This had none of the dirt and roughness of detail that appealed to me in the Russell painting. This wasn't a woman who had to get up and wash her clothes and fix dinner. Yet . . .

"Okay," I said. "I wouldn't get tired of seeing that on a wall, either. But I'm warning you, it will look odd next to my Charlie Russells."

He kissed my ear and laughed.

The American Indian exhibit was in the basement. Sam Hill had, apparently, collected Native American baskets along with his artwork. Lots and lots of baskets. Over the years, other things had been added—some terrific photographs, for instance, and large petroglyphic rocks. Still, the overall effect was a million baskets and a few other things, too.

Here, too, we weren't alone. The family from upstairs was examining the petroglyphs. The oldest, a girl, pulled free of her parents and put her face against one of the Plexiglas display cases.

There was a middle-aged Indian woman on her own. Her face was serious, though it was a face that was more comfortable with smiles than with grimness. There were lines of laughter and weather near her eyes and mouth, and all of her attention was on Adam and me.

It made me a little uncomfortable for some reason. So I turned from the stone carvings near the doorway to the baskets, putting my back toward the woman.

The baskets were extraordinary. In some of them, the designs of almost-stick-figure animals were surprisingly powerful in a way I wouldn't have thought possible with such extreme stylization as required by the weaving.

"It's a good thing I wasn't born back then," I told Adam. "I took an art course in college, and one of the projects was weaving a basket. Mine looked sort of like a disproportionate hammock complete with holes. I never could get the handle to stay on both sides at the same time."

But not even my history-driven passion could keep me interested in the million and twelfth basket, as beautifully made as they were—and I outlasted Adam by a fair bit. These weren't the kinds of baskets used on a daily basis. Most of them were made to sell to collectors and tourists.

They reminded me of a history professor of mine who mourned the loss of everyday things. Every museum, she said, had wedding dresses and christening dresses galore, Indian ceremonial robes and beaded or elk-tooth dresses worn only on the most special occasion. People don't save Grandma's work dress or Grandpa's hunting leathers.

I couldn't help but wonder what Gordon Seeker had wanted us to see here. The family had moved on—I could hear the children talking in the hallway outside this exhibit room. I didn't see the woman who'd been watching us.

I paused by the big chunk of stone near the hall that led to the rest of the basement exhibits. There were several blocks of stone, with petroglyphs incised into their surfaces, in the room. From one, a giant predatory bird glared at me.

"I wonder when this was done," I said, letting my fingers hover over the stone. I could have touched it—others were touching the gray rocks—but I couldn't quite make myself do it. As if the press of my fingers might damage it, when hundreds and maybe thousands of years of wind and rain had not. "And how long it took to carve it."

"These were taken out of the original site when the river was dammed, and the canyon they were in was flooded," Adam said thoughtfully, reading the little card next to the exhibit. "I'd figure it was carved a long time ago, or you'd see more roughness from the creation process. A thousand years almost certainly. Could be ten thousand, I suppose."

We had sandwiches in the museum deli, right next to the Rodin exhibit, then headed out to Horsethief Lake, about fifteen miles west of the museum.

JANICE LYNNE MORRISON WAS A THIRD-GRADE *teacher and a camera nut. Her photos would never grace a museum, but she loved to scrapbook her adventures. This adventure, in particular, needed scrapbooking because she was unhappily certain that her life was about to fall apart.*

They had stopped at a picnic area on the Columbia for lunch—after this it would be restaurants until they reached Lee's parents' house in Wyoming. Everyone had eaten, the remnants of the food were packed away for snacks, and the boys were playing on the rocks.

Lee was in the car taking a phone call. She wasn't sure when she first noticed the phone calls, maybe after school got out, and she was home more often. Her husband worked from home, and it was not unusual for him to get business calls and take them in private. But these calls came at the same time every day—eleven fifteen. When he got off the phone, he would make a great effort to do nice things for her—the kinds of things that someone who was feeling guilty would do. More damningly, he wouldn't meet her eyes, not right after one of the calls. Either he had a bookie or someone on the side.

After their vacation, she would talk to him about it—so she wanted to save all the memories she could.

She couldn't get both of the boys in the shot with the right light, so she kicked off her sandals and waded out into the water a few feet and tried it again. The light hit her digital screen so she had to use the regular viewfinder and put the camera up to her eye. It still wasn't quite right. She needed just a little more field of view. She took one more step back—and there was nothing beneath her feet.

As she fell backward, something snagged her leg and pulled her upstream. She struggled for a moment more, then grew calm. Peaceful. The water rushed past her and took all of her cares away.

Green eyes examined her with interest while some light-colored and fluttery tentacles that formed a fringe around its sharp nose caressed her. It opened its mouth, and she saw long spiky teeth before a wave caught her and pushed her away.

She didn't want to go away from the creature but had no will to fight its need. She staggered out of the water, coughing and choking from the water she'd swallowed. Blood dripped from a gash that wrapped all the way around her thigh just below the line of her shorts. Her head ached, and her eyes burned, but she was calm and happier than she'd ever been before.

It wanted her.

"Mommy, Mommy, are you all right?" A young boy—her son, she thought, what was his name?—held her arm. "Are you all right? Where's your camera?"

She reached out and took his hand—and the hand of the little boy who hadn't said anything, too. He was only wearing his pull-ups and one shoe. Another time, she knew that one shoe would have bothered her. But nothing bothered her anymore.

"Janny?" A man interrupted her before she got the boys to the river, and she frowned at him. Her husband, that was who he was. "Janny, what happened to you? Are you all right?"

He wouldn't let her take the boys, she knew, so she let them go until she understood what the new plan should be.

"Janny?" His voice was soft, gentle, and for some reason, that made her really mad. "Janny, you're bleeding. Did you fall into the river?"

"I need to rinse off the blood," she told him. Her voice came out a little garbled, but she didn't think it would matter. "Can you help me?"

He followed her into the river, though he wasn't happy about it. "It's probably not sanitary, Janny. There's water in the car."

While he argued, she took him deeper and deeper. The monster took him a few feet from where she'd fallen, dragging him under so fast he had no time to cry out.

"Daddy?"

The boys stood on the shore, and when she took their hands again, they followed her in. The habit of obedience and trust stronger than their instincts.

"Mercy."

"Mommy, what happened?" the older one wanted to know.

"Mercy, wake up."

"Daddy went swimming," she told him with a peaceful smile. It wanted Janny, but she hadn't been enough, so Janny had been sent back for more. But the monster was still hungry. "Why don't we go swimming with Daddy?"

I OPENED MY EYES, CONSCIOUS THAT I WAS breathing too fast and that I was drooling on Adam's leg.

"Sorry," I said groggily. "I didn't mean to fall asleep."

"I kept you up too late," Adam said in a tone that was not at all apologetic. "Satisfied" might be a better word. Smug. We hadn't been living celibate before we got married, but it was hard to get much privacy when Adam was pack Alpha and had a teenage daughter. Maybe we should buy a trailer of our own.

"Got to catch your sleep while you can," Adam continued. "I didn't get the full effect this time, but it sounded like another nightmare."

"Oh yeah," I agreed. The sick feeling in my stomach wasn't leaving very quickly. "Creepy in that slow-motion I-can't-stop-this kind of way. I think that Gordon's little talk about the cut on my leg has me thinking about old horror movies."

Coyotes don't make good slaves, he'd said right about the same time he'd said I was river marked. I'd forgotten about it in the oddity of his visit, but it must have stuck in my subconscious and given me that chilling little episode. I wonder what he thought had marked my leg. Maybe someone would tell us more that afternoon.

"I'm assuming since we aren't there yet, I wasn't sleeping for long."

"About ten minutes," he said. "Here's our park."

"It doesn't say Horsethief Lake," I told Adam, as he turned off the highway toward the river and we started down a long, gently bending road after passing a sign that read "Columbia Hills State Park."

"Name sanitized in 2003," Adam told me. "Both the states and the U.S. Geological Survey are PCing geographical names all over the place. Just ask Bran. He'll go on for as long as you want to listen about Jackass Creek—he claims he knew the jackass it was named after."

"Good thing the USGS doesn't speak French, or they'd rename the Grand Tetons," I said.

Adam laughed. "You just know those French trappers were missing home when they named them, don't you?"

The drive through the park took us past an Indian graveyard that was still being used—I could tell from all the balloons and items left on the graves. It looked almost like a birthday party had gone on there, and all of the guests had departed without taking away their presents. There was a tall chain-link fence around the graveyard with "No Trespassing" signs on it.

I can see ghosts. But I've never actually seen one in a

graveyard. Graveyards are for the living. In my experience, ghosts tend to hang out in the same places they did while they were alive.

So what had my father been doing in a campground beside the Columbia all the way out here when he was supposed to be from Browning, Montana?

Calvin Seeker was leaning against a chain-link fence when we parked the car on a gravel lot next to a boating dock. He looked tired and older than he'd appeared last night—like almost twenty. Without moving, he watched us lock up the car and cross the road.

The chain-link fence he was leaning on ran until it met up with the railroad that went along the edge of the water, then it followed the track of the railroad out of our sight around the bluffs. There was a sign behind Calvin, but I couldn't read it.

"Uncle Jim told me to meet you here at noon," he said, a little more politely than his posture indicated. "I'm going to be your tour guide, apparently."

"Thank you," I said.

He shrugged. "No trouble. Sometimes I volunteer to guide people on tourist days during the summer."

He scuffed his shoe in the dirt and gave Adam a wary look. "How did you manage to get in touch with Uncle Jim? He told me while we were waiting in the hospital to see how Benny was doing, but I didn't see him pick up his phone—and I know you didn't get his phone number while we were waiting for the ambulance last night."

"We didn't," said Adam. "We talked to your grandfather."

Calvin came off the fence and stood up straight, his eyes a little wide. "My grandfather?" he asked, sounding startled. "Which one?"

"He called himself Gordon Seeker," I said. "He came by last night, said your uncle had sent him. He gave me some stuff that really helped with my leg."

"Ah, that grandfather." He didn't seem too happy about it, and I was pretty sure it was the thought of Gordon Seeker that had jolted him off the fence. "I should have known."

"Something wrong?" Adam asked.

"Something's always wrong when Grandpa Gordon stirs up the water," Calvin said. He looked at me, then looked at Adam. "Werewolf, huh?"

Adam nodded.

"Okay. Well, if Grandpa Gordon sent you, I'm going to do this a little differently. Did he say why he sent you?" He shook his head before he answered. "What am I asking? Of course not. He'd rather watch us all run around like chickens when the fox comes calling. I guess he thinks it's funny."

"You were at the hospital last night?" I asked. "Is Benny going to be all right? Did he tell you what happened?"

"Yes," Calvin said. He squinted against the sun, and the little gesture let me see the family resemblance between him and the old man who'd come to my trailer. "Benny'll survive. I think . . . I think I should tell you his story after I've played guide if you don't mind. I don't know that it will make more sense that way, but at least you'll know why he wanted you to come out here." He frowned at me and Adam. "I'm not sure why he thinks it's important that you know anything. I might question Uncle Jim, but only a fool asks Grandpa Gordon anything: he just might answer."

He looked out across the river as if for inspiration, and when he spoke again, his voice was low. "My uncle Jim is a medicine man. It runs in the family, usually in sibling lines. None of his kids have the ability to become what he is, and neither did his father. But his uncle did. It runs like that."

"Is Gordon a medicine man?" I asked, trying to work out the lineage. The answer should be no, if Gordon was his grandfather and shared his last name—unless Jim was

Calvin's uncle on his mother's side. Which, I suddenly thought, was probable since they didn't share last names.

"Is the night dark?" Calvin grinned, which robbed his face of its sulky cast and made him look likeable. "Maybe. Maybe not. Depends on what you mean and in whose eyes. He is something, that's for sure. Anyway, I'm Uncle Jim's apprentice. I'm going to start this tour just like I would if you were a pair of tourists, but if I'm doing it right, some things might change along the way." He cleared his throat, looked a little embarrassed, and said, "As inspiration strikes me. Or not.

"So." He took a deep breath. "Welcome to this sacred ground. Speak softly and show respect while you are here, please. Twenty years ago, we fenced it and closed it to strangers because of vandalism. But that made no one happy because these were left behind to share the stories of those who have gone before with those who are now. So the decision was made to make it accessible, but under specific circumstances. If you were to come on your own . . ." He paused and looked at me, and when he continued, he'd lost the practiced flow of his voice. "*You'd* probably be okay. You look Indian. But people here without permission get jail sentences; we are serious about keeping this place safe."

He turned and started walking on a trail, and we followed him through the gate. It was like being in a hedge maze except the hedges were walls of lava and huge rocks.

"This is the Temani Pesh-wa trail," Calvin said, leading the way, though there was really no need for a guide because the path was obvious. "Which means 'written on rock.' The pictograms here were probably painted between five hundred and a thousand years ago."

He took us up a fairly brisk climb, speaking as we walked. "In earlier times, there were a lot of Indians in this area. Lewis and Clark mention stopping very near here, and from their journals, people estimate that there were nearly ten thousand Indians in the vicinity. We do know that one of the many villages was over there."

He pointed back the way we'd come, where, in the distance, a rounded section of land jutted out into the river. From its edges, basalt cliffs dropped several hundred feet to the water below. I couldn't tell from where we were whether there was a body of water between us and the land he'd pointed to. The landmass looked like nothing so much as a wedding cake, complete with a second, much smaller layer in the center.

Just as I was turning to look back at Calvin, I noticed that we weren't the only ones on the trail. The Native American woman who had been in the museum was taking a fork in the trail that we had not. Even as I watched, she crossed behind a big bunch of rock and disappeared into the landscape.

"Twice a year they'd hold a potlatch," Calvin was saying, "a party, to which they invited people from near and far. As part of the potlatch, young men and women of twelve or thirteen would hold their vision quests. Afterward, they would come here and record a reminder of their vision quests upon the rock."

He took us up to a basalt wall of cliffs—a baby cliff compared to the one he'd just pointed out. He stopped but didn't say anything, so I looked up. It took a moment to understand what I was seeing, even though I'd been looking for them. The old paint blended into the rocky cliff as if it belonged there, and I was the outsider. As soon as I saw one, I saw that they were everywhere.

There were dozens, parts of dozens at least. Some of them were clearly identifiable as human or various other animals. Others were impossible to decipher, either because some of the paint had grown too faint or because whatever symbolism they'd used was too alien for me to understand. There were some symbols that were obvious—like flowing water was a series of parallel squiggly lines. Some were less obvious: a red and white target, long wavy lines, circles.

I stepped close, my hands behind my back like a child told not to touch. Hundreds of years ago someone had stood where I was and touched their fingers to the rock. Five hundred years ago. A thousand years ago.

I had the odd thought that Bran the Marrock had been alive when these were painted. Five hundred years I was certain he was. I was almost sure of a thousand.

Still. I wondered if the long-ago girl or boy who had drawn the bold red and white target had known how long their artwork would remain, the last testament that they had once walked the earth.

Beside me, Adam stiffened and took a deep breath. He turned slowly until he looked down where we'd been standing a few minutes ago. I followed his gaze until I saw it, too.

Crouched on a rocky promontory that overhung the lower part of the trail, a red-tailed hawk stared at us. Like the pictograms, it belonged there. But there was something odd about its interest in us. It reminded me a little too closely of the woman in the museum. The bird took flight and passed right over our heads before veering off over the river, then out of sight.

As it flew, I realized that the unease I felt reminded me of my vision quest and the animals who had hunted me, making me unwelcome, until I'd come upon Coyote. A vision quest like those of all the long-ago artists. Maybe, I thought in sudden whimsy, I should draw a La-Z-Boy on one of the rocks. Somehow, I was pretty sure no one would understand that I wasn't vandalizing—just continuing tradition.

If Calvin hadn't been there, I'd have told Adam. I looked over at him and found him watching Calvin with gold eyes that danced with temper.

I put my hand on his arm. Gold eyes weren't a good thing when we were among friends.

Adam put his hand over mine and took a step so he was between me and Calvin. "In your ongoing education as a medicine man, have you ever heard of people who can change into animals, Calvin?" he asked in a surprisingly civil voice.

I frowned at Adam and gave his arm an invisible squeeze. I didn't know Calvin; there was no reason to make him question what I was. Something had happened that I'd missed while my eyes had been on the hawk, and I wasn't sure what it was.

Whatever it was, Adam was pretty mad at Calvin. I wondered if he pulled me behind him to protect me—or to keep me from protecting Calvin.

"No," said Calvin—which was a mistake. He should have learned how to not-lie from his grandfather. Besides, I knew enough Native American legends to know that there were lots of stories about people who turned to animals—and animals into people, for that matter. And he knew about Adam, who was certainly a person who changed into an animal.

Adam smiled, showing his teeth. I couldn't actually see him do it, but Calvin's face told me he had clearly enough. Adam had put away his civilized face and let Calvin see the real one.

"Can't lie to werewolves," I told the young man. "You might as well have shouted, 'Yes, but I don't want you to ask me about it.'"

Calvin swallowed, his fear pressing on my nose like perfume.

"Mercy?" asked Adam.

He was going somewhere with this—and I trusted him as long as his temper held. Werewolves are monsters. I grew up with them, and I loved Adam—and he would never hurt me. That did not apply to people he didn't care about. The faster the situation—whatever the situation was—was defused, the safer for everyone.

Information can sometimes be gotten when the opponent thinks you know all about it anyway. That was what Adam had been asking me to do—tell Calvin who I was.

"I can turn into a coyote," I said. "My mom tells me I must get it from my father."

Calvin's jaw dropped, then his face froze. "Your mother was a white woman," he said urgently. "You can't turn into a coyote."

"Can, too," I said indignantly. It was one thing for me to tell him he was lying—I knew I was right. It was an entirely different matter for him to tell me I was lying.

"Can't."

"Can."

"Can't."

"Can, too."

"Mercy," said Adam with exaggerated patience tinged with humor. He knew I was doing it on purpose. That was okay because he wasn't angry anymore.

"Cannot," said Calvin.

"Knock it off, both of you. Neither of you is five." He glanced at Calvin. "He answered what I wanted to know anyway. That hawk was no natural animal, and this one knew it."

No one reads body language like a werewolf, I thought. And then I realized what Adam was saying.

The blood shot from my head so fast that I had to step sideways to keep my feet—and sideways was three feet down the hillside. Adam jerked me back on the trail before I managed to fall. "Okay?" he asked.

I nodded, though I wasn't sure it was true.

I'd never met another one of my kind. After more than thirty years, I'd sort of assumed that there were no more left, that I was the only one.

I'd also assumed they'd be coyotes like me. Hadn't the old man last night kind of implied that? He'd known I was a coyote, and I'd only told him I was a walker.

I didn't know much about being a walker. Only what Bran had told me, and he hadn't known much—or he'd told me exactly as much as he intended to. I'd grown up thinking the last was true, but over the past year or so had come to believe the first.

"She is a walker," Adam told Calvin. "Coming up with reasons it can't be so doesn't help, and neither does arguing. I should know: I was bitten and Changed by a bandit warlord in Vietnam. Even now, I don't know of any werewolves living in Asia—there are things over there that don't like us, and they can make their dislike fatal. Yet there he was. Mercy changes into a coyote. You can't argue with fact. Just accept it and get over it. Was that your grandfather?"

If Gordon Seeker was a walker who turned into a red-tailed hawk, that would explain why he was able to disappear so effectively. There still should have been a pile of clothes where he'd changed, but being a walker would answer most of my questions.

"Grandpa Gordon changes," said Calvin. He looked as though he had sucked on a lemon as he stared at me.

He didn't not-lie very well, either. Maybe it was something medicine men learned when they were older. I had a feeling that his uncle Jim could not-lie as smoothly as any fae, and I'd seen that his grandfather could do the same. So why had they sent Calvin out with us? Unless they wanted us to share their secrets.

And the reason they might want us to know was tied up with Gordon Seeker, Yo-yo Girl Edythe's prophecy, and whatever had happened to Benny and his sister that Calvin wanted to wait until later to tell us.

Someday, I'm going to meet some supernatural creature who tells me everything I should know up front and in a forthright manner—but I'm not going to hold my breath.

"That hawk wasn't Gordon," said Adam, who could tell a bad not-lie as well as I could. "Who was it?"

If Gordon could change, and the hawk wasn't Gordon, then there were three of us. Three walkers. Gordon had known about me, about my existence, and the only reason we had met was chance. Engineered by Yo-yo Girl, but not by any desire on their part. Fine. They hadn't wanted anything to do with me. I would extend them the same courtesy.

Calvin looked at me a moment and threw up his hands in surrender. "Coyote, huh? Maybe that explains a few more things about why Grandpa Gordon wanted you to see this." He rubbed his face. "Look. Let me take you to see She Who Watches—I don't know if she's something you needed to see or not. Uncle Jim wasn't exactly forthcoming, but she's the best and best-known of the pictograms. Then I'll take you on to the petroglyphs. I'll tell you Benny's story—and I'll give you Uncle Jim's phone number, and you can call him about anything else you need to know, all right?"

It sounded fair enough to me, and Adam nodded.

He turned around and led us back down to where the trail split, and we followed the path of the woman I'd seen earlier. There were more drawings on the rock faces we passed.

"There's no lichen on the places where the pictograms are," commented Adam.

Calvin nodded. He'd calmed down a lot, and his fear no longer made me ache to give chase. "Right. They had some way of clearing off a bare patch and keeping it clean a thousand years later. It might have been something as easy as scraping the rock clean. Lichen needs a certain amount of roughness to grow. There are a few bare patches of rock that were obviously cleared off." He pointed. "But they don't have anything on them. Maybe someone mixed the paint wrong, or maybe they didn't get around to using them. You can see a bit of pigment on some of the bare patches when the light is just right."

"Do you know which tribe the people who lived over there belonged to?" Adam asked.

Calvin shook his head. "When the Europeans came, everybody moved. Lots of bands and a few tribes died off entirely. Most tribes kept their histories orally, and many of those stories were lost. We have some good guesses, but so do other tribes, and their guesses and ours don't always line up."

We turned a corner, onto the same trail down which the woman had disappeared. I could scent her. The trail paralleled the fence. On the other side of the fence were the railroad tracks that ran along the river. The fence and the trail ended abruptly, leaving us in a corner between the fence and a basalt rock wall. On the rock, looking out at the Columbia, was the biggest, clearest pictogram I'd seen. She could have been drawn a decade ago rather than centuries.

She Who Watches looked like a raccoon's face. Two little tulip ears perched on top of her head, and her mouth was open in a wide smile. A square of faded black was set in the middle of her mouth. It might have been a faded tongue or a long-ago attempt to cover up something, but whatever it was, it looked out of place in the rest of the face. Faintly, I could see where fangs had once been drawn in the mouth—and I bet she didn't look so friendly long ago, when those were more obvious.

Most of the pictograms we'd seen were cruder, two-dimensional stick figures. This had depth and real artistry.

"There are a lot of stories about She Who Watches," Calvin said. He opened his mouth and stopped. "But that's not why it was important to come here." He looked startled, as if he'd surprised himself with what he'd said.

"Why don't you tell us the story anyway?" Adam invited. "We have time."

Calvin looked uneasily over his shoulder but there was no one behind us. "All right." He took a deep breath. "All right. It's a Coyote story, so I suppose it's appropriate, right? One of several about how she came to be here—all the ones I know are Coyote stories.

"One day, Coyote came walking up the Columbia and he found this Indian village. He walked among the people, but he couldn't find their leader. So he went up to an old lady making a fish trap. 'Where is your leader?' he asked her.

"'Tsagaglalal, She Who Watches, is our leader,' said the old woman. 'She is up on the hill.'

"So Coyote, he comes up to this place and found a woman standing just where we are.

"'What are you doing up here?' he asked her. 'Your people are down in the village.'

"'I am watching,' she told him. 'I watch to see that my people have enough to eat. I watch so they have good homes to sleep in. I watch to see that they are safe from enemies.'

"Coyote, he thought that this was a good thing. So he took her and threw her up against this rock so that she could keep a watch over her people always."

"I bet there is more to the story," said Adam. "Coyote wouldn't throw her on the rock unless she made a smart-aleck comment or two."

"Well," I said, because he'd been looking at me, "I suppose if I were doing my job, and some stranger came up and started questioning me, I might be tempted to say something a little rude." I'd said quite a bit to Adam over the years, and I saw in his eyes that he was remembering it, too.

"Maybe so," said Calvin. "Let me take you back to the petroglyphs."

He started back down the trail, and I hesitated. I turned

to look at the little corner we'd been stuck in and took a deep breath, but I didn't smell her. I'd caught her scent at the fork in the trail, and there was nowhere else she could have gone. Even if she had climbed over the fence, she'd have left her scent behind.

"Did either of you notice the woman who was out walking the trail a little ways behind us?" I asked. Maybe she'd been the hawk we'd seen.

"What woman?" asked Calvin.

Adam shook his head. "Who did you see?"

"The woman from the museum, from the Indian exhibit there," I told Adam, expecting him to have seen her, too. Adam notices things. Part of it is being werewolf, but a bigger part of it, I think, comes from his time as a member of a Long-Range Reconnaissance Patrol in the jungles of Vietnam.

"A family," he said. "Father, mother, three kids."

"And a middle-aged Native American woman wearing a bright blue shirt with a pair of macaws embroidered on the back," I told him. "She smelled like mint and coffee."

He shook his head. "I didn't see her."

He'd walked right past her.

"What does that mean?" asked Calvin.

"I'm not sure yet," I told him. Calvin couldn't smell a lie. You could see it in his face that he believed what I said. I bet his uncle Jim would have called me on it. Adam gave me a sharp look.

There was a lot going on. Too much of it was mysterious and made no sense at all. And there were two other walkers, at least one of whom had known all about me before we met. The disappearing woman was one mystery too much. Though I was pretty sure she was my mystery and not something engineered by Gordon Seeker or anyone else we'd met there.

"Why don't we go to the petroglyphs, then you tell me

about Benny," I told Calvin grimly. "I'll see if the woman fits in anywhere."

It wasn't his fault. I had the feeling that he was even more in the dark than Adam and I were. Someone was playing games, and I was tired of it.

7

PICTOGRAMS ARE PAINT ON SOME SURFACE, any surface. Gang graffiti are pictograms, but usually the term refers to paints done by ancient man. Petroglyphs are carved into the rock. A lot more effort goes into them, and they take a lot longer to create. Like the displays in the museum, the petroglyphs at Horsethief Lake were on big chunks of rock that had clearly been cut from larger rocks. Unlike the ones in the museum, these were fenced off—look but don't touch.

The first petroglyph I saw at Horsethief Lake looked like a pineapple.

Calvin didn't quite hide his grin when I told him so. "Before the Columbia was dammed in 1959, the river was narrow and deep here, not the wide and tamed thing she is now. There were falls. Celilo Falls. We have photos."

The young man stared out at the river. "You know, I wasn't born then. My mother wasn't even born back then.

Some of the elders still mourn the old river as if she were a living being who died."

"Change is hard," said Adam. "And it doesn't much matter whether it is change for good or ill."

The young man looked at him. "All right. Some of the change was good, some of it not so good. There used to be a canyon. Some people said that there were more petroglyphs on the canyon walls than any other location in the world. I don't know, but there were a lot of them. When it became clear that the dam was going in, an effort was made to save as many as possible. These were displayed at the dam for decades before they were brought here. There are others in the museum and a lot, I suppose, in private collections—the tribes asked people to go in and take what they could as long as they would care for them. The ones left in the canyon are underwater, and I suppose they will be there forever."

We were walking as he talked. Like the drawings on the rock, the carving was primitive. Some of it, like the pineapple person, were like trying to guess what a kindergartner had drawn. Some of them were extraordinary despite the stylization. I could have stayed looking at the eagle for an hour or so. But it was a rock that held a row of mountain sheep that clued me into something.

"I'll be darned," I said. "That's why he sent us to look at the baskets."

The men looked at me.

"Well, maybe not," I conceded, thinking of the woman who'd stared at us in the museum, then followed us to the pictograms. "But those animals look like the ones woven on the baskets. If the only art you ever saw was on baskets and woven blankets, when you decided to carve something, you'd make it look like the baskets."

"When we're through here, you can write to the anthropological journals and tell them your theories," said Adam.

I narrowed my eyes at him. "Stuff that. I'll write a doctoral thesis. Then I can go do what most of the other people with doctoral degrees in anthropology do."

"What's that?" asked Calvin.

"You don't need to encourage her," said Adam seriously, but his eyes laughed at me.

"The same thing that people with degrees in history do," I said. "Fix cars or serve french fries and bad hamburgers."

"This one is the one my uncle told me to point out to you," Calvin said.

The rock had been broken, but the two pieces had been fit together carefully. The creature's face looked a little like a fox—a mutant fox with very big teeth and tentacles. Its body was snakelike. It was like a cross between a Chinese dragon and a fox with the teeth of a wolf eel.

"We don't know as much about these as we do the pictographs," Calvin said. "They could have been carved ten thousand years ago by the first people, or a hundred years ago. We don't know what this one was meant to represent, but we have a name for it. We call it the river devil."

Its eyes were eager, intelligent, and hungry.

I'd seen them before. Bright green eyes in the water that I'd seen in my dream. I blinked, and the eyes were just eyes. No matter how avid they appeared, they were just carved in the stone. But I knew what I had seen.

"Now," Calvin said cheerfully, while Adam watched me out of feral eyes, "there's a Coyote story about a monster who lived in the Columbia in the time of the first people, before we humans were here."

I tried a reassuring smile at Adam, who must have sensed my sudden recognition of the monster on the rock. I mouthed, "Later." He nodded.

It had been a dream, I reminded myself fiercely. Just a dream.

Calvin missed all the byplay, which was fine. "This monster," he said, "ate all of the first people who lived in the river. It ate up all the first people who fished in the river. Eventually, no one was willing to go near the river at all, so they asked the Great Spirit for help. He sent Coyote to see what was to be done.

"Coyote went down to the river and saw that nothing lived near the river. While he was watching, he saw a great monster lift out of the water. 'Ah,' it cried, 'I am so hungry. Why don't you come down so I can eat you.'

"That did not sound like a good idea to Coyote. So he went up into the hills where he could think. 'Hee, hee,' said his sisters, who were berries in his stomach."

"They were what?" I asked, surprised out of my panic over a pair of hungry green eyes in a stupid dream.

"This is the polite version," Calvin told me. "You can ask around if you want to find out the rude version. It is also rude to interrupt the storyteller."

"Sorry." I tried to figure out how berries who were sisters in Coyote's stomach could have a rude version.

"'Why are you laughing?' asked Coyote.

"'We know what you should do,' his sisters said. 'But we won't tell you because you'll just take all the credit like you always do.'

"But they were his sisters, and Coyote was very persuasive. He promised that this time he would tell everyone who was responsible for such a clever plan. At last they told him what to do. Following their advice, he took nine flint knives, a pouch of jerky, a rock, a torch, and some sagebrush and walked down to the river.

"'Come eat me,' he told the monster.

"And it did. As soon as it had swallowed him, he used the flint and stone to light his torch. Inside the monster were all of the first people it had eaten. They were very hungry, having not had food since they had been eaten by the monster. They were also cold because the monster was as chill inside as the river was outside.

"Coyote lit the sagebrush and shared out his jerky among them. He told the first people that he was going to kill the monster. Then, he told them, they would have to find their way out as best they could.

"So he took his first flint knife and started carving his way through to the monster's heart. He hadn't worked very long on the tough flesh before his first knife broke, and he had to bring out his second. The second knife broke, the third, and the fourth. Until at last he was down to his very last knife. But that one cut into the heart of the monster.

"'Run!' he told the trapped people. 'Get out.' And they did, escaping the dying monster any way they could. Out its mouth, out its gills, and out its bottom."

"I thought this wasn't the rude version," I said.

Calvin grinned but kept going. "Beaver was the last to leave. He just barely escaped out the beast's sphincter—and that is why the beaver's tail is flat and has no hair."

I groaned.

"At last it was only Coyote and the monster in the river, and Coyote had the upper hand.

"'I will let you live,' said Coyote, 'only if you promise never to eat anyone ever again.' The monster promised, and Coyote let it live. The beaten river monster sank to the bottom of the Columbia and never was heard from again. The grateful people threw a feast for Coyote, and he ate twice as much as anyone else.

"'Tell us,' the people said. 'How did you come up with such a clever plan?'

"And Coyote forgot the promises he made because he is vain and forgetful. He claimed all the credit for rescuing the people."

Finished with his story, Calvin turned to look at the river devil hovering on the rock. "There's no saying that the river devil and the monster in the Coyote story are the same beast, but I was told to tell you the story after you saw the rock."

"And about Benny," Adam reminded him.

"He's going to be okay," Calvin said. "Physically. The police are giving him a little bit of a bad time because he told them he doesn't remember what happened or where his sister is, and the doctors are having trouble with figuring out what happened to his foot. But Benny's not talking to them because it is none of their business, and they wouldn't understand anyway."

Calvin leaned against the fence that protected the petroglyphs. He looked at us. "I don't see what this has to do with you. Why my uncle and my grandfather think it has anything to do with you. I mean, I understand why he thinks you won't run away from the crazies when we start talking river monsters that eat people. But why is it your business?"

"Good question," I agreed. "I'd be happy if someone had some answers."

"Tell us about Benny," said Adam, who was used to taking responsibility for the world on his broad shoulders. If there was a problem, and he thought he could help, he would.

Calvin looked at him as if he were seeing him for the first time. Maybe he heard Adam's willingness to put his life on the line for a bunch of people he didn't know, too. After an awkwardly long moment, he said, "Benny told my uncle that he and Faith were out fishing, like they do a couple of times a month in the summer. They'd caught a couple of fish yesterday and were about ready to pack it in when something hit Faith's line hard enough that she thought they'd snagged some garbage. She could have just cut the line, but she and Benny, they're good folk. They don't like leaving hooks and line in the river if they don't have to."

A truck was pulling into the parking lot next to Adam's.

It was battered and sported three colors in addition to the bright orange primer, and its motor purred like a happy lion.

"My uncle," said Calvin unnecessarily, since we could all see him getting out of the truck. "So maybe all of us will get some answers."

Adam glanced over his shoulder, then looked at Calvin. "So what did Faith do?"

Calvin, like most people, obeyed Adam's tone of voice without even thinking about it and continued the story as his uncle approached. "She reeled it in, and the line kept coming. She leaned over the boat. Benny, he was leaning the other way to keep the boat from tipping, so he couldn't see what she did. But she said—"

"'There's something funny on the line, Benny. It looks like tentacles. What do you suppose . . .'" Jim let his voice trail off, and then he said matter-of-factly, "And the next thing Benny knows, Faith is in the water. He jumps in after her, and something bumps his leg—he figures that was when his foot went. The water started frothing, and he got the impression that there was something really big in the water. Faith came up to the surface, and he grabbed her in one arm and grabbed a gunnel of the boat in the other. She opened her eyes, and says to him, 'It's so peaceful here,' then her eyes go fixed. Benny, he's seen people die before, so he knows she's gone. About that time, he realizes that there isn't any of her below her rib cage. So he makes the smart decision and drops her body so he can vault into the boat. He lies down on the bottom and feels something that bumps and bobs his boat all over the place. He's gone shark fishing in the ocean, and he said it felt like when there's a fish out there a lot bigger than your boat. At some point he passed out and woke up here and there until you found him."

Jim paused and looked at Adam and me. "After I heard his story, I called in Gordon Seeker because he knows more about this kind of stuff than anyone I know. He listened to Benny's story and decided nothing would do but that he go down to that new campground and check out the werewolf. Whatever he found in your trailer made him believe that you are right in the middle of it. Part of it seems to be that you"—he centered his gaze on me—"are river marked now. Whatever that means."

He didn't sound nearly as friendly as he had last night. But that seemed only natural. For all that he was human, and his cheerful manner was out there for all to see, Jim Alvin had all the hallmarks of an alpha, and we were intruders in his territory.

"So," he said heavily, "now you know what we know. What do you know?"

"We told Calvin a few things," said Adam. "Why don't you give Mercy and me a little time to sort out what we know, and we'll do the same. We have food enough for an army. Get Gordon and whoever else you think might need to know and come down to our campsite in two hours. We'll feed you and talk."

WHEN WE WERE DRIVING BACK TO CAMP, ADAM said, "Did I read you wrong, or do you know more than I do about this?"

"I think 'knowing more' might be a misnomer," I said. "Maybe I have a better handle on the scope of the questions?"

He made a noise halfway between a grunt and a growl.

For thirty-odd years, I'd been alone. For a season, I belonged to Adam and he to me. Sometimes the relief of it was almost more than I could bear.

"The woman I saw at the museum and at Horsethief Lake, I suspect is Faith, Benny's sister. She could, I suppose, be a random ghost, but she seems too interested in us not to be connected to us in some fashion. Benny's sister is the best candidate. I'll ask for a description of her before I tell them—if you think I ought. The only thing knowing who she is might do for them is confirm that she is dead, but I think Benny's story is clear enough."

"I agree," Adam said. "Probably, if she doesn't reappear, there's no reason to bring her up."

"Besides," I said, looking out of the truck at the small orchard we were passing because I didn't want Adam to see my face, "if they have a walker, he'll be able to see her just fine, and she can talk to him."

But Adam knew me, and he put a hand on my knee. "Gordon is probably a walker."

"Right," I agreed.

"And he knew about you before he came into our camp. He just didn't know that you were going to be with me until he saw you."

"Yep," I agreed. The river had a scattering of fishing boats that were dwarfed by a pair of barges traveling upstream.

"They left you to be raised by a wolf pack," he said. "Their loss. Would you rather have had them, or Bran and his pack?"

He wore the pair of dark sunglasses that he sometimes did while driving. He used to wear them more often when the wolves were still trying to hide what they were. And his face was as bland as his voice.

"You have an irritating way of pointing out the obvious," I told him, touching his arm to let him know I was teasing. One of my favorite things about being mated and now married was that I got to touch him whenever I wanted to—and the more I touched, the more I wanted to.

"Good that you find it obvious," he said. "Maybe Gordon and the other walkers had their reasons for staying away, but it doesn't matter anymore. Who do you think is the second walker, the hawk? Is it Jim?"

"Could be," I said, thinking hard. "But I don't have any medicine-magic, almost the opposite, because magic doesn't work on me like it does everyone else. I suppose he could be two things at once. It could also be someone we haven't met as a human yet."

"What bothered you so much about the river-devil petroglyph?" He made the turn into the campground and swiped the card on the box that opened the gate. "All I caught was your shock. I couldn't pick up anything else."

"Remember that nightmare I had on the way to Horsethief Lake?" I said. "I saw something that could have inspired a drawing like that." And I told him what I remembered of the dream.

By the time I'd finished, we were at our campsite. Adam didn't say anything for a while, and I helped him set up to feed an unknown number of people.

"Do you often have dreams like that? About people you don't know?"

"No," I told him. "Usually the people I do know are sufficient to spawn any number of nightmares without inventing any."

He stopped what he was doing and pulled out his magic phone.

Okay, the phone isn't magic, but it does things my computer struggles with.

"Good," he said. "We have a signal. What was your teacher's name? Do you remember?"

"Janice Lynne Morrison," I said.

He glanced at me, a little surprised by my ready answer. I had trouble remembering the names of people I should know. An unfortunate number of my customers were known to Zee and me as Yellow-Spotted Bug or Blue Bus. I've had to check my paperwork to make certain of the names of people I'd known for years.

I shrugged. "Horror has a way of making things stick."

He tapped into his magic phone for a while. If I had a phone that complicated, I'd have to bring Jesse along to run the damned thing.

"There's a Janice Lynne Morrison who teaches third grade at a school in Tigard, one of the Portland suburbs," Adam said with a frown. He turned the phone so I could see its screen. The face that looked back at me was grainy and too formal.

"That's her," I said, my heart sinking to my feet. "What am I doing dreaming about real people, Adam? What am I doing dreaming about their deaths?" I gripped his wrist because I needed to hold on to something solid. "Is it a true dream? I don't do true dreaming. Did I see the future, so I should warn her somehow?" I knew I was babbling, but this was Adam I was babbling to. He didn't mind and wouldn't think I actually expected him to have an answer.

He tucked his phone away with his free hand and let me hold on as tightly as I needed to.

"I don't know," he said. "But we'll find out. Warning her without more information won't help, either. People don't tend to take warnings about monsters who are going to eat them very seriously. Especially when they come from total strangers."

"This is true," said Gordon heavily as he walked around the end of the trailer. "It is why those who know things must sound mysterious. It is like fishing. The mystery the bait, the truth the hook—which is why it sometimes hurts."

"The fish ends up dead," I said dryly.

"Not the ending we are hoping for," Gordon said with a sigh. "But always a possibility." Today he wore jeans and a Dresden Dolls T-shirt.

He looked at me. "Who was your father, Mercedes Thompson?"

"Hauptman," said Adam coolly. "Mercedes Athena Thompson Hauptman."

"Joe Old Coyote," I said, leaning against Adam a little and relaxing my grip on his arm, both signals that I was okay, and he needed to ease up the protection deal, as much as I appreciated it.

"Ayah," said Gordon. "Killed by a car wreck and finished off by vampires. I told him he drove that thing too fast, but he seldom listened to good advice. Do you know who your father was?"

"Just hit me on the head and put me in your basket with the rest of the dead trout," I told him. "Get to the point."

He smiled at me.

"Some people like fishing," said Adam dryly. "Necessary or not."

Gordon laughed. He had a good laugh. "I do. That I do. Still, sometimes in the struggle much is gained that would not be otherwise." Then the amusement faded out of his face. "Sometimes the fish gets hurt. I will tell you a story while you get ready to feed the people who are coming. There will be just three more in addition to those of us who are here." He smiled at my frown. "I am an old man. And old men get to act mysterious. I talked to Jim about ten minutes ago. He and the Owens brothers are coming. Calvin has been set to watch at the hospital, where Benny is showing signs of not being as well as they previously thought. He keeps trying to get out of bed, and they have had to restrain him."

I thought of the way Janice Morrison, whom I would never meet, had walked willingly into the river with her struggling children.

"What do you know of those who are like you and how they came to be, Mercy?" Gordon asked.

"I don't, much."

Adam encompassed us both with a single sharp look, then went to the campsite grill and stuffed newspaper and charcoal into the charcoal chimney. He granted us the illusion of privacy because Gordon obviously wanted to talk to me—but he would listen.

It made me itch, that protective streak of his. But one of the things the past few months had taught me was that it ran both ways. Anyone who tried to hurt my wolf had me to deal with. I might be a thirty-five-pound coyote, but I played dirty.

Gordon grunted in approval. "One time before this, Coyote came upon a village where the chief had a beautiful daughter. Coyote disguised himself as a handsome young hunter. He killed a deer, slung it over his shoulders, and took it to the chief as a gift. 'Chief,' he said, 'let me court your daughter for my wife.'"

"Is this the polite version?" I asked dryly.

Gordon displayed his missing front tooth but didn't slow down his retelling. "The chief didn't know it was Coyote who looked at his daughter. 'Hunter,' said the chief, 'you can court her, but my daughter chooses her own husband.'

"So Coyote began to court the chief's daughter. He brought her fresh meat, tanned hides, and beautiful flowers. She thanked him for each of his gifts. Finally, Coyote went to her father, and said, 'What gift can I bring her that would impress her enough to take me as her husband?'

"'Ask my daughter,' said the chief.

"So Coyote the Hunter went to the daughter and asked her what gift she wanted most of all.

"'I would most like a pool of quiet water where I could bathe in private,' she told him.

"So Coyote, he went out to a quiet place in the woods, and he built her a pool at the base of a waterfall. He diverted a stream so that it flowed down the fall and into the pool. When the chief's daughter saw the pool, she agreed to marry Coyote—still in his guise as a hunter. She welcomed him to her pool, and they laughed and played in it until the woods rang with their happiness." The old man paused. "I think that is enough of the story. It ends tragically, as it usually does when two such different people love each other." There was a sharpness to his tone as he said the last sentence that made it obvious he wasn't just talking about Coyote and the chief's daughter.

I frowned at him. "Lots of people who have more influence over both of us than you do have made that observation. We didn't listen to them, either."

"Is it the werewolf or the Anglo that bothers you?" asked Adam, bringing a bag of premade hamburger patties out of the trailer. Other than his question, he didn't pay any attention to us as he passed by on the way to the grill.

"Wolves eat coyotes," Gordon said, but from his body language, I could tell that our marriage really didn't bother him one way or the other; he just enjoyed stirring the pot.

If he weren't an old man, I had some rude things I could have said to that.

"Yes," observed Adam blandly. "I do."

Yep. That was the one that came to mind. And he didn't even blush when he said it. Maybe Gordon would miss the double entendre. But he grinned cheerfully at Adam.

"Do you know," I said casually, "that the Blackfeet tell Old Man stories and not Coyote stories? The Lakota's trickster is Iktomi—the spider—though he tends to land more on the side of evil than simple chaos."

The old man smiled slyly. "That's because Coyote goes in many guises. And"—he shook a hand at me—"chaos is never simple unless you are Coyote."

"So what did the story have to do with me?" I asked, not really expecting an answer.

"The chief's daughter, who was, for a while, Coyote's wife, had a daughter—and she could walk as coyote or human, as could her sons."

"So I am descended from Coyote. And that red-tailed hawk we saw at Horsethief Lake"—I somehow didn't doubt that Gordon knew about it—"is descended from Hawk."

"Ayah," he said. "A *walker*"—he gave a studied emphasis on the only term I knew for what I was; "avatar" sounded like something that should be running around an Internet multiplayer game or covered with blue paint and

CGI'd into a movie—"is descended from one of these matings of mortal to immortal. But it has been a long time since they walked so freely among us, and for many years now the only way one is born is for both parents to be descended from such a coupling."

"Which is why Calvin was so certain I couldn't be a walker," I said. "My mother, as far as I know, is Western European—mostly German and Irish in descent."

"Ayah," agreed Gordon. "I do not doubt it. Which is why I ask you, do you know who your father was?"

I heard what he wanted me to. I didn't know why he'd decided to play games with me, but I was done. My father had nothing to do with whatever it was that had attacked poor Benny and his sister. Gordon Seckel, whatever he was, was nothing to me.

"He was a rodeo cowboy," I said. If I'd been in coyote form, I'd have had my ears pinned back. "He rode bulls and was moderately good at it. My mother was riding her friend's horse and trying to win enough money to survive. He gave her a place to stay for a while. He was killed in a car wreck before my mother even knew she was pregnant with me."

Adam watched from the grill. His eyes rested on the old man with cool yellow dispassion. I sucked in a breath and tried not to get mad—or let this stranger hurt me with a story older than I was. Emotions seemed to pass easier through the mating ties than words or thoughts. I was learning to control myself a little more now that Adam could feel them, too.

"Yes," said Gordon gently. "I am sure that you are right, of course. Joe Old Coyote died thirty-three years ago on a stretch of highway in eastern Montana." He looked up. "Ah, here they are."

I got the keycard out of the truck. "I'll let them in," I said, and escaped at a jog.

What the old man implied was wrong. If I was tempted

for a moment to believe—to believe that my father might still be alive because Coyote died all the time only to be reborn the next morning—then I had only to remember that I had seen his ghost dance for me. My father was dead. I stretched out and turned my jog into a flat-out run, letting the speed clear my head.

I opened the gate for Jim, who did indeed have Fred and Hank Owens sitting next to him.

"Hop in the back," suggested Jim, once the truck was on the campground side of the gate. "I'll give you a ride on down."

I hadn't ridden in the back of a pickup since I was a kid, and it was still fun. I jumped out before he stopped, just to see if I still could. I landed on my feet but let the momentum roll me backward and carry me back onto my feet again. It was a matter of timing. My foster father had taught me how to do that after he caught me trying to imitate him.

"Teaching her how to do it right, so she doesn't break her fool neck," he'd growled, while my foster mother, Evelyn, fussed, "is likely to be less fatal than forbidding her to do it, because that doesn't work at all."

He had been awesome.

So what if an old Indian thought my father was Coyote? My father had really been Bryan, the man who'd raised me. He'd been there for me when I needed him, until Evelyn died and he hadn't been able to survive the loss. After that, I'd had Bran.

If Bran and Coyote battled it out, I'd put my money on Bran. The thought restored my usual cheery outlook.

I dusted off my backside, and Adam rolled his eyes at me, looking remarkably like his daughter when he did so. "I bet Bran yelled at you for doing stuff like that," he said, but he didn't sound too upset.

"I haven't done it in a long time," I admitted. "Does it still look cool?"

He laughed, ruffled my hair, and welcomed our guests.

We ate hamburgers, chips, and macaroni salad. We made small talk about the weather, the river, living in Washington, living in Montana, living in the military, and thereby gaining a little bit of a fix on the character of people who had been strangers a few hours ago. Eating has been a ritual between allies for nearly as long as there have been people, and all of us were well aware of the subtext.

Gordon Seeker, I noticed, didn't talk much. Just leaned back on a camp chair and watched with an avid gaze that reminded me a little of the river devil. He caught me looking and smiled like the Cheshire cat.

"I think," said Jim finally as he dumped his empty paper plate in the garbage can, "we should introduce ourselves again. To know our allies is a good thing. I am Jim Alvin of the Yakama Nation. My mother was Wishram, my father Yakama, and I possess a little magic of the people." He took his seat on the picnic-table bench where he'd eaten and turned to the Owens brothers.

"Fred Owens," said Fred, though his brother was the one who sat next to Jim. "USMC retired." He glanced at Adam and smiled. "Red-tailed hawk when it suits me. Rancher."

"Hank Owens," his brother said. "USMC retired. Rancher. Welder. Red-tailed hawk when it suits him." He tilted his head at his brother. Evidently it was a family joke because his brother smiled a little. "It was Fred who couldn't let Calvin handle the job on his own."

"We left Calvin—" Jim began to explain, but Gordon interrupted him.

"—at the hospital. I told them."

There was a little strain between Jim and Gordon that reminded me of when there were two Alphas in the room. They might be allies, even friends, but they were waiting for the slightest sign of weakness or aggression.

"Adam Hauptman," said my husband, who was sitting in the second of our camp chairs. "Alpha of the Columbia Basin Pack. Army, honorably discharged 1973. Mate and husband of Mercedes Thompson Hauptman. In my spare time, I run a security firm."

Jim gave him a startled look. I was surprised myself. Werewolves might be out, but the public doesn't know everything. And one of the things that Bran was not telling the public about werewolves was that they were immortal.

"Long time ago," observed Fred.

"Vietnam," said Hank. "You were a ranger in Vietnam."

From my observation post on the ice chest, I watched Adam's face. He'd offered the chair—but I hate the camp chairs. Ten minutes, and my feet are falling asleep.

What was he up to? If Bran found out, he wouldn't be pleased. But Adam always had a reason for what he did. I usually figured it out about five years after the fact. He seemed to be watching Gordon. Maybe it was something as simple as acknowledging that we were all going to be sharing secrets before this was over.

"Nasty time," said Jim.

Adam tipped his water bottle toward Jim, then brought it up to tip his imaginary hat. He looked at me.

"Mercedes Thompson Hauptman," I said, obedient to the look that told me he wanted to move things along. "VW mechanic. Coyote walker mated to Adam Hauptman."

"Gordon Seeker," said Gordon. "But Indian names change from time to time. I have had others. I work a little healing, a little magic, a little of this and that. When I was young, I was a mighty hunter, but it has been a long time since I was young." He eyed Adam. "Maybe even longer ago than when this one was as young as he looks."

"All right," said Adam, when it became obvious that the old man had said all he intended to. "Jim and Calvin told us a few things this afternoon. Namely that we have a monster in the river that has killed at least one person—though the tally is unlikely to stop with Benny's sister. Let me tell you some things you don't know—some of which might not have anything to do with our current problem at all." He told them about the faes' redirection of our honeymoon, including Yo-yo Girl Edythe's prophecy and the otterkin who had been relocated to the Columbia.

Fred frowned and glanced at Jim. "I told you those otters we saw looked odd. Their heads are the wrong shape."

"I have seen them," said Gordon, his voice dismissing their importance. "Prophecy is a weak crutch to lean on."

"Have you met Edythe?" I asked in an interested voice. "Short. Usually looks about ten?"

Gordon raised his eyebrows, and I thought that the answer might have been yes.

I smiled cheerfully at him. "Fae are deceptive. The weaker and more harmless they appear, the more dangerous they are likely to be. Edythe is probably the scariest monster in a raft of scary monsters. I'm not inclined to discount anything she said. And I'm not sure relegating the otterkin to harmless—even though our contact with the fae seemed to be doing it—is very smart."

"They aren't eating people," observed Fred.

"That you know of," I said at the same time that Adam said, "Yet."

He smiled at me. "I'll admit that they don't appear to be part of this—but I don't like that they are here. They were watching Mercy when she pulled Benny out of the water."

"I have a few more things to add," I said. And just then the wind picked up a little, and Benny's sister, Faith, sat down beside me on the edge of the ice chest. I looked at the others—at Fred, Hank, and Gordon, who were supposed to be like me—expecting . . . I don't know. Some sort of recognition, I suppose. But no one jumped up and exclaimed the dead woman's name—or even seemed to see her. Not even Gordon Seeker.

"It wants him," she said. She wasn't looking at me; she was looking at Hank.

"Him who?" I asked.

"Benny." She sighed. "Stupid. I know better than to lean

out over the water like that. But he was stupid, too. I can swim. He should have stayed in the boat. But now . . . it's like the crocodile in *Peter Pan*. It's had a bite of him and wants the whole meal."

"We'll keep him safe," I told her.

Everyone was watching us—or me at least. Adam had stood and was holding up his hand, keeping the others from interrupting. It might not be important—sometimes ghosts could be incredibly stubborn. But sometimes a loud noise or a sudden move, and they disappeared like rabbits.

"I don't know if you can keep him safe," she said sadly. "You know, in the story, all the first people the river monster ate came back to life after it was dead."

"I thought Coyote left it alive?"

She turned toward me, finally, and smiled. It didn't look like a smile that should be on the face of a dead woman. She had a good smile. "There are several versions of that story. When he was a little boy, Calvin always did like the ones in which everyone lived."

She stood up and wandered over to the grill, her fingers passing through the grating, and pressed on the coals beyond.

"Be careful," she told me, her gaze on the coal. "When it marks someone, they belong to it." She looked at Hank again.

"It was always him for me, you know? Ever since high school. But he never had eyes for me." She turned to me in sudden alarm. "Don't tell him that. He doesn't deserve to feel guilty."

"I won't," I assured her.

"And don't believe Jim's mysterious-Indian schtick, either. He's got a Ph.D. in psychology and taught over at UW in Seattle until he retired last year."

She put her hands back on the grill, but this time she didn't go through the grating but kept them on top of the hot metal, tapping her fingers lightly on the grill as if it fascinated her that she could do that without burning herself. I wanted to go and pull them off, even though I knew it couldn't hurt her anymore.

She glanced at the Owens brothers. "And Fred trains cuttin' horses. He's starting to make a name for himself. Hank works with him on the business side, then does welding to help balance the books."

"Why are you telling me all this?" I asked.

"So I remember," she whispered. "Tell them not to call my name. I don't want to stay here like this. Tell Benny I'm okay. Tell him to pick a flower for me and put it on Mama's grave this year for me."

I had never dealt with a ghost quite this coherent before. Usually, they don't even notice me. The few that do don't really seem to be aware that they are dead.

"I'll tell them," I promised, helpless to do anything to make this easier on anyone.

She looked up and met my eyes—and in hers I could see a flicker of violent green, the color of the river devil's eyes. "See that you do."

And she was gone.

Adam, watching me, dropped his hand when I met his eyes.

"Thanks," I told him.

"What the hell is that?" growled Hank. "Who were you talking to?"

"I thought that all walkers could see the dead," I said. "It's why the vampires don't like us."

"Vampires?" said Fred. "There are vampires?"

Jim laughed. "Not all walkers are alike, Mercy. No more than two men wear the same shirt at the same time."

I looked at Gordon.

"That is not my burden," Gordon told me. "Besides, I'm not a walker. Who did you see?"

Calvin had said that Gordon could take animal form, and he hadn't been lying. Still, there were other people who could shift shapes in the Native American stories I'd read. Instead of pursuing what he was, I answered his question.

"She didn't want you to use her name, but could you give me a description of Benny's sister? Before I tell you what she told me, I'd like to make sure I'm talking about the right person."

"No," said Jim coolly. "You tell us what she looked like, and we'll tell you if you get it right."

Okay. I could deal with that. "She's a little shorter than I am and she has muscle. Not casual muscle but the kind that comes from some sort of hard work or sport. She has a little scar just in front of her left ear." I put my finger where the scar was.

"She has a Web site," said Hank hostilely. "Her photo is up on it."

"This," Adam said abruptly, "isn't going to work that way. If you don't believe Mercy saw Benny's sister, nothing she tells you is going to convince you."

"She told Calvin that there was a woman following them at Horsethief Lake." Jim scuffed his boot in the dirt. "She told him that the woman was wearing a dark blue shirt with a pair of macaws on the back before he told her that Benny's sister had been with him on the boat. Beyond that, I don't see what pretending she could see Fai—" He stuttered a little as he switched words. "Benny's sister gains her at this point."

"She loved that shirt," Hank muttered. "Got herself a new sewing machine, one that could do fancy embroidery. That shirt was the first thing she made on it."

"Benny gave her a bad time about the damned parrots," said Fred. "White cockatoos." He laughed and shook his head.

I thought I would have liked Faith if I'd known her while she was alive.

"What did she say?" Adam asked.

"She said that it had a taste of Benny and wanted the rest. I told her that we could keep him safe, but she wasn't convinced of it." I glanced at the men sitting on the bench of the picnic table. "Other than that it was just a few things—and a message to Benny. She wants him to know she's okay, and she wants him to put a flower on her mother's grave for her this year."

I rolled up my pant leg to show everyone the mark I had on my leg. The blood and pus were gone, but it still was a dark brown scab circling my leg. It itched mildly, but I didn't touch it.

"River marked, you said," I told Gordon. "What does it mean?"

He crossed one scarlet boot over his opposite knee and pursed his lips. But before he could say anything, there was the sharp crack of a pistol, and, beside me, Adam jerked.

8

HANK HELD THE GUN LIKE HE KNEW WHAT HE was doing with it. I bolted for him, but no matter how fast I moved, I had to cross twelve feet, and he only had to pull the trigger. But I wasn't the only one moving—his brother hit Hank's gun hand as he shot a second time.

Fred grabbed the gun and jerked it down toward the ground, where Hank spent his third shot. "What are you doing? Hank? Stop it."

Hank didn't get a fourth shot because I grabbed the stick I'd almost tripped over like a baseball bat and hit him in the back of the head, knocking him cold.

I wouldn't have cared if I killed him—and I might well have because the stick I'd grabbed was the fairy walking stick that had followed me—however it follows me—ever since I'd first encountered it.

No matter that it didn't have feet and wasn't alive, it was old fairy magic, and that was apparently enough for it to trail after me like a faithful dog. Though it was graceful and slender, the end was shod in silver and heavy. I might as well have hit Hank in the back of the head with a lead pipe.

Lugh never made anything that couldn't be used as a weapon, the oakman had told me just before he'd used the stick to kill a very nasty vampire. Lugh was an ancient hero of the *Tuatha de Danann*—I'd looked him up later. If the oakman had been right about the walking stick's origins, it predated Christ's birth and then some. It might even be older than Bran.

I dropped the artifact that had been old when Columbus first set foot on the Bahamas on the ground as if it were garbage and returned to my mate's side before anybody else moved.

Hank had shot *Adam.*

Adam hadn't even moved. He'd just slumped over on the stupid camp chair. That told me it was bad. Very bad. I could smell his blood.

As I reached Adam, Gordon was on the other side, plucking Adam off the chair with an ease no old man would ever be able to imitate. Adam was solid muscle and heavy, even in his human form, and Gordon couldn't weigh half what Adam did.

It didn't seem to slow him down, though.

I ripped Adam's shirt open so I could see the damage.

There was a neat hole with a sliver of bone sticking out of his chest. The good news was that his heart was still beating because the blood was pulsing. The bad news was there was no exit hole in his back, and there was too much blood.

"There's no exit wound," Gordon muttered.

"Noticed that," I said shortly. "Got to get it out yesterday." No telling if it was silver or lead, but I had to assume the worst. They all knew Adam was a werewolf, and the silver-bullet stuff was common lore.

I bolted for the truck and the supercomprehensive-when-hell-breaks-out first-aid kit stored behind the backseat in three backpacks. One of them had a surgical kit. One had bandages of all sizes. Another had various ointments and miscellaneous first-aid paraphernalia. I didn't stop to try to figure out which one was which, though they were color-coded. I grabbed them all and hauled them back to Adam.

I dropped them down beside him and knelt by his head—just as Gordon used a very small but wicked-looking black blade to slice into skin because the entry wound had already started to close. That could be good news; wounds made by silver tended to heal as slowly as they did for the rest of us.

"Hold him," grunted Gordon. "Jim, Fred—Hank will keep. He's not dead. Get over here. If he wakes up, we're going to need you all."

"He's awake," I told them. "He'll keep still. Probably better off if everyone else stays back. He'll sense them, essentially strangers, and come up fighting—and the four of us wouldn't be able to hold him if he decides he needs to."

I'm not sure if Fred or Jim had moved toward us when Gordon called them over, but they stayed back out of the way after I told them to. However helpful in getting the bullet out, unconscious was not a good sign. I found an explanation for it when I turned his head and discovered a bloody cut along his temple where the second shot had creased him.

It was already healing, so that bullet, at least, had been lead. Even so, if Hank had hit Adam in the forehead with it, it still stood a good chance of killing him. I owed Fred because I wouldn't have been fast enough.

I stroked my fingers over Adam's face, where he would smell me and know that I was watching out for him, then turned to watch what Gordon was doing. Adam was conscious; I could feel it. But he was trusting me to help him while he did his best to keep his body alive. Even if the first bullet had been lead, it needed to come out, or Adam would be sicker than a kid at Halloween for days until it festered out.

It was about then that I realized the knife Gordon was using wasn't some sort of fancy thing, painted black to make it look military. It was an honest-to-goodness obsidian knife. Stone knives, I remembered inconsequentially from Anthropology 101, were both sharper and more fragile than most steel knives. More important to me than the oddity of the knife was that Gordon looked like he knew what he was doing.

"Remove many bullets?" I asked, just to be sure. I scrambled in the bags until I found the surgical kit and a probe and a pair of forceps.

He gave them a look when I held them up for him. "Usually do this with my fingers," he told me.

Infection wasn't a concern with werewolves—or apparently to Gordon.

"A probe and forceps do less damage when you have to go in deep," I told him firmly. "I can do it if you don't want to."

I had so far in my life avoided pulling bullets out of people, and had no illusions that I'd be good at it. But me with forceps would be better than Gordon's fingers.

He gave me a gap-toothed grin and took the probe.

"Have to work quickly on a werewolf," I told him.

"Healing pretty fast," he grunted, sliding the instrument into the wound he'd reopened with the odd little knife. "Good news, I think, as long as we get the bullet out."

"Dominant werewolves do," I said. "And they don't come much more dominant." Thank goodness. Despite his earlier words, he looked like he knew what he was doing. "You've used a probe before."

He switched hands, holding the probe with his left and taking the forceps with his right. "Only a hundred or two," he said, closing his eyes. "Got it. It's up against his shoulder blade."

A silver bullet doesn't mushroom like a lead bullet does. If it had made it all the way through Adam, it would have left a neat hole going in and an equally neat hole going out. The bullet Gordon pulled out of Adam was squashed and had doubtless bounced around inside and torn up muscle and organs. More painful but infinitely less lethal.

As soon as Gordon's hand was out, I dried my hands on my jeans and hauled out my phone to call Samuel.

"Who are you calling?" asked Gordon.

"A doctor friend of mine," I told him. "And his."

A hand wrapped around the phone, and Adam said hoarsely, "Don't. Not until we know what's going on." He sat up, using his stomach muscles and not his arms. He didn't do it for effect—moving his shoulder would be painful for a while yet.

He looked at Gordon. "Thanks for the surgery. That felt like the fastest extraction I've had."

Gordon raised an eyebrow. "Do you find yourself saying that often? If so, I advise a different lifestyle."

Adam smiled to acknowledge Gordon's point, but when he spoke, it was on another subject. "You said something last night about river marked—about how Mercy wouldn't be a good slave. What's special about that mark? Did the river devil do it?"

He hurt; I could feel just how much. But he wasn't going to show it in public.

"River marked," Gordon said. He looked over to where Fred was exploring the back of Hank's head. "I do see why you are asking. There was once a place where a band of Indians lived. 'Don't go to that village; they are marked by the river,' the people would say. 'If you go there, you will not come back. They will feed you to the river.' All the people of that village wore a brown mark on their bodies, and they obeyed the hungry river in all things. I've forgotten the rest of the story."

"Check Hank," Adam said, his voice only a little more breathy than normal. "He didn't strike me as the shoot first and negotiate later kind of person. Even those crazy jarheads usually need a reason to pull the trigger."

Fred didn't protest the slur, just stripped off Hank's jeans and shirt—and found a dark brown oozing sore across Hank's back that looked a lot like what my calf had looked like before Gordon and his salve had come along.

I jerked up my pant leg. "Looks like what I've got."

"Could have happened when he was coming onshore with our boat last night," said Jim. "He didn't say anything about getting hurt—but Hank's like that. Coyote walkers are immune to the effects?"

Gordon grunted. "This coyote walker, evidently."

And when Hank groaned and started to move, Jim added, "I have a rope in the truck." And he jumped up to get it.

"We don't want the pack here," Adam said very quietly to me, explaining why he hadn't let me call Samuel, I thought. "First—wolves don't do well in water. Second—just think what this thing could do if he controlled a pack of werewolves."

"Wouldn't pack magic stop that?" I asked. If the river devil could control Hank, another walker, maybe it wasn't the walker part of me that had kept it from doing that to me. Maybe it was the pack—or even my mate bond with Adam.

Adam shook his head. "Maybe. But I'm not willing to risk it. Not unless things get a lot more desperate."

"You heal fast," said Jim neutrally as he returned with a rope.

"Werewolves do," I said—and remembered that one of the side effects of rapid healing was an even larger than usual need for food. Adam needed to eat meat—lots of it, the rawer the better. He was holding on to his control, which couldn't be easy with his wound exposed to all of these possibly hostile strangers. Alpha wolves can't afford that kind of weakness. He hid his pain well, but they all knew he'd been shot and they could see the blood.

"I'll get some food," I told him.

"No," Adam said, holding on to my arm before I could go. "Not yet. We'll get this meeting over with first."

He didn't want to betray any more weakness among these people. I supposed I could understand it, but it didn't make me happy. But he was Alpha, and I was his mate. I'd argue with him in private . . . Okay, who was I kidding? I'd argue with him in front of the pack. But not in front of strangers. Not when he was hurt, anyway.

He glanced at the others, who were mostly working on restraining Hank with Jim's rope. Gordon had gone over to supervise the others.

Adam raised his good hand to me, and said quietly, "Give me a hand up."

I did, and tried not to show how much strength it required to get him on his feet. He walked—only a little stiffly—to the picnic table and leaned a hip on it. Apparently, he was satisfied with the job Fred was doing because he didn't say anything until Fred had finished hog-tying his brother.

It is difficult to tie up a person so he can't escape. When I was about ten, a whole bunch of us kids in Aspen Creek, inspired by some movie or other, spent a whole month tying one another up at recess with jump ropes until Bran came and put a stop to it. He probably wouldn't have bothered if we hadn't left Jem Goodnight tied to the swing set after the bell rang. We felt pretty justified because Jem told us that no girl could tie him up in such a way that he couldn't get out of it. "Girls," he'd pronounced, "can't tie knots."

It had taken us three recesses to get it right, but after a

half hour of working on it, it had taken Bran's knife to finally free Jem. I could tie knots, girl or no. Bryan, who'd once been a sailor on the tall ships with sails, had worked with me since I first tied my own shoes.

Adam's phone rang, and he glanced at the screen before he answered it. With a grimace he opened it, and said, "I'm fine, Darryl. Just a misunderstanding." Pack bonds could be a nuisance sometimes, like when Adam had been shot and didn't want the pack to come running.

"You're hurt," said Darryl's voice, and I think the only person who didn't hear him was Jim.

"It's minor."

"Felt like you got shot," Darryl said dryly. "I know what a bullet feels like. You had a misunderstanding on your honeymoon that resulted in your getting shot? We could be there in a couple of hours."

"It was a misunderstanding," growled Adam, speaking slower, as if that would make Darryl more compliant. "Stay where you are. I'll call you in if I need you."

There was a pause. "Let me talk to Mercy."

"*Who* is Alpha?" Adam's voice was a low threat.

"You are," I told him, and snatched the phone out of his hand. "But this is payback for your making poor Darryl watch out for me when you were in D.C. Hey, Darryl. He got shot with a .38 in the shoulder, lead. We're not sure exactly what's going on right now other than the excitement is over for the night. If we need you, we'll call you. Right now, that's looking like it might not be a really good idea."

"Boss man is okay?"

"Grumpy," which was shorthand for hurt, which I wouldn't say, and Darryl would understand that. Wolves never admit how badly they're hurt. "But he's okay. We are safe and not in need of rescue."

"Good enough. I'm keeping the bags packed in case something changes."

"How's Jesse?" I asked. "Has she been throwing parties and living wild?" Jesse made a good change of topic because both Adam and Darryl relaxed as soon as Darryl responded.

"She dyed her hair orange, and it has these glittering purple strings in it," he said, sounding moderately aghast and intrigued at the same time. "I figured since she does it when Adam is in charge, he wouldn't kill me. Does she know that too much dyeing could make her hair turn green?"

I snorted. "Her hair was green. Did you miss it?"

"I forgot," he said. "Maybe not having kids is a good idea after all. Tell the boss all is okay here."

"Will do," I said. "Good night."

I handed the phone back to the wolf who was my mate. "They'll stay home."

He put his phone away without a word, but I could see his dimple peeking out. Jesse's disconcerting the intellectual and physical giant who was Adam's second was pretty funny to think about.

"Sorry," Adam said to the others. "Urgent business, unless you want to be neck-deep in werewolves."

"He knew you were hurt?" Fred asked.

"He's pack," Adam told him. Then, maybe to forestall questions about things Bran didn't want the public to know about werewolves, he continued briskly, "Here's what we need to figure out about whatever is in the river. How much harm is this creature doing? We don't really have a lot of data to go on other than a lot of scary talk about monsters. As the sole representative of monsters here, it is my . . . *obligation* to make certain we are looking at this with a balanced perspective. I am sorry that Benny's sister was killed and Benny injured. However, people are injured by"—he hesitated—"bear attacks, too. Just because something is dangerous does not make it evil. Was it defending its territory? Are we correct that it is a single beast? How intelligent is it? Can we bargain to keep people safe? Should we kill the last or near last of its kind because it has killed a woman and hurt her brother? Is there a way to salvage this situation with no more deaths?"

When you are a werewolf, I thought, it's a little hard to point at another predator, and shout, "It's a scary monster, kill it! Kill it!" I rubbed my calf though it wasn't itching at the moment.

Hank's eyes were open, but he didn't say anything or look at anyone. Instead, he stared at the river with such intensity that I shivered.

"I have a friend in River Patrol," said Fred. "I can find out how many casualties there have been in the river." He looked at Gordon. "Is there any story about how someone is freed from this mark?"

Gordon shook his head. "I do not know. But I will ask around." He looked at Adam. "It is not something you can bargain with, Mr. Hauptman. It is Hunger."

"I'm a werewolf," Adam told him. "People would have said that about me a century ago, too."

"This," said Gordon, "is nothing so benign as a werewolf or a grizzly bear."

Fred, kneeling on the ground next to his hog-tied brother, frowned suddenly at Gordon. "I thought you'd come with them"—he tipped his head toward the trailer, so he meant Adam and me—"until you named yourself Calvin's grandfather. But Calvin Seeker's father's father is dead. I know his mother's father. How is it you are his grandfather?"

Gordon smiled, the gap in front making him look as harmless as I was suddenly certain he wasn't. "I'm an old man," he told Fred. "How should I remember this?"

"I'll vouch for Gordon," said Jim, though he didn't sound enthusiastic or certain of it. "And so will Calvin. I think we ought to get Hank to the hospital, where they can check him. He doesn't seem to be tracking very well."

"I hit him pretty hard," I said, almost apologetically, which was as good as I could do, given that he'd shot Adam. "I didn't realize I'd grabbed my walking stick and not just some random stick until afterward."

"Understandable," said Fred unexpectedly. "My wife would take a baseball bat to someone who shot me."

"Has," said Jim. "I remember. It was Hank that time, too, wasn't it?"

"He didn't mean to," said Fred. "It was in Iraq—Desert Storm. I startled him on sentry-go, and he shot me. Meant I beat him back by a month. He showed up at my house to see how I was, and my Molly chased him around the front yard with my boy's bat until she got him in the backside. Good thing it was a plastic bat, or Hank wouldn't be walking now."

THEY LEFT. JIM, FRED, AND HANK TOOK JIM'S truck with Hank bound and laid out as comfortably as possible in the truck bed, with his brother to steady him. I rode up with them to let them out, and by the time I got back, Adam was alone. He was standing up—I think because if he sat down, he was worried he couldn't get up again.

"Food," I told him.

But he shook his head. "No. Shower. Then food. After I eat, I'll want to sleep. Can't safely sleep covered in blood and risk the wolf waking up without me and panicking him."

He was worried that he'd be weak enough when he slept that he couldn't control his wolf. For the wolf, all the blood would be all it took to wake up defensive and ready to fight. He had a point—the dark hid the worst of it, but there was no denying that he and I were covered in his blood.

"Okay," I said, and ran into the trailer to grab clean

clothes and towels. I got back out and made him get in the truck because "I can't carry you if you go down hard." He didn't argue much, which showed me how badly he was hurting.

We showered together in the men's room, because that was the direction he headed and, well, there was no one else in the campground, so what did it matter which side we went in? The men's room was done in browns rather than greens, but it had the same huge shower stalls with big showerheads. By the end of the shower, he was leaning on me pretty heavily

"Maybe I should have just washed up with a wet cloth and changed clothes," he admitted.

The mark on his chest, where Gordon had opened a path to the bullet, was a dark, angry red, but it would heal as soon as the rest of the damage did. Shift to wolf, food, and sleep would see him right.

"Mercy," he said. "I'll be okay."

I controlled myself because he had enough to worry about without me setting his wolf off. "Sorry. I know you will." I growled a little, not seriously, just enough so he knew I wasn't happy. "I don't like it that you are hurt. I like it even less that it could have been worse."

"Good." He lifted his head into the water. "I'll try to make sure that you always feel that way. My mother used to threaten to shoot my father."

He could barely stand up, and he was making jokes.

I nipped his shoulder. "I can see why she might feel the urge. Tell you what. If you make me mad enough to aim a gun at you—I'll aim for right between your eyes."

"So I won't feel it?" he asked.

I nipped him again, but gently, just a scrape of my teeth. "No. So the bullet will just bounce off your hard head."

He laughed. "Birds of a feather, Mercy."

If Hank had loaded his gun with silver, I might never have heard that laugh again.

Two years ago, silver bullets meant someone had to make them—I'd made my share. After the wolves had come out, suddenly people could buy silver bullets at Wal-Mart. Cops were unhappy about it because silver works pretty slick as an armor-piercing round, but without legislation, anyone who wanted to spend thirty dollars on a bullet could get one. Hank had known what Adam was, and still his gun had been loaded with lead. To me that indicated that he hadn't been planning on shooting Adam—or else he was really broke and couldn't afford the thirty bucks.

Another question occurred to me. Why had he shot Adam instead of Fred, Jim, Gordon, or me?

Assuming he was under the control of the river devil or whatever it was, maybe he or it or they together had decided that the werewolf was the greatest threat. I could understand that reasoning at least as far as Fred and I were concerned. Who would worry about a hawk and a coyote when there was a werewolf in the party? Yo-yo Girl's premonition indicated that Adam was important. Maybe the river devil knew why that was.

I propped Adam against the shower-stall wall and dried him as quickly as I could. I kept a wary eye on him while I did the same to myself and dressed.

"You could shift now," I suggested.

He shook his head. "Not until I eat. The wolf is riled up. Can't protect you, and there's danger around. Too easy to hurt you when I'm like that."

I snorted inelegantly. "Me, fragile? You've got the wrong woman. I don't break; I bounce. Besides, we're mates, remember? Your wolf won't hurt me."

"Not always true," he grunted, as I helped him into a pair of sweatpants. "Ask Bran. Not going to risk it."

"Fine," I said. "Let's get you back to the truck."

"Shirt," he insisted.

"No one is going to see that mark and know you've been wounded." I didn't say that no one would have to as badly as Adam was staggering. Willpower was all well and good, but there were limits. "Anyway, there's no one here to see you but me."

"Shirt," he insisted.

Arguing was taking up energy neither of us had to spare. So I grabbed the button-up shirt I'd brought and helped him into it. The Italian silk shirt looked a little odd paired with the sweatpants, but who was going to look?

Back at the trailer, he sat at the little table and ate with a ferocious and silent intensity. I gave him the last of the hamburger and the thawed steaks before going to work on the frozen stuff. Happily, there was a microwave in the Trailer of Wonders. When I'd finished slicing the frozen meat, I watched the speed with which he was eating and knew it wouldn't be enough.

So I made pancakes on the nifty little stove and had a hot stack waiting for him when he finished the frozen meat. He gave me a look when I set it in front of him, but he ate the pancakes with the same steady rhythm as he'd eaten the rest of the food. Meat was better, but calories were calories.

He finished before I'd gotten the last of the batter in the pan, pushing the plate away so I'd know.

"Okay," I said. "Change already."

"You need to go," he said. "This is going to hurt. Give me about twenty minutes."

I left and waited outside five minutes while our bond let me know just exactly how much pain he was in. Changing for the wolves was bad enough when they weren't hurt. Five minutes was all I could take. I couldn't help him, but I couldn't bear to leave him alone, either.

"I'm coming back in," I told him, so he wouldn't think it was some stranger. The only concession I made to safety was to sit on the far side of the trailer until the wolf heaved himself up on all fours. He started to shake himself free of the last tingles of the change and stopped abruptly. It must have hurt.

"Bedtime," I told him firmly. "Do you need help up?"

He sneezed at me, then trotted up the steps to the bed with only a slight hitch in his gait. If I hadn't been there, it would probably have been a limp, but that he was bothering to hide it from me was a good sign that he'd be okay.

I climbed into bed and settled next to him, touching him gingerly. But he wiggled closer with an impatient sigh, so I quit worrying about hurting him. After a moment, I pulled the covers over both of us. He didn't need them, but I did. The night was warm. I should have been warm, too, especially curled around Adam's big furry self. But I was cold.

I waited until he'd fallen asleep before I started to shake.

He could have been dead. If Fred had been a half instant slower or Hank a smidgen faster.

Mine. He was mine, and not even death would take him from me—not if I could help it.

I WAS PRETTY SURE I WAS DREAMING WHEN I climbed out of the bed, leaving Adam sleeping under a pile of blankets. He looked hot, his long tongue exposed to the air, so I pulled the blankets off him.

I put on my clothes and followed the odd compulsion that pulled me out of the trailer and out to the river. It must have been very late because there were only a few semi-trucks on the highway on the other side of the Columbia.

On the west end of the swimming hole was a big rock formation. I climbed up and sat on the top, my feet dangling over the edge. My toes were ten feet above the river, which rushed darkly along toward the Pacific.

When the man came up and sat beside me, it didn't startle me. His face in shadows, he held out something to me—a piece of grass. I took it and stuck the end in my mouth. From his silhouette, I could see that he was chewing on his own piece, the seed heads bobbing leisurely in the air.

Just a couple of hayseeds in the moonlight. It could almost have been romantic; instead it was peaceful.

We must have been sitting there in a companionable silence for ten minutes before he said, "You aren't sleeping, you know."

I took the grass out of my mouth and dropped it into the river—or that's what I meant to do. A stray gust of wind caught it, and it flew onto the riverbank on the swimming-hole side instead.

"Shouldn't I feel the need to scream and run?" I asked.

"Do you?" He sounded mildly interested.

"No." I considered it. "I am pretty convinced that I *am* probably dreaming, though." Apologetically I shrugged. "Despite your assertion that I'm not."

He looked up at the half-moon and squinted at it, as if he might see something in it I couldn't. "I'd guess that's because you were sleeping when I called you out here. I didn't know if it would work. I can't do a lot of the things I used to do. Still, I am not lying. You are quite awake."

The moon lit the face of a man who'd died more than thirty years ago. A man who had been a ghost, dancing for me in broad daylight. He was handsome and young with a devil-may-care air that was obvious even on such short acquaintance.

"*Are* you my father?" I asked.

He shook his head, the movement emphasized by the grass in his mouth. "Nope. Sorry and all that. But your father was Joe Old Coyote." He pronounced it as two syllables instead of three. Kye-oat not Kye-oat-ee. "He died in a car wreck and a mess with a pair of vampires. They don't like walkers very much, and they liked him rather less than most."

I'd thought I knew why until no one but me had seen the

ghost tonight. If you can see ghosts in the daylight, you can find where vampires are sleeping no matter what magic they use to hide. I'd always attributed it to being a walker, but if the other walkers hadn't seen it, maybe there was something to what Gordon Seeker had been implying so heavily.

"Oh, that," he said, as if I'd spoken aloud. "Just because you *can* see something doesn't mean you *have* to. I'd have thought that anyone who hangs out with werewolves would know that. I mean, who but an idiot would look at a werewolf and think, 'dog.' Yet they do."

"That's pack magic," I told him.

He nodded. "Some is. Sure. But still. Walkers see ghosts, but those two taught themselves not to see the dead quite a while ago in a 'galaxy far, far away.' A man can't fight a war if he can see the dead and still stay sane. So they made a choice."

"You watched *Star Wars*?" I asked.

"Joe did," he answered as if that made sense. "Loved it. A cowboy-and-Indian story where the Indians are the good guys and everyone fights with swords."

"Cowboys and Indians?" I asked while I chewed on the first part of the sentence.

He grunted. "Think about it. Good versus evil. The foe has better armament and seems impossible to defeat—the invading Europeans. The good guys are few in number and restricted to a few bold heroes with an uncanny connection to the Force. Indians."

I'd never thought about it that way, but I supposed I could see where someone might. Of course, people said that "Puff the Magic Dragon" was about doing drugs, too. For me, *Star Wars* was space opera and "Puff" a kid's song about growing up and leaving your dreams behind.

"What about the Ewoks?" I asked. "Aren't they supposed to be the Indians?"

He grinned at me, his sharp teeth flashing white from the moonlight. "Nope. Indians aren't cute and furry. Ewoks were a good marketing ploy."

I took a deep breath of the night air and smelled *him*. The ghost who'd danced for me, then turned into a coyote.

"Why did you dance? I thought you were a ghost."

"That was a ghost," he said. "That was Joe. He worried because you were headed into danger." He slanted a laughing glance at me. "Not that you haven't been in danger any number of times since you were born. But this is different because I'm called to this one for some reason. Things that involve me tend to be chaotic—and chaos can be fatal for the innocent bystanders."

"Not an innocent bystander," I told him.

"But he is your father. He's entitled to worry."

"What did the dance mean?" I asked.

"Not a spell," he said. "Sometimes dancing is a spell—like the rain dance or the ghost dance. This was a celebration dance. An Indian might describe it as 'Look, *Apistotoki*, here is my daughter. See her. See her grace and her beauty. Preserve this child of mine.'" He gave me a sly look. "Or he might describe the dance as 'Look, God, see what I made. Pretty cool, eh? Could you watch out for it?'"

For me. That dance had been for me.

"Tell me," I said, swallowing down the feelings that were roiling around inside me. There was so much I needed to know, and this might be my only chance. "Tell me about Joe Old Coyote." There was something odd going on. Some connection between my father and Coyote, and I couldn't quite figure it out. Direct questions hadn't worked so well; maybe I could get him to elaborate if I went at it sideways. And maybe I'd learn more about my father than my mother had been able to tell me.

The man who looked like my father grunted. "He was a bull rider."

I waited, but it seemed like that was all he had to say. "I did know that," I prompted him.

"Wasn't Blackfeet. Or Blackfoot, either."

That was new information. "He told my mother he was."

"Nope." He shook his head. "No. I'm pretty sure he told her he was from Browning. All the rest was her conclusion."

"Was he from Browning?" I asked. My heart hurt, and I wasn't sure for whom. My mother who'd been so young? Maybe.

"I was bored and lonely," he said with a sly shyness. "So maybe I decided to be just another guy for a while. Maybe. Joe made his entrance at a bar in Browning. He kicked around with some other folks for a while, then entered a rodeo." He made a pleased noise. "Chaos made commercial is a rodeo. He loved it, too. Loved the smells, loved the ache after a good ride, loved fighting the bulls, mostly 'cause those bulls had a good time with him up there. They pitted their strength against his. I could have ridden them for hours, and they could have killed me afterward. But Joe, he was different. Sometimes he won; sometimes they did. Like counting coup. He played by the rules, and they loved him for it."

Coyote had decided to be Joe Old Coyote? Then why did he say he wasn't and speak of Joe Old Coyote in third person?

"So Joe was born in Browning," I said slowly.

"You might say that," agreed Coyote. "Joe usually did."

"Joe was a person you became." I said it as if I were certain, and he nodded.

"Exactly."

"So you were Joe Old Coyote but Joe wasn't you."

"Sort of." Coyote tapped the soil with his hands. "This explaining stuff isn't where my talents lie. I created Joe, then I lived in him until he died. He wasn't me, and I wasn't him, but we occupied the same skin for a while. As long as

Joe walked this earth, I walked it with him—though he never knew that. There were just things he didn't worry about very much—like his childhood. When he died, I was reborn as me—and he was dead."

Maybe it was the night, maybe it was because I was sitting in the moonlight next to Coyote—but suddenly it all sort of made sense. Like that bug-thing in the *Men in Black* movie, Coyote had worn a Joe suit. Unlike the bug's human suit, Coyote's had had a life of his own.

"Joe was real?"

Coyote nodded. "And so is his ghost—even though that is me as well."

I made a command decision not to question that remark. I was feeling like I understood, and a ghost of a real person who wasn't really a person would throw me off my game again.

"If he was born in Browning," I told Coyote, "maybe that makes him Blackfeet. Piegan." I suddenly realized where Joe got his name, and it made me shake my head. "The Blackfeet tell stories about the Old Man, don't they? He's their trickster. It's the Crow and the Lakota in that part of the country who tell Coyote stories. For the Blackfeet, the Old Man plays the part of Coyote. Old Man and Coyote. Old Coyote. Joe, because he was just another Joe."

The man beside me laughed, a soft, pleased sound. "Maybe it does make him Blackfeet. Some anyway. He liked Browning—they know how to party, those Indians in Browning."

"And then he met my mother." My father was a construct of Coyote's boredom. Or loneliness, maybe. It should have made me feel like less of a person, but somehow it didn't. My father had always been this unreal person to me, a black-and-white photo and a few stories my mother told. But I had seen him dance, had heard the echoes of his voice in Coyote's.

Coyote threw his head back and laughed, and I heard

the chorus of coyote howls up and down the gorge, called by his laughter.

"Marjorie Thompson. Marji. Wasn't she somethin'." There was an awed sort of reverence in his voice. "Who'd have thought such a child would be so tough without being hard? If someone could have settled Joe down, it would have been Marji. He thought she was the one, anyway."

"But coyotes don't mate for life, do they?" I tried to keep my voice neutral.

"He would have," said Coyote. "Oh, he would have. He loved her so much."

His voice, sincere and deep, hit me hard. I had to rub my eyes.

"If he'd known about her sooner, he wouldn't have killed the vampire nest over in Billings," he said after a while. "But they needed killing, and he was there. Joe always thought of himself as a hero, you know—not the kind of hero I am, but the Luke Skywalker sort. Rescue the princess, kill the evil villains."

He looked down at the water, and said, as if it were a new discovery, "Maybe *that's* where you get it. I always assumed it was just too much *Star Wars*, but maybe it was genetic." After a moment's thought, he shook his head. "No. I know where his genes came from. I think it must have been *Star Wars*."

"The vampires?" I said tightly.

"Right. He knew taking out that seethe would set the vampires after him, but he wasn't too worried because it was just him. And then Marji came along, and he wasn't thinking about anything. Especially not about vampires. Not until he saw a pair of them talking to her one evening. At that moment he started thinking about vampires pretty damn hard. He let them catch a glimpse to draw them off and led them away on a merry chase. He was doing pretty well until he blew a tire."

He tossed his piece of grass away with a violent gesture, and his grass fell into the river.

"Don't know if the vampires engineered that or not. But they found him when he was trapped, and they killed him."

The story made my heart hurt, but not in a bad way. More like a wound that has just been scrubbed with iodine or hydrogen peroxide. It stung pretty badly, but I thought it might heal better in the end. "So when my father was dead, you were left?" I asked.

"Just me," he said. We sat in silence again for a bit; maybe both of us mourned Joe Old Coyote.

The man who looked like my father broke the silence. "He didn't know about you."

"I know. Mom told me."

"I didn't know about you until a lot later. Then I stopped in to check you out. You looked happy running with the wolves. They looked bewildered—which is as it should be when a coyote plays with wolves. So I knew you were okay." He glanced at me. "Which is what Charles Cornick told me when he saw me watching you. Sent me packing with a flea in my ear." His eyes laughed though his face was perfectly serious. "Terrifying, that one."

"I think so," I told him truthfully.

He laughed. "Not to you. He's a good man. Only an evil man needs to fear a good man."

"Hah," I said. "You obviously never had Charles catch you doing something he disapproved of."

We lapsed into silence, again.

"What can you tell me about the thing in the river?" I asked finally.

He made a rude sound. "I can tell you she's not a poor misunderstood creature. Gordon is right. She's Hunger, and she won't be satisfied until she consumes the world."

She. That answered several things. There was only one. That seemed more manageable than a swarm of monsters that could bite a woman in half and make a man shoot Adam.

“How big is it?” I asked.

He looked at me and poked his tongue into his cheek. “You know? That’s a good question. I think we ought to find out.”

And he knocked me into the river.

9

THE WATER WAS ICY AND CLOSED OVER MY head, encasing me in silence and darkness. For a moment the shock of the fall, of the cold, and of sheer surprise froze my muscles, and I couldn't move. Then my feet hit the riverbed, and the motion somehow woke up every nerve into screaming urgency. I pushed off and up, coming to the surface and sucking in air.

I could hear him laughing.

Son of a bitch. I would kill him. I didn't care if he was Coyote or the son of Satan. He was a dead man walking.

I struck out for the swimming hole even though it meant fighting the river. But for the next mile downstream or so, the riverbank was cliff face, and I didn't want to stay in the river that long: there was a monster out here somewhere.

A toddler walking along the bank could have beat me, for all the forward progress I made. I was only a fair swimmer, strength without technique. It was enough to beat the slow flow of the Columbia, but not by much.

Two otter heads poked up beside me, and I growled at them. Somehow knowing they were fae made them less of a threat than real river otters though I expect the opposite was actually true. I was too busy fighting the river to worry about adjusting my beliefs in accordance to reality.

They disappeared under the water for a few minutes before one popped up again, watching my slow progress with cool appraisal.

"I'd swim faster if I were you," observed Coyote.

Rage fueled my strokes, and I finally made it around the bend and into the shallower, slower water. I swam until the water was waist-deep and staggered toward shore on my feet. Coyote waded in knee-deep and stopped to watch me.

"What did you find out?" he asked.

"That you are a jerk," I told him, my voice vibrating involuntarily with the chill. "What in—"

Something wrapped around my waist and jerked me off my feet, and my head was underwater again. I fought, digging my feet in deep, but it pulled me slowly back out toward the deeper water. I managed to get my face out of the river and gasped for breath. As soon as I got oxygen in my lungs, I screamed Adam's name with a volume that would have done credit to a B-movie actress in a horror film.

Coyote grabbed my wrists, then shifted his grip until his arms were wrapped around my torso. He began to pull me back toward shore, and the strands around my waist tightened until I couldn't breathe.

"Let's see what we caught," he murmured breathlessly in my ear. "It should be interesting."

I didn't hear Adam. He was just suddenly there, a shadow of fur and fang. He closed his mouth on something just below the surface of the water, and his weight on the thing that wrapped around me jerked Coyote and me off our feet and back down into the river. The too-tight bands released me, then Coyote grabbed my arm and hauled me up.

"Run," he said.

But I looked around for Adam. I wasn't leaving him in the river with the monster. The wolf bumped my hip, safe and sound, so I let Coyote pull me out of the river and ran with him as fast as I could up the bank to the steep ridge that separated the swimming beach from the rest of the campground, Adam keeping pace with us. Coyote kept us running about four long strides on the grass before turning around.

The river lay quiet and black, the surface hiding anything that lay beneath.

Beside me, Adam roared a challenge that would have done credit to a grizzly bear. Coyote joined in with a high-pitched cry that hurt my ears, his face exuberant and laughing.

Something wet and squishy rolled down my leg and fell on my bare foot. It looked like a chunk of limp fire hose, if that fire hose was made from the stuff they make gummy worms from and covered with short, silver hair that glittered in the moonlight. One end was all jagged, where Adam had severed it, and the other narrowed, then widened in a ball about the size of a softball.

Something else, neither wolf nor coyote, bellowed like an enraged bull. And the river devil revealed itself . . . herself, if I could believe Coyote. Up and up she rose, like a snake charmer's cobra. Though her body resembled a giant snake's, the overall impression I had was, as it had been looking at the petroglyph, of a Chinese dragon. A huge, ginormous, towering, and ticked-off Chinese dragon.

Her head could certainly have inspired the petroglyph. It was triangular like a fox's, with huge green eyes. Encircling her head at the base of her skull, like a ruff of snakes or petals of a flower, long tentacles twisted and writhed like a wave, not precisely in unison, but not independently, either.

On the very top of her head were two shiny black horns, twisted and rolled back, like a mountain sheep's. From the front, it looked very much like she had a pair of ears.

The full impact of her coloring was muted by the moonlight, and though I could see here and there a hint of green or gold, mostly she just looked silver and black.

She opened her mouth and let out a second angry roar. Unmuffled by the water, it dwarfed Adam's howl, just as her bulk dwarfed the three of us. But it wasn't the sound that scared me.

The front of her mouth was littered with long, spiky teeth—like the petroglyph's had been. Teeth designed to spear and hold her prey. Her back teeth were just as nasty. Not grinders but huge spade-shaped sawing teeth. Teeth that could slice off a man's foot, and she wouldn't even notice until she swallowed.

She threw herself at us, and her head landed with an impact that almost knocked me off my feet again. Tentacles stretched forward—

"The land is mine," said Coyote. "Here you do not reign. Not yet, and not ever." He stepped between us and her, long, saw-toothed knives suddenly in his hands. "Just you try it. Just you try it."

Head in the dirt, she jerked her tentacles back and screamed at him, a wicked, high-pitched sound, while she gave us an up-close and personal view of sharp teeth. Abruptly, she jerked her head back into the river, faster than such a large thing should have been able to move, and disappeared into water that roiled and drove great waves onto the shoreline.

Coyote turned to me. "That big."

I opened my mouth. I was cold and wet, my middle burned where the river devil had grabbed me—and I had nothing to say. He waited for me to find some words, then shrugged and walked down to the indentation she'd left on the ground about fifteen feet from us.

"About six feet from one side of her jaw to the other," he commented. "Nine feet from where her head started until the end of her nose. More or less."

Adam watched him with pinned ears, then sniffed me over carefully. When he was satisfied I wasn't too badly damaged, he grumbled at me.

"It wasn't my idea," I protested. "He threw me in."

The grumble turned into a full-throated growl, and Adam took a step toward Coyote, head lowered and muzzle displaying his generous-sized ivory teeth. I hadn't intended to send Adam after Coyote with my response. I hadn't had a chance to let Adam know just who we were dealing with, not that it would matter to him anyway. I caught Adam by the ruff on the back of his neck in a mute request for restraint.

"Simmer down, wolf," Coyote said absently, making the "wolf" sound like an insult. "I wouldn't have let the creature hurt her."

"Really?" I asked doubtfully. "What could you have done about it if she'd caught me a little faster?"

"Something," he said airily. "Look at all the information we've managed to gather. Hey, did you see those otters? I've never seen otters that look like that."

"They're fae," I said.

He grunted. "Never a good idea to plunk down introduced species without knowing what you're doing."

And he resumed pacing off distances, walking right out into the water. I couldn't have gone that close to the river right then even if my life depended upon it.

"Assuming," Coyote said, "that she strikes like a snake, we can estimate that she struck with half her body length." He held up a finger as if to forestall an imaginary protest. "Yes, I know that a third is probably more accurate, but I believe in erring on the side of caution. Surprising as that might be to some people."

He stopped knee-deep in the water and counted again on the way back to us. "That's not good," he muttered. "That's bigger than I remember. I suppose she might have grown—or my memory is faulty." He pursed his lips and frowned at the indented soil.

"Thirty-two feet from where I stopped to here," he said. "That means between sixty-four and ninety-six feet long. Pretty big."

His eyes traveled down my wet and bedraggled self and landed on the chunk of slimy fire hose at my feet.

"Hah!" he said, trotting over to me. "Good. I thought we might have lost that in the river." He reached down and picked up the piece of the river devil.

"I feel like I'm lost in an anime movie," I said, as Coyote picked the thing up. "One of the tentacle-monster ones." Most of them were X-rated and ended up with a lot of dead people.

Coyote rubbed the thing he held with his fingers, then pulled my shirt up with one hand, ignoring Adam's growl and my "Hey."

Sure enough, there was a swirl of damaged flesh all the way around my waist twice. I'd been afraid to look because these wounds seriously hurt. They looked like acid burns, I decided.

"Mmm," he said, dropping my cold, wet shirt back down over the burns—which didn't help, even though the cold should have worked as an anesthetic.

He took the tentacle in both hands and held it up, comparing it to me—and I saw what he had noticed. The chunk he held was about two feet long and it had wrapped twice around my waist.

"Must be elastic." He started with two fists together and pulled it until he had both arms outstretched. "Yes. Stretchy, all right. What else do we need to know?"

He pulled a knife out of the pocket of his jeans—a smaller, less-threatening knife than the ones he'd pulled on the monster. "Werewolf teeth evidently are sharp enough to make an impression," he murmured. "But steel?" The blade bounced off the rubbery, gummy thing.

"Here," he said. "You hold this end on the ground here." And he grabbed my hand and had me kneel and hold one end of the tentacle while he stretched it out. With tension and the solid earth beneath it, he managed to stick the end of the knife through the flesh.

"Okay. Steel isn't a good weapon," he said. "Good to know."

The small knife went away to be replaced by one of the larger jaggedy knives. Like Gordon's, the knife was obsidian. It wasn't as big as I'd first thought, but it wasn't small, either. It sliced into the tough skin just fine.

"Ah," he said. "Inconvenient because these things are a pain, and they break. But at least they still work."

He looked at me. "How are your hands?"

I looked down at them. "Cold. Wet. Fine?"

He grunted and stood up, tucking the piece of tentacle into his belt. "As I thought. Whatever makes that burn stopped as soon as Adam bit through it—otherwise, he'd be feeling it by now. Means it's magic rather than poison or acid or something. Good for you and Adam, bad for us, I'm afraid."

"Why?" Adam let me use him to lever myself to my feet. His ears were pinned back, and he'd kept his eyes on Coyote in a way that made me a little nervous.

"Because I can do this." Coyote pulled my shirt up and set one hand against my bare stomach.

Icy chill spread from his hands—and the burns disappeared, leaving only my pawprint tattoo. He bent down to take a good look at my midriff and grinned at me. "Coyote. Cool tattoo."

"It's a wolf pawprint," I said coolly, jerking my shirt down over it.

"Still mad about the unexpected swim, huh?" he said, whining a little, a noise that would have been more at home coming from a canine throat. "All in the name of information."

"So why is the magic component bad for us?" I asked.

He looked at me like I was an idiot. "Because we have a

sixty-four- to ninety-six-foot monster to kill—and it uses *magic*."

I had a thought. "Can you fix Hank like this?"

He shook his head. "No. He's not one of mine. But I know someone who can. We're going to need help here, kids."

He pursed his lips and tapped his toes impatiently. "I know. We need Jim Alvin and his sidekick, that Calvin kid, to meet us at the Stonehenge at midnight tomorrow. Tell him to bring Hank. I'll tell him what he needs to do, but he's not going to believe in me. Sad that a medicine man will believe in werewolves, ghosts, and vampires and won't believe in Coyote, but that's what it is these days."

"I don't have his number."

"Where's your cell phone?"

"In the trailer."

He grabbed my hand and pulled a felt-tipped pen out of an empty pocket and wrote a phone number on my hand. "Here. Call him in the morning. If you don't, he'll think I'm just a dream."

He patted me on the head, ignoring Adam's low growl. "Go in and get warmed up." He wiggled his eyebrows at Adam. "I bet you know how to warm her up, eh?"

Adam had very nice big white teeth, and he showed most of them to Coyote.

Coyote veiled his eyes and showed his teeth in return. "Go ahead. Just try it. You're out of your league."

I touched Adam's nose and frowned at Coyote. "You stop baiting him—or I'll call my mom."

Coyote froze, his face blank, and I almost felt bad—except that he'd been threatening Adam. After a moment, he inhaled.

"I'll see you at Stonehenge," he said, and walked off without a look back.

We were most of the way to the trailer when I saw what Adam had done.

"Wow," I said.

A rocket bursting out of the window wouldn't have done more damage. The window and its frame were toast, and a little of the outside skin had been bent up.

At least all the glass was on the outside. "Be careful you don't step on the shrapnel," I told him, taking the long way around the trailer to keep him away from it. My tennis shoes might be wet, but they were proof against a few shards of glass.

In the trailer, I stripped out of my wet clothes and put them in the sack with the bloody clothes from earlier.

"I'm going to need clothes," I said, sorting through my suitcase. When I looked over, Adam had started to shift back to human, so I grabbed clean underwear and a T-shirt and gave him some room.

After I dressed, I found a towel big enough to cover the broken window frame and taped it up using some of the first-aid tape from the kits because I couldn't find any duct tape. I keep a couple of rolls of duct tape in all of my cars. The first-aid tape wasn't the wussy kind, though. This was the stuff that needed WD-40 to get off skin once it was taped down. I hoped the repair people would be able to get it off without damaging the trailer further.

If this kept up, I thought, noticing where a spot of blood had dropped on the carpet—it could have come from any number of things in the past forty-eight hours—we might just be buying a trailer soon. While I was staring at the stain, Adam spoke.

"You could have died." His voice was rough from the change.

"So could you have when Hank shot you," I said, trying not to sound defensive when he hadn't yelled at me. Yet. Adam wasn't the only one who had to learn not to get mad about something that hadn't happened.

He wasn't completely human yet. He knelt on the carpeted floor on the far side of the trailer, his head bowed as he waited for the last of the change.

Even when he was finished, he stayed there, his back to me. "I cannot . . ." he began, then tried again. "When I heard you scream, I thought I'd be too late."

"You came," I told him in a low voice. "You came, and I am fine. When you were shot, I would have killed the man who took your life and not cared. Not even knowing it was not his fault would have made me feel bad about it." I took a deep breath. "And when I knew you'd be okay, I wanted to yell at you for not moving faster, for not being invincible."

"What in *hell* were you doing in that river?" He still wasn't looking at me, and his voice had dropped even further.

"Trying to get out of it as fast as I could," I assured him fervently. I could feel his emotion, a huge tangle I couldn't decipher except to sense the atavistic power of it. "Adam, I can't promise not to get into trouble. I managed it for most of my life, but these last couple of years have more than made up for it. Trouble seems to follow me around, waiting to club me with a tire iron. But I'm not stupid."

He nodded. "Okay. Okay. I can deal with not stupid." But he still didn't turn around. And then he added in a quiet voice, "Or I hope so."

After a moment, he said, "I was not tracking straight through most of this. That was Coyote? The Coyote?"

"That's what he said—and I'm inclined to believe him." I paused. "It also appears that he is . . . or some aspect of him was . . . my father. It was complicated. I understood it, mostly, but I had to think a little sideways to do it."

Adam laughed. It wasn't a big laugh, but it was a real one. "I bet."

Adam was trying to come down from the wolf's anger. I tried to find something to say that didn't hurt me and wouldn't make him mad.

"I guess Coyote playing at being human is why I am a walker, even though Mom's not Indian," I said.

"Your father's not dead," he said. "Your mom is going to be . . ."

"Yeah," I agreed, clearing my throat and trying to sound casual. My father wasn't dead—and he was. Had I really even had a father? Better to think about my mother.

"As much as I have this pressing urge to get back at Mom for orchestrating our wedding without consulting me, I can't do that to her," I said, looking at my bare feet. They'd been inside the wet shoes long enough to gain that wrinkled look and corpselike color. "She really loved Joe Old Coyote and . . . Curt is wonderful. But Joe, he rescued her, he treasured her."

I thought of Coyote's voice as he talked about my mother, and added, "I'm not sure that Curt could compete with the man she remembers—maybe even Joe couldn't. And Joe is dead, really dead." I cleared my throat. "He wasn't really Coyote, just a suit Coyote wore for a while. Real to himself and everyone around him, but in the end he was a construct, and Coyote . . . Mom would figure it out eventually. But by the time she did, Curt might not be waiting around."

Adam stood up then and came over to me. He put both arms around me. He didn't say anything, just held me.

"My life used to be normal," I told his shoulder. "I got up. Went to work. Fixed a few cars, paid a few bills, and no one tried to kill me. My father was dead; my mother was six hours away by car—I could even manage to make that trip last eight or nine hours if I worked at it."

"Argued with your back-fence neighbor," Adam said, his voice very gentle.

"And watched him when he wasn't looking," I agreed. "Because every once in a while, especially after a full moon hunt, he'd forget that I could see in the dark, and he'd run around naked in the backyard."

He laughed silently. "I *never* forgot you could see in the dark," he admitted.

"Oh." I thought about it for a while. "That's pretty good. Not quite up to my slowly eroding Rabbit, but you get points for that."

Adam was a neat and tidy person, the kind of man who walks into a room and straightens the paintings. For years I used the junker car in my backyard to exact revenge for high-handed orders I had to follow. Had to follow because they weren't just high-handed—they were smart. When I was particularly annoyed, I'd remove tires—never all four—and leave the trunk open or one of the doors, just to bother him.

He, evidently, had run around naked to bother me. I thought about that a moment more.

"Thank you for the years of entertainment," I said.

"No trouble," he responded in a serious voice. "Now that we're married, are you finally going to do something with that car? Like tow it away or store it somewhere out of sight?"

I took a deep breath—and my lungs seemed to be working just fine with the awful my-father-who-wasn't-my-father lump in my stomach gone.

"I'll think about it," I told him. "Maybe you should put it on your What I Want for Christmas List?"

"You okay now?" he asked.

"Okay."

He tightened his arms and lifted me off my feet. "Mercy?" he growled into my ear.

I wrapped my legs around his waist. "Yeah," I said. "Me, too."

Adam could have died last night. I could have died twenty minutes ago. I wasn't willing to waste a moment more.

At some point in the night he kissed my pawprint tattoo and laughed. "Did you really tell Coyote this was a wolf print?"

"To you, it is a coyote print," I said firmly. "For him, it is a wolf print. Only I and my tattoo artist know for sure."

I WOKE IN THE MORNING TO THE SOUND OF Adam's stomach growling under my ear.

"Sorry," he said. "Too many changes and not enough food."

I patted his hard belly and kissed it. "Poor thing," I told it. "Doesn't Adam treat you right? No worries. *I'll* go feed you."

My head bounced when Adam laughed.

"Let's go find someplace to eat breakfast and get some groceries." And then he proved that even when he was distracted, he still listened to me. "And some clothes for you."

WHILE I WAS DRESSING, I NOTICED THE NUMBER written on the palm of my hand and remembered I was supposed to make a phone call.

"Yes?" Jim's voice was wary.

"Coyote told me to call you," I told him. "He said that you wouldn't believe that he was real unless I did."

The man on the other side of the phone didn't even breathe.

Adam grinned at me as he buttoned up his shirt.

"How is your husband?" Jim asked politely.

"He's fine." Even the red mark was gone. How fast a wound healed varied from wolf to wolf and wound to wound. As Alpha, Adam tended to heal even faster than most. I'd expected that to change since we were so far from the pack, but evidently it hadn't.

"How are Hank's head and Benny's foot?" I asked.

"Hank is okay. Once we got him away from you, he seemed to recover a bit. Though he has a concussion, it's not a bad one." He cleared his throat. "Fred told the doctor Hank took a fall. The doctor seemed to think it might involve a pipe or tire iron, but Hank told him it was a fall, too. Fred is keeping an eye on him. Benny has been tranquilized ever since he tried to get up and leave the second time. He seems perfectly happy."

"So we're meeting you at Stonehenge? Coyote seemed pretty sure something could be done for Hank."

"You are very casual about meeting Coyote," he said. "Maybe we both just had a dream."

"You're the medicine man," I told him. "You should know better than that—and be casual, too." Maybe that wasn't fair. "Eventually, anyway. I'm married to a werewolf, and I've met Baba Yaga. At least Coyote doesn't fly around in a giant mortar."

"Baba Yaga? No. I don't want to know." Jim sighed. "Maybe I should go back to teaching school about crazy people instead of being one. Yes. I'll see you and your husband at Stonehenge at midnight. The memorial is supposed to be closed after dark, but I have a few contacts. Indian sacred ceremonies usually work, but I have a few more tricks up my sleeve if I need them."

ADAM DIDN'T APPROVE OF WAL-MART.

"There is a department store back in The Dalles," he said with a touch of grimness as we walked through the doors into the warehouselike building.

"Do they still call them department stores?" I wondered aloud, then shrugged it off. "Doesn't matter. Wal-Mart is the Happy Shopping Grounds for the financially challenged. *And* those who ruin clothing on a daily basis. I don't care about ripping up five-dollar T-shirts. And destroying twenty-dollar jeans hurts less than eighty-dollar jeans."

He growled, and I really looked at him.

The bright lights over our heads flickered and gave his skin a slightly green cast. That was the fault of the cheap bulbs, but the tension in his neck and the hunted expression were different. Too many strangers, too many smells, way too many sounds. A paranoid person—or an Alpha wolf—might feel like he couldn't make sure no one blindsided him in a place like Wal-Mart.

"Hey," I said, coming to a stop. "How about I shop here, and you head over to the grocery store and grab some food? I'll shop in peace, and you can pick me up in forty-five minutes."

He shook his head. "I'm not leaving you here alone."

"The only thing that wants to kill me is in the river," I told him, trying to keep my voice down, but the woman pushing a cart past us gave me an odd look. "I've been shopping at Wal-Marts for most of my life, and I've never been assaulted in one." I narrowed my gaze at him though I kept it focused on his chin. "As long as it's not demons, fae, or sea monsters, I can also take care of myself pretty well. I'm not helpless." And suddenly it mattered very much that he not treat me like some ninny who needed to be protected at all times, someone who would stand around waiting to be rescued.

He saw it in my face, I think, because he took a deep breath and looked around. "Okay. Okay."

I stood on my tiptoes and kissed his cheek. "Thank you."

He kissed me back. Not on the cheek. By the time I'd recovered enough to process information, he was striding out the door, and everyone in view was staring at me.

I flushed. "We just got married," I announced, then felt even stupider, so I hurried to escape in the aisles.

The Wal-Mart in Hood River wasn't as big as any of the three in the Tri-Cities. But it had jeans and shirts, and that was all I was worried about.

I grabbed four dark-colored T-shirts and three pairs of

jeans in the proper size and headed for the dressing rooms. I didn't need to try on the T-shirts, but I never buy jeans without putting them on first. It doesn't matter what size they say they are—some of them are shaped differently than others.

The lady working the dressing rooms gave me a bored look, handed me a plastic "6" and a "1," and sent me in. Apparently, they were out of "7"s.

The only other occupant of the rooms was a harried mother and her teenage daughter arguing about how tight the girl's jeans were. They stood in the larger area in the center of two rows of small rooms in front of the big mirror.

"They are fine, Mom," the girl said in the long-suffering tones used by put-upon teens everywhere, probably back to the dawn of time.

"You'll sit down and the seat will split, just like happened to your aunt Sherry when we were in high school. She has never gotten over it."

"Aunt Sherry is a . . . Well, anyway, I am not Aunt Sherry. These are mostly Lycra, Mom. They're *supposed* to fit tight. Look."

I squeezed past the girl, who was doing deep knee bends.

I found an empty room, then tuned them out. I don't know about normal folks, but if I wanted to, I could have listened in on the conversations of everyone in the store. I'd had to learn early to ignore them or I'd have gone crazy. Adam paid *attention* to all that noise because he worried about safety, but I wasn't worried enough to put up with the discomfort.

The first pair of jeans had a puzzling bulge halfway down my thigh on the left leg. I tried turning around to see if it was just my imagination, but the left-leg bulge stayed where it was.

The teenager and her mother had left the changing

rooms when I went out to look in the bigger mirror, so I had the whole thing to myself. Unless I'd mysteriously gained a lump on the side of my thigh, there was a problem with these jeans.

I went back into my room and pulled them off. Then I checked in the smaller mirror to make sure that I *hadn't* suddenly mutated. To my relief, without the jeans, my thighs looked like a matched pair. The river mark was still curled around my calf—I'd have to remember to ask Coyote if he could get rid of that one, too.

The second fit better, no odd bulges, and my butt didn't look bigger than it ought to in them—but it had fake pockets on the front. I *use* my pockets. No-pocket jeans are only slightly less irritating than thong underwear.

The third pair didn't fit as well as the second one had, but they had pockets that worked. I could live with them. If they bothered me too much, I'd just wear them to work until they were ripped and greasy enough I didn't feel bad throwing them away.

I had fifteen minutes to pay and get out to the parking lot. I hung up the rejects and pulled my own pants on. I buttoned them just as something dropped onto my shoulders, knocking me to my knees. I caught a glimpse of a blade in the mirror and grabbed the hand that held it even as I fell.

I jerked my head back hard and pulled the hand forward at the same time—connecting with some body part that was also hard, a chin, I thought, though I couldn't be sure. Her chin, because it was a woman's body that had hit me. I slammed her wrist on the wooden bench along the back wall, and the brass-bladed knife fell out of her hand.

I dropped my hold on her, grabbed the knife, and tossed it back up through the hole in the ceiling she'd come from: I didn't want to be caught with a knife in Wal-Mart. I was the wife of the Alpha of the Columbia Basin Pack—knife fighting was not an acceptable activity. If she tried to crawl back up there and get it, I'd use the time to run out to the main store, where cameras could catch me defending myself against an armed foe.

"You leave her be," she said. "Finders, keepers. She belongs to us."

The river devil? I thought, but I had no chance to ask her.

She ignored the knife and threw herself at me. I let her momentum pull me to my feet and carry us into the larger area between the changing rooms. The big mirror showed me her face—it was the odd woman who'd been staring at Adam and me the day before yesterday at the restaurant. I'd been right. She had been fae—more specifically water-type fae, because she smelled of it. Dollars to doughnuts, she was one of the otterkin.

She fought like an otter, too. Coming in close—inner circle—fast and furious, trying for my throat with fingernails and teeth. Fortunately for me, we were not in the water, and she was not an otter but a fae—though she smelled like both.

Glamour has never made sense to me. It is a kind of magic the fae use to change their appearance. According to Zee, the ability to use glamour is what makes a fae a fae instead of some other kind of thing that uses magic. Glamour is an illusion—but not. Because with glamour, a twenty-five-pound otter is a hundred-and-forty-pound woman.

Tactics that work really well for an otter don't work as well for a human, not even a human with a knife—particularly since I have a brown belt in karate. I was *not* helpless. The thought that Adam would never again let me out without a keeper if I got hurt made me determined to win this fight.

In the couple of minutes we engaged, I ended up with a bunch of bruises—including what was going to be an awesome shiner from where she ran me into a doorknob—a split lip, and a bloody nose. On the other hand, I broke *her* nose, and while she grabbed it, I got a really good kick into her ribs. If she didn't have a broken rib out of it, she had one or two cracked ones, which should slow her down some.

I heard the footsteps behind me and the flushed face of the formerly bored changing-room lady appeared. At the sight of us, she exclaimed, "*What's going on here?*"

The otterkin woman screamed—not in terror but in anger. Then she turned into an otter and ran up the wall into the ceiling and was gone.

As the fae woman's scent faded from *here* to *was here*, I turned to the clerk. Her mouth was opened unattractively as she stared up at the ceiling.

"You don't get paid enough to deal with this," I told her firmly. I didn't borrow authority from Adam for fear that it would worry him, but I know how it sounds and can imitate it when I have to.

"She's gone and won't be back." I looked around, and except for a dent in the drywall where her knee had hit the wall, there wasn't any extra damage. There was blood all over, but I was betting that Wal-Mart had cleaners to get all sorts of things out of their carpets.

I grabbed the jeans I wanted as well as the T-shirts. I put the darkest T-shirt up to wipe my nose. It hadn't been a hard hit, and it had mostly stopped bleeding.

"I'll just go pay for this," I said. "You can put those other jeans back where they go, then call someone in to clean up."

I walked out like I knew what I was doing and paid for the clothes—with cash so there was no awkward name-left-behind-at-the-scene-of-the-crime thing. The clerk was too occupied looking at my split lip to notice that one of the shirts was bloody. As I took the receipt, I noticed a general migration toward the changing room on the part of the employees. At least one of them looked old enough to be a person of authority.

I smiled at the clerk and tried to look innocent, grab my bags, and make a quick getaway.

"Honey," said the cashier, who was half my age. "You get rid of that man. You don't have to put up with being a punching bag."

"It was a woman," I told her. "And you are absolutely right."

I walked briskly out of the store and kept going across the parking lot as I called Adam. "I saw a sandwich shop in the little mall above Wal-Mart," I told him. "I'll meet you there."

"It's a little early for lunch," he said. We'd eaten breakfast just before he'd dropped me off at Wal-Mart.

"You're a wolf," I informed him. "You can eat anytime."

"What did you do?"

I heard a siren and hoped that it wasn't someone coming looking for me. I made my brisk walk a little brisker. "Got in a fight with my girlfriend, apparently." I hung up before he could ask me anything else.

The nice lady at the sandwich shop had been happy to fill a plastic bag with ice and accepted my story about a jealous girlfriend with a sympathetic ear (I kept my wedding ring hidden). She made me two large chicken sandwiches, and I paid for them and a pair of juices.

When Adam drove up, I was watching the police cars at Wal-Mart—it must have been a slow day—with the ice bag wrapped in my new bloodstained black T-shirt. Bloodstains on a new black shirt were more a matter of texture and smell than color.

"I think we ought to go back to the camp," I told him.

He pulled the ice down from my eye and took a good look before he let me put it back up again. Then he examined my hands, and brought my free hand up to his lips so he could kiss the bruises. He led me to the truck and buckled me in.

It was a good thing that there weren't many cars in the parking lot, or he'd never have gotten the big truck back out of it. I never had that problem with my Rabbit.

He didn't say anything, just drove the quarter of a mile toward the highway on-ramp in silence. I made it mostly to The Dalles before I broke.

"I didn't know anyone wanted to kill me when I made you leave me alone."

"I smelled fae," he said neutrally—the sneak. That was why he'd kissed my knuckles.

"She jumped me in the changing room," I told him reluctantly. I'd known after the doorknob hit my eye that I wasn't going to be able to hide the fight from Adam. Not that I'd really been planning on keeping the attack secret; it had just been an option I'd wanted to keep open if I could. "I think it was one of the otterkin—and she was the weird lady from lunch the day before yesterday."

"Did you leave the body?" he asked.

"No body," I told him. "I wasn't trying to kill her. And once I got rid of the knife, I was pretty sure she couldn't kill me. She wasn't any stronger than a normal human." I thought a moment. "I don't think so, anyway. As soon as the clerk came in, she glamoured back to otterkin and left through the ceiling. She might have used magic to get up there, but otters are pretty agile."

He squeezed his nose. Then he laughed. "I guess you proved your point," he told me. "You can take care of yourself."

"I wonder why the otterkin are trying to kill me?" I said.

"I don't think that we'll call in the fae to help us against the river devil," said Adam. "I think the chances are that they may come down on the wrong side."

"You were thinking of asking the fae for *help*?" I squeaked. Help was even worse than a favor.

He gave me an exasperated look. "I said I wasn't."

"It sounded like you might have been before I was attacked."

"You're trying to distract me," he said. "You don't need to. I'm not going to yell at you because you were attacked—especially since you won the fight."

"She ran away," I said.

"Without accomplishing her purpose. That's losing in my book. Especially since you got rid of her knife before she stuck it in you."

I gave him a wary look, but he honestly didn't appear upset.

"Mercy," he said, "in a fair fight between near equals, I'll back you every time. It's the demons, vampires, and river devils I worry about, and I'm working on that."

I could live with that if he could.

10

UNLIKE THE MARYHILL MUSEUM OR SHE WHO Watches, Stonehenge was a place I had been to many times over the years. It's right on the way to my mom's house in Portland. Sam Hill had been told that the henge at Salisbury had been used for human sacrifice and decided that it was a fitting memorial for the men who were sacrificed in World War I.

Adam and I parked the truck next to a deserted orchard down by the river and walked over hill and dale to the high place where Sam Hill's conceit looked out over the gorge.

I never could decide if Stonehenge was beautiful, spiritual, or merely a roadside oddity. Certainly it was impressive—a massive exact-sized replica cast in concrete of a place half a world away.

The original Stonehenge took about sixteen hundred years to build. The one at Maryhill took a little more than ten years to complete. It is a monument to commemorate thirteen young men of Klickitat County who died in a war nearly a hundred years ago, a silent testament of a man who knew how to dream big, and, I'd been told, a magical collection site of great power to those who knew how to access it.

I'd always taken that last bit with a grain of salt. After all, I'd have thought a powerful place would have attracted witches or something nastier (and there is not a whole lot nastier than a black witch), and in all the years I'd been visiting, I'd never seen anything dangerous. The other reason I'd doubted was because I am pretty good at sensing magic—and it had never felt any more magical than my garage.

In the night, it was different.

The minute my foot landed on the flattened area around the monument, I could feel the pulse of magic under my feet. Adam sensed it, too—though werewolves don't usually feel magic other than their own. He lifted his head and took a deep breath.

"I thought this was an awfully public place to be meeting," I told Adam. "You can see up here from all the way over the river on the main highway. Suddenly, though, Coyote's desire to meet here makes better sense. I've heard talk of ley lines since before I could walk—Bran might be a werewolf, but he understands the working of magic even if he doesn't do witchcraft or wizardry himself."

I paused, frowning. "I don't think he does, anyway. I've been here a lot over the years, and this is the first time I've ever felt magic."

"Ley lines?" said Adam. "I can feel something." He closed his eyes and breathed in, as if trying to pick up that little bit more that isolating his senses might give him. "Ley lines, huh? Feels like someone stroking my hair in the wrong direction."

"Is that a good thing or a bad thing?" I asked.

He snorted. "No flirting. We're here on business."

We'd come early; my husband, the eternal tactician, had

determined that would be the better course. I liked those two words together. "My" and "husband."

"What are you grinning about?" he asked.

I told him, and he grinned, too. "Hopeless," he said. "You are hopeless. We are supposed to be getting the lay of the land, not making goo-goo eyes at each other. I suppose it won't do much harm, though, since it has already been scouted." He tucked his arm around me and nodded toward the tall stone outer ring of Stonehenge, where a pair of hawks perched, watching us.

"Ah," I said. "But are they enemy scouts or friendly ones?"

"Friendly," said Jim Alvin, coming out of the shadows like . . . well, like a good Indian scout. "Hank found that as a hawk he can better resist the river devil, so we thought it would be safer for everyone if he stayed in his feathered form."

It takes a lot to sneak up on a coyote—upwind, silent, and cloaked by darkness and stillness. From Adam's expressionless face, I knew he hadn't sensed Jim, either. I reached up and tipped an imaginary hat to him. "Are all medicine men as adept at sneaking around as you are?" I asked.

In one of those coincidences that happen only once in a while, Calvin came tromping down the gravel driveway, making as much noise as any human possibly could. "Uncle Jim? Are you around here somewhere? I parked the car where you told me—" He stumbled over an uneven spot in the road. "And why can't we use flashlights again? Because we *want* to break our necks?" That last was said quietly; I'm not sure he intended anyone else to hear.

"Not all of us," said Jim unnecessarily.

"Where *are* you?" Calvin asked.

He couldn't see us though we were no more than forty feet away, and the half-gone moon lit the night. I tried to imagine what it would be like to wander around the night half-blind to everything around you.

Vulnerable.

No wonder people look for monsters in the dark.

"We're over here," Jim said, and Calvin changed his trajectory. About half the way over, he saw us. I could see it in his body. Evidently his uncle could, too. "The Hauptmans are already here. Hank and Fred are waiting in the monument."

Calvin increased his pace. "Everyone is early. Do we have to wait until midnight?"

"We'll see. The earth is rich tonight," Jim said. "Waiting for us."

"Nature abhors a vacuum," I said. "Why aren't there nasty things out here sucking up this magic?"

"Because it is ours," said Calvin.

"Shamanistic—not accessible to witch, wizard, or fae?" asked Adam in fascinated tones. "I've heard about this kind of place, but never with any detail. I assumed they'd be hidden places."

"Not accessible to other kinds of magic users without a lot of work," said Jim. "And more time than they are allowed—this is a pretty public place. My grandfather cleaned out a coven. Burned the whole town to do it, and Maryhill never recovered—but they haven't tried again. I'm not sure that the fae can't access it; but if they do, they probably can find a place nearby that is more private and almost as powerful. Ley lines are lines—they don't just stop in one place. From what I've heard, a wizard wouldn't hurt anything, but I've not seen one here."

"The power was here before Stonehenge," said Calvin, "but the construct seems to make it more accessible. There are a couple of places near here that were more traditional places of power and probably were better before Sam Hill built this here."

"Did Coyote tell you what he wanted you to do with all this magic?" I asked.

"Coyote?" asked Calvin, "Who is Coyote?"

"Coyote," said Jim dryly.

Calvin smiled uncertainly, blinked a couple of times, then seemed to get it. "Coyote?"

Then he looked at me. "She knows Coy—" He broke off midword, staring at me.

"Damn," he said in awe. "Oh, hot damn."

"Watch your mouth, boy," Jim said.

"Freakin' sh—" Calvin bit off the last word. "That's why. That's why you are a walker when your mother is white. Coyote is your freakin' father."

I don't know why his reaction offended me. "No. I have it on the best of authority that Coyote is not my father. *My* father was a Blackfeet bull rider who died in a car wreck before I was born." I wasn't completely sure that Coyote wasn't my father—but I knew that he didn't think so—and I wasn't claiming him if he wasn't claiming me.

Calvin frowned at me.

"I am not," I said clearly if through my clenched teeth, "Coyote's daughter."

Jim took a deep breath. "Glad that's cleared up. Yes, Coyote told me what he wanted me to do. It's all set up inside the circle."

"Let's go see it, then," Adam said. He took Calvin by the arm, and said, "Follow me. I'll keep you on your feet."

We walked past the heel stone, a sixteen-foot-tall monolith just a little northeast of the rest of the monument and under the continuous ring of cement-formed stone that was the outer edge of the henge. I looked up warily when we walked underneath the cement slab where both hawks were perched.

They were about fifteen feet over our heads, and my inner coyote was sure that wasn't far enough away. We were loud, too; the fine-textured gravel wasn't conducive to quietness.

"Hawks hunt by day." Adam's grip on Calvin had shifted upward until he just rested a hand on his shoulder, but he was talking to me. "As long as Hank doesn't have a gun, wolf trumps hawk at night."

One of the hawks screamed an insult back, and Adam smiled, an expression that was as full of challenge as the hawk's cry.

"Anytime, hawk," he said. "Anytime."

He was still ticked off about being shot, I thought. Come to think of it, I wasn't too happy about that, either.

"Calvin and I came about an hour ago," Jim was saying, ignoring the prefight exchange, "and set up what we needed with flashlights. Coyote was pretty firm about no visible modern technology for the ceremony." He looked at Calvin, and I was sure he could see in the dark a lot better than his nephew. "Flashlights were mentioned particularly. But I'm an old man and a big believer in 'work smarter, not harder,' so we came up with the truck."

Stonehenge consisted of the heel stone, a pair of concentric circles—the first the ring of lintel stones held up by standing stones, the second a ring of monoliths maybe eight or nine feet tall—and an inner court.

The inner court was shaped somewhat like a horseshoe with the open end pointed northeast—at the heel stone, in fact. The outer rim of the horseshoe was delineated by five huge sets of stones, each made of two standing stones holding up a lintel stone. They always reminded me of those staples used in furniture building with a small band and tall legs. There were two on each side of the horseshoe and one in the center; all of them are taller than the outer ring, and the center one was taller still. Inside these massive rock sculptures was another set of the monoliths, following the horseshoe pattern.

On top of all of the monoliths, both in the inner court

and the outer, were wide, clear glass containers that protected the fat, white, unlit candles inside of them. The candle wicks were mostly blackened, indicating that they'd been used before.

In front of the tallest of the massive cement-pretending-to-be-rock staplelike things, there was an altar—eight or ten feet long by three feet wide and two feet high.

A few feet in front of the altar, the wood for a small fire had been set on top of what looked like a circle of two-inch-thick coarse gravel, much darker and coarser than the gravel already there. I bent down to touch it, and Jim spoke.

"Tomorrow morning, when we can see, we'll come clean up," he told me. "The gravel will make it easy to erase any sign of fire. We don't want to give anyone ideas and have a bunch of teenagers lighting fires up here at night. It will also make sure that the fire doesn't spread. Grass fires happen this time of year, but I don't want to be responsible for one."

Adam had climbed up on a monolith to take a closer look at the candles, a casual pull-up that hinted at the strength he kept in check. He dropped to the ground and dusted his hands. "Hard to light from down here."

"We kept the stool I used to put them all up there." Calvin had stayed near Adam but kept taking surreptitious glances at me. Then he frowned. "Mercy? Is that a black eye?"

I reached up to touch it.

"She got into a fight in Wal-Mart," Adam said. Someone who didn't know him probably wouldn't hear the amusement in his voice.

"What?"

"She was attacked in Wal-Mart."

"You should see the other woman," I said. I noticed we were missing someone. "Where's Jim?" He'd been talking to me just a minute ago. I'd have thought that the noisy gravel would keep him from sneaking around. Apparently, I'd been wrong.

"He's gone to wash and change." Calvin said. "There's a little building over there, used to be a tourist shop, but it's been closed for a few years now. Jim has a key. I'd better start lighting the candles. It takes a while."

"We can help." Adam took a cigarette lighter out of his pocket. Adam didn't smoke, but he took being prepared to a whole new level.

"I only have one stool," Calvin apologized.

"That's okay." Adam moved behind me, grabbed my hips, and lifted me up over his head and onto his shoulders.

"Hey," I said indignantly.

It would have gone a little smoother if he'd warned me first. As it was, I had to scramble a bit for balance. He waited until I was steady, then patted me on the hip.

"I don't need a step stool," Adam said, walking over to one of the monoliths and handing up a lighter. "I have a Mercy."

Even with the three of us working on it, lighting the candles took a long time. I'd never noticed how many of them there were before. More than thirty, I thought, maybe even fifty of them.

When we were through, there was a Christmasy air provided by dozens of white candles. By happenstance or design, we met Calvin at the last standing stone, right next to the altar. Adam set me on the ground while Calvin finished the last light. In the short time, the magic in the ground had grown, and it jumped at me like an eager flame when my feet hit the gravel. I staggered a bit, and Adam, probably thinking I was still off balance, put a hand on my shoulder to steady me.

Calvin climbed off his step stool, put his lighter in his pocket, and folded up the stool. "I'm going to take this over to the parking lot. Meanwhile, Uncle Jim asked me to tell you that you need to take the shape of your beasts."

"Do you know what Coyote has us doing?" I asked.

Calvin dropped his eyes. "No."

I snorted before he could say anything. "Don't bother. You are without a doubt the worst liar I have ever met. Good for you. But you might keep it in mind and compensate for it. Cultivate a mysterious air and don't answer the things that might tempt you to lie." That was what Bran did. Even Bran couldn't lie to a werewolf. I didn't think he could, anyway.

"How long do we have?" Adam asked. "Walkers may be able to flash between shapes, but I take more time."

"I didn't know. Sorry. I should have told you before I started on the lights."

"If they want us here, they'll wait for us," I told Adam.

"Yeah," Calvin agreed. "I'm pretty sure that this ceremony needs both of you." He took a step away from us, then stopped. "Hey, Fred told me you were asking about deaths on the Columbia. He asked me to check into it, so I asked a friend of mine who's a cop on the river. He told me that in the past three weeks there have been twenty-six people who are presumed drowned between the John Day Dam and the one at The Dalles, not including the family of four that was reported missing late this afternoon when their car was found at a state park on the Oregon side of the Columbia. That's more people than we've lost on the river in the last five years combined."

"What family?" I asked.

"A stockbroker and his elementary-teacher wife and their two young children," he told me.

"Lee and Janice Morrison." The dream had been real. I could have done something about it. Surely I could have done something.

"That's right. Did you see today's paper?"

Adam's hand was on my shoulder. "How long had they been missing?" he asked.

"Two days."

Before my dream. I'd seen something that had happened in the past. No chance of doing anything. It should have made me feel better, but it didn't.

"I think," said Adam softly, "it is safe to say that this is something that needs to be hunted down and killed."

Calvin nodded. "Word is that there is an FBI team working on the idea that we have some sort of serial killer on the loose. They're being quiet so far; they don't want to encourage the killer or panic anyone. My buddy was pretty interested in why I was asking. I told him it was because of Benny and Faith." He looked at me. "That way I wasn't lying to him."

"Let's go change," I said. I didn't want to think about Janice and her family anymore. They were gone, and there was nothing I could do for them.

HAD WE BEEN HOME WITH THE WOLF PACK around, we'd just have stripped and changed, but I wasn't comfortable stripping in front of strangers anymore. Even if I'd been willing to, Adam would not change in public.

Bran had requested the wolves refrain from changing where others could see. The werewolves were beautiful—but the change is horrific. No sense in scaring people with what they were, Bran said, not when the wolves were still trying to be tame for the news cameras.

So we left Stonehenge and climbed over the drop-off just beyond, which hid us effectively from Calvin, Hank, and Fred—as long as the hawks stayed on the far side of the henge.

Still, we were exposed. There were no trees nearby, and we could see all the way down to the river and beyond to the highway—miles and miles. Darkness ensured that no one down there could actually see us, but it felt like they could.

Beside Adam, who was doing the same thing, I took off my clothes, folding them tightly to discourage any bugs attracted by the leftover warmth. I stuffed my socks in my shoes.

"I'll stay human until you've shifted," I told him. So I could guard his back or run interference if I had to.

Shifting to coyote wasn't without its cost. I could do it several times a day, but eventually I wore out. I could also stay human for a long time—months if I had to. Wolves are different.

Werewolves are moon called. They have to change during the full moon, and it is harder for them to control the wolf during that time, too. However, a lot of werewolves only shift during the full moon—two or three days a month. The shift is painful and takes a lot of energy. Shifting more than a couple of times a week was beyond a lot of wolves' abilities. Adam had been changing much more than that lately.

His shift was a lot slower than usual—and it looked as though it was a lot more painful, too. I sat beside him on the pad my folded-up clothes made. Maybe I should have left my clothes on, but since, tonight at least, I wasn't wet, it wasn't cold. I stayed close to him, but not so close I'd touch him inadvertently and hurt him.

The pulse of Stonehenge's magic was growing more regular, like a beating heart. I thought it was getting even stronger, too, but that might have been because I was sitting on the ground. My own heart sped up a little until it kept beat with the magic. It wasn't unpleasant, just disconcerting.

"Mercy?" Calvin called.

"Not yet," I told him.

"How long?"

"As long as it takes," growled Adam, his voice hoarse and deep as he was caught halfway between wolf and man.

The flow of magic paused, as if it had heard him, then took up its beat again. I didn't like it.

"Are you all right?" I asked, very quietly.

He didn't say anything, which I took as answer enough.

His breathing grew labored until I started to be seriously worried for him.

"It's the earth's magic," Coyote said, sitting down beside me on the side opposite Adam's struggle.

Adam growled, a hoarse and pained sound that was nonetheless a threat.

"No harm to you or yours," Coyote told him. "I stand guard for you. They were supposed to tell you to change before you came here. I suppose the instructions got garbled in the translation from Jim to Calvin. Mother Earth does not change easily—that is an aspect of water or flame. Earth magic is interfering with his change, but it shouldn't make it impossible."

Impossible wasn't good—but I buttoned my lips because even I knew that intent and will played a part in any kind of magic. No sense putting doubts into Adam's head until he really failed to shift.

"What are we doing tonight?" I asked Coyote to give myself something else to think about.

"Probably wasting our time." He didn't look at me but stared out over the world spread beneath our feet. I noticed that he seldom spoke directly to me. Half the time it felt as though he addressed the open air instead.

"And if we aren't wasting our time?" I waited a minute, trying not to listen to Adam's struggles because he wouldn't want me to hear him. I could feel the claustrophobic panic that he was repressing. He couldn't afford for me to panic, too. "Come on, Coyote. It isn't a secret because even Calvin knows."

He laughed, slapping his leg. "Point to you. Fine. Fine. I'm hoping to call a little help. We aren't what we once were, and some of us never were much for interfering with people. But Raven is curious, and Otter should feel he has something at stake." He paused, glanced at me, and continued, "Nice black eye, Mercy. Upon reflection, Otter might be on the wrong side. That would be unfortunate."

"You're calling the others like you?" I asked.

"There are no others like me," he returned. "None as handsome or strong. None as clever or skilled. None with so many stories told about them. Who was it brought fire down so people could roast their food and keep warm in the winter? But I'm hoping to call the others, yes."

"Other what, exactly?" I asked. "Just what kind of creature are you?" The fae, some of them, had set themselves over the early residents of Europe as deities. The Coyote stories never had that feel to them. Coyote was a power but not one who asked to be worshipped.

"Have you read Plato?" he asked.

"Have you?" I returned because the idea of Coyote reading *The Republic* or *Apology* was absurd and somehow totally believable because of its very absurdity.

"You are familiar with his theory of forms," Coyote continued without answering my question.

"That our world isn't real but a reflection of reality. And in the real world there are archetypes of things that exist in our world, which is how we can look at a chair we've never seen before, and say, 'Hey, look. It's a chair.' Because in the real world, there is an object that is the epitome of chairness." I used my history degree about twice a year whether I needed to or not.

"Close enough," he agreed. "I am the reality of all coyotes. The archetype. The epitome." He smiled out into the darkness. "You are just a reflection of me."

"They should have called you Narcissus," I told him, trying not to flinch at the sounds that Adam made. "Too bad *you* aren't the enemy we need to defeat. We could just put out a mirror for you to admire yourself in."

"And then they wouldn't call you Mercy anymore," he said. "Your name would be She Who Traps Coyote." He reached over and took my hand, and said in a low voice, "It won't be much longer. But I'd wait until he invites you to look before you gaze into his eyes."

"Are your sisters really berries in your stomach?" I asked him.

"Ah," he said delightedly. "You need to find someone to teach you the rude versions of my stories. They are much more entertaining. Modesty prevents me from telling stories about myself."

I laughed, as he meant me to.

"My sisters aren't speaking to me right now," he finished with great—and I suspected entirely feigned—dignity, "so it does not matter what they are."

Beside me, Adam rose with a snarl. I lowered my head to show that I was no threat. After a bad change, it would be a few minutes before Adam had a leash on his wolf. To my surprise, Coyote bowed his head as well.

"I like this man, your husband," he told me. Maybe it was an explanation. "He would have attacked me for putting you in danger—even though the wolf knew exactly what I was. And yet, when you asked him to have patience, he did. It is proper that men listen to the counsel of women."

"Like you listen to your sisters?" I said, as the wolf put his nose just under my ear. I tilted my head to give him my throat. Sharp teeth brushed against my skin, and I shivered.

"Wise women," Coyote agreed. "But sometimes pushy and easy to rile. I think they need to develop their sense of fun. They do not agree with me, so maybe they are not so wise as all that, eh?"

Adam shook himself hard, his ears making a flapping sound—a signal.

I turned to look at him, and he jerked his nose up toward the monument. I changed into my coyote self—which did seem to take a little more effort than it normally did—and followed Adam up the hill, Coyote striding beside us.

At least he wasn't Baba Yaga or Yo-yo Girl, I thought.

GORDON WAS TALKING QUIETLY WITH CALVIN and Jim when we walked into the henge's circles. Jim was barefoot, dressed in new dark jeans and a long-sleeved shirt that looked to be blue in the light of the candles, though my coyote eyes are not always trustworthy with color at night. Gordon's boots, for instance, looked black, but I thought they were probably the same red boots he'd worn the rest of the times we'd seen him. He wore a flannel shirt over a plain T-shirt.

"I was beginning to think that it was time to leave," said Gordon coolly, as we approached.

"Earth magic isn't the best thing for a change when you're a werewolf," Coyote said. "Which is why I told Jim to make sure he was a wolf when he got here."

"You said to tell Mercy to bring the wolf," Jim said, sounding irritated. I was beginning to think that everyone sounded like that after a while of dealing with Coyote.

Calvin's eyes widened, and he looked as though he expected Jim to get hit by lightning.

Coyote just laughed. "Mercy, you go sit up on the altar, would you?" He looked up at the hawks. "You two go sit next to her."

Gordon didn't seem awed or surprised by Coyote, either. "Whatever you do in front of Hank, the river devil will see."

"Let her watch," Coyote said indifferently. "But if nothing else happens tonight, I think I can get Hank fixed. Hawk owes me a few favors."

I hopped up onto the altar next to the hawks a little hesitantly. There was a bronze plaque on top, but it was too worn to read in the dark. Adam hopped up beside me and curled around me protectively, keeping the bulk of his body between me and the other predators.

"Adam," said Coyote, "not being Aztec, we are not going to sacrifice your bride on the altar. She just can't be touching the ground when Jim performs the dance. However, should Wolf answer this call, it would be disastrous if your head were higher than his. Usually he shows up in human or humanlike form, but he is one who often prefers his wolfskin. Would you mind taking a position just in front of the altar, between it and the fire?"

Adam snarled soundlessly at the hawks, a clear warning, and slipped off the altar to sit where Coyote had asked him to.

Gordon's eyebrows had risen almost to his white hair. "A polite Coyote?"

Coyote growled something in a foreign language.

"I thought you were not her father," Gordon said placidly. "That makes him not your son by marriage."

"Say, then," said Coyote, "I respect him and don't fancy getting in the middle of a dogfight tonight if I can help it. Now let us get this done."

He changed. His shift was even faster than mine, I thought, though I couldn't be sure. Between one blink and the next, there was a huge coyote the size of a Saint Bernard. He stalked over to the monolith that was on one end of the horseshoe and hopped up on top of it.

Gordon looked sour, then he became the largest eagle I have ever seen in my life, and I've seen some huge golden eagles. As a bird, he stood taller than the man he'd been. I couldn't say what color his feathers were though they looked as if they were several shades darker than the hawks'. Then he spread his wings, and I realized Gordon wasn't an eagle after all. No eagle ever had a wingspan that large.

"Thunderbird," said Calvin reverently. "Grandfather said you were Thunderbird, but that was when he was calling me by my father's name more often than not."

Thunderbird.

The bird leaned forward and rubbed that wicked sharp-looking beak against the side of Calvin's head. Since Calvin's head stayed on his shoulders, I had to assume it was a gesture of affection. With a movement that was half hop and half flight, he landed on the monolith opposite Coyote. He made the standing stone look a lot smaller. Gordon, who was Thunderbird, nudged the candle until it was situated where he wanted. The candlelight turned his feathers a warm dark chocolate. He rocked back and forth a bit, stretching his wings out, then settled into stillness.

Calvin brought out a rolled-up rug, a small drum, and a beaded parfleche bag. Parfleche—untanned hide—was more commonly used by the plains Indians than the plateau Indians like the Yakama, I thought. However, I supposed a medicine man could use whatever implements he wanted to.

Calvin set the bag to one side of the prepared but as-yet-unlit fire. Then, with great formality, he unrolled the carpet, aligning it with the altar stone. He took the drum with him to sit next to Adam.

Jim stood in front of the carpet and closed his eyes. It looked like a prayer, but whatever he did caused the magic to sit up and take notice—I could feel it even through the cement I perched upon.

He stepped onto the carpet and held a hand over the stacked wood. "Wood," he said, "who swallowed the flame of the Fire Beings, it is time to burn."

When the little fire burst into flame, Adam flinched a bit, but it didn't seem to surprise Calvin or Jim.

Jim gave a small nod to Calvin, who began to play the drum. At first he played with a simple, one-handed beat. It wasn't a steady sound but tentative and irregular—until he caught the beat of the magic that ran beneath us. He stayed with that for a while, then began to speed up, accenting the simple beat with grace notes. When the magic followed his additions, he switched up the cadence to a driving, syncopated rhythm. And the magic followed his lead.

The wind chose that moment to pick up and throw

smoke from the fire into my eyes. I blinked but I must have gotten some ash in with the smoke. Putting my muzzle down on top of the stone, I scrubbed at my face with my paws. It helped. I lifted my head as soon as I could see—and I was alone.

11

I STOOD UP IN A PANIC, THE BEAT OF CALVIN'S drum still strong—but the bond between Adam and me was strong and reassuring. It gave me courage to stay where I was, take a deep breath, and look around to see if I could figure out what had happened to everyone else.

The fire burned, the candles were lit, and the night sky overhead was clear and star-spangled. However, there was a thick fog at ground level, and I could see nothing beyond the outer ring of the henge. About that time I realized that I was in my human shape, wearing the clothes I'd taken off and carefully folded a little while ago. They felt real under my fingers—even the slight roughness where I'd dripped a little mustard on my jeans that afternoon.

But I was pretty sure this was a vision. I couldn't think of any other reason that I could still hear the drum.

The rising hair on the back of my neck told me that somewhere, someone was watching me. I couldn't hear or smell them, but I could feel eyes on me.

Maybe they were waiting for an invitation. "Hello?"

"Hello, Mercedes."

I turned around and found that there were four women walking in through the largest of the staple-shaped rocks. All of them were dressed in identical white doeskin wedding dresses complete with fringe and elk teeth. Their feet were bare and callused, and the pale dust from the light gray gravel covered their feet as if they had been walking in it a long time. They smelled clean and astringent, like sage or witch hazel, but sweeter than either.

I was no expert on native peoples, despite a bit of heritage searching while I was in college. But I was sufficiently well versed to know that each of them was from a very different tribe, despite their too-beautiful-to-be-real features. The first woman looked Navajo or Hopi to me—or maybe even Apache. Her skin was darker than any of the others', and her features were soft. She wore her hair in Princess Leia–like buns on either side of her head, which I thought was a traditional Hopi style—the style of one of the Pueblo Indians, anyway.

The second woman had the rounded, low cheekbones of the Inuit, and her eyes crinkled at me in a friendly fashion. Her hair was separated into two thick braids that hung down to her shoulders.

The third woman looked like someone from one of the Plains tribes, though I couldn't pinpoint exactly what made me think so. Her face was a little less soft than the first two, her gaze clear and penetrating. Like the second woman, she wore her hair in a pair of braids, but hers hung down past her waist. She had bone earrings in her ears—the only one of the four to wear jewelry of any kind.

The fourth woman wore her dark hair pulled loosely back from her face, but otherwise it was free to flow halfway down her back. It was thick and wiry, like the mane of a wild horse. I could not tell what people she was from, except that she was Indian. Her features were sharp, her nose narrow, and her lips full. She was the one who spoke first.

"Mercedes is not a proper Indian name." Her tone, like her words, was critical, but not emotionally so. I'd have expected to hear such a tone from a woman in a market looking at fruit. She pursed her lips briefly, evidently considering my name. "She is a mechanic. We should call her She Fixes Cars."

The first woman, the one who might have been Hopi, shook her head. "No, sister Bringer of Change."

The woman who looked like one of the Plains Indians but not quite Crow, Blackfeet, or Lakota, frowned disapprovingly. "Rash Coyote Who Runs With Wolf. We could shorten it to Dinner Woman."

The merry Inuit woman laughed. "Mercedes Who Fixes Volkswagens, we have brought you to see us since our brother would not bring us to see you."

"Your brother?" I asked carefully. I was still standing on the altar, which had me looking down on them. That felt wrong, so I stepped off onto the sand and the magic in the ground promptly turned my knees to rubber.

"Coyote," they said at the same time, while the Inuit woman kept me from falling.

I couldn't help but think that it would be a bad thing to sit on the ground if just standing on it had this much of an effect. I sat on the altar and pulled my feet up.

"We cannot tell the future," said the sharp-featured woman whose tribe I couldn't place at all. "But we know what our brother is planning. Would you tell him that it is very dangerous, but it is also the only thing that we could think of that might work?"

"What is he planning?" I asked.

"We can tell you here." Inuit Woman sat beside me but left her feet on the ground. "But he can't tell you until he rids himself of her spies. That's actually why we brought you here—that, and we wanted to get a look at you. He

Sees Spirits—you know him as Jim Alvin—has opened this way between us for a short time. Coyote needed privacy to speak to the others, to Hawk and Raven, to Bear and Beaver, and to the rest. We decided that you should know what he says."

"River Devil," said the Hopi-Navajo-possibly-Apache woman, "is a creature who lives in your world and ours at the same time. In ours she is immortal, but she can be killed in yours. Once she is dead, she cannot go back unless she is summoned. But at that time she returns bigger and more dangerous than before. The last time our brother confronted her, he trapped her rather than killing her in the hope that it would be more effective than killing her had proved." I decided she was Hopi, and as I did so, her features changed just a little until there was no possibility of her being anything else.

"Who would summon that thing?" I asked.

The Inuit woman shrugged. "There will always be fools, and the river devil can be persuasive to the minds of men."

The sharp-featured woman.

"Cherokee," I said, suddenly certain I had it right.

She smiled a small secret smile, the kind that always makes me want to smack Bran. "If you like." She tilted her head, and said, "River Devil is Hunger because living between worlds for those without a hold in either is costly. She must consume food for both her aspects: meat for the flesh and for the spirit."

The Hopi woman continued, "All life is rife with possibilities. Seeds have possibilities, but all their tomorrows are caught by the patterning of their life cycle. Animals have possibilities that are greater than that of a fir tree or a blade of grass. Still, though, for most animals, the pattern of instinct, the patterns of their lives, are very strong. Humanity has a far greater range of possibilities, especially the very young. Who will children grow up to be? Who will they marry, what will they believe, what will they create? Creation is a very powerful seed of possibility."

The Plains woman who was not Lakota, Crow, or Blackfeet said, "River Devil feeds on possibilities."

Inuit Woman reached up to place her hand on her sister's shoulder. "She feeds on the death of those possibilities. For this reason, she must feed upon people rather than animals, animals rather than plants. But best of all, she loves to feed upon children."

"She feeds on the end of possibilities," corrected the Plains woman—Shoshone, I decided. She looked Shoshone to me. She smiled as if she'd heard me think it aloud. It was a big smile, like her brother's. "The greater the possibilities, the better her hunger is sated. When she is full, she must digest her prey both here in the world of spirits and also there in the world of flesh. While she is doing that, she is vulnerable."

"Coyote and his kind—Hawk, Bear, Salmon, Wolf, Thunderbird, and others—they have more possibilities than even a newborn child." The Cherokee woman turned in a graceful circle as if to encompass all that Coyote and those like him were. "If Coyote can persuade enough of them to allow River Devil to consume them, they may be enough to force the river devil to overeat. And she will be helpless until she digests them all."

"While she is helpless, someone needs to kill her." The Inuit sister looked at me with her big dark eyes, and I knew, with a sinking feeling, who they were talking about.

"What about Fred or Hank?" I asked. Adam couldn't do it. His strength might make him a better candidate, but werewolves don't swim. I wouldn't risk Adam to the river.

"They are vulnerable to the river devil's mark," she said. Then she paused and addressed my unvoiced thought. "I do not know about the werewolf. Alone, he would be like the others, but his pack might keep him safe . . ."

"Or she might gain the whole pack." The Hopi woman

shook her head. "No. That would not be wise. Nor is water the werewolf's element for all that it is an element of change."

Shoshone Woman said, "She must die, then. As she eats, she grows in power. If she does not die before she digests such a meal as our brother will provide, she will be much, much more destructive than she is now."

"What about an airstrike?" I said. "Or nuclear weapons? I know people who might be able to get the military in on this." Bran could. He might not be out—but he knew how to get things done when he wanted to.

Hopi Woman shook her head. "No. Modern weapons will not harm her. Only the most simple thing, a symbol of the earth that opposes her water: a stone knife."

"Our time is short now," Cherokee Woman said. "You must go back."

Shoshone Woman touched my cheek. "Tell our brother he is wise, that we have no further words of wisdom to add to his."

"He says that you are not speaking to him," I said.

She laughed, but it was a sad laugh. "Coyote doesn't usually lie, but sometimes he forgets. It is he who is angry with us. We gave him advice he did not like, and he got mad."

Cherokee Woman narrowed her eyes at me. "We told him nothing good could come of letting Joe Old Coyote take the Anglo woman to his bed."

Inuit Woman smiled and touched my leg. "Obviously, we were wrong."

"Coyote is like the river devil," I said. "Right? He walks in both places. So why doesn't he eat everything in sight?"

"Coyote walks in one world at a time," Cherokee Woman told me. "He can do this without being trapped because we wait for him here, and you and his other descendants anchor him there."

"Coyote understands that the Universe is all one." Shoshone Woman's voice was indulgent.

"Coyote," said Hopi Woman dryly, "doesn't much worry about understanding anything, which is why he understands so much."

"What happens when the river devil eats them? Coyote and the others." In the stories, Coyote died and was reborn the next day, but there was an air of resignation that clung to these women that hinted at something more dire this time.

They exchanged looks that I could not read.

"We don't know." Inuit Woman stared out into the fog that surrounded us. "As I told you, it is not given to us to know the future. We are merely wise advisors."

"It may be that this is the last time for Coyote to walk your world," said Cherokee Woman in a low voice. "So much has changed, it is impossible to know what those changes mean."

"There are some who do not walk either world any longer." Shoshone Woman's eyes glistened with tears. "River Devil is of both worlds and so could send them back scattered into the universe."

"Do not worry about that which cannot be changed." Hopi Woman sat on the ground and patted my tennis shoes. "Even if Coyote is not reborn with the morning sun, there is always hope of a new dawn. Come now, sisters, it is time to send her back."

"I think she looks like me," said Shoshone Woman. "What do you think?"

AND HER WORDS STILL RANG IN MY EARS WHEN I found myself back where I had started. Time had passed—I could tell because Jim was kneeling on the rug feeding tobacco leaves into the fire. He sang, the words unintelligible to my ears, but not foreign.

Adam licked my nose, then nipped it—he'd noticed I was gone, then. I'd ask him later if my body had disappeared with me or if it had just waited there for me. I nuzzled him to let him know I was fine.

One of the hawks—Fred and Hank were hard to tell apart when they were human; as hawks I figured I might have a fifty-fifty chance—fluttered his wings and cried out softly. We were apparently bothering him.

Adam hopped up on the altar where I was sitting and stepped over me with his front paws. He lowered his head and showed the hawk his teeth. Both hawks retreated to the far edge of the altar because neither was stupid, and maybe because Adam had great big teeth.

I glanced first at Jim, who seemed to be very focused on his song and on feeding the last of the tobacco leaves into the fire, then out at Coyote and Gordon—who were gone.

Adam licked my ear, then lay down between me and the hawks. His front paws hung down over the front of the altar, and I suspect his back paws were off on the other end. The three feet of cement that was the width of the altar was generous for me but wasn't nearly enough to hold a whole werewolf.

Jim closed his eyes and held up his right hand. When he closed his fist, the drumbeat stopped—and with it, the overwhelming pulse of magic. It was like someone had pulled the plug at a nightclub, and all the music stopped. As suddenly as if someone had slammed a door, Stonehenge was as mundane as an exact model of a neolithic calendar could be.

No magic, no mystery, just a gray cement monument that suddenly had a lot more people in it than there had been when the drum had been sounding.

Gordon and Coyote in their human guises were standing in front of the monoliths they'd started out on top of. Between us and them, six Indian men I'd never seen before stepped away from the monoliths.

One man, who looked no older than Calvin, was in a three-piece suit. Adam had taught me to recognize good suits, and this one was several thousand dollars of very nice. Another, like Gordon, was wearing a modern cowboy look, though his was toned down a fair bit. Brown boots, jeans, earth-tone striped shirt, and a brown Montana-style (narrow-brimmed) cowboy hat. Iron gray hair was braided tightly and fell over his shoulder and almost to his knees.

The other four wore traditional native garb, though unlike Coyote's sisters, no two of them were dressed alike. There were two in hunting leathers of slightly different styles. The older one, whose wrinkled face and white hair made Gordon look like a young man, wore leathers that were nearly as pale as the doeskin Coyote's sisters had worn. Except for the fringe around the shoulder seams, his leathers were very plain. The other man's hunting leathers were a rich dark brown with ornate quillwork around his neckline. There were stains on his clothes, as if he'd gone hunting many times wearing that particular shirt and leggings.

The third man in native dress wore leather leggings, but his loose shirt was made of patterned red gingham and tied with a hemp belt that ended in a fringe to which tiny brass bells were tied. His hair was cut straight around his jawline.

The fourth had a red cloth wrapped around his head, almost like a turban, from which maybe a dozen brownish red feathers stuck straight up. He wore a beaded breechclout that reached his knees in front and back. His shirt was a striped cotton that looked to have been loomed by hand rather than machine from the slight irregularity of the weave.

I got a really good look at his shirt because he walked right up to the altar and grabbed the hawk nearest me, one hand confining the wicked talons. He pulled the bird hard against his body, trapping the wings with his arm, and the sharp beak with his hand.

"So," he said, his voice heavily accented. "She tries to steal my hawk's will."

"As I told you, Hawk," said Coyote. "Can you fix it?"

The man holding the bird gave Coyote a cold stare with eyes as sharp as those of the animal who took his name. The hawk left behind made a soft noise, like a baby bird in the nest.

"I do not approve of you, Coyote. You have always been more concerned with the two-legged people than the people in fur."

"I was asked to help. Would you have refused the request of the Great Spirit?"

Hawk snorted. "You were doing it before that. And look what has happened." He let go of the hawk's talons to make a sweeping gesture. It didn't matter because Hank was limp in his grasp. "There are cars and roads, bridges and houses until the earth cannot breathe. It would have been better had the Great Spirit stopped with the first people."

Coyote sneered, just a little. "As I'm sure you would tell him."

"I'm telling you," said Hawk.

He reached down and grabbed a handful of dirt and small gravel. He tossed it into the air, and the wind caught it, held it. He held the bird up over his head, and the wind blew the handful of earth against the hawk, who cried out when it hit him.

He threw the bird up in the air, gave Coyote another cold look, and disappeared. The bird dropped, and Hank landed in a naked human heap on the ground. Naked meant that it was easy to see that the mark was gone.

Beside me, Fred, also in human skin, scrambled off the altar and over to his brother. Jim, now seated on the rug and looking exhausted but fascinated, motioned to his apprentice, and Calvin took off at a run, presumably for clothes, but I wasn't certain.

"Hawk is impetuous," said the man in the suit. "And I don't like agreeing with him." His casual gaze traveled around Stonehenge in mild curiosity. It passed over Adam and me, then returned. Pale blue eyes that looked wrong and somehow utterly right in that oh-so-Native-American face focused on Adam.

"Ah," he said, striding over in the same no-nonsense ground-covering way that Adam used to cross a crowded room. "This is the werewolf."

Adam got slowly to his feet and shook himself lightly. As he stood on top of the altar, his head was level with the collarbone of the suited man—who could only be Wolf.

"I had heard of your kind," Wolf said.

I glanced at the other men there, but they seemed to be happy to let Wolf take center stage as Hawk had done a moment ago.

"Werewolf." Wolf frowned. "I had thought it an abomination when I heard it first. Wolf trapped in the same skin as a human—always in opposition with each other. And in some ways it is abominable. But look at you. You are beautiful."

I thought so, too.

"How is that different from our walkers?" asked Coyote in an interested tone. "They carry both spirits, too."

"No," said Wolf absently, still lost in his examination of Adam. "In our descendants, there is only one spirit that expresses itself as either human or animal. This is different. The wolf is mine, and the man not at all. And yet it works."

He touched Adam, and I felt it through our bond, felt Adam's wolf come forward to meet Wolf. Adam was wary but not alarmed, neither dominant nor dominated.

Wolf's hands traveled all over Adam's head and neck, like a judge at a dog show. Adam showed no sign that it bothered him though it bothered me. Adam was mine.

"The perfect predator," Wolf purred, leaning forward and rubbing his cheek possessively against Adam's cheek.

I may have let out a disgruntled yip.

Wolf glanced over at me with cool blue eyes, and his mouth curled up in the beginnings of a snarl.

"That one is mine," said Coyote. His tone was casual, but there was steel behind it that turned the simple comment into a warning.

Wolf looked at Coyote and reached out to swat me with the back of his hand—and Adam caught that hand in his teeth. Wolf spun back with a hiss, and Adam released his hand—but there was blood. Adam flattened his ears, stepping between me and Wolf. He wasn't quite snarling, but he'd made his position clear.

"Do you see this," Wolf said. "Abomination. Wolves do not run with coyotes."

"It's a romance as old as time," soothed Coyote. "Rules are set up for the good of society. But as soon as you make a rule, someone feels the need to break it. If it helps, most werewolves mate with humans. Even worse, I would think, than one of my coyotes."

Wolf took a step toward Adam. "She is your mate?"

I couldn't tell if that made it better or worse, and I don't think Wolf knew, either. His hand had quit bleeding already. Adam hadn't done much more than break through the skin. It had been a warning and not a real attempt to hurt Wolf. I'd like to think that Adam was too smart to take on something like Wolf—but I was afraid that wasn't true, not if he thought Wolf would hurt me.

I regretted that yip of possession even though I was pretty sure that I'd do it again in the same circumstances. I didn't like anyone except me having their hands all over him. There had been possession in Wolf's touch, and Adam belonged to me.

"You have left her with the river's mark," said the cowboy Indian in the earth-toned clothes. His voice was silky smooth and beautiful.

"I have, Snake," said Coyote. "Because I have killed the

river devil before, she cannot take over Mercy as she does everyone else. But Mercy is now something of interest to the river devil, something that we've already proved can get her attention and bring her to where we want her in pretty short order. The river devil doesn't like its prey to get away from it, and she wants it back." He looked at me. "There are a lot of miles of water between The Dalles and John Day."

And it hadn't taken her ten minutes to find me when Coyote threw me in the river. He'd been right: we had learned a lot from that.

Calvin had returned from wherever he'd gone. He had a couple of blankets, which he gave to Fred and Hank. Hank took one with a nod of thanks; but Fred just changed back into a hawk and flew up to perch next to one of the candles on a nearby standing stone.

The old man in white hunting leathers said, "I think it might be better to let River Devil have her way. When she has eaten the whole world, it can be made anew again."

"You sound so certain," said Gordon in an interested voice. "Are you? I don't think it is as easy as all that."

The old man growled at him, a big rumbling sound that was somehow fitting coming from that fierce old body.

"Friend Bear," said Coyote. "Change is not bad. Change is just change. Startling to those of us who go away, then come back after a long time, yes. But it is not evil."

"Look at the pollution." Bear took a breath as if he could smell smog out there a hundred miles from anywhere. My nose is very good, and I would have called his bluff if I could have talked. "The roads, the railroads. Look at the houses upon houses that destroy hunting ground and leave only a tiny fraction of the forests free. Wolf has said that Mother Earth cannot move underneath the cement and steel, and I say that he is right."

"There are things that are bad," Coyote said. "But there were bad things then, too. Starving times. Freezing times.

Times of sickness. There are good things here." He waved a hand at Wolf. "Look at the clothes you wear. That suit is silk and wool woven in a fashion that was not possible a few centuries ago. All change brings bad things and good things to replace the bad and good things that were before. It is natural to look back and say it was better before—but that does not make it true. Different is not worse. It is just different."

"There is some truth in what you say, Coyote." Wolf was petting his suit jacket with the same sort of possessiveness he'd shown toward Adam.

"I don't like it here," said the man in the darker leathers; he sounded unhappy and uneasy.

"Bobcat." Coyote liked this one. I could tell by the tone of his voice. "There are good hunting grounds here; you just have to find them—as was always true. The sun is still warm, and flowers still smell sweet."

"You should take him to Disneyland," suggested Gordon. "Or I could. I like Disneyland."

The purely human contingent had been very quiet up to this point. But now Calvin spoke. "If you give it a chance, I think you would find it isn't horrible here."

The man with the belt with the brass bells put an arm around Bobcat. "The problem is this, Bobcat. Things change whether you want them to or not—unless you are dead." His voice was hoarse, like a three-pack-a-day-for-twenty-years smoker. "Don't hold so hard to the past that you die with it."

He looked at Coyote. "There is no sense in this, though. We have all agreed to do as you asked, or we would not be here. Where and when?"

"As Raven says," agreed Coyote formally. Then he described how to find our campsite in a way that ravens, bobcats, wolves, snakes, and bears could find it. When he was finished, he said, "As for when, the sooner the better, I think. Tomorrow?"

"After dark," said Jim. "Calvin says the FBI are looking for whoever is responsible for the killing field that this river has become. You don't want them showing up at the wrong time." He looked at Raven, and said, "Warriors with bang sticks who are river marked is a bad idea."

Raven smiled at him. "I do know who the FBI are," he told Jim. "Coyote is not the only one who still wanders."

While they were talking, the others had left. Some of them seemed to walk away, but I saw Wolf disappear, probably because he did it while still staring at Adam. Who belonged to me.

"Thank you, Raven," said Coyote, after a quick glance to see that the other animal spirits, including Gordon, were gone.

"We may all die forever tomorrow, old friend," said Raven. "But it will be interesting, anyway."

ADAM AND I LEFT TO CHANGE AND GET DRESSED, too—but I was the only one doing any changing. Adam's panicked gaze met mine as I was putting on my jeans.

"Hold on," I told him. "There's help about."

I pulled on my clothes, stuck my shoes on my feet, and grabbed Adam's clothes as fast as I could. Then I bounded back up the hill, hoping like heck that Coyote hadn't already vanished like the rest of them.

Why I was so sure that Coyote knew anything about werewolves was a mystery to me, but it seemed right. He'd known Adam would have trouble shifting when the earth magic was singing.

The candles were all out. Jim and Calvin were gone; Fred and Hank had left before we'd headed out to change. Stonehenge looked deserted.

"Coyote?" I called.

"Mercy?"

I'd been almost certain he was gone, but he and Raven

had apparently been sitting on the altar playing a card game in the dark. Hard to believe I'd missed them, but Coyote was that sort, so I didn't worry about it. I had other things on my mind.

"Adam can't change back. Would the earth magic have done something that keeps him from shifting?"

"He can't change back to human?" Coyote folded up his hand of cards and set them on the bronze plaque, giving us his full attention. "That's awkward, this being your honeymoon."

"He can't change," I said, ignoring the last sentence. "Is it the earth magic? Will the effects go away after we leave here?"

Coyote considered it. "The earth magic shouldn't do anything unless directed by a shaman, and I think Jim likes you."

Raven gave his head a birdlike twitch. "It wasn't Jim, and it wasn't the earth magic." His voice left no room for doubt. "Your werewolf bit our Wolf, remember?"

Raven grinned at me, a big warm expression that was infinitely reassuring though I could think of no reason I should trust him. "Wolf takes things like that personally. But he's not one to cling to his angers, either." His face became a little pensive. "Not like Owl."

Coyote snorted. "He still bearing a grudge for that? That happened a long, long time ago."

"How was I to know that it was his favorite thing?" Raven's eyes twinkled with starlight. "It was shiny." He glanced at me. "But it was heavy, so I dropped it in the ocean. It was an accident."

"You think that this is something Wolf did?" I had a good grip on the ruff around Adam's neck. It was a habit I'd developed over the past few months because I found it reassuring.

Adam didn't look worried or nervous, but he wouldn't,

not in front of people who were essentially strangers. I was doing the worried and nervous for both of us.

A werewolf can stay wolf for a while. A couple of days, no trouble. A few weeks . . . well, not so good, but most of them will be okay afterward. Months were possible—one or two. After that, he would be all wolf with no human. Bran's son Samuel had experienced that, and his wolf had behaved in a mostly civilized fashion for a couple of weeks without losing it, astonishing everyone. It was unlikely that Adam, who had not seen his first century, could do the same.

"How long?" I asked.

Coyote sighed. "Mercedes, it takes power to pull forward Adam's wolf so strongly that his human half cannot change. We . . . None of us has a lot of that kind of power over here anymore, which is probably why Wolf did it: to show that he is not to be trifled with." Coyote looked at Adam. "He could have killed you had he desired. It would have been easier. After tomorrow's battle, I should be very surprised if Wolf's punishment does not fade away. It would be easy to be angry with him—but he and the others have agreed to sacrifice themselves. It is, I think, unlikely that he will return to this place soon after that."

"If ever," agreed Raven quietly. He had picked up all the cards and laid out a solitaire pattern. Spider, I thought, or some variant. "So give him his dignity and don't worry."

"Thank you," I told them both. I started to go, then I remembered something. "Hey, Coyote?"

He had just scooped up the cards again and was in the middle of shuffling. "Yes."

"Your sisters told me to tell you that they thought your an was a good one."

"Did they tell you what it was?" He resumed shuffling, there was a rapidity to his movement that told me he eeling something strongly.

"Yes." I took a deep breath. "Weak link here, I think. But I'll do my best."

He smiled. "Yes, I expect you will."

WHEN SOMETHING WOKE ME UP FROM A SOUND sleep in the middle of the night, I assumed it was Coyote again. This time I woke Adam up, too.

"Someone wants me outside," I told him, tapping my head. "I think Coyote might want to talk again."

When I got out of bed, I tripped over the walking stick. I picked it up gently, instead of swearing at it, and leaned it against the wall. Swearing at ancient artifacts seemed a little unwise. Not something I'd do unless I'd carefully considered all the possible effects.

Adam and I made our way out to the swimming hole, where the call was coming from. But it wasn't Coyote.

Out in the darkness I could see her—or at least her wake. The roiling water burbled and swirled as she swam in lazy circles.

Mercedes Thompson. Her voice was in my head.

I sat down on the ground with a thump, in the faint hope that it would somehow make it harder for her to get me into the water. Coyote had been too precipitous in declaring me immune to her charms. Perhaps she couldn't make me drown my own children—and Jesse, thank goodness, was a hundred miles away. But she could call me out to her, and she could speak to me.

I thought as hard as I could, *Go die.*

Mercedes, she said again, her voice like a cool liquid in my head, giving me the mother of all ice-cream headaches. *Are you listening to me? Do you see what I want you to see*

"Do you hear her?" I asked Adam.

He looked out toward the river.

"No." I tapped him, then tapped my head. "She' here."

His teeth gleamed white in the darkness.

MacKenzie Hepner was eight years old as of four days ago. She was supposed to be in the tent with her little brother, but something had woken her up. She hitched up her nightgown and waded in the cold water. On her arm she could see the mark that that weed had left when she went swimming too far out in the river, and her stepdad had to swim out and rescue her. It made her reconsider how she felt about her stepdad. He hadn't even yelled at her, just hugged her. It took her a while to figure out he was scared, too . . .

Do you see what I want you to see, Mercedes?

My breath started coming in panicked gulps. I hadn't been just dreaming about the ill-fated Janice and her family. The river devil had fed me the details afterward. Maybe that hadn't been on purpose. Maybe. But they had been real, and this eight-year-old named MacKenzie was real, too.

I hid my forehead against Adam and told him what was happening, giving him the words when she gave words to me, describing the rest. He whined unhappily.

Gesture to me if you see what I want you to see. Did you see her?

Evidently, she couldn't read my thoughts. Like Bran, she could only shove things at me.

MacKenzie's feet were numb, and the rocks made the bottoms hurt. She shouldn't be out here in the river in the dark. She knew it was against the rules—

I waved my hand weakly. I didn't want to know any more about a child who was going to walk into the river and get eaten.

I will let her live.

"She says she'll let the child live," I told Adam.

He got it, I think, before I did, because he lunged up and ed at her—at me, then bumped me with a hip in a order to go back to the trailer.

I felt her laughter. She'd seen Adam's reaction. She knew I'd heard her.

Bargain. A bargain. A bargain. You for her. You come die tonight, and I will let the little girl and her little brother live.

Adam planted himself between me and the river devil.

"She offers a bargain," I told him. "Me for the little girl—and apparently her brother. If I die, they won't."

Adam looked at me, his heart in his eyes.

"She's eight," I told him. "Just. Yesterday her stepfather proved that he might be okay. She's willing to give him a chance. She has a younger brother that she could go get and bring with her." I swallowed. "What would you do, Adam? Would you die so that little girl could live?"

I knew the answer—and from his body language, so did he. Then he looked at the monster out in the water and back to me with a flicker of his ears. He couldn't do it because she didn't want him. I couldn't do it, either. No matter how much I wanted to. Without me, Coyote's plan wouldn't work.

"Would she lie?" I said, while the river devil chanted her promises in my head. "I'm worth more to her than the child, I think. She knows about Coyote and his interest in me, and it worries her. But after I'm dead? Would she keep her word? Who would know?"

"She would keep her word." Coyote came up to stand beside Adam. "I can't let you do it, anyway."

"I know. Your sisters made it clear that you need me."

Adam whined again.

"I'll tell you about them," I promised. I'd forgotten to let him know what had happened; we'd both been tired.

Choose, Mercedes.

"For an ancient evil, she speaks awfully good Englis
I said.

"She's been eating English-speaking people." Co
sat next to me.

"Can you hear her?" I asked.

He shook his head. "No. She can't mark me."

"Could you save her?" I asked Coyote. "Could you save that little girl? Didn't you carve the way for the waters to flow and move mountains? Raven hung the stars."

"That was a long time ago, under the Great Spirit's direction," he said, sounding sad. "I'm on my own here."

"Why doesn't the Great Spirit take care of this?"

"Why should He?" Coyote asked. "All that is mortal dies. Death is not such a bad thing. What would be a bad thing would be living without challenges. Without knowing defeat, we cannot know what victory is. There is no life without death."

"I like my god better than I like yours," I told him.

"Don't you know, child? He is one and the same." Coyote watched the river devil wait for my response. "The Great Spirit has given us our wits and our courage. He sends helpers and counsel. He sent me to you, didn't he? I talked to my sisters tonight. It was a good thing."

"Can you save this girl?"

"Do you know where she is?"

"A campground near the river," I said. But was it a campground? There were a lot of places you could just go camping. "No."

"Then no."

"Damn it," I said.

You or they die. Bargain. You die, they live.

"Is there anyone else who could take my role?" I asked.

"None that I know of. I was surprised that you were not controlled by her mark. You are the only creature who is wholly of this realm that I have seen resist her."

"If I weren't here, what would you do?"

He sighed. "One of us would take your place. But there are only seven of us who can or will help. I believe that a time will come when the Great Spirit will send us back out into the world again, entrusted with tasks to accomplish.

But many of us were hurt when the Europeans swept through here. Disease took so many of our children, then the vampires singled out those who managed to survive and brought more death upon them . . ." He sighed. "We were allowed to retreat and lick our wounds—and for many it will take the Great Spirit to pry them out of their safe dens." He scuffed his bare foot on the ground, rolling a rock a dozen feet. "I won't lie. We may not have enough to do what we need, even with you. Without you?" He shook his head.

Mercedes. The demand was angry and impatient.

I picked up a rock and chucked it in the river as my answer.

Coward to save yourself at the expense of a child. You shall see what you have done.

I learned a lot in the next fifteen or twenty minutes. I learned that MacKenzie's little brother was named Curt, like my stepfather. He was four—and marked as MacKenzie was, so he didn't fight when his sister carried him on her hip out into the river. As a treat especially for me, I think, the river devil released her hold on their minds before she killed them. But maybe it was because MacKenzie's screams had her parents tearing out of their tent and into the water after them.

I learned that I could have exchanged my life for four people's lives. Four.

12

I DIDN'T SLEEP. WHAT WAS THE POINT? I COULD have nightmares while I was awake just as well as when I was asleep.

I had made the right decision, the only decision. But that didn't make it any easier to live with the deaths of four people I could have saved.

I fed Adam, and when he grunted at me, I fed myself, too. I had to keep my strength up. If four people had died to give me a chance to help kill the river devil, it wouldn't do to fail because I hadn't eaten.

About 5:00 A.M., when the first pale hint of dawn touched the sky, Adam and I got in the truck and headed back up to Stonehenge. Without Adam to converse with nd nothing much to do, I would drive us both crazy if we ayed at the campsite. Stonehenge needed to be cleaned I could do that and save Jim and Calvin some work.

had been nearly 2:00 A.M. when we'd packed up that ing, and Jim had looked like a man who'd been rode hard and put away wet. I didn't expect him to arrive until a more civilized hour. But he and Calvin drove up about ten minutes after I finally found the step stool so I could get high enough to remove the candles from the tops of the standing stones. Chin-ups on forty-five monoliths (I counted them while contemplating how to get the candles down) had struck me as too energetically taxing when I had a monster to kill later.

Calvin waved at me and hopped in the back of the truck to grab two boxes. He jumped back out and trotted over while Jim got out of the truck and shut the door.

"Hey," said Calvin. "Didn't expect—" He saw Adam and stopped dead. "Uhm. What's wrong with him?"

Even happy werewolves are scary in broad daylight if your eyes let you really see what they are. Adam was not a happy werewolf.

"Wolf took offense at the bite," I said. "So Adam can't change back to human right now."

"Jeez," said Calvin. "That sucks—and it's your *honey-moon*." Then his face flushed darker with embarrassment.

That was not what had Adam's hackles up, though. I'd told him about Coyote's sisters after Coyote left. And whispering very quietly what the plan to kill the monster was. Adam couldn't talk to tell me what he thought. I knew that he understood that it was the best plan we could come up with. I also knew that he didn't like it. At all. Amazing what body language can convey.

"Coyote is sure it is temporary," I told him, getting the next candle down while Calvin started to set them in the boxes he'd brought. The boxes were like the ones moving companies use to pack glasses, with cardboard inserts that kept each of the candles separate from the others. "Jus don't look him in the eyes, okay?"

It took us about an hour and a half to get the pl cleaned up and looking the way it had before we'd cc

Hardest was getting the coarse dark gravel out of the much finer pale gravel.

"You could have used a plywood board," I told Jim, who was sitting on the altar criticizing Calvin and me while we picked up gravel one piece at a time and put it in a wheelbarrow.

"No," he said. "I could not have. The fire had to rest on earth. Even the gravel was cheating a bit."

"Next time." Even Calvin the Ever Cheerful was getting grumpy. "Next time I vote we put the fire on the ground. I'll dig it out afterward and put fresh gravel that matches the original back over the top."

Jim grunted. "That is more work. We did it that way for a few years until I started to do it this way."

"What about a gunnysack?" I asked. "Something porous but not so loose a weave that the big gravel can drop through. Or use gravel that would blend in better with what is already here."

"Might work," agreed Jim. "But then what would I use to keep my apprentice busy? I suppose I could do what my teacher did and teach him beading."

"I'll pick up gravel, Uncle, thank you," Calvin said meekly.

The medicine man laughed. "I thought you might feel that way."

I STOPPED AT THE GAS STATION IN BIGGS AND got a pair of ice-cream cones—banana and strawberry—and a notebook. We ate the ice cream in the truck until Adam was finished with his strawberry cone because I couldn't feed myself and Adam and drive at the same time.

As I drove back over the bridge, still licking my banana cream, I could see the Maryhill Campground, full of trailers, and RVs. Had MacKenzie been staying there with her family? Or had they been somewhere more private? I hadn't noticed any other campers. But if it had been the Maryhill Campground, Coyote might have been able to get to her in time to save her while I kept River Devil busy. If she'd been at the Maryhill Campground, and we had known where she was.

I drove back to camp and started writing. A letter to my mother and one to each of my sisters. I did not, of course, mention Coyote. A long letter to Samuel and Bran. A letter to Jesse. A letter to Stefan. A lot of pages that I'd burn if I survived the night.

Jesse called Adam's phone while I was in the middle of writing the letter to her. He brought his phone to me so I could answer it—after a little fumbling.

"I need Daddy," Jesse said intensely. "Now."

"He can't talk." Adam put his chin on my leg.

"I don't care. Take the phone to him in the bathroom."

"He's a wolf, Jesse," I told her patiently. "He can't talk. Is there something I can do for you?"

"Why is he a wolf?" she said, sounding shocked. "It's your honeymoon."

"Jesse. Much as I'd love to discuss my honeymoon with you—what do you need?"

"It's Darryl," she wailed. "He's impossible. Auriele left to do something or other, and he says I can't go shopping. My favorite store has a four-hour sale, from noon to four, and he won't let me go."

Jesse, to my certain knowledge, had never cared about shopping. There were other things she did worry about, and I could think of only one of them that would put that frantic tone in her voice.

"Gabriel wants to go do something," I interprete
"Maybe a movie? Darryl would be an inconvenience, a
you thought if you figured out something that he would
do, he'd let you do it without him."

"Darryl's right here, you know?" she said.

"Your father might have bought your story, but I doubt it," I told her. "Where are you going?"

"Darryl critiques movies," she said. "Loudly. *During* the movie, and Gabriel . . ."

Gabriel had changed in the last half year. He'd been kicked out of his house by a mother he loved (and who loved him back—that was part of the problem) and held captive by a fairy queen. Things like that change a person. Mostly he was a little more wary and a lot more somber.

Gabriel was living in the house that replaced my old one, so he and Jesse were now neighbors. But he'd lost the easy confidence that everything would turn out right—once he'd seen the monsters being monsters. Around some of the werewolves he was very . . . cautious. Adam didn't seem to bother him, but Darryl did.

"How about Kyle and Warren?" I asked. Warren had that whole aw-shucks-ma'am going for him and was nearly as good at hiding his dominance as Bran. People tended to like Warren, and he and Gabriel got on just fine.

There was a little silence. "Kyle's *important*, Mercy. He and Warren can't just take the time to go to a movie with a couple of kids."

I laughed, and Adam sneezed. "Did you hear that, Darryl? Kyle's *important*."

"Good to know someone is important around here," he grumbled. He wasn't angry, though. Darryl had a Ph.D. and worked in a federally funded think tank as an analyst of things too complex for most people's brains. He and his mate, Auriele, had become Jesse's de facto babysitters when her mother left because female werewolves were few and far between: Adam's pack only had three. And Darryl was Adam's second in command, a wolf more than up to taking on anyone who might try to hurt the daughter of the Columbia Basin Pack's Alpha.

"I'll call them," Darryl said. "Now that I know what the trouble is. You could have told me, Jesse."

"I didn't want to hurt your feelings," Jesse muttered. "It's not that he doesn't like you."

"I know exactly what it's about." Darryl's voice was so deep it rumbled. "It's okay. I don't mind scaring people. I especially don't mind scaring your boyfriends."

"Everything good now?" I asked.

"I guess," Jesse said.

"If Kyle and Warren can't go, check with Samuel and Ariana."

"I'll do that," said Darryl.

"Love you, Jesse." I kept it casual. "See you." Probably. Maybe. The death of eight-year-old MacKenzie in the wee small hours this morning had taken the edge off my usual optimism.

"Tell Daddy he better not spend the whole honeymoon in wolf shape," Jesse said. "Love you both."

Adam had been reading my letter. I finally figured out how to hang up his phone, then met his eyes.

"I'm not planning on dying," I told him. "But, Mr. Always Prepared for Anything, there are things I'd like to tell people if I do."

Like I loved them. Like someone needed to watch out for Stefan, who still didn't seem to be doing too well. Warren had called with an update a couple of days ago and reported that Stefan's people seemed to be better. Stefan had collected a couple of people in Portland, but he was still too thin. Warren and Ben would be taking turns dropping by and feeding Stefan themselves, but that was a temporary fix. And someone needed to wait about ten more years, then track down the grown-up kids who belonged to that poor trucker who'd been framed for murders committed by a vampire and tell them he hadn't suddenly gone crazy and killed a bunch of innocent people. Those kinds of things needed to be taken care of if I wasn't there to do it.

Adam was restless and angry, so I sent him out to hunt

something. Maybe killing something would make him feel better.

I wrote his letter while he was gone. When I was through, I lay down on the bed and tried to figure out some other way out of this disaster.

Calling the werewolves for help was out. The fae . . . Zee was my friend. I could call Zee. I considered it. Was it a good idea?

Not if the river devil could mark the fae, I realized. Fae were not proof against magic. I'd seen a fairy queen force other fae to worship her—and some of those had been fairly powerful.

If the river devil could suborn Zee . . . I've only seen Zee without his glamour a couple of times, and it was impressive. More impressive was the way the other fae treated him: wary respect—even from the Gray Lords themselves. If he had to obey the river devil, it would not be a good thing.

So. Coyote and his kinfolk were going to get themselves eaten. And Heaven help anyone left if I didn't kill the monster. I was going to swim over and try to take it out with a flint knife—presumably Coyote would provide that.

Scuba gear might be good.

I seemed to remember . . .

I went to the bench in the kitchen area and pulled up the cushion and set it aside. The hard top of the bench opened, revealing two complete sets of snorkeling gear. I'd noticed it when I was exploring the trailer, and now it made me wonder just how much Yo-yo Girl had seen in her vision. It wouldn't have been Adam who put them there.

I know a couple of adrenaline-junkie werewolves who scuba, but none that snorkel. It is not, strictly speaking, necessary to be able to swim when scuba diving, where sinking and rising are controlled by weight belts and an air-filled vest.

I pulled out a pair of water socks that looked to be my size and the smaller of the sets of fins. The snorkel I left where it was. My old college roommate had spent an entire summer trying to teach me to snorkel. We proved that the fins greatly increased my speed in the water and that the snorkel greatly increased the chance of my drowning myself.

Hank Owens called as I was closing up the compartment under the bench and asked for Adam.

"He's out running," I told him.

"Would you give him my apologies, ma'am? First time I've ever shot a civilian."

"You didn't shoot him on purpose," I said.

"Not to argue, ma'am," he said gently, "but I pointed my gun at him and pulled the trigger. That's as 'on purpose' as it gets."

I sensed we could argue back and forth all day. "Fine. I don't think you owe him an apology. He won't think you owe him an apology, but I will tell him you offered it. How are you doing? That sand-and-drop thing Hawk did to you didn't look very pleasant."

"No, ma'am. But I'm fine."

"Good."

"Thank you for conveying my message, ma'am."

"You're very welcome."

By the time Adam came back, I had decided that Coyote's plan stood as good a chance as any and that I was as prepared as I was going to be.

"Catch anything?" I asked.

He shook his head. Then he shook everything else.

"Hank called to apologize for shooting you."

He flattened his ears.

"That's what I told him. But he seemed to feel the need, so I told him I'd let you know."

I had done all I could. If we stayed here, all I was going to do was lapse into a funk that Adam was only too likely to joi

"Hey, Adam? Let's go out to lunch." This might be n

last day on earth, and I refused to spend it moping around. Even if I'd had to let four people die this morning to preserve my life. I swallowed down my gorge.

Adam woofed in agreement to my proposal and escorted me out to the truck.

We ate takeout. Most restaurants don't let dogs in. We drove to the first pretty place I saw and ate fast-food tacos with flowers blooming all around us. The seagulls mostly left us alone because of Adam. When we were through eating, I bundled up the garbage and lay down with my head on Adam and went to sleep, soaking up the heat of the day like a balm to my soul.

And I didn't dream at all that I remember.

I woke with Adam licking my face—it felt a little hot. I don't sunburn much, but falling asleep in the middle of a hot summer afternoon just might do it. I touched my face with my fingertips, but it didn't seem sore, just warm.

"You ought to use sunscreen if you're going to sleep outside like this. Someday you might not have a fairy godfather to come and take care of the sunburn." Coyote sat next to us, chewing on a piece of grass. "Are you ready?"

I don't know how long I'd been there, but the sun was nearly down. I sat up. Dinnertime had come and gone, but I wasn't hungry. The werewolf would be another matter.

"Adam will need more food," I said, eyeing my mate sideways. "But yes, I'm as ready as I'm going to get."

"Why are you looking at me like that?" he asked.

"I didn't know that you also played fairy godfather."

"It's a secondary thing," he said modestly, bouncing to his feet. "Let's go get some food."

OYOTE RODE IN THE BACKSEAT AND ATE TWICE
t Adam did—and that was saying something.

've got knives for you," he said, licking the salt from st french fry off his fingers.

"Knives?"

"Yes. Last time I did this, it took nine blades, so I brought you twelve. They are obsidian—be careful you don't slice yourself while you're at it. My sisters made the sheath and the knives, so they are as sharp as any knife I've seen. Remember, obsidian is brittle and doesn't hold an edge forever, which is why I brought you so many."

"All right," I said. I realized that I hadn't lied to Coyote back in the little park: I *was* ready. The nap in the sun with Adam's heartbeat in my ear had steadied me, had given me courage. Succeed or fail, I would do my best to make sure that the river devil died tonight. That was all anyone could do.

THERE WERE SEVEN OF THEM WAITING FOR US AT our trailer. Evidently, Hawk had decided to help as well. They'd let themselves in and helped themselves to food, drink, and—from the looks of it—every sweet thing in the place. It looked like an invasion of pirates. If I'd known what they liked, I'd have brought back a couple of dozen doughnuts.

Dark was falling.

No one said much, but when the sun touched the western horizon, clothing disappeared as they garbed themselves in things suitable to war. Like the old clans of the Scots, for most of the tribes of the Americas, war meant as close to naked as makes no never mind. Apparent age dropped away, and the animal spirits who walked out to the river with me wore bodies as smoothly muscled as any werewolves. They also were furred or feathered as their aspect demanded, and their heads were those of beasts—their true shapes, as beautiful and strange as anything I have ever seen. It reminded me of the Egyptian gods; I' never thought about the similarity before. They w armed, too—all but the birds, who would fight the ba from the air in their animal forms.

There were no passive sacrifices here. They would go fighting, but none of them seemed to believe that they wouldn't go down.

They all knew the river devil better than I.

I wore my old blue tank swimsuit with a soft leather sheath packed with obsidian knives. The sheath wrapped around me like a snug Miss America sash or one of those old bandoleer bullet belts. The knives were stuck in and held tightly by the pale, well-tanned leather of the sheath. They didn't look a great deal like normal knives—or even the knives Coyote had drawn to drive the river devil back to the water. These were knives like the one Gordon had used to dig the bullet out of Adam. Using them would be more like using the blade of a box cutter than anything else. There was no handle, just a blunt side that was safe to hold and a very sharp side for cutting.

Over the top of the bandoleer I wore one of Adam's dark gray dress shirts. No sense advertising our plans.

Coyote nodded at me, and I walked out into the river. Adam paced unhappily back and forth on the shore just beyond where the river devil had landed, so he would be out of her reach. He hadn't been happy about agreeing to stay out of the river, but he wasn't stupid. We couldn't risk that she could gain control of him as she had Hank.

The plan was for me to stay safe until it was my turn to act—but still we needed me to be the bait that drew her in close. We'd decided, Coyote and I, that I should go in no farther than knee-deep, which put me about fifteen feet from shore. So close, Coyote was confident he could grab me before she pulled me out into the deep water. Knee-deep meant the entirety of the river mark on my leg was underwater. Raven took to the skies to see if he could spot er from the air when she came, though it was unlikely. e night-dark river didn't give up her secrets easily.

was ready. Ten minutes came and went.

othing happened. Nothing except that I was getting

cold. And scared because I'm not stupid. Somewhere in this river was a monster who wanted to eat me, and I was daring her to do just that.

I looked at the shoreline, but no one seemed impatient—except Adam. Even with him, it was not so much impatience as growing frustration. Raven waved, and I waved in return before the feeling of having nothing to watch my back made me turn around again.

"She's not stupid," I muttered to myself as I stared at the dark water. "She's got to be wondering what I'm doing going out into the river again after this morning." I tried to put myself inside her head. "I wouldn't come to her to save a child, but now I'm cavorting about in the water. 'Is this woman merely stupid?' she'll wonder. 'Is Mercedes the bait for one of Coyote's traps?' He's killed her before, but she is stronger now and he weaker. Even if it is a trap, what does she have to fear?" I hoped that she would be more arrogant than suspicious.

"Maybe she can sense the assault team on the shore." I thought about it for a minute. "But that shouldn't worry her. None of *them* think they have a chance of killing her. She probably doesn't think they can, either."

Their fatality had surprised me a little. I know a bit about warriors and testosterone—and Coyote and his friends were the first and definitely had the second. Good warriors understand how to assess risk, but they also tend to beat their chests and brag a bit. Coyote certainly didn't seem to eschew bragging, but no one was predicting victory here.

After a half hour, I decided that knee-deep wasn't working. I took a deep breath and held it, listening intently to the river. Nothing—or at least nothing I could distinguish from the normal sounds. The problem was that there was too much noise. Water brushing the shore, night birds and insects hunting food or mates, even the highways all work to camouflage any sound the river devil might make.

I stared out at the far shore and imagined her out there, watching me and waiting. I took another step out, feeling the ground under my feet start to drop off. Another step, and I was abruptly waist-deep.

From the shore, Adam howled. I turned around and waved to them to show that the move had been voluntary.

"Knee-deep isn't working," I said. "I thought I'd try a little deeper." Two steps was all it had taken—I was still quite close to shore.

An otter head popped up about ten feet from me, looking smug. He couldn't hurt me here in the swimming area, according to Uncle Mike. But where the otters were, quite often the river devil was as well. I lost my nerve and turned to go back—and something wrapped around one ankle and hauled me through the water like a water-ski boat. Something that might have been Coyote's hand brushed mine, then was gone.

I spread my body out, trying to create as much drag as I could, even as I fumbled with Adam's shirt, trying to get it open enough to get at the knives. I knew what she was doing; I'd seen her do it to others. I had no intention of being her meal, but I wasn't sure if I'd have time to do anything to stop it.

I had to try. If I died first, the whole enterprise was at risk.

So I concentrated on the advice Sensei Johanson had once told me was the first and most important way to win a sparring match: "Be ready."

The river devil had pulled me deep under the surface, and it was dark. I was watching for her, and I saw nothing—but I felt the change in the currents of the water as she opened her mouth.

You, I shall consume with much pleasure, the river vil told me. *And then I shall know how you defy me when other mortal thing has. I shall learn and, learning, v stronger.*

Mercy! It was Adam, his voice a roar in my head overwhelming her words so I could move again.

More by luck than by skill, though I was trying to feel for anything I could grab, my free foot caught the outside of a tooth that was longer than my shinbone, and I grabbed another upper tooth with my left hand and stopped myself, arching my body away from her.

Mercedes. His voice was a howl of grief that I couldn't answer, not if I wanted to save myself.

I remembered, from seeing her head above the water, that the teeth in the front of her mouth were spiky and stuck out almost like the quills of a porcupine. They were also long, and I hoped that she couldn't open her mouth wide enough to engulf me as long as I kept my feet braced on the outside of her lower jaw and my grip on the upper tooth.

You make things harder than they should be, she told me. *You are caught and cannot get away.*

She snapped her teeth together with wicked speed—but I am wicked fast, too. I bent and straightened with her. The water helped as well. When she snapped her mouth closed, the water pushed out.

She changed tactics and tried to use her tentacle to shake me loose. I noticed that this close to her, the tentacle seemed to be operating a little less efficiently, like a rubber band that was too loose. It could hold on to me, it could pull me—but it couldn't push me.

I didn't know why she didn't try to grab me with another tentacle. Maybe she was just too angry right now. But when she did, I was dead. If this stalemate lasted much longer, I was dead anyway. My abilities didn't extend to breathing water, and I'd been underwater for a while.

On a particularly hard jerk, I took a chance and stopped resisting with my legs. She was pulling so hard that she yanked my legs up past her upper teeth. She quit pulling a soon as she realized what she had done, but too late. She already given me enough slack to twist my tentacle-cau leg around one of the long spikelike teeth at the front of her mouth. The next time she pulled her tentacle, she'd be pulling on her own tooth instead of my leg.

All well and good, but if I didn't get air soon, all the cleverness in the world wouldn't help me. I wiggled until I was on top of her muzzle instead of in front of it. I'd managed to pull open Adam's shirt while she was hauling me to her, and now I slipped a knife out of the bandoleer and sliced the tentacle just around my ankle.

Her tentacles must have been extremely sensitive. Just as she had when Adam freed me, she jerked her head up out of the water. Since I was on top, the motion catapulted me out of the river, off her head, and into the air. I landed about fifteen feet from where I'd started and plunged back into the water. She'd thrown me upstream, so the current would bring me right back to her. I broke surface again just about the time she let loose with a shriek that hurt my ears.

She saw me and dropped back into the water, disappearing under the surface. I swam as fast as I could, but, not being a fish, I was pretty sure I was going to be food.

Something grabbed my shoulders and I screamed, reaching up to grab whatever it was as it yanked me out of the water. I quit screaming as the river devil's open mouth appeared on the surface of the water below my toes, which were now about five feet in the air. My hands closed around two leather-covered steel-strong bones that could only be the legs of a very, very big predatory bird.

My food, my *food. Thief!* The river devil's voice in my head made me tighten my grip on the great bird's legs and draw my feet up as far as I could.

He shouldn't have been able to bear my weight, even as big as he was—and with his wings outspread, he was huge. But he wasn't just a thunderbird—he was Thunderbird—and I supposed that made a difference.

The river devil broke the surface but had misjudged her [illegible] because Thunderbird swooped sideways at the last moment. She hung where she was a moment before toppling sideways and crashing into the river like a whale breaching. Thunderbird carried me to the river's edge and dropped me, gently, next to where Adam should have been waiting.

And wasn't.

"Adam," I shrieked, wiping the water out of my eyes. She couldn't have him. He was *mine*. I staggered into a run toward the river about the time Adam emerged, knocking me over and drenching me further with the water held by his fur.

I swore at him. "You have got to stay out of the water," I told him through gritted, chattering teeth. "If she gets you, she won't have to bother killing me—she can make *you* do it."

It scared me. I understood why he'd done it, understood it viscerally, but he had to stay out of the river. I tried to roll out from under him, but a big paw on my shoulder held me down and he snarled at me.

That's when I realized that I wasn't dealing with Adam. Adam knew why he had to stay out of the water. But the wolf didn't understand, and the wolf had taken over.

We didn't have time for this. I had to get my fins on and be ready to swim out to wherever the river devil was when she went comatose.

I heard a war cry—someone had made it out to her.

"Adam," I said. "Let me up."

Instead, he lay down on top of me. Damn Wolf. If Adam had been in his human shape, the wolf would never have gotten this much of an upper hand.

But I knew how to deal with this—if I calmed down, he would, too. He was responding as much to the frantic beat of my heart and my fear as he was to seeing me jerked underwater. He hadn't seen me fight underwater wit something I couldn't see, where I could only feel tho sharp spiky teeth and—that wasn't going to help me q down at all.

I closed my eyes and sought that calm place I'd learned to find in the dojo. It came in handy both when working on engines and when dealing with unhappy customers.

It took longer than it might have because I couldn't help but listen to the sounds of the battle I couldn't see, but eventually my pulse settled down, and I was relaxed under Adam.

"Okay," I told him. "I'm okay. You need to get off of me before I'm squished."

The wolf growled.

"Adam," I said sharply. "Get *off* me."

He closed his yellow eyes and took a deep breath.

"Adam?"

When his eyes opened it was Adam who looked back at me. He stood up and backed off.

"Thank you," I said, rolling to my feet a little less gracefully than I meant to.

Out in the river there was a feeding frenzy going on. There was blood in the water; I could smell it even though I couldn't see. I could hear the cries of the birds—Hawk, Raven, and Thunderbird as they attacked from above, but the devil was too far out in the middle of the river. Even with my night vision, I had trouble seeing what was going on. I grabbed my water socks and pulled them on my feet, ignoring the rough tear that wept blood on the foot I'd managed to brace on the river devil's teeth.

The fight was moving gradually toward the little swimming hole, and I felt Adam's attention focus as he figured out what she was doing. Our bond allowed me to understand it, too: she was herding them into the cove because she didn't want anyone to escape, and it would make it [illegible]asier for her to locate body parts if she missed anything.

It would make my job easier, too.

[illegible] was worried I wasn't going to be able to get Adam to [illegible]e back in the water. I was pretty sure I was going to be [illegible]ed—

[illegible] was close enough I could see her bright green

eyes—which meant that Adam and I were too close to the river.

"Come on," I said. "Let's—"

There was a tremendous splash and her head lifted out of the water. Speared on her teeth was a man with a canine head. She opened her mouth as a single tentacle pulled him off the teeth that impaled him. She threw him into the air, and, tipping her head back, caught him in her rear teeth and chewed him to bits.

Adam collapsed, like a puppet whose strings were cut. Coyote howled a tribute.

She had eaten Wolf.

I didn't know what had happened to Adam. He was breathing, his heart was steady—he was just unconscious. I was kneeling beside him, looking for any injury, when pain rushed over me, and I understood why he'd fallen.

My skin was on fire, and I felt as if someone had poured boiling water over me. I screamed, stumbling to my feet. And this time it was I, tears sliding down my wet face, who howled a tribute—and Coyote who died.

It didn't last long after that. I think that when they were all alive, they'd been able to harry her, to play off one another's strengths. But as they died, they lost the ability to distract her.

Raven died trying to keep Snake alive—the distraction allowed Snake to drive his spear deep into her side, but not deep enough. Watching her, I realized why she'd only grabbed me with one tentacle—she could only use one of them at a time. The unused tentacles bobbed about her head as if she had thick wire hair. She dove on top of Snake, and I didn't see him again. The only ones that seemed to b[illegible] remaining were Thunderbird and Hawk.

Thunderbird dove like an F-15, striking with both [illegible]oned feet extended. I'd seen him score a deep furrow[illegible] her nose a few moments before. But this time, she wh[illegible] her tentacle around his legs and snatched him out of the air and into the water.

Suddenly she shrieked—neither she nor I had seen Hawk, and he'd managed to take out an eye while she was concentrating on Thunderbird. But Hawk's talons were stuck, and she dove abruptly. For a moment, the river was still, and Thunderbird floated alone on the surface, bobbing gently with the current. Then he disappeared under the water, tugged by something underneath him.

Wait until she surfaces and is still, Coyote had cautioned me as he ate a couple of fast-food burgers in the backseat of the truck—one greasy sandwich in each hand. *If there aren't enough of us to cause her to go belly-up, there's no sense in you dying, too.*

I'd asked him what to do if she didn't react the way he'd hoped.

Maybe then it might be time to bring in the nuclear warheads, he'd said. For all that there was a smile on his face, I had been pretty sure he hadn't been joking.

I stripped off Adam's shirt. When I saw blood, I realized that Thunderbird had opened up a good slice under one arm when he rescued me. Under the circumstances, I wasn't going to complain. I checked the knife belt. There were a few knives missing, but I still had eight left. Hopefully, that would be enough.

I waded out into the river until I was knee-deep, then put on the long, bright pink fins. And then I waited, nearly in the same spot as I'd waited before.

I'd have expected that the water would keep the smell of carnage to a minimum, but I could smell blood. Something bumped my knee, and I fell over backward trying to scramble away in my clumsy fins, landing with a splash on my backside. The bandoleer jerked and I grabbed the otter with one hand and threw him as far as I could before I stood up. I checked the sheath, but it seemed to be okay except for a bite mark on one edge. There were still eight knives.

A long, pale shape appeared on the surface about ten feet from me. It waved lazily back and forth as the current caught it. It was joined by another and another, then her head appeared—half her head anyway, the rest lurking beneath the water—one eye skyward and her mouth open wide. Finally, her body surfaced, limp and huge. Really, really huge. I was pretty sure it was longer than Coyote's estimate of ninety-odd feet.

Showtime.

I waded out, ignoring the otterkin who were circling me. If they could have attacked me before this, they would have. Whatever the fae had done to this cove, it was serving my purposes now.

As soon as the water was thigh-deep, I dove forward and let the fins do the work of getting me to the river devil.

I'd expected that I would have to chase her downstream, but her greed for the last bit of flesh kept her in the backwater of the swimming cove. It didn't matter for my task—but if I was successful, it might mean that I'd have a lot easier time getting back to Adam.

I noticed that there were flashing lights on the big highway—someone had seen a disturbance over here, I thought. We'd known there was a good chance that people would notice eventually. If I killed her, then it wouldn't matter. If I didn't, it would likely give her a whole slew of victims, but I wouldn't care. Coyote might, just *might*, come back from the dead—but I wouldn't.

Her body floated about three feet above the river surface, the pectoral fin stuck straight up in the air. I couldn't get to it from the underside. I swam around her head—because it was the shortest way—but I tried not to look too closely at her open mouth. Her bad eye, the eye Hawk had hit, was the one that I could see.

I don't know how long she'll stay somnolent, Coyote

had told me on the way here. *I don't even have a best guess. All we can do is feed her everyone we can and hope it is enough.* Then he'd grinned. *She might sleep for a week digesting me alone.*

Something brushed against me, and I spun to look, expecting an otterkin. But it was just a feather. A feather as long as my forearm attached to a piece of skin and caught between her teeth. I swam faster.

Her topside was rougher than her underbelly had been. I might have been able to scale it, but I didn't have to. A spear sunk deep into her flesh gave me an easier way up. I pulled off my fins and gave them to the river before I started to climb.

Her skin was cold and faintly mucous. She smelled like fish and magic. I'd thought she would have big scales, but they were small, even finer than a trout's on her underbelly. On her back, they were more like a snake's. I put my hand on the base of her pectoral fin and measured out four hand spans, then I pulled out one of my knives and made the first cut.

I held my breath as the skin parted reluctantly, but she was still as death. If it weren't for the faint pulse beneath my knees and the fluttering of her gills about three feet in front of me, I might have thought she was already dead.

The first knife made it through the tough skin before it lost its edge. I didn't notice at first, wasting precious time dragging the dull rock against her unyielding flesh. By the fourth knife, my cut was nearly a foot deep and twice that wide. I braced it open by tucking my knee in the fissure while watery pink blood filled the bottom. I had to stop and empty it out a couple of times so I could make sure that the knife was still cutting.

You have to get it wide enough to get to the heart, Coy-
had told me, holding his hands about two feet apart. *doesn't have ribs—she's a fish. But she doesn't need*
Her flesh is made of magic as much as flesh. That's

why the steel didn't work, that's why bullets won't work, that's why a grenade wouldn't work. I'm not sure a nuclear strike would work—but it would be interesting to try. Of course, after that no one could use water from that river for a hundred years or so . . .

The otters swam around, tugging at her tentacles and doing something with magic—I could feel it. Fae magic felt different to me from the magic that kept the river devil alive. They were trying to wake her up.

I kept looking out on the beach, but Adam hadn't moved.

What are you doing, Mercedes? Her voice rang in my head, and I froze, certain that I'd failed, that she was awake.

You are not strong enough for the task you were given, she said. *You should have come to me this morning and let those children live. At least then your death would mean something.*

The tissue under my blade was surging with the beat of her heart, a sign, Coyote had told me, that I was close. I switched to a new blade—I had three left—and kept working.

My hands were cold and numb, and I'd slipped a couple of times. There was at least one cut that would need stitches if I survived. The new blade broke. I tossed it at one of the otterkin and hit it in the head. It chittered at me, and I stuck my tongue out at it as I grabbed another knife.

Two left.

Not enough, Mercedes, she said. *Not good enough. Poor Coyote died in vain and took with him the last of the spirit warriors who walk our Mother Earth. You fail, but don't worry—you won't have to live with your failure.*

That blade dulled. And then there was only one. Had she moved underneath me?

I took it out and went to work. It would either be enou or it wouldn't. The ankle that she'd grabbed me by throb in time with the beat of her heart. The hip attached to ankle ached dully—I must have pulled a muscle in it. The cut under my arm burned every time I moved my hand.

And the tissue parted, exposing her heart.

It didn't look like any heart I had ever seen—it was black and veined with gray, and the magic of it was so strong it stung the tips of my fingers.

It's no use trying to stab her heart. Coyote had chewed for a while, then swallowed. *It's too hard. You need to go for the connective tissue.*

So I did. There were four webs of gristle that held the heart in place. Once I took care of that, the veins and arteries were soft enough I could pull them out with my bare hand, or so Coyote had assured me.

I set my knife to the first of the webs—and right about that time, she woke up.

13

SHE DIDN'T AWAKEN ALL AT ONCE—OR ELSE I'D hurt her badly enough that she couldn't react right away. The first thing she did was stretch. When she did, her pectoral fin fluttered and hit my hand, knocking the knife out of my hand. I watched it hit the water and disappear.

The otterkin all pulled back into a semicircle about fifteen feet from her. Under me she writhed, and the back half of her body disappeared underwater. I was going to have to jump and get swimming if I wanted a chance to live through this.

Yes, Mercedes, you should run now, she said. *I like to chase my prey.*

Instead, I grabbed the edges of her skin and dug my fingers in so she couldn't knock me off. Coyote died to giv
me this chance, and I had failed him. MacKenzie, wh
would never grow older than eight years and four days
had died to give me this chance, and I had failed her
her family. Faith Jamison had come to me, and I had
her, too.

I had failed them all. But they were dead; they wouldn't care. Adam would care.

I wasn't going to go down without a fight. Not with Adam waiting for me.

A single tentacle snapped back and hit my shinbone with a crack, and the pain didn't touch me. I flattened my hand just as I would have to break a board and hit her heart. My form sucked because I was trying to stay put on a slippery fish who wasn't cooperating, and I might as well have hit her with one of Thunderbird's feathers. I reached in and pulled on her heart with my fingers and got nothing except for a mild zap of magic that felt like I'd grabbed onto an electric fence.

I needed a weapon, something that could penetrate the river devil's magic, and all I had was my bare hands.

Her struggle to wake up pulled me underwater, making it obvious, if I needed to be reminded, that if I changed to a coyote to gain teeth, I'd never manage to stay on her long enough to do anything. I wasn't even sure I *could* change to a coyote—Coyote was dead I had *nothing.*

I was up and out of the water again when a stray thought brushed across my awareness.

Lugh never made anything that couldn't be used as a weapon, the oakman had said.

Maybe I did have a weapon.

Jump, the river devil urged. *Run. Swim for shore. I might even let you make it all the way if you swim fast enough. Or maybe I'll decide that living with your failure would be a punishment more fitting what you have attempted here.*

I opened my hand, and said, "Come on. Now. I need ou." Then I reached behind my hip and grabbed the silver-d-oak walking stick.

he river devil writhed, and the section I was on lifted p out of the water. I used the force of her movement nine as I stabbed down with the end of the staff. As ed it down to the heart, I saw the silver-shod end re-form into a spearhead. The spear slid six inches into her heart and stopped as if it had hit something solid. As we began to drop back to the water, the river devil twisted, rolling upright.

All the metal in the staff flared white-hot. My feet slipped off the slick side of the river devil, and instinct had me grab the shaft with all I was worth, even as the heat seared my hands. I doubt I could have held on for another second, but a second was all it took.

The staff started to shift relative to the monster, and I thought my weight was pulling it out, but a frantic look showed me something else, just before water closed over my head.

The staff had sucked the heat from her flesh, turned her black heart to white ice. The weight of my body had given more torque to the staff; the heart cracked and pulled loose from the river devil's body.

Somehow, I ended up under the river devil, and she carried me to the bottom, which was not too deep. I wiggled and pulled to get out from under her—it would be too ironic to end up dead after all of this, dead in less than six feet of water.

I lost track of the walking stick, but that was all right: it would be back. Once I was free, it took me almost too long to decide which way was up. I finally went limp and assumed that up was the direction I floated. I surfaced eventually. Had we been any deeper, I might not have.

There were chunks of ice melting in the water. They reeked of magic and blood and I avoided touching them as I swam very slowly back to shore. When the water was too shallow to swim, I crawled. Getting to my feet was just wa
too much work.

I struggled out of the water and found a last spur
strength to get to where Adam lay. With a hand buri
his thick fur, I had enough courage to roll over to l
the river devil. She was floating still, her body movi

the motion of the water. The wound I'd made was still there; it wasn't healing.

"Adam," I said to his unconscious body. "Adam, we did it."

I put my forehead down on his side and let myself believe.

"I should let you live," a man's voice snarled, unconsciously echoing the river devil's words—or maybe he'd heard her, too.

I looked up to see a man standing between me and the river. His features were all wrong, like a bad drawing. Almost human, but not quite. He wore a dry pair of jeans and a WSU sweatshirt, but his feet were bare. He had a ragged beard that was a slightly darker color than his hair. Though there had been all sorts of emotion in his voice, there was none on his face. It was peculiarly blank, like a particularly strong form of autism: a trait, I decided, with two examples to draw from, that must be common to all otterkin.

"What?" I asked him stupidly because his words didn't quite make sense.

"You blooded one of Lugh's creations in the heart of a creature even older and more magical than the walking stick is," he said. "I should just let you live with what you have made. But you must pay the price for killing our creature, she whom we awakened at great cost from her deep sleep."

I was too tired for this. I hurt. There wasn't any part of me that didn't hurt, but especially my hand where I'd hit the river devil's heart. Actually, both hands throbbed wickedly from grabbing the staff while it was hot. The leg that the river devil had smacked with her tentacle ached, too, hat kind of deep ache that told me I'd suffered real dam-e. I was also bleeding from quite a collection of slices cuts. It belatedly occurred to me that my weariness t stem from blood loss as much as the energy I'd ded killing the river devil.

ı woke her up." I could sit up, I told my body firmly.

It protested, but finally managed. I was going to pull my legs up, too, but, after the first attempt to do so, I decided to leave them where they were for the moment.

"It took us two months and all our magic—and you just killed her? Arrogant vermin interfering in something that is no business of yours." He was holding something in his right hand, I thought, but I couldn't tell what because it was slightly behind him, and I couldn't make my body move again to see what it was just yet.

"That's right," I agreed. "I killed her. It seemed like the proper thing to do at the time—as she was killing a lot of people. Why did you release her?"

"She was ours," he said indignantly. "She was sleeping in our home." He paused, contemplating that, I think, though it was hard to read thought in his face. When he spoke again, his voice was a soft croon. "So beautiful and deadly, my lady was. We woke her up to see her beauty living—and, as we petitioned her to do, she hunted humans until we all fed in the wealth of her hunting. She was everything our hearts could desire. She fed us and we her. She was our weapon of perfect vengeance."

The brush next to him rattled a bit, and more people came out of the bushes. One of them was the woman who had attacked me in Wal-Mart, and she was holding her bronze knife. She was crying, which looked really odd on her blank face.

Uncle Mike said there were seven of them, but I only saw six.

"There should be one more of you, shouldn't there?" I asked.

"One was sacrificed when our Goddess came to life," said the man.

I thought of the dream I'd had, the one where I'd ea an otter. I'd been river marked then. It never occurre me that that dream, too, had been a true dream.

Behind him, all of the otterkin's mouths moved

same time, as if they were mouthing his words as he spoke them. They brought with them an air of menace that was not entirely owed to the weaponry they carried.

There was one big man in the group. I noticed him because over his shoulder he was carrying a big, dark, and shiny stick shaped something like a golf club. I didn't recall ever seeing a shillelagh in the flesh before.

"He died, our brother, exalted by the gift his sacrifice brought to his people." The bearded man who was apparently the spokesman for them all paused again. It didn't seem to be an affectation for emphasis, but something integral to his speech. Maybe he was translating, or maybe his thoughts were just that slow. "And you have ruined that."

He swung whatever he'd been holding behind his back at me without much warning. But I'd been watching for something of the sort, and I surged to my feet, my weight entirely on my good leg. I caught the blade of the bronze sword on the walking stick that had been lying just under Adam's body instead of buried in the river devil because that was where I needed it to be.

It hurt. If I hadn't been so worried for Adam, who was unable to protect himself, I doubt I could have done it. Even so, I knew it was useless. There were six of them and only one battered, damaged me. But I'd made a promise in my letter to Adam, and I was determined to keep it.

The bronze sword flared with an orange light and broke. Whatever magic it had held wasn't up to dealing with Lugh's walking stick.

Then something really disconcerting happened. The walking stick buried its suddenly sharp-again end in the otter-kin's throat with no help from me. The lunge it made forced e to come down hard on my bad leg. I might have blacked a bit after that.

opened my eyes and found myself face-to-face with earded otterkin, my cheek resting in the dirt and his blood. He was laughing at me as he died.

My ears started to work about then, and I realized that there was a battle taking place behind me. I heard Adam's baleful, softest growl, the one he uses only when he is beyond angry. The power of his rage lit my soul with its singular goal: none of the otterkin would survive this night.

He was awake, and that meant I was safe. I started to turn over, but there must have been something really wrong with my leg because the moment I tried to move it, I passed out again.

When I opened my eyes again, I was looking at a dead otter instead of a dead man. His blood was still warm, so I couldn't have been out of it for too long. There was no sound behind me, but I knew better than to try to turn over.

"Adam?" I asked. My voice was weak and had this annoying quiver in it. When no one responded, I didn't ask again. Exhaustion should have made me numb, but I hurt too much for that. I should have been triumphant, but I hurt too much for that, too.

For a bare instant, I was afraid that the otterkin had somehow hurt him. I *reached* for the bond between us with all of my heart—and found him nearby, changing from wolf to man. Relieved, I settled in to wait for him, absorbing his fear for me, his rage, and his love with something approaching euphoria. If I could feel all of that, I wasn't dead, and that seemed as remarkable an accomplishment as I'd ever achieved.

I MUST HAVE SLEPT FOR A LITTLE, BECAUSE THE blood under my cheek had cooled and there were gentle hands running over me.

"Adam," I said. "You need to get some clothes on befor those police officers get down here." I'd been hearing th sirens approaching for a few minutes.

"Shh," he told me. And as if a curtain had been d

back, I could feel his feverish need to make sure I was okay. He'd sounded so calm, so sane—when he was none of those things.

"Please?" He needed something to help him, or he was going to kill anyone who came within a dozen feet of me. Sometimes the thought had occurred to me that Adam dressed so civilized in his silk shirts and hand-tailored suits as a shield against the wildness within him.

Besides, if the police showed up to find Adam naked, they were going to have some sort of strong reaction—and Adam needed everyone to be as calm as possible.

He hesitated.

"I'm okay," I told him. "Really I am." I tried to move, then rethought what I'd said. "Okay. I hurt, and I think my leg is broken. And maybe my hand. But I'm not going to bleed to death, and I think we'll have an easier time with the police and the FBI and whoever else is about to descend upon us if you are wearing jeans."

"I don't want to leave you here," he said. "And I'm not moving you without a more careful look."

"If you can't put jeans on and be back here in under a minute, I'd be surprised," I told him. Then I had a bright idea. "I don't want anyone but me seeing you naked," I told him, a little surprised that it was the truth. "Not when I can't defend my claim." It was stupid, and I knew it—but I also knew he'd understand.

"Damn it, Mercy," he said—and then he was running.

I found myself smiling as I heard the door of the trailer open and realized I was smiling into the face of the otterkin whose eyes were clouded with death and whose blood made the ground sticky under my face. Tomorrow, I'd have ightmares about that, maybe. But tonight, he was dead, d I wasn't. That was good enough for me.

t was a good thing the otterkin apparently turned back otters when they died. If the police had come here and found six human bodies, we might have had a lot of trouble. The walking stick dug into my ribs, and I tugged it out from under me, regarding it soberly.

I'd figure out what I'd done to the walking stick in time. How bad could it be? The oakman had used it to kill a vampire, and it hadn't changed. Whatever the walking stick had become, it couldn't be as bad as the river devil.

THE REST OF THAT NIGHT WAS KIND OF FUZZY.

Adam, dressed only in a pair of jeans, examined me carefully to make sure I hadn't damaged anything that moving would make worse. Then he picked me up and carried me over to the camp chairs, where he'd laid out one of the blankets to bundle me up in. He called his office and had them remotely open the gate and let in the cops—who were gathered outside the gate like hornets at their nest.

He was cleaning my face, very gently, when the police came in and all sorts of official cars drove to us.

Adam did the talking, implying a lot of not-quite-true things without ever lying. Everyone got pretty tense when Adam introduced himself as the Alpha of the Columbia Basin Pack. But they seemed to find it perfectly acceptable to hear that a few people believed that the recent spate of deaths by the river were not the work of a human serial killer but of a real monster.

In the interest of privacy, he told them, he couldn't reveal who called him in.

One of the sheriff's men murmured, "When I first met him, he was with Jim Alvin and Calvin Seeker." From his words, I was pretty sure he was the one who'd given us a ride back to our campground when we'd found Benny, bu
I could only look out of one eye at this point, the other ha
ing swollen shut.

At the sound of Jim's name, the local cops all lo

wise and quit asking questions. One of them murmured, "Native American medicine man," to the FBI agents, and suddenly no one asked Adam any more questions about why we were here. Apparently, no one wanted to create an incident with the Yakama Nation.

The less the officials knew about magic, fae otterkin, and Coyote, the more likely they would be to attribute all the deaths to a prehistoric creature—I'd heard one of the FBI say that phrase when talking on his cell phone to someone—and go home. More important to me at this point, they would let me go home, too.

I closed my good eye, and when I opened it, Adam had a cup of hot cocoa and was making me drink it. I fussed at him for waking me up until I got the first mouthful down. It tasted really good, and it was hot.

"Where's everyone else?" I asked when I was done because it looked as though we were alone.

"Down staring at the river devil." Adam set the mug aside and kissed me gently on the forehead. "They got pretty excited when they realized it was still just lying there. They have about three minutes before I take you to the emergency room."

He was holding on to civilization by the skin of his teeth. A proper mate would be meek and subservient until he recovered.

"I don't want to go to the hospital," I whined. I didn't want to move for at least a hundred years now that I was finally warm. If I didn't move, I didn't hurt. Much.

"You don't get a choice." His voice was oh-so-calm, but I could feel the huge storm that lay behind all that control.

"I killed the nasty monster. I think I should get to say ," I told him. To my embarrassment, tears welled in my s. I had to blink fast to make them go away. I was done, eserves left at all. I just couldn't bear any more tonight.

ou are in shock," he said grimly. "You need stitches

in half a dozen places, and your leg is broken. Where do you think you should be going?"

"Home?"

He sighed, leaned forward, and rested his forehead on mine for a moment. "I'll take you home tomorrow," he promised. "Tonight, you're going to the emergency room."

THEY CUT MY OLD SWIMMING SUIT OFF ME AT the hospital, where a tired-eyed female doctor and a pair of nurses (one of them a man) scrubbed, stitched, stapled, and otherwise abused my body. I made them leave Adam's dog tags on my neck. The doctor *and* both nurses flirted shamelessly with Adam even though he was now wearing a shirt and shoes with his jeans. But Adam didn't seem to notice, so that was okay.

By the time the sun rose, I had a bright pink cast on my leg and orders to have it checked over by an orthopedic doctor ASAP. The tibia was certainly broken, so was my kneecap, and the X-rays also showed a suspicious-looking shadow on my ankle. I had more stitches than a Raggedy Ann doll and hands wrapped up like mummies. Not only was my right hand broken, but both hands were sliced, diced, and burned. I had two black eyes. The first was the remnant of the fight in Wal-Mart. I had no idea when the second one happened. Maybe it was when the river devil landed on me after she was dead, or before that, when she was flopping around. I didn't feel it when it happened, and I wasn't feeling it anymore because I also had the best drugs in the known universe. I was very happy and didn't care much that my leg still ached. It wasn't just the drugs that made me happy; the river devil's mark was gone.

Once I quit hurting, Adam lost the soft edge in his vo[illegible] that worried me so much, and his eyes darkened until t[illegible] approached their usual color. Of course, once I quit [illegible]

ing, I also quit worrying about Adam losing control and killing someone he'd feel bad about later.

"Hey," I asked Adam, as he took the paperwork the nurse handed him, "is this the hospital they took Benny to?"

So Adam rolled me through the hospital in a wheelchair to go visit Benny. When we got to his room, Benny was sleeping deeply in his bed, a tired-looking woman was drowsing in a tired-looking chair, and Calvin was sitting in the wide windowsill staring out at the dawn.

One of the wheels on the chair had a squeak; it caught Calvin's attention. He turned his head, then darn near fell off the window.

"What happened to you?" he asked. Then, his expression lightening, he said fiercely, "Did you do it?"

"We are minus one monster," I said, accidentally waking the woman in the chair—and Benny, too.

"Pain meds," murmured Adam in explanation of something. I think it was the giggling. "As you can see, taking out the monster was a close-run thing."

"Tell me," said Benny.

So I did. At some point—near where I was trying to climb up the river devil, I think—Adam sat on the floor next to the chair and leaned his forehead against my thigh. There was another chair in the room, so I wasn't quite sure why he was sitting on the floor. The drugs had fuzzed our bond, so it took me a moment to feel the sick fear that racked him.

"Walking stick?" asked Calvin, distracting me from Adam's distress.

I blinked at him. I couldn't remember if the walking tick was supposed to be a secret or not.

"It's an old fae artifact that attached itself to her while was risking her neck to save a fae she knows," Adam ered, and I could tell he wasn't happy about remem- me trying to save Zee, either.

"He was a friend," I reminded him.

"She does stuff like this all the time?" asked Calvin, looking at Adam with respect.

Adam lifted his head, and his eyes were yellow again— but his voice was only a little rough. "To be fair, it's usually not her fault. She doesn't start things."

"But it looks like she finishes them," said the woman holding Benny's hand. I was going to jump out on a long limb and assume that she was his wife. I must have said that aloud because she nodded. "Yes. I am. I have to thank you and your husband for saving Benny."

"He saved himself," I said in surprise. "Didn't someone tell you the story? He was smart."

"And lucky," said Benny. "If you hadn't found me when you did, I'd have died."

I leaned forward. "Did they tell you what your sister said to me?"

"Jim did," said Calvin.

"Did she want me to put flowers from her to Mom on the grave, or from me to Fai . . . to my sister?" Benny's voice was a little fuzzy. Maybe they were giving him painkillers, too.

"I don't know," I told him. "Maybe you should do both."

"Would you finish the story?" Calvin asked, a little plaintively. "You'd just dropped the last knife and stabbed the river devil with a fae artifact that turned into a spear."

"Right." So I told them how its heart had turned to ice, and the walking stick burned my hand. "And then I swam back to shore."

"With a broken leg?" asked Adam.

"Pretty neat trick, huh," I said smugly.

"Really good drugs." Calvin's voice was dry.

Adam's face was hidden against my leg again. This ti he had one hand wrapped around my good ankle. other hand dug into the tile on the floor. The tile cr with a pop.

"You're going to cut yourself," I chided him.

He lifted his head. "*You* are going to be the death of me."

I sucked in my breath. The sudden surge of fear I felt at that thought broke through the happy glaze I'd been enjoying. "Don't say that. Adam, don't let me do that."

"Shh," he said. "I'm sorry. Don't cry. It's all right." He rose to kneel beside me, wiping my cheeks with his thumbs. "Werewolves are tough, Mercy. I'm not the one who almost died tonight." He sucked in a breath. "Don't you do that ever again."

"I didn't do it on purpose," I wailed miserably. "I didn't want to almost die."

"It's the drugs," said Benny wisely. "They make me say things wrong, too."

"So what happened to the—what did you call them?—otterkin?" asked Calvin.

Since I'd already told them about the walking stick, I told them about what it had done to the otterkin and what the otterkin had said about it.

"You can ask Zee what he thinks." Adam had regained enough control that his eyes were his usual chocolate brown. He regarded me a moment, and added, "Later, when you are not quite so happy. He might not understand about the good drugs."

"He might not understand about me killing one of the last six otterkin. There were supposed to be seven, but I think the river devil ate one of them when she woke up." I yawned. "I don't think killing them was quite what Uncle Mike had in mind when he told us to check up on them."

"I don't know," said Adam. "Uncle Mike can be pretty oblique when he wants to."

"The Gray Lords might come after me." I frowned at Adam. "That might come back to bite the pack. The Gray Lords aren't always very precise about where they aim their wrath."

"If the wrath of the Gray Lords lands on the pack, I'm

happy to claim the credit for it. You killed one of them, and I killed the rest." Fierce satisfaction sizzled in his voice.

I touched the curve of his jaw with my broken hand. "Good. I wouldn't be surprised if some of the body count that's going to be attributed to the monster is actually theirs. It sounded like they'd been eating people anyway." She had been feeding them, the otterkin had told me. And they had been feeding her. A lot of the fae had at one time or another eaten human flesh. I suspected that the otterkin were the people-eating kind of fae. "They were bound not to hurt anyone in the swimming area of that campground—and they moved away from there."

"Who is Uncle Mike, and what are the Gray Lords?" asked Calvin.

"You might as well tell him," I told Adam. "He's a medicine man and ought to know things like that."

ADAM DROVE US BACK TO THE CAMPGROUND. Once there, he wrapped me in a blanket in the passenger seat of the truck, which he'd left running with the air-conditioning on. The air-conditioning was for me, and I was pretty sure the blanket was for him—the shield that he wished he could put around me, Jesse, and the pack, so we wouldn't come to harm.

"We could wait until tomorrow to leave," I told him. "You look tired. I'm not as bad as I look."

He kissed me. "Mercy," he said, "you are every bit as bad off as you look. I was there when they did the repair work. The drugs they gave you in the hospital are going to wear off before long, and the replacements aren't nearly as good. I want you home when that happens. This campground is crawling with reporters and all sorts o[illegible] official personnel who want to study the Columbia Riv[illegible] Monster. I really don't want to spend a night here. [illegible] most importantly"—he made a sound that was ha[illegible] sigh and half a laugh, then whispered in my ear—"I'm afraid of what will happen if we stay one more day on our honeymoon. We'll give it six months, and I'll take you somewhere—San Diego, New York—hell, even Paris, if that's where you want to go. But I need to get you home today."

He shut the door and went out to pack up our campsite. I dozed a little before the sound of a truck woke me up. There had been lots of cars and trucks driving in and out—Adam hadn't bothered to shut the gate after we'd left for the hospital. But the rumble of this engine was familiar. I had to blink several times to clear my vision and confirm it was in fact Jim Alvin's truck. He stopped several times along the way to our campsite, talking to various officials. He had a smile on his face, so I expect they were people he knew.

He parked his truck, then stopped to talk to Adam for a while, too. Finally, he came to the truck I was in and opened my door.

He took a good look and whistled through his teeth. "Calvin told me he thought you'd done it by the skin of your teeth—and I think that might be the only skin you have left."

"Have you seen Coyote?" I asked.

The smile in his eyes died. "No. But you know that he'll either show up again or else he's off in the other camp playing with his friends. Coyote always comes out all right in the end."

"Other camp?"

"With the people who have gone before him," he said.

"What about Gordon Seeker?"

"It will work out all right in the end, Mercy." He hit the de of the doorframe lightly with a knuckle. "I wanted to nk you for doing what I couldn't."

blinked at him a bit, sorting through my muddled hts until I found the one I wanted. "It took us all."

"Yes," he agreed. "But I still have two good legs and most of my skin."

"'Sall right," I assured him earnestly. "I'm not feeling any pain right now."

He looked at me intently, then smiled. "What tribe are you from, Mercedes Athena Thompson Hauptman?"

"Blackfeet," I told him, the answer coming automatically. "Who told you about the Athena part?"

He smiled mysteriously. "Some things are better kept secret. Blackfeet, eh? Are you sure it's not Blackfoot?"

I frowned at him.

"I think you are taking something precious home with you from this trip," he told me. "Remember who you are. Good dreams, Mercy. I'll call you if I see Gordon or Coyote if you will do the same."

"All right." I closed my eyes because they wouldn't stay open any longer. "If your car doesn't work, bring it on by."

He laughed and shut the door.

ADAM WAS RIGHT ABOUT THE DRUGS: BOTH THAT they would wear off and that the replacements in the amber plastic bottles wouldn't do as good a job.

"Next time I go out to kill monsters," I told him as we came into town, "you should do a better job of stopping me."

He took my bandaged hand and kissed it. "I promised you that I wouldn't do that. Next time, pick a monster who doesn't live in a river or ocean, and I'll be more help."

"Okay." I paused and thought about it. "I don't want a next time."

He sighed. "Me, either."

If I could have moved without moaning, I'd have leane against him. I settled for leaving my hand on his thi where he'd put it.

“But if there is,” I told him, “and evidence suggests that there will be—I’d rather fight monsters with you than with anyone else I can think of.”

“I have a confession to make,” he told me. “I wanted to wait until you were a little closer to your usual fighting weight, but I don’t think it will work.”

“You found a cute waitress, and now you want a divorce,” I said.

He laughed. “No. But I’ll look for one at the next available opportunity.”

“Cool. I found a handsome nurse, but I think he liked you better than he liked me.”

“Seriously,” he said. “I did something I shouldn’t have.”

I was still feeling a little muddled, so I’m not sure if my sudden insight came from our mating bond or from the fact that he sounded a little too much like my mother did when she told my little sister that she’d found her diary and read it. Since I’d told Nan that she shouldn’t write anything down she didn’t want someone to read, I’d been surprised by how upset my mother was. Turned out that Nan figured that if someone was going to sneak and read her diary, they deserved what they got. It took her about ten minutes to convince Mom she wasn’t dealing drugs to pay for her abortion.

“You read the letters,” I said, doing my best to sound offended.

“I read the letter you wrote to me.”

I yawned, and it sort of ruined my pretense of indignation. I patted whatever part of him I could reach. “That’s okay,” I told him. “It had your name on it.”

We drove for a while more before he spoke again. “I ove you, too.”

I smiled at him without opening my eyes. “I know you ”

dozed a little, and, before I knew it, we’d pulled into

Adam's driveway. Someone would have to back the thing out, but it wouldn't be me, so I decided not to worry about it.

The screen door opened, and Jesse bubbled out.

"Dad. Hey, Dad. Why're you home early? Someone from your office came and left a big package that says it's a wheelchair in the garage. Is that what it is? Why did we get a wheelchair?"

I opened my door and contemplated the difficulties of making it down to the ground while Adam hugged Jesse. If we'd been in my Rabbit, I could have gotten out on my own, because my Rabbit doesn't have a three-and-a-half-foot drop to the ground. Not that it would have done me much good, though. I wasn't going anywhere on my own anyway.

Jesse looked up, and her jaw dropped. "Dad," she said in a horrified voice, "what did you do to Mercy?"

UNCLE MIKE WAS NOT HAPPY WHEN I CALLED HIM the next morning and told him we killed all the otterkin. He did listen when I told him what they had done, though. I gave him an inventory of the damage to my person (I'd quit taking anything but over-the-counter painkillers and was feeling whiny).

"*How* many stitches?" he asked when I was through.

"One hundred and forty-two," I told him. "And four staples. And *all* of them itch."

It wasn't so bad when I had a distraction. Since I couldn't do anything, that meant talking to people. I was home alone right now—which was why I'd decided to call Uncle Mike and fill him in.

"And do you know, when you have a broken hand and a giant cut under your arm, crutches don't work, and neithe does a wheelchair unless you have a minion to wheel yc around. My good hand is burnt, so I can't even turn circle

"I think I'll pitch it to the Gray Lords as suicid

werewolf," he said after a long moment of silence. "Anyone who hurts you in front of Adam is too stupid to live anyway."

"Adam only killed five of them. I killed the other one." I paused. "Okay, not quite. I was holding the walking stick when it killed him."

There was a long pause. "Oh?"

I told him about using the walking stick to kill the river devil, what the otterkin had told me afterward, and how the walking stick had killed him.

"You quenched Lugh's walking stick in the blood of an ancient Native American monster?"

"I screwed up?"

He sighed. "What else was there to be doing? If you hadn't used it, you'd be dead—and there would be a monster loose eating people. But there's no denying that it's not a good thing. Violence begets violence—especially when there's magic involved."

"What should I do with it?"

"What *can* you do? Try not to kill anyone else with it."

"Can I give it to you?" It wasn't that I was afraid of it—I didn't even know what was wrong with it. It was that I had failed to keep it safe. It should go to someone who would take better care of it.

"We tried that before, remember?" Uncle Mike said. "It didn't work."

"The oakman used it to kill a vampire. Why didn't that do anything to it?"

"I don't know," Uncle Mike said. "But if I were to guess, it would be because it wasn't the oakman's walking stick—it was yours. Intent and ownership are pretty powerful magic."

"Oh." I remembered the last thing I needed to talk to about. "About your trailer. Do you have a favorite shop? If not, I know a few people."

SIX DAYS LATER I WAS CHANNEL SURFING IN THE basement TV room when I heard someone set foot on the top of the stairs.

"Go away," I said.

I was tired of everyone, which was ungracious of me. But I don't like being dependent—it makes me cranky. I needed someone to carry me upstairs and downstairs. I needed someone to help me outside and inside. I even needed someone to help me into the bathroom because none of the bathroom doors were big enough for a wheelchair. It hadn't been so bad when Adam was here, but he'd had to leave two days ago and tend to some disaster in Texas. He wouldn't have gone, except that it had something to do with some hush-hush government installation, and he was the only one in the company with high enough clearance to deal with it.

Today was particularly grim as I'd gone to a doctor's appointment where I'd hoped to get a walking cast—and instead had been told I had to stay off the leg entirely for at least two weeks. Warren had carried me and my wheelchair down the stairs and then proceeded to hover. I finally asked him to leave me alone in a manner that I'd have to apologize for when I was through feeling sorry for myself—and when Jesse got home from her date, because I'd left my cell phone in my coat, which was upstairs in the kitchen. The only phone in the basement was down three stairs. To top it off, my leg had objected to all the abuse and now wouldn't quit throbbing. The acetaminophen wasn't cutting it. So I was sitting in front of the TV with my eyes leaking, and I didn't want any witnesses.

The feet on the stairs just kept coming. I was supposed to be alone in the house, but Adam's house generally ha pack members showing up at all hours anyway.

"I said—"

"Go away," said Stefan. "I heard you."

He didn't increase his speed, which was kind of him because it let me wipe my eyes before he could see me.

"I'd turn around," I said with some bitterness, "but my doctor tells me that I've been damaging my hands, and I'll have scarring if I keep it up. So I can't even make the damned thing go in circles anymore."

Stefan stepped around in front of me and turned off the TV so the room was shrouded in darkness. He crouched so he was eye to eye with me.

"Warren called me as soon as the sun set," he said, brushing my hair back from my face with his thumbs. "He said—and I quote—'It's time to pay up, Stefan. We've been trying, but we're all out of options.'"

I raised my chin. "I'm fine. You can tell Warren they can all have the rest of the week off. They don't have to stick around and cater to me. I'll be fine." I'd figure out a way to get me and my bent leg cast in and out of the bathroom myself. Somehow.

"Mercy," he said gently. "It's not that they don't want to help—they can't. You've told them all to leave you alone. With Adam gone, you're the highest power in the pack, and they can't gainsay you. Warren told me that they were down to leaving you with pack members he couldn't be happy about."

That had never occurred to me. And explained why Auriele and Darryl hadn't been back, even after I'd sent them an e-mail apologizing for yelling at them. I know e-mail apologies are lame, but it was the only way I could be sure not to grump at them some more.

"You need to tell them they can come back to the house nd talk to you—and help you do whatever you need. Just you would help them if they needed it. Warren asked me xplain that they certainly understand the need to snap narl a bit."

Chagrined at my stupidity, I nodded.

"But not tonight," he said. "Tonight you have me. Would you like to go for a stroll? It's still pretty warm out. I brought over some games if you'd rather. I believe you are partial to Battleship."

I sighed in resignation. "I have to go to the bathroom."

He hauled me in and out without embarrassment—on his part anyway. Then he took me for a walk down by the river. He carried me because the ground was too rough for a wheelchair. It could have been uncomfortable, but he paid no attention to the forced intimacy, so I didn't have to, either. I'd been trying to be as little trouble as possible, so the only time I'd been outside since we'd gotten back from Maryhill was to go to doctor's appointments.

"You look better," I told him. It was true; he was still on the lean side, but he no longer looked like a stiff wind would carry him away.

"I took a trip to Portland last week and brought back a couple of people," he said, sounding sad. Vampires didn't hunt for their sheep, the people they would keep in their menageries, in their own territories. "I tried to find people I thought would blend in with the rest, but we're still having territorial negotiations. I need a few more, but I'll wait until things settle down. Warren said that he and Ben were happy to continue to be food until I didn't need them anymore."

I patted his shoulder. "I hate being dependent, too. It sucks."

He gave a rueful laugh. "We do seem to be in the same boat, no? I suppose we must work on being gracious and grateful until we can do for ourselves. Someday the wheel of fate will put us in a position to be of use to them, and we will remember how much easier it is to give help than it to accept it. Now, why don't you tell me of your adve tures? I've heard quite a bit from Warren, of course, b prefer to get the story from the source whenever poss

So he walked and I talked until I was hoarse and cold. Then we went inside and played Battleship.

"B-7," I SAID.

"Miss." He was gloating because he was working his way down my last and biggest ship, and I was still looking for his two-peg patrol boat. "C-2."

"Hit and you know it," I grumped.

He looked at me, then his eyes focused over my shoulder.

"D-4," said Coyote.

Stefan came to his feet, and said, "Who are you?" at about the same time I turned my chair around regardless of scarring my hands up, and said, "Am I glad to see you. We were worried."

"Of course you were," Coyote told me. He stared at me a moment. "Mercy, what did you do to yourself?"

"River Devil and otterkin," I said.

His thumb brushed under my eye, and he held it up. "You are leaking, Mercy. Maybe you need a few more stitches."

I laughed and wiped my face. "All my stitches come out in four more days. I thought you were dead."

"I was," he said. "That's what the plan was. Don't you remember? Why do you have a vampire in your basement?" He narrowed his gaze at Stefan, and with ill-concealed hostility said, "Vampires kill walkers."

"Mercy," said Stefan, "is this Coyote?"

"Yep," I agreed. "Stefan, meet Coyote. Coyote, meet Stefan Uccello. He's a friend of mine."

Coyote's gaze grew noticeably colder. "I remember you."

Stefan smiled at me. "I have not battled with any walk- for a hundred years or more. But I think that it would be for me to take my leave until your guest is finished. ave your cell phone?" I held it up; he'd retrieved it when we came in from our walk. “Call me when he leaves. I promised Warren I wouldn’t leave you alone. I will tell him that you said he could come back tomorrow.”

“Thank you,” I said, meaning it.

He kissed my cheek, ignoring Coyote’s throaty growl. Then he disappeared.

Coyote straightened, staring at the place where the vampire had been. “I’ve never seen one of the blood drinkers do something like that before.”

“Stefan is special,” I agreed. “I’m so glad you’re back. How did the others fare, do you know?”

Coyote took Stefan’s chair and sat down with a groan. “Thunderbird—Gordon Seeker—was the only one who beat me back. Surprised both of us. There aren’t any more Thunderbird walkers, and we were certain that he would never return with no one to anchor him. Just goes to show you that no matter how old you are, life can still surprise you. Do you have anything to eat? It’s been a few days.”

“In the fridge,” I told him. “Help yourself.”

He did. He carried me and my wheelchair up to the kitchen and made himself a huge sandwich, poured a glass of milk, and sat down with me. I told him about killing the river devil and the otterkin. I also told him about how worried I’d gotten about the walking stick.

It hadn’t done anything since killing the otterkin, but there was an eagerness, a shadow of violence, that seemed to lurk around it. I had noticed that when I was at my most prickly, the walking stick was usually somewhere nearby. Maybe it was my imagination—I wouldn’t have told Adam, for instance, without better evidence. But Coyote ran more on instinct than logic, so I thought he’d understand. I think I hoped he’d have some sort of suggestion for me, but h[illegible] just listened and nodded while he ate. I even told him abo[illegible] coping with a broken hand and a broken leg while a pack [illegible] werewolves tried to take care of me despite myself, and [illegible] him laughing milk out his nose. My leg still hurt, my stitches still itched, and Adam was still all the way in Texas, but somehow I felt better anyway.

Coyote told me a few stories about himself. He used the rude versions, too. Potty humor shouldn't be funny to anyone over the age of twelve—and then only to the male half of the species. But somehow it was different when Coyote told it, both sly and innocent at the same time.

He leaned forward and touched my nose. "You're tired. I'd better get going."

"Stop in again," I invited him.

Coyote looked around the kitchen, then he looked at me. "You know, I think I will." He got up and, behind my back, said, "That is very beautiful."

I turned as far as I could in my wheelchair and saw that he'd picked up the walking stick, which must have been lurking around. He gave it a Charlie Chaplin swing.

"I don't think I've ever seen anything more gracefully etched or cleverly carved," he said. Then he looked at me and smiled, waiting for me to understand.

"Would you," I said carefully, remembering what Charles had taught me about guests and things that they admired, "care to accept it? It has delighted me for many days, as have you—which makes it a fitting gift for such an honored and welcomed guest."

He smiled at me as if I had been exceptionally clever. "But it's gotten a bit dangerous recently, yes? We shall have marvelous adventures, this walking stick and I."

I'd given it back to the fae quite often when it first came to me—and it had always returned. But somehow, I thought that it would stay with Coyote.

"Take care of yourself," I told him. "And tell your sisters 'hi' from me."

"I'll do that," he promised, opening the back door. He stopped in the doorway and turned back to me.

"You tell your mate that I expect him to take care of you," he growled.

"I will." I smiled a little. "Have fun."

"Oh, I will," said Coyote. He shut the door, but I heard the last bit anyway. "I always do."

MERCY'S LETTER TO ADAM

Dearest Adam,

If you are reading this, I guess it means I didn't make it out this time. Damn. I was really worried about this one, and if there had been any way out of it, I'd have found it.

Words aren't my best thing, not when it's time to tell you how I feel—but you know that. I'm much better with actions than explaining myself. I think it's because I don't think in words about you. How can I reduce what I feel for you to mere letters on a page? "I love you" doesn't seem big enough somehow, and everything else I tried (you can go through that little garbage can under the sink if you want to see the drafts of this letter) sounds like really bad poetry, which is even worse, so I'll just stick to the simple words. I love you, Adam.

I want you to know that I fought to get back to you. I didn't take the easy way out. I didn't give up. I fought this death because I had you waiting for me on the shore. If it had been possible to drag this puny mortal flesh back to you, I would have done it, if I had to crawl to do so. I would have walked through Hell to get back to you, and only failed because of the weakness of my body, not of my heart.

Don't push Jesse away. She needs you more than she's willing to admit. I was going to tell you to go hunt down a woman who will love you, but I find that I'm not a big enough person to do that. Still, don't feel guilty when you do, okay? And don't leave her waiting for years (like you did me) because you think you are too old, too Alpha, too whatever. Just make sure she treasures you properly.

Love you,
Mercy

#1 *NEW YORK TIMES* BESTSELLING AUTHOR

PATRICIA BRIGGS

"[Briggs] spins tales of werewolves, coyote shifters, and magic and, my, does she do it well."

—USATODAY.com

For a complete list of titles,
please visit prh.com/patriciabriggs